Dedication

For Julie Winslett. Your words always bring a smile to my face.

Acknowledgements

Things are upside down in the world right now, and each person is being affected differently. Still, my tribe is with me in one way or another. Candy, Chris, Jen, Kendall, Kerstin, Nikki, and Riley, together we will get through this.

With this book, I asked my readers for names. So, here's a huge shout out to those who suggested names I used in this book: Candy R, Josie K, Lita B, Michelle G, Milgia S, Natasha K, Samantha K, and Tarah D

I love this cover so very much. Wander Aguiar is a fantastic photographer, and Jay Aheer took the photo of Dylan and made it Maveryck. Thanks to all of you for bringing my Mayhem to life.

Thank you to Yanka for the Russian translations.

A huge shoutout to the man. Life hasn't been easy the last year, but you've continued to support me and my dream. I love you.

"Now hear another monstrous sight: Beware:

The sharp-beaked hounds of Zeus that never bark"

~ Aeschylus, "Prometheus Bound", 5th century

BC

DOUBLE THE MAYHEM

THE HOUNDS OF ZEUS MC
BOOK 2

BY FAITH GIBSON

Copyright © 2020 by Faith Gibson

Published by: Bramblerose Press LLC

Editor: Jagged Rose Wordsmithing, Candace Royer

First edition: April 2020

Cover design: Jay Aheer, Simply Defined Art

Cover photography: © Wander Aguiar Photography

Cover model: Dylan Horsch

Back cover photo: Kris Meier – Animal Photography

Russian Terms

Otvali! - piss off
Mudak - asshole
Printessa - Princess
Cho ty khochesh', suka!! - what do you want, bitch?
Ty cho ebanuti?" - what are you, fucking crazy?
svoloch' - bastard
mor cectpa - my sister
blyad' - whore

Prologue

2048

"Ah, Tatiana. So nice of you to join us. Take one step closer and I slit his throat."

She stopped walking, but she was smiling. She took in the scene before her, letting the calm before the storm settle into her body. This moment had been the one she had trained for all her life. The culmination of years of hard work. Years of training to become one of the best assassins the world had ever seen.

"Thank you," she said to the other woman.

"What the fuck are you thanking me for?" The blade at the male's throat loosened just a fraction. It was no longer cutting into his skin but was still close enough that one flick of the wrist would end his life.

"For helping me get what was rightfully mine. With everyone out of the way, I can now take over the family business."

The other woman scoffed. "Like you would know anything about that. You were trained to be a killer, not head of a Russian mafia."

She grinned, cocking her head to the side. "So you think. So *he* thought. By keeping me in the dark, I learned so much more than shooting a gun. Or taking a punch. Or how to make it so the bodies were never found. You see, he taught me how to be invisible. I learned how to hide. How to listen. How to find all the best places in the manor where voices carry. Where to stash money so no one else could find it. Where to place listening devices that recorded everything. I have to say, fucking my cousin? There's not enough bleach in the world to wash that image from my brain." She gave a full-bodied shiver. "But why now?"

"I knew you had something to do with me getting kicked out of the house! I should have killed you then. Instead, I bided my time. Put a plan in motion to destroy you and those you care about."

"Too bad your plan didn't work. Your days of treachery are over." Fire ran through her veins as she prepared to fight.

"You think so?" When the other woman turned, she was holding a sai in one hand and a short sword in the other.

"Yes. I do." Tatiana held her empty hands out beside her thighs.

The other woman sneered. "As you wish."

CHAPTER ONE

Maveryck

WHAT A CLUSTERFUCK. As one of the mercenaries for the Hounds of Zeus, Maveryck was damn good at his job. He never went in half-cocked. He studied his mark. Then studied them some more. Maveryck had watched Anatoly Volkov for a couple weeks. Had studied the men guarding the three-story home and surrounding acreage. Taking out several security personnel was easy for a shifter. His stealth and strength were no match for humans. He, however, wasn't immune to bullets. Before today, Volkov had been protected by three men. Today? There were at least eight. Instead of fighting through the ones guarding the exterior doorways and alerting those protecting Anatoly in his bedroom, Mav stripped, stowing his clothes and boots in the special bag designed to carry his gear, and shifted into his eagle, flying from the trees to the rooftop. From there, he shifted back, redressed, and slipped into a third-floor window. He thanked Zeus the windows were older and had no screens getting in his way.

Mav hadn't noticed any women at the compound other than an older woman who was probably the housekeeper, but the room he entered most likely belonged to Valkov's daughter, Tatiana. Mav had yet to set eyes on the only female in Valkov's family. The scent of wildflowers had him momentarily forgetting his mission while he searched the room for the cause of the fragrance. If Tatiana had been in her room, Mav would have incapacitated her. He didn't kill innocents.

We don't know she's innocent.

His Gryphon was right. Being the daughter of a mafia boss meant the woman had been raised in a world of drugs and violence. Was she immune to all of it? Or had she been groomed to take her father's place?

Let's hope she's innocent, because I want to shift into our lion and roll around in that scent. It's too intoxicating.

Again, his Gryphon was right. It *was* intoxicating, but Maveryck didn't have time to ponder why that particular odor was so distracting. Voices from below broke him out of his stupor, and after inhaling deeply, he crept to the door and listened for signs of guards in the hallway. Finding the third floor empty, Mav eased his way down the staircase, stopping every few steps to listen. The only conversation he heard came from below, and although he didn't speak Russian, the words didn't sound urgent.

The lion was close to the surface, but Mav pushed back against it. He needed to remain in control, at least for the moment. When the coast was clear, he edged his way down the hall to where the mark's bedroom was located. The conversation continued, and Mav slowly turned the knob, pushing the door open enough to see into the large room. Two guards were sitting at a table, not paying attention to their surroundings. No one would expect the threat to come from above; instead, they assumed an assassin would be taken out by those guarding the lower points of entry. Volkov wasn't visible, but he was speaking to the guards from the *en suite* bathroom.

With their attention on their boss, Mav extended his claws and silently stole across the carpet. Before either one could alert Volkov, Mav struck, slashing across their necks with the swiftness of his predator.

"Did you hear what I said?" Volkov asked.

Maveryck strode into the bathroom. "Yeah, I heard you."

"How did—?" Mav cut off the man's words. Volkov grabbed his neck, blood spurting between his fingers. Anatoly's eyes darkened briefly before they glazed over. Maveryck didn't hang around to make sure his mark was dead. Nobody came back from having their carotid artery ripped open. Moving to the window, Mav flipped the locks and raised it and looked outside to see where the guards were. Two of Volkov's nephews were standing at the edge of the lawn, bickering. One of them jumped when the dirt around his feet sprayed outward from a gunshot. The bullet exploding hadn't been loud, so whoever was shooting at Volkov's nephews was using a suppressor. Who the hell would be shooting at those two?

"You bitch! I will kill you!" Viktor Volkov hissed.

Bitch? Was it Tatiana shooting at her cousins? Interesting. As much as Mav would like to get a glimpse at the woman whose scent was so heady, he didn't have time. He undressed and stowed his things so he could shift. He should probably move to a room toward the back of the house, but he didn't want to

5

chance taking the extra time. While the brothers were preoccupied, Mav gripped the bag in his beak and took off toward the woods. It wasn't until he had shifted back and was on his bike, riding away from the estate that he realized he should have driven a car. Shots from a handgun hit the ground all around, and Mav rolled on the throttle. He didn't breathe easy until he put a couple miles between him and the compound.

That had been too damned close. Being a Gryphon, Maveryck "Mayhem" Lazlo wasn't easily shaken by much, but being shot at when the job should have been an easy in and out had his shifter cursing him. Loudly. He ignored the beast within as he drove his bike as hard as he could without laying it down, steering around the curves leading away from the Volkov compound. He'd encountered guards inside the house he dispatched without trouble. Taking down Anatoly Volkov had been uncomplicated once Mav found the man on the toilet. At least when he released his bowels upon death, he'd been in the right place.

You're not funny.

I'm fucking hilarious, he quipped back at his Gryphon.

We almost died, so no, you're not.

Almost being the operative word.

Yes, he was being flippant, but such was the life of a mercenary. The Hounds went into dangerous situations every time they took on a new job. This one was no exception. He knew the Russian mob boss had plenty of protection surrounding the house. It was the one in the woods he had missed. What he couldn't figure out was how that happened. Having retreated the same way he'd entered the house, no one should have seen him leaving. His bike had been hidden well, and he hadn't shifted back to his human form until he was a good distance from the house.

Someone saw you.

Yeah, no shit.

Mav eased off the throttle when he didn't see anyone following. Another thing he couldn't figure out was why Volkov was being guarded so heavily today. Mav had watched the compound for weeks. Studying who came and went. Someone had tipped the man off that there was a contract on him, and Mav needed to find out who that was. He needed to call Ryker and give him a heads-up, because if one contract was compromised, all the others could be as well. He was less than four hours from home, so Maveryck rode without stopping except for gas, opting to have a face-to-face with his oldest brother, who was the President of their MC, as well as the one who gave them their assignments.

The Hounds of Zeus wasn't only the name of their motorcycle club. It was the name the god Zeus had given the Gryphon shifters he created to watch over humans, contrary to what history taught. Only Gryphons were allowed to be members of the MC. This ensured their true nature was kept secret. It also meant all those who rode in the club had the same "serve and protect" mentality. Their MC wasn't about running drugs and guns. They didn't have a clubhouse full of half-naked women there to service their more carnal needs. The Hounds were all about family. His consisted of two loving parents, six sisters, and four brothers. One of those brothers was his twin, Warryck. War had recently quit his job as a college professor and after a twenty-five-year absence had reentered their lives.

That alone was almost enough to consider his life perfect. Almost. If it wasn't for that one summer day four years ago...

Maveryck sucked in a breath as the needle pierced his left nipple. "I hate you," he seethed as his younger brother, Kyllian, laughed at his pain.

"Come on, Mav. It's not my fault you lost the bet." Kyllian "Kayos" Lazlo was younger by a few years, but he wasn't the brother closest to Mav. That honor went to Warryck, his twin. Maveryck tried not to think about the other part of his soul, because when he did, he got all tied up in knots.

Maveryck ignored Kyllian while the tatted blonde gave him after-care instructions for his new metal. It wasn't like he didn't know how to take care of piercings considering the myriad he had in his ears, his nose, and his eyebrow. It wasn't even the first one he'd gotten somewhere sensitive, but he wasn't about to tell her that. Mav did like blondes. He really liked blondes who could appreciate a nice Prince Albert, and by the way she kept eyeing his crotch, he had no doubt she would really appreciate his. But Mav had another blonde waiting for him. One he was pretty sure was in it for the long haul.

After paying the woman and giving her a large tip, he pushed Kyllian out the door and proceeded to wrap a muscular bicep arm around Kyllian's neck. "You're a pain in my ass."

Kyllian twisted out of the hold and skipped backwards down the cracked sidewalk. "Ready to go another round?" he taunted. Mav sucked at video games, but this time, he'd lost shooting pool. When they were younger, Mav and War spent their days outside, running through the woods close to their home, swimming in the lake, playing ball, and riding motorcycles when they were old enough. Kyllian and Hayden, their youngest brothers, preferred to hang out playing video games. Mav knew better than to take bets placed by either one of his younger brothers, but his pride often got in the way.

"I'm running out of places to pierce. Besides, Ryot has called church tonight."

"But it's Tuesday."

"Doesn't matter. If our brother calls church, we go."

Sutton Lazlo, father to Maveryck and his siblings, had been President of the Hounds of Zeus. Sutton was retired from both the Army as well as the police force. A hardass who took his position in society seriously, Sutton was tough on his boys, but he was fair, and he loved them and wasn't afraid to tell them so. He wasn't afraid to let them know when they fucked up either. When Sutton decided to go undercover twenty years prior, he handed over the gavel to his oldest son, Ryker.

Climbing on his black and chrome bike, Mav grinned, thinking about the pretty blonde waiting for him at home. He had a ring picked out and couldn't wait to give it to her. "I'll see you later," Mav called out to Kyllian. His brother gave him a two-fingered salute and fired up his own bike, headed the opposite direction.

When Maveryck got home, Jenna's car wasn't there. She hadn't mentioned going anywhere after work, but she might have stopped at the store on her way home. Mav parked his bike in front of the garage since he had to go back out in a couple hours. When he stepped into the living room, something seemed off. The house was too quiet, and his heavy boots echoed on the hardwood floor. He walked toward the bedroom, pulling his phone out to call his female. When he saw he had a text from Jenna, he smiled. He had turned the *ringer off while getting his piercing and had forgotten to turn it back on. He opened the text, but when he saw the words, Mav sat on the bed so he wouldn't fall.*

Jenna: Mav, I need some space. I'm leaving to find myself.

That was it. No other explanation. No saying when she'd be back home. Mav threw his phone across the room, the plastic and glass shattering into hundreds of pieces, and his Gryphon took over.

Maveryck did his best not to think of that day, but every once in a while, the memory slipped back in. He had thought he was finally getting what his parents had. Sutton and Rory were the perfect couple. They were a team. Even when Sutton had been President of the Hounds, he still turned to his mate for advice. Aurora Rose Lazlo was one of the smartest, fiercest females Mav knew. He wanted a partner in his life who was as strong and loyal as his mom. He thought he'd found that in Jenna. He'd been wrong. Four years later, and she hadn't made contact with him one time. He could have found out where she was, especially now that Lucy, War's daughter, was working with the Hounds. Lucy was skilled in all aspects of computers and could have easily tracked down Jenna, but Mav didn't need to know where she was. That knowledge wouldn't change the fact that she'd walked out without looking back.

Maveryck did his best to focus all his time and attention on being the best at his job. He took any job that came their way, no matter how dangerous it was. He didn't have a death wish, but he also didn't have anyone waiting and worrying whether or not he came home at the end of the day. Instead of going home to

10

an empty house, Mav drove to the Hounds' compound to fill Ryker in on his mission.

The structure the Hounds called home wasn't a typical MC clubhouse. Sutton had bought a building close to the house he and Rory bought when they moved to Upstate New York, and together with Ryker, they had turned it into a home away from home. There were bedrooms located in the back where visiting members could stay, or those single members could hang out if they chose to do so when they didn't want to be alone. Gryphons weren't solitary creatures by nature, and having their brothers to talk to was common among them. Rory had designed the kitchen, and she often cooked for the Club. Ryker spent more time there than he did at home, so it wasn't a surprise to find him in the garage talking to Hayden, one of their younger brothers. Hayden was the resident mechanic. He built bikes from the ground up and had orders from all across the country for his machines.

Ryker didn't move from his spot when Mav climbed off his bike. He narrowed his eyes and asked, "Why didn't you call?"

Mav ran his hands through his long hair after removing his helmet. "We might have a problem."

"Did you not complete the mission?"

"I did, but they were waiting on me."

Hayden stood and moved away from the bike he was working on, wiping his hands on a grease rag. "How's that possible?"

Maveryck stared at his oldest brother. All jobs came through Ryker. He was part of Nexus – a network of exterminators who took contracts based on location and specialty. Where some were assassins who

11

took out individuals such as pedophiles, rapists, and murderers, the Hounds were mercenaries who focused on The Ministry – the religious zealots responsible for bringing the world to its knees over thirty years ago. That wasn't something they were paid for, nor did they advertise going after the cults. The Hounds also took contracts on groups the government had trouble corralling, such as human traffickers and motorcycle clubs who thought they were above the law. That wasn't to say they didn't go after individuals like mafia bosses. According to Ryker, there was no shortage of assassins, but when a contract was left open too long, he would take it to get the offender off the street.

Ryker scrubbed at his beard. "The only way it could happen is if someone is posing as a Nexus member."

"I thought the vetting process was foolproof," Mav said.

"Nothing in life is foolproof. I'll need to talk to Proxy and get their read on the situation."

"Can you trust them?" Hayden asked.

Ryker frowned and blew out a breath. "As much as you can trust a contact for a secret group of killers. It wouldn't be in their best interest to allow the wrong sort into the network. If word gets out, they're the ones who have the most to lose, since it cuts into their profit." According to Ryker, he didn't know who his contact was other than their alias. He didn't know if they were a man or woman, since their voice was always distorted. Maveryck didn't like that this unknown person or persons knew all about the Hounds while they knew nothing about the contact. It was one of the few things he and his older brother disagreed on.

"I'm going home. There's a bottle of whiskey calling my name." Mav didn't bother saying goodbye. He'd relayed what happened, and now it was up to Ryker to figure the shitstorm out. Mav didn't envy his oldest brother. Being the President came with too many obligations and responsibilities. Mav liked having the freedom to hop on his bike without having to answer to anyone. If he had a woman, she'd have to enjoy being on the back of his Harley, or it just wouldn't work. Jenna had liked… Nope, not going there.

Not going there ever again.

CHAPTER TWO

Tatiana

TATIANA RELEASED ANOTHER pissed-off breath as she closed her left eye and peered through the scope of her rifle with the right. She was supposed to be on the beach sipping mai tais while cabana boys in skimpy bathing suits catered to her every whim. *She* was supposed to be wearing a skimpy bathing suit. Instead, she was lying on the hard ground dressed in camouflage as she scanned the area around the compound of one of the biggest pieces of shit known to man. But when Anatoly Volkov called on her, she obeyed. Not that she had a choice in the matter. He had raised her. Trained her. Taught her everything she knew. Therefore, she belonged to him.

Anatoly was fifth generation Volkov Russian mob. When his father screwed things up with the Odessa Mafia in the late 1900s, Anatoly cut ties with the man and moved the family from California to the East Coast. The world would be better off without Anatoly in it, but he was still her father.

So what? He trained you to be a killer. Someone to protect the Volkov empire. Not run it.

No matter how smart she was, Tatiana would

never be allowed to sit at the head of the table all because she was female. Her father taught her how to protect the family by being invisible, but what he didn't realize was he taught her too well. She'd spent hours spying on Anatoly and his comrades. She knew as much about the family business as did her three asshole cousins, but when the time came, Mikael, the oldest brother, would step into *her* father's shoes.

When Anatoly somehow caught wind of a hit put out against him, he called her, demanding she rush back home, even though he had a small army protecting the fortress he called home. She'd been in line to board her flight, but she turned around and left the airport so she could do her duty to protect the man. Instead of standing guard outside his bedroom, Anatoly insisted two of his men remain inside while Tatiana searched the area around the compound. Not finding anything or anyone who shouldn't be there, she decided to remain stationary in case someone was watching her. That was how she came to be lying on her stomach, rifle aimed at the back door. Five others were stationed around the perimeter of the large structure. Two of those being her cousins, Ivan and Viktor. Her cousins who were supposed to be inside with her father.

"Come in, Peacock," Ivan said, using the stupid code name he'd given her. Speaking of assholes.

"What?"

"You haven't reported in."

"Because there's nothing to report."

"Do I need to send Viktor to help you?"

Tatiana snorted. "Viktor couldn't find his ass if I drew him a map."

"You are such a bitch," Viktor spat. *Oops.* She should have known he would be listening.

"Truth hurts, Little Cousin." Tatiana couldn't help getting another dig in at the youngest of the three brothers. Ivan and Mikael were both over six foot, but Viktor was shorter than Tatiana who barely graced five and a half feet. What he lacked in height he made up for in attitude, and it wasn't pleasant.

Ignoring her jab, Viktor taunted, "You're supposed to be the best. You should have seen something by now."

"You do know that catching someone unaware requires stealth. Stealth requires silence. Something I'm not allowed at the moment because you two can't mind your own damned business. Then again, you probably don't know that, or you'd leave me alone to do my fucking job."

"Do you kiss your mother with that mouth?" Viktor goaded.

Tatiana sucked in a breath and turned the scope toward the back of the house where Viktor was leaning against a tree. Taunting was one thing, but bringing up her mother was sinking to the lowest level of the nine circles. Releasing the air from her lungs, Tatiana squeezed the trigger. Dirt and debris danced around her cousin's feet.

"You bitch!" Viktor glared toward the hill, searching to find where the silenced shot had been fired from. "I will kill you."

"Not if I get you first," she promised.

"Stop it. Both of you," Ivan demanded. He was smart enough to fear her temper. "If something happens to Anatoly because of your pettiness..."

Tatiana turned the scope away from the house when a commotion caught her eye. Several birds scattered from the trees on the north side of the compound, a large eagle among them. Tracking the larger bird's movement, Tatiana pulled away from the scope then readjusted her eye when she noticed the eagle gripping something in one of its talons. What looked like a bag of sorts was dangling beneath it. "What the...?" The bird disappeared as it dipped down between some branches of the tall evergreen. Jumping to her feet, Tatiana draped the strap of the weapon over her neck and took off running in the direction the bird had dropped. As she rushed through the woods, she removed her pistol from the holster at her hip, flipping off the safety. Being an expert in all manner of firearms, she didn't need to look at the 9mm as she pulled a silencer from her pocket and screwed the attachment on.

"Have the others checked in?" she asked as she scanned the area.

"*Otvali!* I know how to do my job," Ivan hissed.

"*Mudak,*" Tatiana mumbled.

"What the fuck did you call me?"

Shit. Tatiana did her best to always use English, but when her cousins pissed her off, she sometimes let a Russian term slip. "Why are you two outside? You're supposed to be guarding Father."

"Did you see someone? Where are you going?" Ivan asked his own questions as she ran out in the open for a few yards before slipping back into the cover of the trees.

Ignoring her cousin who was now calling for the others to check in, Tatiana slowed her steps as she neared the spot where the bird dove. Her heart was beating in her ears as she rested to catch her breath. Walking as quietly as possible, Tatiana scanned the area, gun gripped in both hands.

The roar of a motorcycle engine echoed off the cliffs in the distance, and she took off at a sprint toward the road leading away from the compound. Just as she broke through the tree line, a black and chrome bike thundered away, ridden by a large man with long, blond hair escaping from beneath his helmet. She didn't have time to unhitch the rifle, so taking aim, Tatiana shot at the man until the magazine of her pistol was empty.

"Fuck!" she exclaimed as she lost sight of him. "Ivan, get to the house. Now!" If her intuition was correct, her father was dead. Her role – her only job – was to protect her father. Protect the Volkov name. Sometimes that meant eliminating a threat. Tatiana had taken her first life at age sixteen. Without a mother around to teach her any differently, Tatiana learned to compartmentalize between ending a life and living one. Her father had tried to tell her emotions had no place in the type of life they led. Anatoly had an *us or them* mentality, and he considered anyone not in their family to be *them*. She didn't think that way. She couldn't. If she allowed herself to be nothing but a machine, she'd turn out like him and her cousins. Tatiana was her own person, and Russian mafia or not, her father couldn't take that from her.

With nothing to be done about the man on the motorcycle, Tatiana turned toward the house and ran. She was halfway there when her cousin's voice nearly pierced her eardrum. Tatiana was never taught their native tongue, but that didn't stop her from learning it on her own. She hadn't gone ten feet when her cousin's curses let her know her fears were confirmed. Still, she didn't slow until she was inside.

"Some fucking guard you are, Tatiana!"

"This isn't my fault. I was following orders, Viktor. You were there when Father told me to scan the perimeter. I was also there when he ordered you and Ivan to stand guard outside his room. So, tell me why you two were outside?"

"Enough!" Mikael shouted, running a hand through his hair. "I'm the one who told Viktor and Ivan to guard the side door."

Tatiana tried to shoulder past her cousin, but he blocked her way. "You don't want to go in there, Cousin."

"Get out of my way, Mikael. I need to see him."

Mikael exhaled loudly and stepped aside. Tatiana rushed into her father's room and stopped several feet away from where two guards were lying on the floor of the bedroom. A crimson stain spread around them, soaking into the golden carpet from having their necks sliced open. When she didn't see her father, she stepped carefully over the guards and moved toward the bathroom. That was where she found Anatoly, sitting on the toilet, with his neck also cut.

"How is this possible?" she asked.

"That's what we're trying to figure out. I have Ivan looking at the video feed," Mikael said.

"I only saw one man," Tatiana muttered.

"What man? What are you talking about?" Viktor demanded.

"I chased a man through the woods, but he got on

19

a motorcycle before I could reach him. I emptied my gun, but he was too fast."

"So, you failed to get your father's murderer? What good are you?"

"Me? I'm not the one who let him get in the house!"

"Enough! Viktor, you and Ivan wait for me in the study. I need to have a word with Tatiana."

Tatiana stood and faced her cousin, already knowing her fate. With her father dead, Mikael was now head of the family.

"Your father kept you close because you were his daughter, but unlike him, I have no use for a female guard. However, your skills can be useful elsewhere. I know this has always been your home, but seeing as how you and Viktor can't get along, I think it's best you make other living arrangements. I'll see to it you're given enough money to get started in a new city. As long as you do as I say, you will remain under my protection."

Tatiana bit back a laugh. She understood the ways of the family. It didn't matter that she was Anatoly's daughter. It made no difference everything should go to her as his only offspring. Mikael was now head of the family, and as such, the compound and all assets were his to control. Unless she took them from him by force. *Yeah, you and what army?* As for his protection, she knew all he had to do was put word out that Tatiana was a traitor, and there would be a target on her back.

"It is your job to find your father's killer. Since you saw him and failed to take him out, you will not stop until you find who did this and finish the job. Once that is accomplished, you will remain on the payroll in the capacity of assassin. But let me make myself clear, Cousin. Should you refuse, I will make sure word gets out that you are no longer a Volkov."

"I understand." She understood so much more than he realized. "I'll go pack my belongings." With one last look at her father's body, Tatiana left the room. She should feel bad the man was dead. She did, but not the way a daughter should grieve the man who brought her into the world. Tatiana's life hadn't been easy nor happy, but it was constant. She knew what to expect. In his own way, Anatoly had protected Tatiana, but now he was no longer there as a buffer between her and her cousins or anyone else who felt she wasn't fit to be part of their family all because she was a woman.

To avoid passing the office, Tatiana took the back staircase to her bedroom on the third floor. Her clothes, toiletries, and weapons were the only items she intended to take. Those and the one photo she had of her and her mother. Anything else would serve as a dark reminder of the life she'd been forced into at a young age. She had more shoes than one woman needed, but they were necessary in her line of work. Being an assassin often meant disguising herself, and besides that, she really liked shoes. It took almost an hour and several trips to her car, but Tatiana was loaded and on her way out the door.

Either luck was on her side, or Mikael had kept his brothers occupied. Either way, Tatiana was able to escape the manor without running into Viktor. Or Marta. Not having to say goodbye was a blessing. The cook-slash-housekeeper had to know by now Anatoly was dead. Tatiana knew Marta was one of Anatoly's mistresses. Tatiana learned long ago the woman wasn't her friend. She refused to teach Tatiana to cook, saying the *Printessa* had no place in the kitchen. Considering she said it with a scowl, Tatiana knew Marta wasn't a fan. The woman had other reasons not to like Tatiana, but those were best left in the past.

Mikael said he would give her enough money to move out, but what he didn't know was she had put most of what her father paid her into a separate account. Anatoly kept tabs on her money, but she explained the lack of funds was due to her wardrobe and weapons for the jobs he sent her on. Mikael, who had been mentored by Anatoly, now had access to her information. He would be able to trace her using her phone, but since she was still employed by the family, she couldn't toss it. Since he could track her, she didn't bother going farther than the first nice hotel she came to. She would consider an apartment once she figured out how she was going to get away from the family. But first, she had a killer to catch.

Tatiana didn't unpack her car other than taking the suitcase which contained a few sets of clothes and toiletries, her case which concealed her rifle, and her computer. After the day she had, Tatiana wasn't ready to start the search for the assassin. She wanted to strip down, grab a bottle of wine, and take a nice, long bath. Besides, she had no idea where to begin looking for the biker.

If she'd been using her rifle, she could have used the scope to get a better look at the man. The only thing she was sure of was his long, blond hair. He wasn't wearing a motorcycle club vest, so she couldn't track him that way. Tossing her things onto the king-sized bed, Tatiana unpacked her clothes and put them in the dresser. Next, she lined up the shoes she'd included at the bottom of the closet next to the rifle case. She reloaded the pistol, chambering a bullet, and made sure the safety was on. Her stomach rumbled with hunger, so she called down for room service.

While she waited for her steak dinner and bottle of wine, Tatiana flopped down on the bed and stared at the ceiling. Her father was dead. Now that she had time to really think about that, she expected the tears to fall. They didn't. Why would they when he had never shown Tatiana an ounce of love? From the time her mother died, Anatoly made it his mission to train Tatiana as a soldier.

Her childhood had been stolen from her. Her teenage years were nothing like what she imagined other girls her age got to experience. Attending high school. Going on dates. Tatiana had never been kissed, but that was her choice. It wasn't until she was sent out of town on jobs that she finally had sex, thinking one-night stands were better than not having companionship. She lost her virginity when she was twenty-one, but she never allowed men to kiss her. That, to her, was more intimate than sex.

Getting away from the watchful eye of her father was the main reason she'd been looking forward to going on vacation. Alone. She'd been surprised when he didn't argue against her going to such a tropical location by herself.

None of that mattered now. He was gone. Mikael was in charge, and she was on her own. That didn't mean she wasn't expected to toe the line. She just had to figure out how to do so while finding a way to separate herself from her cousins. *Good luck with that.*

24

CHAPTER THREE

Natalia

FIVE DAYS AFTER her father had been killed, Tatiana was still hiding out in her hotel, trying to figure out her next steps. When her cell phone rang, she expected it to be one of her cousins. She wanted to let it go to voicemail, but she didn't want to experience Mikael's temper. When she looked at the caller ID, it showed an unlisted number. Still, she answered. An electronic voice introduced themselves as Nix. Tatiana was freaked out and hung up. This Nix immediately called back, and when Tatiana let it roll over to voicemail, the person left a detailed message explaining how they knew everything about Tatiana including the fact that she needed a job to get away from her cousins. Nix offered her the chance to put her assassin skills to work while continuing to search for the blond biker.

She didn't return the call, but then a package showed up at her hotel the next morning. Tatiana was intrigued. Included was a birth certificate for someone named Natalia Jones. A passport and driver's license had been issued in the new name, along with a flash drive. Tatiana didn't dare insert it into her own laptop for fear it would crash her system. The note included

25

assured her it was safe, but she didn't trust the note.

Tatiana took the flash drive to a local internet café and risked their computer. The information provided included files showing a new bank account set up in her new name, as well as everything she needed to escape her cousins and begin a new life. In exchange for this new identity, Tatiana had to agree to work for an organization of assassins. If, after joining, Tatiana found she changed her mind, she could revert back to her old name, and Natalia Jones would no longer exist.

Being born into a family of Russian mafia royalty meant she had been trained from an early age in all things guns, money laundering, and family. She'd taken to guns like a fish to water, and she knew how to hide her money from everyone, including her family. *Especially* her family. If what Nix promised was reality, Tatiana had someone helping her disappear for good.

Taking a leap of faith, because the alternative of working for the family the rest of her life wasn't an option, Tatiana agreed to the terms set forth in the contract.

Just like that, Tatiana Volkova no longer existed.

Natalia left New Woodland and moved farther north, using the advance Nix gave her. She rented a small house, having closed her eyes and pointed to a location on the map. After getting settled, she cut her hair and dyed it lavender. Natalia had a new name, so a new look to go with it felt right. She would like to have chosen her own name. Natalia wasn't bad, but Jones was so… plain. Maybe that was the point. It was one of the most popular surnames, so she had become one in millions. Easier to hide who she was.

Nix gave Natalia a couple weeks to acclimate to

her new surroundings before sending her a contract. Since she had experience assassinating whoever Anatoly considered a threat to the family, Natalia felt comfortable accepting it, wanting to dive into her new role. She was ready to see the zeros in her bank account rise significantly, and she could only do that by accepting jobs.

The first one was closer to home than she had expected. Natalia worked the mark the same way she did her previous hits. She spent time watching the man. Learning his patterns. Assessing the best time to hit. It had been almost too easy, and after the job was complete, her bank account grew. Nix gave Natalia a few days before sending another file. She accepted each one she received since they were all straightforward. Now, almost three months later, Natalia was perched atop an apartment building across from her latest assignment.

Exhaling slowly, Natalia squeezed the trigger of her rifle. Her mark dropped, but something seemed off about the way he fell. Looking through the scope, she searched for signs of anyone in the room who shouldn't be there. A shadow crossed the window, and she had her answer. Someone else killed her mark or at least was in the room with him. She had spent weeks surveying the man she'd been contracted to kill, and his schedule had remained the same every single day. No one came in except for the kid who delivered groceries, and he only went out on Thursday morning to visit his mother. Natalia guessed even pedophiles had families. "Damn it," she hissed under her breath, breaking down her rifle.

Natalia didn't want to take the chance of being

caught by whomever had been in the apartment, but she needed to make sure he was dead, or she wouldn't get paid. *You might not get paid anyway.* Before crossing the street to the mark's building, Natalia stowed her rifle case, which looked like an ordinary briefcase, in the trunk of her rental. As was her usual routine, she had parked a couple blocks away.

The weight of her knives against her wrists, which were hidden by a fashionable, long coat, was comforting. Her blonde wig and sunglasses hid most of her features were someone to see her going in the building. Natalia scanned her surroundings, looking for anyone out of place. Staking out the mark's home had given her insight into the type of people who strolled down the crowded sidewalk in the busy area of New Albany.

As she neared the apartment, an imposing figure made his way toward Natalia. He scanned the area much the same way she did. He was dressed casually. His jeans were worn, hugging him tight in all the right places. Thick forearms covered in ink led to nice biceps, which were straining the sleeves of his white T-shirt. Natalia's eyes were hidden behind dark sunglasses, so she was able to study his face as they passed one another. She'd never seen eyes that blue, and if she weren't on assignment, she would have been sorely tempted to turn around and follow the man. Pretending to adjust her sunglasses, Natalia pressed the side of the right leg, snapping a photo of the man to look at later. Being an assassin paid well and afforded her some useful equipment.

His clothes were too tight and exposing to hide weapons, so she was pretty sure he wasn't anyone to think twice about in regards to her mark. She would definitely think twice about him in other ways when this mess was over with. Natalia did like taller men with muscles. Then again, most men were taller than her five-five frame.

When she reached the apartment building, Natalia didn't slow. She entered the lobby like she belonged there, bypassing the elevators for the stairs. Although she was wearing a disguise, she didn't want to be caught on the security camera in the lift. When she reached the door where her mark lived, she tried the knob. Finding it locked, she pulled the picking tools out of her coat pocket. Within seconds, the tumblers clicked, and she turned the knob with her gloved hand. Silently, she eased into the entryway, her senses on high alert.

As she peered around the wall separating the hall and the main lounging area, Natalia froze. The man wasn't moving and never would again. Instead of a hole in the center of his forehead, blood pooled under his head from the deep gash across his throat.

"Fuck!" Natalia had seen this cause of death before. The same large laceration that killed her father and his guards had taken out this man. Was Anatoly's killer taunting her? Had he been following her, waiting for the right moment to take her out, too? If so, her new identity was compromised.

Pulling out her phone, Natalia snapped a few pictures for Nix before she turned and exited the apartment. Retracing her steps, she pulled her gloves off, shoving them in her pocket after she left the building through a back entrance, and nonchalantly strolled down the sidewalk to a coffee shop. Caffeine on top of the adrenaline coursing through her veins wasn't a good idea, but she required a moment to gather her thoughts before calling Nix. If someone else had killed him, Natalia wouldn't get her fee. But why would someone else have taken him out? Had Nix double-dipped on the contract? They – because she still didn't know if Nix was male or female – had never screwed her out of a deal before, so why would they start now?

Nix never dictated how Natalia did her job. She could take a considerable amount of time watching, waiting until the opportunity was perfect, as long as she got the job done. Two weeks wasn't out of the norm, so had whoever contracted the hit got impatient and hired someone else? A quarter of a million was a lot of money to pay twice.

She got her caramel macchiato and left the busy shop, sipping her drink while walking back toward the hotel where she'd holed up. Her bags were already packed and waiting in the trunk along with her weapon's case. Once a job was complete, Natalia didn't wait around. She left the area and went home to decompress.

Natalia waited to make sure she wasn't being followed, and then she rang Nix on the burner phone.

"Myshka?" they answered, using Natalia's callsign. "Did something happen?" Of course, they would ask that, considering Natalia never called after a job. She sent a photo with proof the job was done. She hadn't sent the photos yet.

"Was this an open contract and you forgot to tell me?" Natalia kept her eyes on the road in front of her instead of scanning the streets for another assassin.

"No. I check the contracts continuously until it's closed. Again, did something happen?" The distortion didn't mask the irritation coming through the phone.

"Someone got there before I did. The mark's neck was sliced almost through. I took the shot, but the mark was already falling."

"Did you take pictures?"

"Yes. I'll send them to you when I stop."

"I'll be in touch." Nix disconnected before discussing payment.

"Damn it!" Natalia slapped the steering wheel. She needed a vacation now more than ever. She was good at her job, and no, she didn't regret the people she killed. Natalia had a code, and she researched the marks before she pulled the trigger. She refused to have innocent blood on her hands, only taking contracts on the worst of the worst. Serial killers. Rapists. Pedophiles. Human traffickers. Natalia refused to take out someone's husband because they were cheating. She also refused to take an open contract. Too many assassins in one place was not a party in her book.

Just as she merged onto the interstate, the burner phone rang. "Yes?"

"I double-checked. The contract was not open. The client doesn't know it wasn't you who made the hit, so you'll still get your money."

"Then what the hell, Nix?"

"Someone probably found out about his proclivities and decided to take matters into their own hands. Regardless, the contract is complete, and the world now has one less child molester, and we still get paid. That's a win in my book."

31

"I don't need company on my jobs."

"The money will be wired as soon as I have the photos." Nix hung up before Natalia could complain further. She shouldn't fuss; she was still getting paid. But what if she'd pulled the trigger two seconds earlier? Would the actual killer come looking for her? That had been too close for comfort. What she couldn't figure out was why, if it wasn't an open contract, had there been someone else there? As long as she got her money, it didn't matter. Natalia drove out of the city, and when she had several miles between her and the dead body, she pulled over and sent the photos to Nix. Less than ten minutes later, her phone pinged with the payment notification. Breathing only slightly easier, she headed toward home.

Home. The large estate where she'd grown up ceased being home the second her mother died when Natalia was six. What had once been her sanctuary quickly became nothing more than a military school. The area around the compound was her training field. Her father pulled her from public school and brought in a tutor. The few friends she'd made quickly faded from her mind, and her three cousins were the only ones close to her age she associated with.

In the beginning, she didn't mind hanging around the three boys, but as they got older, she became aware of the resentment. Both hers and her cousins'. She resented them because they were taught the business side of things. They resented her because her father trained her to be his protection. She had the best of everything where weapons were concerned. Killing was the only thing she knew, and she had a job making lots of money doing what she was good at while ridding the world of scum like her latest mark.

Now, home was in Upstate New York, hundreds of miles away from where she grew up, though sometimes it didn't seem far enough. The bungalow-style house was nestled between rows of trees, hiding her from nosy neighbors. She didn't have to worry about sneaking her weapons into an apartment building. She could've found something larger, but it was just her. No roommates. No family. No pets to come home to. She'd thought about getting a dog, but that wouldn't be fair to the animal.

After spending her life having her every move not only dictated but watched, it was nice to come home to solitude where she could do whatever she wanted. The only thing missing was a partner. Even if she were to eventually retire, she would have to lie to whomever she settled down with about her past, and that was something she refused to do. Relationships built on lies, even those by omission, were doomed from the start. Natalia couldn't see a husband in her future as much as she longed for a family of her own.

As she turned into the driveway, the perimeter lights came on. Natalia might have a new identity, but she still looked over her shoulder. When she agreed to work for Nexus, Nix assured Natalia nobody besides the company knew who she really was. The paperwork had created a whole new person complete with a history going back to when she was "born." Assurances or not, being an assassin meant she was constantly on guard, and that didn't stop just because she was at home. Her alarm system was top-of-the-line. Any movement inside or outside alerted an app on her phone. The app also allowed her to make sure the cameras were online. No one visited, and nobody was ever supposed to be there besides herself, but she was too paranoid not to check a couple times a day. All her mail went to a PO Box, so her home address wasn't in any system other than Nexus's.

When Natalia noticed an envelope on her front porch, her first thought was Nix. They were the only ones outside the realtor who knew where she lived. Still, whoever had dropped off the package had done so without triggering the alarm. Not bothering to unpack, Natalia opened the app on her phone and checked inside the house. The cameras didn't show any intruders, so she rewound the feed to try and pinpoint when the breach happened. When she found it, Natalia felt only marginally better. A drone had dropped the package off, not flying low enough to set off the sensors.

Natalia didn't bother looking for gloves before she picked up the envelope. If someone went to that much trouble to reach her, they were smart enough not to leave fingerprints or DNA. She didn't tear into it right away. Instead, she got her luggage and weapons out of her car and took them inside. Natalia went about her routine of tossing dirty clothes into the washing machine, securing her rifle in the gun safe in the back of her closet, and then taking a shower. Dressed in her favorite terrycloth shorts and an oversized T-shirt, Natalia unpacked the rest of her things and stowed her bags in the guestroom closet.

It was going on four in the morning, but she was too wired to sleep. Natalia poured herself a glass of wine and sat down at the kitchen table, eyeing the envelope. She took several sips before using a knife to open the package. She upended the envelope, and a stack of photos slid out onto the table, spreading apart like a hand of cards. Shuffling through the pictures, she had a nagging feeling about the subject matter. The man reminded her of the one she'd passed on the sidewalk hours ago. This one had longer hair that was lighter blond, and his beard was shorter, but his build was the same.

Natalia retrieved her laptop and downloaded the photo she'd taken using her sunglasses. When it loaded, she compared that picture with the ones she'd been sent. Either it was the same man, or he had a twin. One of the photos showed the man with a group of bikers, all wearing the same motorcycle club vest. *The Hounds of Zeus*. She checked inside the envelope, but there was nothing inside to indicate who had sent the photos or why. She assumed it was Nix, but why was more concerning than who at the moment. She studied the photos as she finished off her wine. Natalia had just set the glass down when it hit her – the man who had taken out Anatoly had been blond and rode a bike. Was this the same person who'd killed her mark before her bullet could do the job? The killing strike had been the same, and she didn't believe in coincidence. Now, all she had to do was find this biker.

And do what once you find him?

That was the million-dollar question.

CHAPTER FOUR

Maveryck

OUT OF THE thousands of days Maveryck had been alive, there were a handful which stuck out in his mind more than others. One was the day Warryck walked away from the family. Another was the day War graduated from college, and Mav and the other Hounds rode with him to get revenge for his wife's death. Jenna texting to let him know she was leaving was on his list. Until today, the most recent was six months ago when he took out Anatoly Volkov. Now, he would be adding today to the list.

Maveryck was pissed. No, he was beyond pissed. Ryker assured him the shitshow at Volkov's compound had been a fluke, but coming close to having his head blown off by a sniper had him seething. Not only would he no longer take contracts for single hits, he was going to have a long talk with his older brother about any of the Hounds taking them. It was obvious they could no longer trust Nexus.

Mav schooled his expression as he left the apartment. He didn't need to give anyone reason to pay attention to him. Well, no more attention that he usually got for a male his size. With his long beard and all his ink, he stood out. He kept his eyes peeled for someone who didn't belong in the area. If whoever had taken the shot was worth their salt, they wouldn't make it obvious they were an assassin. When a short blonde walked toward him, Mav couldn't help but appreciate her toned legs strolling the sidewalk like a runway model, if runway models were on the short side.

He was used to women checking him out, so when she adjusted her sunglasses, he wasn't surprised. What did surprise him was his body's reaction to her. He experienced a sense of déjà vu when the scent of wildflowers met his nose. If he hadn't been reeling from nearly getting shot, he might have turned around and followed her. It had been too long since he'd had sex. For the last four years, he'd not bothered with women other than one-night stands. Those he made sure were out of town, away from the family. He didn't want to give any woman the wrong idea of his intentions, and he sure didn't want a woman knowing where he lived or that he was in an MC. There were too many females who loved the idea of getting with a biker.

Against his better judgment, he turned and watched the woman strut down the sidewalk. There was something about her that called to him. If Gryphons had fated mates, he might think that was what was urging him to go after her. Since they didn't, he chalked it up to the Gryphon being unsettled. His beast remained quiet, so Mav kept walking. He couldn't go after her anyway. He had to get out of the area and away from any and all CCTVs in the vicinity. More importantly, he had to get home and have a talk with Ryker. Again.

When he reached his bike, he slung a leg over the seat, and settled the helmet on his head. He was ready to be home and hit the road for pleasure. War and his female, Kerrigan, were settling in. Now that War was officially a Hound of the MC persuasion, it was like old times. Maveryck liked Kerrigan, and he didn't mind when she joined them on their rides. When she thought the twins needed time to themselves to reconnect, she hung out with Rory or Lucy. The females of the Lazlo family had welcomed Kerrigan. It was easy to like the fiery redhead.

When he pulled up at the clubhouse, he was surprised to see so many bikes in the parking lot considering it was almost two in the morning. He had checked his phone before he left New Jersey, and there hadn't been any messages. When he stepped off his bike, he checked it again. Seeing no missed calls or messages, he ran his hands through his short hair and headed inside. Mav had cut his hair after the Volkov fiasco. If the shooter was going to come after him, he thought it would be best if he looked different, so he changed his appearance somewhat. Instead of shaving his beard, he let it grow longer. He started growing his facial hair back when he was presented with his patches, and he'd never shaved it off.

"Mayhem, how'd it go?" Ryker asked, using Mav's MC name. The Hounds got quiet, waiting for Mav's answer.

"It was another fucking Volkov situation. We've gotta talk about these singular hits. Something's not right."

"What happened?" War asked, stepping up to clap

38

his twin on the shoulder. Fuck, but Mav could use a hug. He knew the other Hounds wouldn't blink twice at the two of them embracing, but he'd wait until they were alone.

"I just about got my head blown off by a sniper rifle. If I'd been one second slower..." Mav shook his head. "This is bullshit, Ryot. And that's the last time I'm taking a contract. Someone at Nexus is either fucking with us or fucking up. Either way, I'm done." Maveryck strode to the bar and snagged a bottle of whiskey. He chugged down several mouthfuls, not caring about the others drinking from the same bottle, and then wiped his mouth with the back of his free hand.

"That is a problem, but we'll talk more about it tomorrow."

"Why are you all gathered so late?"

"Hawk and Spyder have been scoping out Josiah Talbert's compound, and we were waiting on you to get back so you could ride with us." Ryker motioned to Hawk. "Tell us about the layout."

The Hounds gathered around the oak table in the room where they held church – MC meetings. Hawk spread out a hand-drawn picture of the compound. "It's set up like an Old West town with rows of buildings on both sides of the street and a church at one end. Behind the main buildings are cottages where the people live, with couples living on one side and single people living on the other. The outbuildings and barns are at the north end of the property. There's a larger house where Josiah lives, midway between the single homes and the outbuildings. There are two roads leading in and out. This one takes you right into the town, and the other one is close to the outbuilding." Hawk pointed to the map as he explained the layout.

Spyder stepped up next to Hawk. "The cottages are basic wooden structures, but there's a shit-ton of them, like a neighborhood. The buildings lining the street where the church is have everything you would see in the Old West with the exception of a saloon. As far as I could tell, there's no drinking allowed. We'll go in this way, stopping about a mile out so they don't hear us."

"The layout is almost identical to Gideon's former location. Exactly how many people live here?" Mav asked. There had been over two hundred at Gideon's compound.

"Best guess? Three hundred. This isn't just a town where people live in harmony sitting around singing 'Kumbaya.' This could very well be a military installation if it weren't for the civilians. Most of the men dress as if they're ready for battle. Black fatigues, black T-shirts, and military-grade boots. They don't carry weapons out in the open, but we did get a glance at the inside of the warehouses. All of them are full of crates." Spyder pointed at where the large outbuildings were drawn on the map.

"What's in the barns?" Ryker asked.

"Vehicles. Trucks of all sizes, as well as ATVs. There was a lot of movement, like they're gearing up for something."

"It's about three hours away, and if we leave now, we can still get there before daylight." Ryker turned to Mav. "I know you've been through some shit, so if you want to sit this one out, I'll understand."

"Fuck that. I need something to take my mind off

the last few hours." Mav replaced the cap on the whiskey and put the bottle back.

"You sure you're up to it?" War asked. His twin wasn't being condescending, so his words didn't piss Maveryck off.

"I'm sure."

Ryker pounded a fist on the table. "Hounds, let's ride. Havyck, you and King take the SUV in case we need to get someone out of there."

Their youngest brother didn't argue. Maveryck would have if Ryker told him to drive a cage. He was still pissed and needed the feel of the wind on his face to ease the anger.

While the others were headed to their bikes, War hung back. "Come here," he said, opening his arms. Mav didn't hesitate to let his twin wrap him in a tight embrace. Now that War was back, Maveryck couldn't remember how he'd gotten through the last twenty-odd years without him. They only hugged a few seconds, but it was enough.

"Thanks. You don't know how much I needed that."

"Probably as much as I did." War grinned and patted Mav's cheek softly.

Riding was as necessary as breathing for Mav, but racing the wind beside his twin the past few months had enhanced each experience. Mav loved his other brothers, but War was the other half of him. The bond hadn't gone away while they were apart; it had only been muted. And even though War had Kerrigan in his life, he was part of the MC, and that meant Mav got to spend a lot of time with him. Seeing the Hounds' colors on War's kutte was something he never really expected but always hoped for. Now, they both were Hounds in every sense of the word.

They didn't wear their vests when they were on a mission. There were plenty of biker clubs across the country, and the Hounds didn't need to advertise which club they belonged to as they rode into other territories. The Hounds had chapters all around the world, but they were spread out. Thus, the reason their chapter needed to ride four hours away to investigate the cult. Since this particular group was part of The Ministry, they would figure out a way to take it apart.

As they were loading up, Mav looked around. "Hey, where's Pop?" Sutton usually rode with them whenever they went after the cults.

"Rory got back from Texas last night." Ryker didn't need to explain further. Their mom had been down south visiting a couple of their sisters, and Ministry or not, Sutton wasn't going to let his wife come home after a long trip only to have him leave straightaway. He had turned the MC over to Ryker, but he was still involved in their mission to take down the Ministry. He and Rory were in charge of finding temporary homes for anyone being held in the groups against their will.

The Hounds rolled out with Ryot and Mayhem, being Pres and VP, leading the way. The other members were stacked behind them, and Havyck and King brought up the rear in the SUV. Mav would like to ride alongside his twin, but when they rode in a large group, they all stuck to rank formation, even if they weren't wearing their colors.

Maveryck let the cool night air wash over him. Riding to and from jobs alone wasn't nearly as soothing as riding with his Brothers. The roar of the engines always turned heads, whether they were on the highway or on backroads. Tonight, with little traffic, the rumble wasn't quite as loud, but it was still impressive. When they pulled off the highway to refuel, the Hounds paired up at the pumps before moving off to the side of the parking lot. Spyder and Hawk had already been to the compound earlier in the week, so they took the lead positions.

Twenty minutes later, the group turned onto a backroad a mile away from where Josiah Talbert's compound was located and parked off to the side. Since they weren't sure what they were going to find, they walked the rest of the way in instead of shifting. When they got to the tall, chain-link fence surrounding the property, the Hounds paused and listened. Being early, they hadn't expected to hear much of anything, but it was eerily quiet.

Hawk stepped to the middle of the pack. "If we walk straight that way, we run into the back of the church."

"You mean that big-ass building?" Ryker was looking where Hawk pointed.

Hawk nodded. "Yes. It's the largest structure on the compound with the exception of the warehouses. It's even larger than the barns."

Mav's beast had been restless ever since they were almost shot, not bothering to speak. Until now.

It's too quiet.

I agree.

We should shift and take a look around.

Not our call. This is Ryot's deal. You know that.

I do, but we need to shift.

43

Mav was almost afraid to shift. With his beast being so antsy, he was afraid he might lose control. That hadn't happened since Jenna texted that she was leaving. Then the Gryphon came forward, and Mav had come close to tearing his house apart. If it wasn't for the vaulted ceiling in his living room, he would have.

"Are you with us?" Ryker asked Mav.

"Yeah, sorry. Just listening to the quiet." Shifters had sensitive hearing, and there were different levels of stillness. This one was right up there with the silence after a snowstorm.

"That's what we were discussing. If there are three hundred people here, there would be some type of noise. Since Hawk and Spyder are familiar with the layout, they're going to shift and do a flyover."

We should go with them.

No, we shouldn't.

It didn't take long for their two scouts to return. When they shifted back to their human forms, Hawk was shaking his head. "They're gone."

"That's impossible. You were just here a few days ago." Ryker ran his hands through his hair, pacing back and forth. "Are you sure there's no one left?"

"There could be a few people hiding out. But the warehouses and barn doors were open, and they're all empty."

"Fuck!" Ryker's head transformed to that of his lion. He shook out his long mane, rumbled low in his throat, and then shifted back. "We need to search every inch of that compound. If there's one person left, I want them found. I promised Mac..." Ryker turned and walked off. The other Hounds waited for him to get his thoughts together. Mac's boyfriend had supposedly been taken from Gideon's compound to this one.

Ryker stalked back to the group. "Spread out. I want every inch of this compound scoured."

The Hounds took off, and when they entered the small town, Mav and War branched off together. A couple hours later, they all reconvened. Not one person had been found.

They didn't have to wait long for Ryker to give the orders of next steps. "Rev, I want you, Shadow, Ace, and Ripper to stay here. Search for any clue as to where they could have gone. Tank, go back to the clubhouse. I'm gonna call Lucy in to help. Mayhem, you come with me. We need to talk about your last assignment. Everyone else can go home for now, but be ready to ride at a moment's notice. As soon as we get any scrap of information, we're going after these fuckers."

Maveryck was ready to go home and get some sleep. But Ryker was right; they needed to figure out what the hell was going on with their contracts. Sleep would have to wait.

CHAPTER FIVE

Natalia

AFTER TOSSING AND turning because her mind wouldn't shut off, Natalia finally got a few hours' sleep. She might have slept longer, but something woke her. Easing her hand under her pillow, Natalia wrapped her hand around the grip of her Glock. The weight of the weapon in her hand was as comfortable as her favorite pair of boots. Being in a small house should make her feel safer than living in the three-story manor, but here, she was alone with only herself to rely on. Natalia slid out of bed and padded barefoot to the front of the house, listening before she entered the living room. Her computer beeped, and Natalia lowered her gun. The notification was the one she received when Nix had a job for her. *Well, tough shit.* Natalia wasn't ready to take another contract. She had promised herself a vacation, but the photos still spread out on the table had put a halt to that idea.

Opening her laptop, she clicked on the tiny icon on the bottom right of the screen and entered her login information. Once it went through the encryption process, the message appeared. She might be a new operative, but her contract stated she could accept or decline any job. She briefly scanned this one, and just as quickly declined. Closing out of the program, she went into the kitchen and placed a pod in her coffee maker. While she waited on it to brew, she opened the fridge, looking for something to eat. Crap, she really needed to get groceries. Natalia grabbed a bag of cheddar cubes and the caramel creamer.

Having grown up with a cook, the past few months had been full of takeout and frozen dinners. The few times she'd attempted to make something for herself, she'd relied on online videos for direction. The dishes hadn't turned out that badly, but they weren't gourmet, either. She had also turned to videos to show her how to properly wash her clothes after shrinking one of her favorite skirts. Who the hell didn't know how to sort clothes at twenty-six?

With her coffee and sad breakfast in hand, Natalia sat down at the table and focused on the photos. The man from the sidewalk was ruggedly handsome. Piercings and ink adorned his body, but it was his eyes that captivated her. The blue wasn't pale and soothing; it was bright and enticing. His hair was somewhere between brown and blond, and that was throwing her off from connecting the two men. If the biker who took out Anatoly had cut his hair, it was possible the blonder locks had been trimmed off leaving the shorter, darker hair.

Opening the internet, Natalia searched The Hounds of Zeus. What she found wasn't information on a motorcycle club. Instead, pages of Greek mythology popped up, explaining how the Hounds were synonymous with Harpies. Natalia didn't see the MC using a bird-like woman as their symbol, though.

She pulled one of the photos closer and studied the back of the vest. The logo, or whatever bikers called their symbol, looked more like two gryphons surrounding a skull. She clicked on the images tab, and several photos populated of the bikers, but when she clicked on the individual photos, no club information was linked to them, which she found odd. Natalia searched biker clubs in the area, and several had websites or there were news articles written about them. Not the Hounds.

Hmm.

Even the ones who proclaimed to be one-percenters had an internet presence. Natalia got sucked into the world of bikers, and after a couple hours, she knew more than she ever thought she would. That still didn't help her with the Hounds. Her computer skills were only as good as the next person's. Meaning, she didn't have special hacker skills. Whenever she was researching her next mark, she relied on Nix to send her the information. Natalia thought about asking Nix if they'd sent the photos, but if they hadn't, she didn't want to open that conversation. If Nix had, though, what had been their reason? Did they want her to know who had taken out her father? And if so, what good would the information do her? Did they expect her to get revenge?

Did she want to get revenge? Mikael had tasked her with that very thing when he sent her away from her home. Several months later, she was doing everything but what he commanded. And why wouldn't she be? He didn't control her life. Besides, she had already admitted to herself she was glad her father was no longer of this world. When he was first killed, her life was turned on its axis being kicked out, but now? Natalia was doing something she was good at. It might not be what most people would consider an honorable profession, but to her it was. She was taking out the trash. Getting rid of the worst humanity had to offer. If taking the life of a pedophile meant children were safe from that horrific abuse? Yeah, she would say she was proud of her job. Maybe Anatoly had done her a favor in training her to kill. It beat sitting behind a desk answering a phone.

Maybe the man who took out her father had also done her a favor. That didn't negate the fact that the man from the sidewalk had been in the vicinity of her last job. Nix assured her the contract hadn't been an open one, so how did someone else end up killing the man? And why was this same man in the area? Thinking back to the way both Anatoly and her mark had been taken out, it was clear the killer didn't use guns. He preferred a knife or some other sharp object. Knives were easier to conceal. When she looked close at the photo of Blue Eyes – because she couldn't keep calling him the man from the sidewalk – he could have hidden his weapon of choice in his boots. And that made it easier to get in and out of the area quickly. He didn't have to break down a rifle. He didn't have to find the perfect vantage point from which to take a shot. No, he preferred to be up close. That made him all the more dangerous.

Why did that excite Natalia? It should make her want to run fast and run far. It didn't though. He was the type of man she could have a relationship with. Natalia imagined meeting up for coffee for the first date. Instead of talking about their favorite music and movies, they could compare kills. They would make a killer couple. She snorted at her pun. There was no way a man like him would want a woman who looked like her. Sure, she was cute like a pixie, but she had seen the types of women bikers went for. Curvy, big-breasted women with bigger hair. Ones who probably knew how to dance on a pole or at least on top of a bar. Natalia had never danced a day in her life. Was she stereotyping? Yes. She was also being realistic.

Putting aside the crazy fantasy of being Blue Eyes "old lady," Natalia decided to forget about the man and the photos for the time being. She had crap she needed to do, like laundry and grocery shopping. She still wanted a vacation in a tropical location, and the mysteries would be there when she returned. Logging into her bank account, Natalia knew to the penny how much money she had, but she checked her balance every single day. Nix had the ability to wire money into the account since they had set it up, so it only made sense they could withdraw funds as well. Call her paranoid, but with the way this last job had gone, she considered opening a separate account.

Her mind went back to Blue Eyes, and Natalia picked up the photo she had taken. He looked right at her when they passed on the sidewalk, one side of his mouth tilted in a smirk. Did she even register in his mind? Maybe, but she'd been wearing a disguise. He had seen a sharply dressed woman with shoulder-length blonde hair and dark, red lips. Was that his type? He couldn't tell what was hidden beneath her coat other than her legs. If he was the one who took out her mark, he probably checked out every single person he passed, considering a bullet had been shot into the same room he'd been in. Had he taken a contract only to find out someone else was after the same man?

Gah! Natalia's mind was spinning. She needed something else to think about, and when her stomach growled, that did the trick. She put her empty mug in the dishwasher and gathered the photos and her laptop, taking them to her bedroom and storing them in the safe in her closet. Not that she thought anyone would break into her house, but her paranoia was working overtime. Natalia kept her pistol close by at all times, so she placed it on the back of the toilet while she took a shower. With her hair being so short, all she did was run a towel over it before combing it with her fingers. Her color had faded, so she made a call to the hairdresser while putting on her makeup.

The weather was turning cooler, but still, she dressed in a pair of khaki shorts and a sleeveless, lavender blouse. While showering, she decided today would be a good day for a pedicure. If she was going on vacation, her toes needed to be as bright as her bikinis waiting to be worn at the beach. With that thought in mind, Natalia slipped on her favorite leather sandals, put her gun in the hidden pocket of her large purse, and headed to town.

When Natalia picked the spot on the map, she contemplated living in one of the smaller hamlets, but she squashed that idea, because everyone knew everyone else as well as their business. She had a new identity, but she didn't want to stand out among a small group of people. Instead, she chose to live close to New Troy. It wasn't one of the largest cities in the state, but it was large enough she could come and go without anyone recognizing her if she ventured into the downtown area. Plus, it had shopping. Natalia had always loved clothes. And shoes. She wasn't one of those people who liked to order things online and have them delivered. No, she liked to browse the stores and try on different outfits. She could spend hours at the mall.

Now that her account wasn't being monitored by her father or cousin, Natalia could spend as much time and money on fashion as she chose. Wearing disguises on her jobs made it that much more interesting. She took every opportunity to become someone different, and why not? It not only kept her identity hidden, but it was also fun. When she worked for her father, he wanted it known who had taken out his enemies. Sure, that put a bullseye on Natalia, but that was the price of being his assassin. She wondered who Mikael had named in her place. Having run, she was now the one being hunted, of that she had no doubt. You didn't leave their branch of the Volkov family unless you were dead.

After shopping for a few hours, Natalia stopped off and enjoyed her pedicure. She closed her eyes and relaxed while the women chatted in their native language. She paid for the deluxe treatment, getting a hot stone massage and exfoliating scrub. The chair vibrated against her back, rolling against her muscles, keeping her on the fringe of falling asleep. She sat under the dryer and flipped through the latest gossip magazine while the polish dried. With her toes now painted "Berry Fairy Fun," she got into her car to head to the grocery store. She had just started the ignition when her phone rang. It was her hairdresser letting Natalia know she'd had a cancellation. Forgetting groceries, she pulled out of the mall parking lot and headed to the salon.

Natalia had only been to Vicky twice, but the stylist had done such a great job on both the cut and color that Natalia vowed never to use anyone else again. Natalia had dyed her hair once when she was younger. Back then, her darker locks reached halfway down her back. When her father saw the bright red, he had Mikael hold her down while he chopped it off. He didn't stop at a bob. Anatoly cut her hair so close to her scalp he might as well have shaved it. It took a couple years to grow back out, but she never let it get that long again. And she never colored it. Not until she was someone new.

When Natalia was seated, Vicky brought her a glass of wine and made small talk with the other stylists and patrons about her children and theirs without badgering Natalia to share about her own life. That was another reason Natalia returned. The first time she sat in the chair, Vicky caught on to Natalia's need for privacy. Natalia preferred to remain silent rather than come up with a lie about where she worked and why she had no family.

While Natalia had plenty of stories she could tell, they would have her sitting in jail were she ever to talk about her experiences. That couldn't happen. So, instead of fabricating a cover story, she closed her eyes and kept quiet. It was times like this when Natalia second-guessed her profession and living a lonely existence. She had no friends. She didn't talk to her neighbors. Natalia didn't talk to anyone really. Spending time in the chair with Vicky was probably the most socialization she got.

Vicky touched Natalia's shoulder. "What do you think?"

Natalia opened her eyes, admiring the brighter pastel color. "I love it. I feel more like me. Great job, as always."

Vicky removed the cape, and Natalia followed her to the desk to pay. "Would you like to schedule an appointment for next time?"

Natalia shook her head. "I'd better not. My work schedule is kind of crazy." She handed Vicky enough cash to pay for the cut and color plus a nice tip. She didn't use credit cards if she could help it. After saying goodbye, Natalia turned toward the deli next door. She'd already decided to put off grocery shopping until the next day. With her sandwich in hand, Natalia made her way toward her car when the rumble of motorcycles cut through all the other noise around her. She turned toward the sound, and within seconds, a group of bikes rode down the street. She rushed to her car and jumped in, hoping to catch up with them. They might not be the right club, but if they were, she would be one step closer to finding Blue Eyes.

The bikes got caught at a long red light, giving Natalia a chance to get close. Only these men weren't wearing vests with logos on the back. Natalia pulled up beside them in the inside lane and glanced over at the man sitting next to her. He was built, but he wasn't quite as muscular as the one she was looking for. The hair hanging from beneath his helmet was dirty blond, so the color was right, but he didn't have a beard. As if he could feel her eyes on him, the man turned to look at her. He smiled at her, pulled his black sunglasses down and winked before turning his attention back to the road. The light changed, and the bikes took off. Since they didn't appear to be associated with a club, Natalia turned her car around and headed home. As she drove, she wondered what it would be like to ride on the back of a bike, arms wrapped around the rider. She wasn't scared of much, and she had a feeling she would love the sense of freedom riding a motorcycle brought.

If she could just find Blue Eyes, she might get the opportunity. *Sure, you will. Is that before or after you ask him if he killed your father?*

Chapter Six

Maveryck

WHEN MAVERYCK AND Ryker got back to the clubhouse, they headed straight for the bar. Mav did the honors and poured them both a glass of whiskey. "Tell me exactly what happened," Ryker said.

"I had just taken out the mark when a bullet lodged into the wall behind me. The only reason it isn't in my brain is because the man fell against my leg and knocked me off balance."

"And you didn't wait around to see if anyone showed up?"

"No. Not after what happened with Volkov."

"Did you see anyone in the vicinity who shouldn't have been there?" Ryker sipped his liquor, eyes boring into Mav's. Maveryck was used to his older brother's form of interrogation. He could probably recite the questions verbatim.

"No. There was a pretty blonde, but she wasn't carrying a sniper case."

Ryker rolled his eyes. "You don't carry—" His phone pinged, and Ryker glanced at it. "It's a contract." Mav sipped his whiskey while waiting for Ryker to read over the offer. His brother glanced up, frowning.

"I'll be right back." Ryker disappeared into the office, and when he came back, he was carrying a small stack of papers.

"Take a look at this." Ryker handed the documents over.

Mav set his glass on the bar. "What's this one? Another mob boss?"

"Close. It's Anatoly Volkov's daughter."

Mav's head snapped up. "Tatiana Volkova? Who would put a hit out on a mafia princess?"

"Probably someone whose family member she took out. According to these documents, she was her father's assassin."

Maveryck read through the file, then read it again. Nothing in the report matched the image he had in his mind of the woman.

"She might have been the one shooting at you when you took her father out."

Fucking hell. Mav didn't kill women. "I'm gonna need more intel. If she's taking out her father's enemies, she's doing the world a favor. Did you accept the contract?"

"Yes, but not to actually kill the woman. We need to find her and see if she takes out innocents as well as her father's enemies. Well, I guess they're her cousin's enemies now. If not, it makes no sense why Nexus would accept the contract."

"Another reason not to trust them." Maveryck studied the one photo included of the woman. In it, she was standing outside her home with two of her cousins. "When was this taken? Do you know?"

"About three months before you killed Volkov according to the date."

The woman in the photo was slender, standing approximately five-four or five-five, considering the height of her cousins. Chestnut hair fell just past her shoulders. Her clothing was boring. Not what he would expect someone of her status to wear. Then again, he hadn't expected her to be an assassin. Maveryck thought back to the way her bedroom smelled like wildflowers. The pastel colors of her walls and bedding fit with the image he had of her before reading this report. Now, it didn't fit at all.

"Do you want to go after her, or do you want me to put someone else on it? You said you weren't taking any more one-offs," Ryker asked.

"I'll take this one. I have a feeling there's more at play here than disgruntled family."

"I thought you might. Where are you going to start?"

"Where I left off – at their estate."

"Do you think that's wise? She shot at you once."

"Someone shot at me. We don't know for sure it was her. But I need to get close enough to follow her, and she'll leave home at some point."

"Just watch yourself. I know better than to ask if you want backup."

"I'll be careful." Mav gathered the papers and photo. He had some planning to do.

"Keep me posted," Ryker said. "I'm going to get Lucy to see if she can gather any intel on Nexus in the meantime."

"Can we still trust them?"

"I'm not sure, but something isn't right. I feel it in my gut." Ryker glanced down, something he rarely did. Sutton had impressed upon the brothers the importance of looking someone in the eye when speaking to them. The fact that Ryker looked away worried Maveryck.

Still, Mav agreed something wasn't right, but instead of discussing it further, he said goodbye and headed home. The roar of his bike wasn't enough to keep his mind from wandering to the woman in the photo. Something about her expression was off. He knew her older cousin Mikael had taken over for Anatoly, but that didn't mean the man employed Tatiana in the same capacity her father had. She was good enough to be their enforcer but not good enough to rule the family. Maybe she hadn't wanted to rule. *But she wanted to kill people?*

Mav couldn't cast stones at the woman. As far as he knew, she only went after others in the Russian Mafia. What little he had read about them was they broke bonds with the larger groups in their native land when the apocalypse happened. Men like Anatoly Volkov weren't any better than men like Gideon and Josiah Talbert. They all tried to form their own groups which worked outside the rules of right. The Ministry didn't kidnap people to sell for profit, but they might as well. They brought people in under false pretenses and then brainwashed them into believing the Ministry's way of life was the only way.

They kidnapped Kerrigan.

That they did, so who was to say the Ministry didn't make it a habit of kidnapping others? But that wasn't Mav's mission at the moment. He had to find Tatiana Volkova and find out if her life was worth saving.

Instead of taking his bike back to New Woodland,

Mav loaded his SUV with all his surveillance equipment as well as enough clothes for two weeks. He doubted it would take that long to find the woman, but once he did, he was going to follow her. It was his job to ascertain whether or not she deserved death. Yeah, some might call that a God complex, but it was the truth of what he did. There were mercenaries out there whose moral compass didn't point north, but the Hounds' did. They were created to protect humans, not take their lives if they didn't deserve it.

Some might also have a problem with their victims not receiving a trial for their crimes, but the contracts Mav and the other Hounds accepted were for repeat offenders, or men like Anatoly who traded in drugs, guns, and humans. They were men who were among the vilest of humans. Did his daughter know about her father's dealings? Mav had never taken out a female before, and he really hoped Tatiana Volkova wouldn't be the first.

Four and a half hours later, Maveryck checked into a hotel. It was a thirty-minute drive to the Volkov manor. Since he was already familiar with the location as well as the setup, all he needed to do was get close and watch. He had equipment such as infrared goggles, a camera with a long-range lens, and a drone that could get in close for jobs where the mark lived in a less rural area. Here, he wouldn't need those things. Not as long as Tatiana remained there. Instead, he would rely on his eagle to get him close enough to watch. He needed the woman to go about her business so Mav could see what she did outside her home. Did she still work for Mikael, killing their family's enemies? Or was she taking other contracts? Killing innocents?

Mav didn't bother unpacking. He kept his clothes in his duffel in case he needed to move out quickly. Not wanting to be seen around town more than necessary, he ordered room service.

When it was a couple hours before daybreak, Mav left the hotel and drove to a park on the opposite side of the tree line that backed up to the Volkov property. He had found an abandoned service road the last time he was there, and it allowed Mav to park his car well off the road. After undressing and stowing his clothes in his bag, Mav shifted into his eagle and took off toward the house. He found a limb where he could leave his bag, and then got closer to the house. He found the same tree he'd sat in the last time and got comfortable.

Unlike their Aves counterparts, the Hounds' eagles could shift into whatever size suited their need. The Hounds also had the ability to call upon one or more of the elements. Maveryck was an earth shifter; therefore, his wings were reddish-gold. Being an earth shifter, he connected more with his lion, but he never discounted his eagle. The earth was his to command, but he only did so as a last resort. Gryphons had been around since the beginning of time and had yet to be discovered by humans who weren't supposed to know of their existence with the exception of those they took as mates. They had to be careful with shifting and calling on the elements. In choosing a mate, they had to make sure that human wasn't going to expose them. Gryphons had the ability to alter a human's thoughts, so if they felt their mate couldn't keep their secret, they "helped" them forget the truth. It was one thing he regretted most about the way Jenna left. She knew his secret. Maybe it was time to find his ex-girlfriend and take care of that.

But first, he had to find Tatiana.

MAVERYCK WAS AT a loss. He sat on the Volkov place for five days with no sight of Tatiana. On the night of the fifth day, he flew past her window. He hadn't seen a light on in her room the whole time he waited, so he was desperate. Shifting back to human, he entered her room. The furniture was there, but most of her clothes were missing from the closet. The scent of wildflowers was almost nonexistent, like she hadn't been there in a while. It wasn't like he could ask someone where she was.

Actually, he could.

Not knowing where the housekeeper's room was meant he had to go door-to-door, but that was exactly what he did. When he found the right one, he prayed the older woman didn't sleep in the nude. Luckily, she was dressed in a gown. Mav padded with the stealth of his lion to the woman's bed. He leaned over and put one hand on her mouth, the other on her shoulder to keep her from moving.

Using his Gryphon's power, he said, "I'm going to ask you some questions, and you aren't going to scream. You will answer truthfully, then I will be on my way. You will forget I was ever here." The fear in her eyes dissipated, and her body relaxed. "Where is Tatiana?"

"Mikael sent her away to find her father's killer,"

the woman said calmly.

"And did she?"

"We don't know. The girl disappeared."

"What do you mean 'disappeared?'"

"She left the hotel, destroyed her phone, and he hasn't heard from her since. He's got people looking for her."

Shit. What if Mikael was the one who put the hit out on his cousin?

"Forget I was here."

Mav turned to leave and stepped on something soft. Looking down, he saw a child's shoe. He hadn't seen any kids in the house or on the grounds, but he chalked it up to the woman having a grandchild there at some point. He left the same way he entered, then flew back to where he parked his SUV. After dressing, he drove to the hotel. If Tatiana fled, there was only one way to find her, and that was with Lucy's help. It was late, and he didn't want to bother her or Tamian, so he opted to call her in the morning.

His first order of business was to take a long, five-day-overdue shower. Having lived on mice and rabbits for the last few days had been necessary, but now he was ready for a fat steak and possibly a nice lobster tail to go with it.

It had been a long time since Mav had visited a casino, but he was fairly close to New Atlantic City. Since most casinos had gourmet restaurants inside, he figured he'd get his steak and then do a little gambling. If he was lucky, he might find someone to get lost in for a few hours. The Diamond Eyes proved to be just the place he was looking for. After devouring one of the best meals he'd eaten in a long time, Maveryck found a blackjack table and threw down a couple hundred dollars. While both blackjack and poker were games of luck depending on the cards laid, he found poker to be tedious. Players took too long to decide whether the risk was worth it.

He was up a few hundred when a brunette sat next to him. He gave her his best smile, one she returned. Mav played a few more rounds, waiting to see if there was a spark between them. She was pretty enough, but her perfume was too strong. Her laugh a little too loud. Those things had never bothered him before. Not when all he was looking for was a warm body for a few hours. Something was holding him back. He had dismissed every single woman who had made their intentions known, and he couldn't figure out why. He was out of town, away from home, just the way he liked it when he found someone to have sex with.

He knew his dick wasn't broken, because he rubbed one out every night before he went to sleep and again every morning in the shower. It had only been several hours since he'd taken himself in hand and painted the tile wall with his release. No, it wasn't his dick that wasn't onboard with any of these women. It had to be psychological. With his mind preoccupied with those thoughts, he colored up then took his chips to the cashier. Mav had made more than enough to pay for his meal, so he called the night a win, even if he was going to bed alone.

Morning came much too soon, but Maveryck sat up against the headboard and called for room service. He wasn't ready to leave New Atlantic City. He needed his niece's help, and if she could get answers quickly, he would rather not be on the road in case Lucy found evidence of Tatiana still near the city. It wasn't too early, so he called her.

"Hey, Uncle Mav. What's up?"

"I need your help. Remember the Volkov hit?" Lucy knew all about what her family did for a living. She used her computer skills to help them on their jobs as well as in their search for the Ministry. Ever since spending time with her mate's Clan down in New Atlanta, Lucy had wowed them all with what Julian Stone had taught her in such a short time. The Gargoyles of the Stone Society he'd met were all honorable. Some of them were lucky enough to have gorgeous females for mates. Thinking of Tessa, Tamian's sister, he waited for his dick to plump in his briefs. Nothing. *What the hell?*

"You mean that shitshow where you almost got your ass shot off? I remember," Lucy said, the scowl coming through in her voice, bringing Mav's thoughts back to where they should be, not on another male's mate.

"We got a contract on his daughter, Tatiana Volkova. Thing is, she's disappeared, and I need your help finding her." Mav told Lucy everything he knew about the woman as well as what the housekeeper had told him.

"I'll get right on it. Are you headed home?"

"No. I'm going to hang out here for a bit, just in case you find something. If it looks like it'll take more than a few hours, I'll hit the road then."

"Okay. Sit tight, and I'll call you back in a bit."

"Thanks, Luce."

"Later."

Mav turned on the television while he waited on

his breakfast. Switching to the twenty-four-hour news channel, he closed his eyes and listened to the newscaster talk about current events. When they broke in with an amber alert, Mav opened his eyes and turned the volume up. He had a soft spot for kids, and it broke his heart whenever he heard of one being abducted. A knock on the door took his attention away from the television. When he was sitting down with his breakfast, the report on the missing child was flashing the phone number across the screen for the local police, the New Philadelphia PD, as well as the child abduction hotline. The missing child's photo was in the top corner. A sweet-looking little girl was smiling in the picture. Mav took a moment to pray to Zeus the child would be found unharmed.

While he ate his breakfast, Mav let himself imagine having a child of his own. He often thought it might be selfish to wish for a family considering the type of work he did, but his parents made it work with eleven kids, and he and his siblings had never wanted for anything. So no, he didn't think it was selfish to want what Sutton and Rory had. If only he could find someone to spend his life with. Maybe that's why none of the women at the casino had held his interest. Maybe Mav was ready – again – to stop looking for hookups and to find the one for the long haul.

Mav sent another prayer to Zeus. This time, it was for himself.

CHAPTER SEVEN

Maveryck

MAVERYCK WAS BONE tired and ready to sleep in his own bed. He left New Atlantic City with a plan, and as soon as he arrived back in New Troy, he drove straight home. He had planned to stop at Lucy's, the large manor she now shared with Tamian. The Gargoyle had been instrumental in rescuing Lucy when she worked for the Global Intelligence Agency. Maveryck and a few other Hounds had the pleasure of meeting and working alongside several Gargoyles. Before that incident, he had heard tell of the other shifters but had never met one. Like the Hounds, Gargoyles had been created to watch over humans, and Maveryck admired Tamian. He was Prince to the Italian Gargoyle throne, but the male was down to earth. Most importantly, he treated Lucy like the queen she would one day be.

He had already given Lucy all the intel he had on Tatiana, and she hadn't found anything relevant on the missing woman, so he drove to his two-story house instead. The weariness from the last week began to set in, and Maveryck needed a little downtime. When he walked into his house, he didn't bother to unpack. He stripped down to his boxer briefs and fell face first onto the bed. Maveryck hadn't had a chance to pull the covers up when his phone rang.

"Mom, I'm beat. Can whatever it is not wait until I've

had a few hours' sleep?"

"No. I'm afraid it can't. Son, you need to get here now. And drive your car." Rory hung up without another word.

"My car?" he asked the dead phone, throwing his legs over the side of the bed. Fuck. Mav scrubbed a hand over his face and stood, pulling on the clothes he'd shrugged off less than two minutes earlier. He made his way through the house and grabbed the keys off the kitchen counter. On the drive to his parents' house, he tried not to worry about why he'd been summoned. If it was a medical emergency, surely Rory would have said so. When he arrived, there was a strange vehicle parked out front. He pulled in the driveway, and before he had his SUV in park, his father was waiting for him.

"Pop, what the hell is going on?"

"Jenna's here," Sutton responded cryptically.

"What?" Instead of coming to his house, his ex was at his parents' place. Mav didn't get a chance to ask Sutton for more information because his father was already walking toward the front door. It had been more than four years since Jenna walked out of his life without so much as a goodbye or a fuck you. Well, that wasn't exactly true. She had told him she was leaving via text message – after the fact. Sutton led the way to the living room where Jenna was seated on the sofa, looking a little less put together than she'd always been when they were a couple. Before he could ask her what she wanted, she stood and faced him.

"They're all yours," Jenna said, shoving a manila envelope in his hand then strolling out the door without looking back.

"What's all mine?" Mav asked her retreating back.

"Maveryck," Rory called, getting his attention. As soon as he turned around, Mav froze. Two towheaded little boys were sitting on the floor playing with toy trucks.

"What the ever-loving hell?" he muttered.

"Language," his mother chastised.

Sutton clapped him on the shoulder. "This is Major and Marshall, and according to those papers in your hands, they're your sons."

"What?" At the mention of their names, both boys turned their eyes toward Maveryck. He didn't have to read the papers to know they were his kids. Looking at them was like looking at him and War when they were that age. At least from the photos he'd seen. Like him and War, these boys weren't identical either, but they were close. One had more freckles across his nose, and he had a cowlick in his front hairline. Instead of running after Jenna like he wanted, Mav squatted so he was on their level. "Hey there," he said softly, not wanting to scare them right away with his gruff voice.

"Which one of you is Major?"

The one with the cowlick pointed at his chest. "Me. I'm the oldest."

"By five minutes," Marshall whispered.

Mav laughed and fell back on his ass. He was a father.

To twins.

Fuck.

"So…" Maveryck stared at the boys who stared back. He didn't know anything about kids, even though he'd just been thinking about having one of his own. Now he had two. Holy fucking hell, he had kids. "Uhm, are you hungry?"

"Can we get pizza?" Major asked.

"That's for special days," Marshall said to his twin.

Maveryck frowned. What the fuck constituted a special day? "We can get pizza. You know why?" The boys just stared at him. "Today's really special."

The twins continued to stare at him, and Mav stared back. Shit. Now what?

"Boys, let's go in the kitchen and find a snack. Your dad can work out supper later." Rory gave Mav a pointed look. He just shook his head and watched the twins dutifully follow their grandmother out of the room.

"What the fuck, Pop?" Mav, still seated on the floor, looked up at his dad.

Sutton held out his hand and pulled Mav to his feet. "Since you weren't home, Jenna brought the boys here. Their birth certificates are in the envelope along with their medical records and a letter signed by a judge turning over custody to you. She's given up her parental rights. She wrote you a note, but it's a piss-poor explanation, if you ask me."

Maveryck removed the contents of the envelope and opened the short letter.

Maveryck,

You deserve more than a text saying goodbye or a note telling you about your sons, but I've never been good with words. I found out I was pregnant but didn't know how to tell you, so I left. I tried so many times to call, but I couldn't find the courage. You'd never said you wanted kids, and you'd also never asked me to marry you, even after three years. Time got away, and then I had them. I did the best I could by them, but it wasn't easy. I realized recently they need you more than they need me. Especially if they turn out to be like you. Don't worry about me sharing your secret.

They're good boys, and I know you'll be better for them and give them what I can't.

Jenna

Mav folded the note and shoved it back in the envelope. He agreed with his dad. It was piss-poor. He scanned the documents, and sure enough, Jenna had signed the boys over to him. He looked at their birth certificates. Jenna had given them his last name, which was good, but neither one had middle names. The twins had been born... *Shit.* "Their birthday was two months ago. But that doesn't make sense.

70

She would have been—"

"About six months pregnant when she left." Sutton lowered his voice. "If those boys weren't the spitting image of you and War when you were little, I'd be concerned they aren't yours. I mean, she didn't look pregnant."

"No, she didn't. It wasn't like she wore baggy clothes, and I saw her naked. We had sex right up until she left."

No, you didn't.

Yes, we did. Didn't we?

No. You were out on jobs, and she was already asleep when you came home.

"Fuck. No, we didn't. No wonder she left." Mav scrubbed a hand down his face. "We hadn't had sex for a few months, now that I think about it. But that doesn't excuse her not telling me. What the hell am I going to do?"

Sutton clapped Maveryck on the shoulder. "The best you can. I know they're a surprise, but you have me and your mom to help. And your brothers are going to be wonderful uncles. Right now, we need to get your house ready. Jenna left a few boxes, but it doesn't look like four-year's worth of stuff. Let's go through them and see what's missing, and then you and I will go shopping. Rory can watch over them for the time being."

"I'm a dad," Mav muttered.

Sutton nodded solemnly. "Yes, you are. Now, come on."

Mav followed Sutton into the kitchen where the twins were eating grilled cheese sandwiches. Major's cheeks looked like a chipmunk.

"Did you try to eat the whole thing at once?" Mav asked.

Major just nodded, doing his best to chew. When it didn't work, he opened his mouth and spit out the half-eaten sandwich. Mav looked at Rory who rolled her eyes. She took Major's plate and dumped the food in the garbage before putting another sandwich in front of him. "Try eating this one a bite at a time. Nobody is going to take your food,

Major. I promise."

Mav frowned at his mother, but she shook her head. Why did his son think someone was going to take his food? Marshall had his sandwich cradled in his hands in front of his little body like he was guarding it with his life. If Jenna had starved them, he was going to beat her ass. He'd never hit a woman before, but these were *his* sons. It hit him then that these two precious beings were his children. He made them. He was too pissed at Jenna to give her any credit. Because of her, Mav had missed the first four years of their lives. Missed their first words. Their first steps. Their first—

They're here now. Snap out of it.

Mav pulled out the chair next to Marshall and watched his boys eat. They didn't look sick or like they'd been abused, but sometimes the scars were on the inside. He wasn't going to interrogate them on their first day with him. Even he knew better than that. He needed to be subtle, and if it came out they had been mentally abused or neglected, Mav would get them the best help available.

"Can we ride your motorcycle?" Major asked when his sandwich was finished.

"How do you know I have a motorcycle?"

"Mommy told us you did," Major said.

"I do have one."

"Can we ride it?" Major was full of questions, but Marshall was still staring at his sandwich. He'd only taken a few bites.

"Not today, but you better believe I'll take you for rides. First thing we need to do is get a bedroom set up for you.

"Are we gonna live here?" Major asked. It seemed he was the spokesman – spokes-kid – for the two of them.

"No, you'll live with me in our house. I'll take you there in a little while, but first I need to get you beds and stuff. Do you guys like superheroes or sports or trucks?"

Major shrugged and said, "I guess."

"No, I meant which one do you like best?"

72

Major looked at his twin, but Marshall didn't say anything. "Uhm… trucks?" Mav's heart broke. If his kids didn't know what they liked… *Fuck!*

"I tell you what. You two finish eating, and I'm going to go look through the things your mom brought. I'll be back in a few minutes." Mav stood and pressed his hand to both their heads, touching his sons for the first time. Something in his heart settled.

Sutton followed him to the porch where two small cardboard boxes were sitting next to booster seats. One box was filled with worn-out clothes, and the other contained a few toys. Mav closed his eyes, unable to stop the tears from falling. "How… how is this all they have? Pop? These are my boys. My sons, and this… these two boxes are all they have?"

Sutton pulled Mav to his chest and wrapped his strong arms around his son. "They're here now. Everything's going to be okay, I promise you that. Come on. Let's go make sure they have the best bedroom two little boys have ever seen."

"I need to call War. He'll want to know." Mav wiped his eyes, refusing to look at the sad boxes at his feet.

"All your brothers will, but I don't think the twins need to be bombarded with all that, do you? Hayden and Kyllian can be a handful."

"You're right, but maybe they can be removing the furniture from the boys' room so we don't have to do that later."

"That's a good idea. Let's go tell your mom and the boys we're going shopping, then you can conference call your brothers on the way to the store."

The boys were sitting huddled together on the sofa in the family room watching cartoons. Mav smiled, because he and War sat the same way when they were little.

Rory grabbed Sutton by the hand and led him into the kitchen. She was whispering, but Mav could tell his mom was itching for a fight. He knew she wasn't mad at the boys

73

but mad at their situation. He wasn't happy with Jenna, but he was thrilled that his two little men were where they belonged – with him. He gave his father time to calm Rory down before joining them.

Keeping her voice low, she said, "I'm going to kill her. I'm going to find that bitch and tear her apart with my claws."

"Mom? What is it?"

"*What is it?* She kept our babies from us for four years. Four years! She had no right," Rory seethed.

"No, she didn't. And you'll have to get in line with the claws. I'm not satisfied with that note she left. Don't get me wrong. I'm glad she gave them up, but I want to know why now. But right now, I need to go shopping and get furniture and toys and clothes. That's going to take all afternoon. Then, I'm going to take them home and make sure they are comfortable. While Pop and I do that, I'm going to ask the others to get started removing the stuff in their room so things will go faster."

"You're welcome to stay here, you know." Rory had just returned from seeing two of his sisters and their kids who also had little ones of their own. His female siblings, all six of them, were in their eighties. Since they were Gryphons, they didn't look much older than Mav. Then again, neither did his parents.

"I do know that, and I appreciate it. But I want them settled at home as quickly as possible. I'm going to need your help in the next few weeks, because *kids*. I know nothing about them. While I'm gone, please take a look at their medical records and make sure there's nothing we need to be concerned with immediately."

"I can do that. As soon as you get their room set up, give me a call, and I'll bring them to you."

"Thanks, Mom."

Mav walked back in the living room and knelt in front of the twins. "Do you want bunk beds or twin beds?"

74

"Whassa bunk bed?" Marshall asked softly, his pale eyebrows dipping between eyes the same blue as Mav's.

"It's where the beds are stacked on top of the other. Here, let me show you." Mav googled a picture and showed it to them. "There's those, or…" He showed them a picture of a room with two twin beds. "These. Which ones do you like best?"

"We don't have to share?" Major asked.

Mav swallowed hard. "No, buddy. You each get your own bed. So, what's it going to be?" The room across from his was large enough to accommodate either.

The twins looked at each other, but neither one spoke. It was like they were having a silent conversation. Mav knew that was impossible, because they wouldn't get their Gryphon until they reached puberty, if they got it at all. Even then, they shouldn't be able to communicate telepathically. Maybe they were just so close they didn't need words.

Major pointed to the twin beds. "Those ones."

"You got it. Do you have a favorite color?"

"Blue," they responded together.

Mav chuckled and tucked his phone away. As he did in the kitchen, he pressed his palms to the sides of their heads, relishing their softness. "Got it. Okay, Pops and I are going shopping. You'll have a new bedroom before you know it."

"And pizza?" Major asked.

"And pizza. Be good for your grandmother."

"Okay," they said in unison.

Maveryck met his dad outside. Sutton looked up and tucked his phone in his pocket. "I'm going to drive my truck so we can haul more furniture. I figure Halston's would be the best place since it's close to the Bed and Bath place."

"Yeah, that sounds good. I'll meet you there." Mav got in his SUV, and as soon as he was on the road, he called his own twin.

"Mav? What's up?"

"You're not going to believe this shit. Rory called as

75

soon as I got home and told me to haul ass to her house. When I got there, Jenna was waiting."

"Mav, that's… I don't know what it is. Is it good? Bad?"

"It's twins."

"Twins? She's pregnant? Was she coming to rub it in your face or something?"

Mav grinned even though he was still freaking the fuck out. "No, twins as in I have a set, and they're four. Major and Marshall. War, they're the sweetest things you'll ever see in your life. I'm a father. Me. A dad!"

"Congratulations, but I'm curious as to the rest of the story."

Mav told his twin the gist of what happened. When War finally stopped offering to hunt Jenna down, Mav said, "We'll discuss that later, because I will be going after her for more answers. Right now, Pops and I are headed to get them some furniture and clothes. I'm calling the brothers to see if they'll go clear out the bedroom across from mine. I want to get the boys settled as soon as possible."

"What do you need me to do? Hang on." War told Kerrigan the short version of the story.

"Put it on speaker," she told War. "Mav? What can we do to help? Do you need us to go shopping or go babyproof your house or something?"

Maveryck's heart warmed. War was blessed with such a thoughtful mate. "Since they're four, I don't think babyproofing is necessary."

"War said you're getting furniture. What about clothes or toys? We can do that for you."

"If you want to get them some clothes, that'd save me time, and I'll pay you back as soon as we get to my house."

"Just let me know what sizes, and we'll take care of it."

Mav rattled off the sizes he'd noticed on the clothes in the box. "You might want to get some the next size larger too. What little Jenna left wasn't in good shape, and I don't even know if they fit properly. Shit, they need shoes too. War, please call Rory. They're with her right now, and she can look at what they're wearing to give you the size. And jackets. And gloves and beanies, and—"

"Breathe, Brother. Kerrigan and I have this. You just worry about the furniture."

"Thanks. I... Zeus almighty. I don't know anything about kids, War."

"No, but our mother does, and so do King, Ace, and the Rev. Plus, you've got the rest of us. These two boys have more uncles than they'll know what to do with."

"And they have me and Lucy," Kerrigan added.

War murmured his agreement to his mate then continued, "Now, go do what you have to, and we'll meet you at your house later. I love you, Mav. It's going to be okay."

"I love you too. And thanks. Both of you."

Mav was still in shock, but War was right. He and his boys were going to be just fine.

Chapter Eight

Natalia

NATALIA WAS GLAD to be home. She had been torn between taking a vacation and looking for the biker. The vacation finally won out, and Natalia spent the next week traveling to Fiji. She had rented a private bure situated over crystal-clear waters. While it offered her a modicum of privacy, she hadn't realized that traveling alone would be so lonely. All around were couples enjoying the sun and water of the Pacific. Her cabana boys in skimpy swimsuits turned out to be island boys in dress shirts and khaki shorts. They were nice enough to look at, if you went for the college-aged surfer type. She didn't. She compared them to Blue Eyes with his broad chest, biceps that stretched the arms of his T-shirt, and jeans that molded to thighs as big as her waist.

Eating dinner alone at home was the norm, but eating solo in a fancy restaurant had been miserable. All around was laughter. Dancing. Soft touches. Light kisses. Love. She would have been better off getting a remote cabin in the woods. Natalia tried to make the best of her situation. She sunned on the beach. Went snorkeling. Browsed the cute shops. Joined in the local dance and storytelling night. All-in-all, it was worth the money to see such beautiful waters surrounded by lush greenery. When she stopped feeling sorry for herself, she welcomed the island experience and found the locals a pleasure to talk to.

Now she was home and feeling a bit adrift. She gave herself a day to reacclimate to the time difference by lounging on the sofa and staring at photos of a certain biker. What was it that was so compelling about him? Was it the fact that she'd been sent the pictures anonymously? Maybe it was the mystery surrounding his identity. Or the fact that he could possibly be her father's killer. Whatever it was, it was driving Natalia crazy.

When she finally logged onto her computer, she had several emails from Nix, all contracts. She also had another email in her Nexus account, but the sender's identity was blank. She figured there had been a glitch in the system, and Nix's codename had somehow been left off. Regardless, she opened the message and when she saw who the mark was, her breath caught. Natalia stood so fast she almost dropped her computer.

Why would someone want to take him out? What had he done that warranted his life snuffed out? She couldn't do it. But if she didn't accept the contract, someone else would, and she couldn't let that happen. Could she? She didn't know this man. Didn't know one thing about him, except now she knew his name – Maveryck Lazlo, a.k.a. Mayhem. Natalia placed her laptop on the table before detouring to the kitchen for a glass of wine. She needed alcohol.

She declined the other contracts Nix sent and focused on this one. Natalia took a gulp of merlot, needing the wine to hit her system quickly. She wasn't a nervous person. Natalia prided herself on being calm in all situations. But this… this was something she knew – one way or another – would change her life. *Why?* That she didn't know, but she felt it in her gut. Women's intuition was a real thing. She had relied on it over the years when taking out her opponent, and it never let her down. She clicked the accept button then got busy reading what little information had been included.

One thing that shocked her was how close to her he lived. The address noted was less than twenty minutes from her home. She opened a new browser and entered his address. When it populated, she clicked on the street view. The house was a surprise. Natalia hadn't imagined a biker living in such a nice place. Then again, she knew nothing about him, like what he did for a living. According to her research, motorcycle clubs tended to deal in drugs and guns, much like her father had. Did this one follow suit? Or were they in the minority the way some clubs touted doing good for the community? If he had a contract on him, the man had obviously done something to warrant taking a look at.

Natalia was excited. Normally, when she took a contract, she was anxious to get the job done. With this one? She couldn't wait to do surveillance. To follow the gorgeous man and see what his life was about. Maybe she would get close to him and find out firsthand the type of man he truly was. How else was she going to determine whether or not he deserved a bullet?

There was no time like the present to get started. Natalia sent the information to her private email and shut down her computer. Since she was doing recon, she opted for one of her casual disguises, which included a long, brown wig and frumpy clothes, much like the way she used to dress at home when her father was alive. She chose to wear green contact lenses. Not that she planned to get close enough for the man to see her eyes.

Her car was nondescript, so she didn't worry about it being recognized or remembered. As she drove by the house, her stomach fluttered thinking about the man moving about inside. Did he have a wife or girlfriend in there with him? The information she'd received didn't mention either, but that didn't mean he lived alone. Natalia couldn't imagine a man as virile as him going without companionship for very long. Would he consider having someone like her in his bed? She had never had a problem finding one-night stands, and they had always commented how pretty she was. But those men weren't Blue Eyes. They weren't Maveryck, the hot-assin biker.

With his house being in a neighborhood, there wasn't anywhere Natalia could park without being conspicuous. She drove around, looking for realtor signs, hoping to find an empty house she could use, but she didn't find any. She was going to have to figure out another way to get close to him. Now that Natalia knew the name of the motorcycle club and the address of the clubhouse, she drove there next.

When the GPS indicated she had arrived at her destination, Natalia looked around. She had been expecting something different than the large, brick building with its paved parking lot. Bikes lined up in a neat row was the only indication she had the right place. Natalia drove past and made a U-turn before pulling into the parking lot across the street. The business, a lawyer's office, was open; therefore, she couldn't sit there long. At least not during their hours of operation. She searched for security cameras. Not seeing any, she turned her attention to the building across the street.

Farther back in the lot was a large garage. The doors were open, and there was a man working on a motorcycle. Natalia pulled out her binoculars to get a better look. He was squatting with his back to her, but from what she could tell, he was built much like Maveryck. His hair was covered by a bandana, but he wore the black leather kutte with the MC's rocker and colors on the back. *Look at you, using the lingo.* Natalia rolled her eyes at herself. When he stood and turned around, Natalia gasped. It was the same man who had winked at her when she followed the group of bikers after getting her hair done. What if her mark had been in that group? Damnit, she might have been close to Blue Eyes and didn't know it.

The side door to the brick building opened, and two bikers walked out on either side of a woman. One of the men had his arm around the woman. At first glance, the couple appeared to be in their late forties, maybe early fifties, while the other man looked to be a little younger. The older biker

81

walked the woman to her car, and the younger straddled one of the Harleys. The woman didn't look like a skanky broad. She looked… normal. She had on jeans and a button-up blouse. The only indication she was an "old lady" was the black riding boots on her feet.

Natalia was pretty sure this woman was not a random chick, but more likely the biker's wife by the way he couldn't keep his eyes off her. He tenderly kissed the woman before setting his forehead to hers, smiling as he said something. She smiled back and placed her hand on his cheek. *Wow.* He kissed her again before putting her in the car. The man watched her pull out of the parking lot, remaining there until she and the biker following her were out of sight.

A car door slammed, and Natalia jerked the binoculars away from her eyes. She searched for the owner of the car to find a man in a suit walking into the lawyer's office. He glanced back over his shoulder to where she was sitting before going inside. Time was up.

Reluctantly, Natalia left the area and drove around, thinking. She knew looks could be deceiving. But that couple appeared so in love. Maybe the biker was a criminal and his woman didn't know it. Maybe they were both criminals. There wasn't a rule that said bad people couldn't fall in love. Hell, if she thought about it, most people would consider her a criminal. *That's because you are.* Just because she got paid to take out the trash didn't mean it wasn't illegal. What right did she have to take the life of another? None really. Didn't make it right just because that's how she'd been raised. But it was all she'd ever known. All she knew how to do. She couldn't very well go get a desk job with her current resume, not that she would want one. She did what she was good at. It paid well, and so far, her conscience had been clear. At least since the jobs she had taken for Nix. She didn't want to think about the men she'd killed when her father first trained her.

Was she a bad person?

Natalia didn't think so. She didn't hurt good people. She had the capacity to love, although she hadn't loved anyone since her mother died. Not Marta. Not her father. Especially not her cousins. That was a sad realization. Maybe one day she would find someone who would be able to accept her for who she was. Love her in spite of the things she'd done. Maybe someone like—

That sound she was becoming familiar with echoed from somewhere close by. Natalia put on her blinker and pulled over into the nearest parking lot and waited. Six bikers motored past, and Natalia pulled out behind them. This time, the men had on their vests – kuttes – with the colors of a skull with a Gryphon on either side. She couldn't tell if Maveryck was among the group. She didn't crowd them, keeping a few cars between her and them.

Natalia followed them for twenty minutes, until they pulled over at a quaint Mexican restaurant. She turned into the strip center next door and parked where she could keep an eye on them. Six of the sexiest men she'd ever seen pulled off their helmets and strode into the building as a unit. All of them were built, some more than others, and there was no denying they were confident in their skin. While nice to look at, they weren't the man she was after. *Where are you?*

NATALIA KNEW SHE was getting reckless, driving her car by the clubhouse every day and parking across the street every night. She was running out of time. If she didn't find Maveryck Lazlo, Nix would probably give the contract to someone else. Natalia had responded to the email, stating she was on the job, but it was taking more time than usual to find the mark. Nix didn't answer, but Natalia continued looking for the man.

After a while, she believed Maveryck belonged to a different chapter. That didn't make sense, considering the other men in one of the photos with him came and went from this particular clubhouse. Maybe he was on vacation, or off on a job somewhere. Whatever the case, Natalia was losing hope of seeing him. She wasn't giving up though. Since she couldn't find Maveryck, she had been watching the other bikers. None of them had been involved in secret meetings outside their clubhouse. Most of them went home at the end of the day, and to her surprise, some even had women and children waiting on them. As far as she could tell, these were family men who happen to ride motorcycles.

After a week of wasting gas and good disguises, Natalia decided to focus on one of the other bikers in case he led her to Blue Eyes. If all else failed, she would stop him and just ask if he knew Maveryck. Natalia was going to make up some lame excuse about wanting to reunite with him after a night together, praying Maveryck didn't have a wife at home who would come after her.

And she knew exactly who she was going to follow. One she had yet to tail. The biker who winked at her was at the clubhouse every day. If he figured out she was tailing him, she would lay on the charm and hope the wink he gave her meant he liked what he saw. It was probably rude to use the man to get to another one, but if she didn't find Maveryck soon, someone else would be gunning for him. Literally.

The biker she'd chosen to follow didn't make her wait long. He pulled out of the clubhouse lot and headed in the direction of Maveryck's house. Instead of pulling into Maveryck's neighborhood, the man drove to a house a few miles away, pulling his bike around back of the house. Natalia thought she would have to wait for a while as he went inside, but he returned from around back to the detached garage. When the door opened, an SUV backed out. Natalia was sitting a few doors down, and when he drove past, he looked right in her window. She couldn't see his eyes, but there was no doubt he saw her. *Shit!* There went the element of surprise. Now, she looked like a stalker. Maybe that wasn't a bad thing. She could play that up to her advantage. She turned the car around and followed, doing her best to keep her distance but not far enough back she lost him.

The vehicle turned onto the street Maveryck lived on, and Natalia kept going straight. She drove around half an hour before taking a chance on driving by Maveryck's house. When she did, she found the SUV parked in the driveway. Either Maveryck was home, or the other man was taking care of his house for him. Natalia was used to straightforward jobs. This was the first time she'd had trouble locating her mark. Not that she considered him a target. Not for her. Maybe her best course of action was to walk up to his front door and knock. No, then she would have to admit how she knew about the contract. She had his address, so maybe she could mail a copy of the contract to him, leaving out some damning information about herself. If she overnighted it, he would get it tomorrow, and that would warn him without giving herself away.

With that decision made, Natalia headed home. She had no idea what she was going to tell Nix. This would be the first time she hadn't completed a job. Not that she had been planning to pull the trigger. Not without knowing more about Maveryck Lazlo. Maybe she would warn him but continue looking for him. Someone thought he warranted death. She hadn't observed any of the others doing anything illegal. As she sat waiting most nights, Natalia researched more on the various biker clubs. She'd been under the impression they all had illegal undertakings keeping their clubs afloat. That wasn't true. There were clubs comprised of retired military. Some claimed to be Christian clubs riding for Jesus. There were those whose members were cops and firefighters. These clubs, on the surface, did good in their communities. Raising money and doing their best to help those less fortunate around them. Maybe the Hounds fell into that category.

As soon as she was inside her own home, Natalia removed her disguise and dressed in her normal clothes. Since she didn't want Maveryck to know she was in the area, Natalia would have to drive for a bit to a post office in another town. Tugging on a pair of skinny jeans and a long-sleeved T-shirt, she slid her feet into a pair of ankle boots. She fluffed her hair where it had been flattened under the wig of the day. Once she looked presentable, Natalia sat down at her laptop and opened the contract, copying only the part stating who the mark was and the other identifying information Nix had sent on Maveryck. Then she opened a blank document and typed out a short note.

Dear Mr. Lazlo,

It has come to my attention you have a price on your head. After much consideration, I do not feel as though you deserve to be targeted. Let this serve as warning to watch your back.

Natalia didn't know how to sign the note, so she left it as it was. Short and to the point. It would buy her some time to actually lay eyes on the man. Once she did that, she would be able to follow him and determine for herself the type of man he was.

CHAPTER NINE

Maveryck

THE CONVERSATION WITH Maveryck's other brothers was nothing short of manic. Ryker remained silent, while Hayden and Kyllian talked over each other. Ryker finally ordered them to be quiet so he could ask pertinent questions. He assured Mav the three of them would have the bedroom cleaned out. He also promised the three of them would be staying long enough to help Mav and Sutton unload the furniture and assemble the beds.

It took longer than Mav anticipated to choose the boys' bedroom furniture. Sutton finally grabbed him by the shoulders and assured him the twins would be happy with whatever he chose. They were only four and weren't likely to care much about whether the beds were oak or maple. Next, they went to the home goods store where he chose fun superhero bedding with blue sheets.

With both their vehicles loaded, Mav turned in a circle, looking at the stores in the vicinity. "They need toys."

"That's being taken care of. Let's go get the furniture set up." Sutton didn't give Mav time to ask questions. He got in his truck and pulled out of the parking lot with Mav standing like a statue. He tried to think of anything else the twins might need, but War and Kerrigan had the clothes covered. Sutton said toys were being taken care of. He knew they needed other things, but his brain had stopped functioning properly. His phone rang, and he panicked, thinking it was Rory.

"Mom?"

"Get your ass in your car and follow me," Sutton commanded.

"Right. Got it." How the hell was Mav supposed to take care of his boys when his head was spinning?

His brothers' bikes were parked at the curb, leaving room for Mav and their dad to back their trucks into the driveway. Ryker was already helping Sutton remove the beds from the back of his truck. Hayden and Kyllian grabbed the dresser next, none of them waiting on Maveryck. He followed after them, and when he got to the twins' room, he was pleasantly surprised to see it had been cleared out and vacuumed.

"How do you want the room arranged?" Ryker asked.

"Let's put the beds on the far side with the dresser over here. The toybox can go in the corner next to the closet." Maveryck had rearranged the room several times over in his head, and this was the best use of space he came up with. "I'm going to toss the new sheets in the washer."

For as nervous as he was, Maveryck was equally as excited. He went outside to his SUV and grabbed all the bags. He had just closed the lid on the washing machine when a large hand gripped his shoulder.

"How you doing, Son?"

Mav turned, leaning against the dryer. "Nervous. Excited. I'm ready to make up for lost time, but shit, Pop. I've got a job to do. How am I going to go after Tatiana Volkova with two boys?"

"The same way every other working parent does their job; you get a babysitter. Your mother and I will be more than happy to watch the twins if you need to leave." Maveryck had filled his father in on the latest contract while they were shopping for furniture. "It's not like you'll be taking them to a daycare where a stranger is watching them.

Rory is going to fight you anyway about spending time with them, so look at it as doing her a favor while you continue with your job."

"I don't want them to think I'm abandoning them, though."

"They won't think that. Now, they may think that about Jenna. You need to find her and have a sit-down as soon as possible. You also need to find out if she's shared our secret. We need to know where her head is. Most importantly, we need to understand why she chose now to bring the boys to you."

"I need to give Lucy a call. See if she can locate Jenna. I didn't see an address in the papers she left."

"Didn't you leave the package with your Mom?" Mav nodded. "Okay, I'll give her a call. Have her doublecheck before you get Lucy involved in something else. We need her focus to be on Josiah's whereabouts and your Tatiana."

"She's not my anything," Maveryck muttered.

His dad got a contemplative look on his face. "Warryck probably didn't think Kerrigan was his anything when you started looking for her, either."

"Why would this Volkova woman mean something to me other than a paycheck?" Sometimes Mav wondered how his father's mind worked.

Sutton scratched his chin. "It's just... your life is changing. War quit his job, and then *Bam!* He found his female. You now have the twins, so..."

"Bam?" Mav laughed. "Sometimes I wonder about you, old man."

Sutton cuffed him upside the head. "I may be older, but I can still kick your ass." Maveryck had no doubt about that. Sutton Lazlo was a force to be reckoned with. "Come on. Let's see how your brothers are faring."

Less than two hours later, the twins' bedroom was set up with freshly laundered sheets hiding underneath the new comforters. War and Kerrigan had just arrived with clothes and quite a few toys. Hayden and Kyllian tore into the toys, removing the packaging. The two of them praised War and his female for getting some "really cool shit."

"Yeah, well, don't break the cool shit before the twins get a chance to play with them," Sutton admonished.

Kerrigan showed Maveryck all the clothes they had bought, separating them into different sizes. Mav would have to get the boys to try them on to see what did and didn't fit before he washed them. When he held up a pair of Aquaman pajamas, he turned to his own twin. "Aquaman?"

"Hey, don't look at me. Kerrigan picked those out."

"What? He's the hottest of the bunch." Kerrigan shrugged, grabbing them from Mav and folding them back up. War rolled his eyes at his feisty redhead before tugging her to him and kissing her soundly. Mav was happy for his brother, but he felt the tinge of longing in his chest whenever he was around them.

"Thank you all for everything. I'm going to call Rory and have her bring the boys home," Mav said. "I'd like to give them at least tonight to settle in before introducing them to everyone."

"You're kicking us out? We want to meet the little dudes." Kyllian was normally laid back. Nothing could bring him down, but he was clearly upset.

"I want you to meet them. I just don't want them overwhelmed with a houseful of people on their first night home. I want to get them comfortable with me and being in a new place. I have no idea what life has been like for them up until now, but I have a feeling it wasn't as good as it should have been. So, please. Give me tonight. You can come back tomorrow."

"Your brother's right. Besides, there will be plenty of nights in the future where he'll be off on a job and will need you to watch over the twins." Sutton began herding everyone toward the front door.

Mav hugged Kerrigan then each one of his brothers.

Even Ryker went in for an embrace instead of a fist bump. Having his own daughter back in his life had loosened the male's attitude. When it came time for him to say goodbye to War, everyone walked outside, leaving the two of them alone in the house.

War pulled Mav to him. "I'm so happy for you, Brother. I can't wait to meet the little guys."

"Thank you. I want you to meet them. They look just like we did when we were that age."

"Yeah?"

Mav wiped a stray tear. "Yeah. I just hope they aren't as rowdy as we were. I'm not Rory."

"No, but you are their father. The three of you are going to be fine."

Mav smiled. He prayed his twin was right. He wanted to be the best dad to his boys. As he stepped outside and saw the faces smiling back at him, he knew he wasn't in this alone. He had one hell of a support system. "I'll see you all tomorrow."

Sutton waited around until the others were gone. "You ready?"

"Definitely." Maveryck called his mom and told her to bring his boys home.

"WHOA! THIS IS our room?" Major's eyes were wide as he turned in circles, taking in his new bedroom. Marshall was waiting at the door, peeking in. "Marsh! Look, toys!"

With that little nudge from his brother, Marshall charged into the room and fell to his knees beside Major who was pulling all the toys out of the container Mav had bought. It wasn't a cheap plastic toybox, but a wooden chest. Hayden had removed the lid and hinges, storing them in the attic until the boys were older and could open and close the heavy lid without hurting themselves.

"Which one do you want?" Major asked.

"Uhm…" Marshall stuck his finger in his mouth as he looked over all the toys. "I like this one." He picked up the Aquaman action figure.

"I'll take this one," Major said, choosing Superman. He placed the toy on the bed nearest him then proceeded to put the rest of the toys back. Maveryck enjoyed some of the new action hero movies, but the older ones with both the Marvel and DC characters were still his favorite. When the world fell apart thirty years prior, most movies and television productions had halted. The movies of that era remained mainstream for years, until the entertainment industry got back up and running. He was glad his boys enjoyed the toys, but he was confused as to why Major was putting the other toys back. Maybe Jenna only allowed them to play with one thing at a time.

"You can play with all of them, if you'd like. We'll just make sure to put them away before you go to bed," Mav instructed. Both boys looked at each other before turning and looking at their dad.

"We don't have to pick just one?" Major asked.

"No, Son, you don't. You have to share them, but all those toys are yours."

"Wow!" Marshall's eyes were big. He scooted closer to the toy chest and got on his knees looking down into the box.

"I'm going to order pizza. What kind do you like?"

The twins did that thing where they stared at each other without speaking. Major looked up at Mav and asked, "Are you our daddy?"

"I sure am. Did… Uh, did your mom talk about me? Did she tell you anything about me? You knew I had a motorcycle."

They shook their heads in unison. Fuck. They really had been thrown in the deep end. "Hang on. I want to show you

92

something." Maveryck rushed to his room, choosing two photos of him and War, and one of all the brothers. Dropping to his knees next to the boys he held out the first one. "This is me and my twin, Warryck. We call him War. And then there's this one." Mav handed them the frame and waited.

"That's us!" Major said.

"No, that's me and War when we were little. See how much you look like me and your uncle?"

They both nodded. Marshall took the photo and brushed his index finger over Mav's young face in the picture. When he looked up at Maveryck, his eyes were glossy. "Who's this?"

"That's me, Buddy. You take after me, and Major takes after his Uncle Warryck." When Marshall kept staring at Mav, he cleared his throat, which was clogged with emotion, and showed them the last photo. "And these here are your other uncles. That's Ryker. Me and War are next, and that there is Hayden and Kyllian," Mav said, pointing out each male. "You'll get to meet your uncles tomorrow. If that's okay."

"I get to see War?" Major asked.

"Yes, and his girlfriend, Kerrigan. They're the ones who bought your toys and clothes. And my other brothers helped set up your room today."

Major handed the frame back to Mav. "Uh, can we have peppernoni?"

Maveryck grinned. "You mean pepperoni?" Major nodded. "You sure can. I love pepperoni." Major's smile was huge, like Maveryck had told him the best secret in the world. "I'm gonna let you two play while I go downstairs and order the pizza. Just yell if you need anything. Or, if you want to, you're welcome to come downstairs with me and your grandparents. Whatever you want."

"Okay, Daddo."

Daddo? Maveryck laughed out loud, startling the twins. "Daddo. I like it." He stepped out of the room, but instead of

93

heading downstairs, he peeked back around the corner to watch the boys. They were digging in the toybox, whispering and grinning. With their arms full, they climbed on one of the beds and began playing. Maveryck's heart melted.

When they first arrived with Rory, the boys stood in the middle of the living room like little statues. Maveryck showed them around the house, leaving their room for last. The twins held hands as they followed their dad, silently taking it all in. He wondered if they were naturally quiet, or if their new situation had them shy. He hadn't really talked to them much, but he decided to wait until his parents left to try and get to know them better. Rory and Sutton were sitting in the living room, waiting for him to come back downstairs. His mom was being surprisingly hands-off. He appreciated that more than she could know. They were his boys, and the three of them would figure out their own dynamic.

"I'm ordering pizza. You two want to stay and eat with us?"

"Do you want us to stay?" Rory asked.

"Of course. The boys want peppernoni. What do you two want?"

Sutton barked out a laugh. "Zeus, but they're cute. Just get extra of whatever you order, and we'll eat it."

Maveryck pulled out his phone, placing the order with the little mom-and-pop pizza place a few miles from the house. When he was finished, he sat down and sighed.

Rory pulled the envelope containing the boys' information out of her purse. "There's an address on one of the forms. I don't know if it's Jenna's current address, but you can have Lucy check it out. As far as medical conditions, I didn't see any. From what I observed, they're two healthy little boys. They aren't rambunctious, but that might be because they're in a new environment. They were perfectly behaved while you were setting up their room. Too behaved for boys their age, if you ask me."

"Maybe it's the calm before the storm? I'm not going to

complain if they don't tear the house apart," Mav said. He knew there was something going on. Maybe Jenna had been stern with them, expecting them to be on their best behavior all the time, but in his heart, he knew it was more than that. He intended to find out what. He didn't express his suspicions. Instead, he asked his mom about her trip to Texas. She was gushing about her two newest great-grandbabies when the doorbell rang.

"Boys, pizza's here," Mav called upstairs. Within seconds, little feet pounded down the stairs.

"Pizza! Pizza! Pizza!" they yelled together as they ran into the living room, only stopping when they hit Mav's legs.

Mav looked at his parents, rolling his eyes. "And there's the thunder."

Chapter Ten

Maveryck

MAVERYCK COULDN'T BELIEVE the difference in the boys once they got their bellies full of pizza. They were still well behaved, but they became chatty. Maybe it was because he assured them they weren't ever going to have to move again. The subject had come up during supper when Rory asked if they shared a bedroom at home with their mom. Major said they had "a buncha" bedrooms, probably meaning they'd moved a lot. They were only four, for Zeus's sake.

The adults tried to keep the conversation light, staying away from heavy topics such as Jenna's boyfriends, which there seemed to be a few of, and whippings, which there seemed to be plenty of. Mav had to leave the room more than once so the boys didn't catch on to his mood.

Leave it to Major to change the atmosphere when he asked his grandmother, "Why does Pops call you Rory? Is it because you roar?" Mav snickered, but his mom let out a low rumble from her lion. Major's eyes got comically wide, and Marshall fell out of his chair. When she held out her hand to Marshall and hummed, he fell onto her lap, laughing.

Major turned to Sutton and asked, "Pops, can you purr too?" Of course, Sutton obliged the boy. Not with an actual purr, since lions didn't do that, but he did hum. When Maveryck added his own rumbles, the twins jumped up and down, pumping their fists in the air.

Mav did them one better. He got up and left the room, and when the twins couldn't see him, he let out a roar. The boys came running into the other room looking for the sound. Maveryck jumped out from behind the door, and yelled, "Boo!" The kids screamed then fell into each other, laughing hysterically.

"Daddo! That wasn't funny!" Marshall fussed when he could catch his breath. "I almost peed."

Maveryck ushered them into the living room where his parents were sitting on opposite ends of the sofa. They'd already agreed the kids could watch cartoons. Maveryck hadn't bought a television for their room. He thought they were too young for that. The boys plopped down on the sofa between their grandparents. Rory brushed Marshall's hair off his forehead. "Did Daddo scare you?"

"Uh huh. I almost died!"

Major leaned around Sutton, looking at Maveryck. "Is that why mommy called you an animal? Because you're loud like a lion?"

Maveryck blanched, but he made sure to keep a smile on his face for his boys. "Maybe. And maybe it's because I like playing in the woods." He glanced at his parents to see if they agreed with his answer. He would eventually tell the boys about Gryphons, but not until he felt they were old enough to keep the secret. His dad nodded, and Rory smiled before answering Major's earlier question.

"Major, your Pops calls me Rory because that's my name. Aurora Rose Lazlo. Rory is short for Aurora."

Major ran his finger along Sutton's arm where the vibrant rose tattoo sat prominently on his forearm. "Pops has you on his arm."

"He sure does."

"Do you have a bottle colored on you?" Major searched Rory's skin for any tattoos.

Rory frowned. "A bottle?"

"Yeah. Pop comes in bottles." Major's little face was so

97

serious Maveryck hated to laugh, but he couldn't help it.

Rory smiled down at Major. "You're correct, but no. I don't have a bottle. Your Pops used to be a policeman, so I have his badge on my shoulder. Whenever he was out catching bad guys, I had his badge with me to remind me I was safe." Maveryck studied his mother. That was the first time he'd heard why she got that particular tattoo. It was the only one she had representing his father. On the opposite shoulder, she had the dates of all her children and grandchildren. "Guess I'll be headed back for more ink," she said, winking at Mav.

Sutton shifted where he sat. "It's getting late, so your Grams and I are going to head home." Maveryck had a feeling his mom's words had touched something in his dad, and he needed to get her alone. It didn't bother him to know they still did it for each other. He wanted that type of connection after being with someone for over eighty years.

Marshall climbed onto Rory's lap and whispered something in her ear. When she looked down at him, tears glistened in her eyes and she nodded. He threw his little arms around her neck and squeezed tight. When he let go, Major was there to hug her, too. Sutton held out his hand and helped Rory to her feet. He pressed a soft kiss to her temple. Maveryck and the boys walked them to the door.

"We'll see you tomorrow." Since his brothers were coming to meet the twins, his parents were coming back too.

"Bye, boys." Sutton said.

"Be good for your Daddo," Rory added.

"We will." Major nodded like a little bobblehead.

"Bye, Pops. Bye, Grammy Rose," Marshall whispered.

Rory teared up again. "Bye, my darling boys."

When Maveryck closed the door, he looked down at his twins. "So, how about after you take your bath, we have popcorn and a movie?"

"Yeah!" they yelled together. Major grabbed Marshall's hands, and they danced in a circle. Maveryck was glad to see

them feeling more open, and he prayed he could always keep them as happy as they were in that moment.

Instead of putting the twins in the hall bathroom tub, Mav took them into his *en suite* where he had a larger, jetted tub. He didn't know how old kids had to be to leave them alone while they played in the water. Seeing as he hadn't been around many children, he wasn't going to take a chance. He grabbed them some underwear and their new pajamas while the tub was filling. It dawned on him as they splashed around that he didn't have kid-friendly soap or shampoo. He mentally put it on the list of items to get at the grocery store. He had plenty of food in the house, but he wanted to get things they enjoyed. He wasn't going to feed them junk food every meal, but he wanted them to enjoy their meals, too.

When their skin was wrinkled from being in the water so long, Maveryck helped them get dried off and into their pajamas. Since they were going to eat popcorn, he didn't make them brush their teeth. He told them to grab a couple toys to take downstairs, and while they were playing in the living room, he got the popcorn ready. It was too late for them to drink soda, or pop, as Major called it. He poured them some juice in cups with lids and straws Kerrigan had been smart enough to buy. He pulled up his online movie account and flipped through the animated movies. The boys hadn't seen any of them, but they had seen some of the superhero movies. He thought they were too young for those, but he was still learning about what was appropriate for boys their age. They settled on a movie with little yellow creatures with huge eyes. With a son on each side of him, Mav held the popcorn in his lap and got lost in their laughter.

When it was time for bed, the boys went without a fuss. He helped them brush their teeth in the hall bathroom, and when they went into their bedroom, he moved the clothes off the bed. "We'll need to try these clothes on you tomorrow to see what fits. But for now, I'll just set them out of the way."

Major took the bed closest to the door, and Marshall climbed on the other one. Maveryck sat down on the edge of Major's bed. "I know we haven't talked a whole lot, but I want you to know I'm really glad you're here with me. I promise to be the best dad I can. I have a lot to learn, but I think we're going to be okay. I love you both so much."

"Love you, Daddo," Major said.

Marshall didn't return the sentiment. Instead, he whispered, "Can we have hugs?"

"You can have all the hugs you want, Buddy. You never have to ask for them, okay?"

Marshall nodded then launched himself from his bed into Maveryck's arms. Major snuggled against Mav's side, wrapping his little arms around Mav's waist. He held them for long minutes until Marshall wiggled down out of his lap and returned to his bed.

"I'll be right across the hall if you need me. Goodnight, my boys."

There were two nightlights plugged into the electrical sockets, so there was a little light in the room. Maveryck left their door open, and when he went to his room, he did the same. He wanted them to know he was there for them, even across the hall. He made his way downstairs, turning off lights and making sure all the doors were locked. Mav picked up the envelope which contained the boys' information and took it to his bedroom. He took a quick shower, put on some sleep pants, then sat propped against the headboard and read over every document, making note of Jenna's address. After reading through them another time, Maveryck tried to figure out what went wrong four years ago. Why had Jenna left without telling him she was pregnant? If they weren't his, he might understand, but they were. Major and Marshall were his sons. He didn't need a paternity test to know that. He could look at them and see they were his. *Or Warryck's.* They looked like him and his own twin, but War had been off in his own world at the time.

Even if he hadn't been, Mav trusted War like he trusted no other in this world. His twin would never betray him in such a way.

At least she gave them cool names.

That she did. Can you tell if they have Gryphons inside them?

No, not yet. But I do know they're ours.

Ours. Mav should have known his Gryphon would claim them too.

As Mav thought back to his time with Jenna, giggles came from across the hall. He didn't worry about them not being asleep. It was their first night in a new home, and if they were laughing, that meant they were content with where they were. It was so much better than crying. Mav put the documents back in the envelope and set it on the nightstand. Sliding down under the covers, he reached over and turned off the lamp. He didn't know what time the boys would be up, but they had a full day ahead of them tomorrow, and he needed at least a little sleep to be ready to deal with a houseful of Lazlos.

When Mav woke the next morning, there was a slight weight against his chest and back. He opened his eyes to find blond hair in his face. One of the boys was snuggled against his front, and the other was tucked against his back. Puffs of air hit his bare skin as little snores came from whichever twin was spooning him from behind. He didn't want to disturb them, but his bladder was insisting he get out of bed. Raising his head, Mav noticed it was already going on nine, so it was time they all got up. Easing his way from between them, Mav pushed the covers down and slid to the end of the bed. When he turned to look at them, the twins had moved to the middle of the bed and had wrapped themselves around each other. He padded to his nightstand and picked up his phone. He took a picture of the twins cuddled together. It wasn't the first one he'd taken. When he met with Jenna, he was going to ask for any and all pictures she had of the boys.

He hadn't been there to see their first four years, but he wanted to have whatever evidence of their lives he could.

Leaving the boys asleep, Maveryck headed to the kitchen to start breakfast. He figured all kids liked pancakes, so after he started the coffee pot, he set about making pancakes, bacon, and eggs. He was flipping the last batch when four feet pounded down the steps.

"Daddo! We're starving!" Major all but yelled.

"Well, it's a good thing I cooked you some breakfast. I hope you like pancakes."

"Pancakes! Pancakes!" They danced around chanting. Mav laughed at them, glad he made the right decision.

"All right. Climb on up in your chairs." Mav plated the food and set it in front of their eager faces. They were too short to reach the table properly, so he told them to hold on. He went to the living room where his mom had left their booster seats. "There, that's better," he said after putting their butts in their seats. He poured them some milk before fixing his own plate. While they ate, he told them their plans for the day. "After we eat, we're going to try on your new clothes. Then we're going to go to the store. All your uncles will be coming by later to see you, and I figured we'd make a party out of it. We'll grill some hotdogs and burgers."

"And cake? We get cake?" Major asked.

"'Cause you said it's a party," Marshall added.

"We can get cake. Since I missed your birthday, we'll make it a late birthday party."

"Yeah!"

"Cake!"

Mav shook his head, grinning. He couldn't remember the last time he'd smiled so much, and it felt good. Really good. After they'd both devoured their breakfast, he helped them clean the syrup from their hands and faces, then they tried on their new clothes. Kerrigan hadn't bought double of everything, and for that he was glad. He wanted the boys to have their own identities. The smaller sizes fit, so he put the

102

larger sizes away for when they grew into them. Once they had chosen what they wanted to wear for the day, he loaded them in the SUV, placing them in the new car seats he'd bought, and they headed to the grocery store.

Why he thought that was a good idea, he didn't know. Having them at home was one thing. Trying to corral two rambunctious four-year-olds in a crowded store was a lesson in patience. He thought about putting them in the shopping cart, but there was no room with all the food he was buying, so he did his best to get them to hold onto him or the cart. He had tossed several bags of chips into the cart when he noticed Marshall was missing. "Marshall? Marshall!"

Oh, Zeus. He'd only had his boys less than twenty-four hours, and he'd already lost one of them.

Fuck!

CHAPTER ELEVEN

Natalia

INSTEAD OF TAKING the package to the post office, Natalia waited until three in the morning and drove to Maveryck Lazlo's home, putting the envelope in his mailbox. Hopefully, he or whoever was watching his house would gather the mail sooner rather than later. She needed him to be aware of the contract. Why? She could only assume it was because she didn't think he deserved death. At least, not yet. Everyone died. But not everyone did so at the end of a sniper rifle. *Or a fricking sharp knife.* Natalia didn't think she could do her job if she were required to make the kills close up, the way her father died. The way her last mark had been taken out.

She'd gone to bed as soon as she returned home, but sleep hadn't been easy to find. She couldn't stop thinking about the biker couple. The tenderness she had witnessed between the two. Nor could she explain why she felt the Hounds of Zeus were good people. Maybe she hadn't followed them long enough. Hadn't dug deep enough. Nothing about the men she had followed screamed criminals. If Maveryck was a bad man, she had given him a reason to cease his criminal activity, at least for the time being. If he was a good man, she had given him fair warning to watch his back. She wanted there to be good behind those blue eyes. Eyes that haunted her sleep in the form of dreams.

Natalia had never fixated on a man the way she did Maveryck. What was it about him she couldn't let go of? It wasn't only his looks. He was the type of man women wanted to bed and men wanted to be, but he wasn't the first of his type she'd met. Or even taken to bed. She'd only passed him on the sidewalk. They hadn't touched. She hadn't been close enough to catch a hint of cologne or body wash. She hadn't heard his voice. Was it a deep baritone? Or would it be a lighter tenor? What did he sound like when he laughed? Did he have something or someone in his life who gave him a reason to laugh? Was he a gentle lover or the type of man who liked to fuck hard?

She had none of the answers, and that was what was eating at her. Natalia wanted to know what made Maveryck Lazlo tick. Now that she'd warned him, she should accept another contract to give her something else to focus on. Because giving one stranger all her thoughts was doing nothing positive for her. Sitting up in bed, Natalia pulled her knees to her chest and wrapped her arms around her shins.

While debating what to do with her day, she picked at the already chipped polish on her toes. That decided one item on her list. She loved having her toes painted, but she couldn't do it herself to save her life. When she tried, she ended up with more polish on her toes than her nails. Plus, it never lasted more than a day. The grocery store was also on her list, because she was determined to cook something that didn't come in the frozen section or out of a box. Natalia rolled out of bed, and after a quick shower, she pulled out her laptop and opened the webpage of a television chef who was all about quick and easy recipes. After finding several she thought she might be able to accomplish without burning down the kitchen, Natalia made a list of ingredients.

The trip to the nail salon didn't take long since she only went in for a polish change. The grocery store was next. She grabbed a cart and her list and started in the fresh produce section. Having plenty of money in the bank, Natalia didn't worry about prices too much, but as she subconsciously totaled the items in her cart, she wondered how families with several kids could afford to eat healthy. Some of this shit was expensive. She maneuvered her way down each aisle, since she didn't know where half the stuff she needed was shelved. She was searching for the spices when a little boy ran around the corner, barreling into her cart. He fell on his bottom with an *"oof."*

"Are you okay?" Natalia asked, squatting to check on him.

He stared at her with wide eyes. "Your hair is funny. You look like a lollipop," he said, grinning.

Natalia couldn't help but smile back. "I do, huh?"

The little boy nodded. Natalia helped him to his feet. "What's your name?" he asked.

"Natalia. What's yours?" She probably shouldn't be so chatty with a runaway child, but he was just too cute. His mom had to be somewhere close by.

"Marshall? Marshall!" a man's frantic voice yelled from close by.

"I'm here with the lollipop!" Marshall grinned at her again.

"But we've already passed the candy—" A gorgeous blond rounded the corner, his frantic demeanor morphing into that of relief when he found the boy. Kneeling, he said, "Marshall, you can't run away like that. I was worried."

"Sorry, Daddo. I was just looking."

Maveryck Lazlo, the man she was searching for, was there in front of her. Natalia stood entranced as he hugged his son. One of his sons. There was another child hanging onto their cart, and from what Natalia could tell, they were twins. They didn't appear to be identical, but they were darn close. The one who wasn't Marshall had more freckles across his nose, his face was fuller, and he had a cowlick in his bangs. They both had the same piercing blue eyes as their father. And if there were kids, there was a Mrs. Lazlo.

Maveryck finally noticed Natalia. "I'm so sorry, Miss…?"

"Her name's Tolly!" Marshall said.

"Natalia," she corrected.

Marshall squirmed, and Maveryck set him on his feet. His brother stepped closer and peered up at her. "Lolly?"

"Tolly," Marshall said.

"Lolly," his brother volleyed.

"Lollipop!" they sang together, giggling. "I told you, you look like a lollipop," Marshall declared.

Natalia couldn't help but laugh. She turned her eyes from the boys to their father who was staring at her, and her smile faded. "I'm sorry. He ran around the corner straight into my cart. I was just making sure he was okay."

"No, no. I appreciate that. You just…" Maveryck cocked his head, eyes narrowed.

"Well, if everyone is okay, I'll let you get back to your wife."

"No wife," Maveryck muttered. Well, wasn't that interesting? But there had to be a mother out there somewhere.

"We're having a party. It's for our birthday. You wanna come? We're having cake," Marshall asked.

"Oh, uh." Natalia glanced at Maveryck, who was still staring. "That's really sweet of you, but I need to get home. Thank you for the offer, though."

"You're pretty," Not-Marshall said.

"Why, thank you. What's your name?" She couldn't keep thinking of him as "Not-Marshall."

"Major. I'm oldest."

Marshall rolled his eyes, and Natalia grinned. She bet that was a thorn in Marshall's side.

"It's nice to meet you. All of you, but I really should be going." Natalia had to get away from Maveryck Lazlo and his adorable twins before she did something regrettably stupid.

107

"Come on, boys. Let's let Natalia finish her shopping. We still have to go get a cake."

"Cake!" both boys yelled and did a funny little wiggle dance. Natalia couldn't have stopped the laugh that left her throat if she tried.

"You have some adorable boys, Mister...?"

"Maveryck. Lazlo. Mav. Uh, just Mav. And thank you." Maveryck stumbled over his words, and if she hadn't seen the blush come over his cheeks, she wouldn't have believed this big, strong biker was capable.

"You're welcome, just Mav. Boys, I hope you enjoy your party." Natalia ruffled Marshall's hair and turned her cart to head away from so much temptation.

"Bye, Lolly!" one of them yelled, and the other followed up with, "Bye, Tolly!" Giggling, they started chanting, "Tolly, Lolly, lollipop." Natalia grinned to herself as she headed straight for the checkout counter without turning to see the boys enjoying themselves. No way was she finishing her shopping list, not with her mark so close. The smart thing to do would have been to accept the invitation to the party. That would give her a chance to observe the man close up. Since Maveryck didn't extend the invitation, she didn't think he would appreciate her saying yes to his son.

"Come on, boys. What kind of cake do you like?" Maveryck asked as they walked behind her to the bakery. That was odd. Why didn't he know what kind of cake his own kids liked? Against her better judgment, Natalia turned to watch father and sons. Maveryck looked back over his shoulder at her, his expression one of confusion.

"Chocolate!" the twins shouted in unison.

"Ma'am, are you ready to check out?" the cashier asked. Natalia apologized and began setting her items on the conveyor belt. After loading her things in the back of her vehicle, Natalia had to make herself turn the engine over and drive away. She wondered if Maveryck – Mav – had found the envelope. Did he realize he was in danger? And if so, why was he out in public with his kids?

God, but those boys were cute. As she drove, Natalia allowed herself to daydream about being their mom. Not that she would dream of replacing their current mom, but damn. All that energy? Maveryck had his hands full, that was for certain. He had been visibly worried about Marshall when he wasn't within sight, so maybe Maveryck had found the information she left. No, that didn't make sense. If he had, there's no way a father who cared for his sons would willingly put them in harm's way, unless he thought the contract was a joke. Maybe she should go to his house and tell him it was one-hundred-percent true. But then she'd have to tell him how she knew it wasn't a joke.

Natalia didn't want those boys to be in danger. As unsure as she was about their father, Natalia knew she had to do something to protect the twins. But what? She had already warned Maveryck. That was the best she could do. Wasn't it?

When she arrived home, Natalia put away the few groceries she'd managed to purchase. Her plan to cook now took a back seat to her worry about the twins. Okay, maybe she was worried about their father, but that was stupid. She didn't know him. Her phone rang. Not her personal one, but the burner she used for work. No doubt Nix was calling for a report.

"Hello?"

"Myshka, is there a reason you're turning down all contracts? I know you wanted a vacation, but we need you back in the field."

"What are you talking about? I'm on assignment. I know it's taking me longer than normal to complete the job, but I've only just located the mark today. I still have to do recon."

"What assignment?"

"The one you emailed to me. The one I accepted."

"When was this?"

Natalia pulled up the assignment and looked at the time stamp. She relayed the exact date and time.

"I did not send you that contract, Myshka. Who was it from?"

"Well, that's the thing. There was no contact information. I thought it was probably a glitch."

"Forward it to me immediately. And wait for me to get back to you before you proceed further." Nix disconnected without saying goodbye.

Oh, God. What if this wasn't a legitimate contract? What if she'd found Maveryck Lazlo and taken him out? Natalia went to the bedroom and got her laptop out of its hiding place. She forwarded the email to Nix. Instead of shutting it back down, she left it open in case Nix emailed her back. Natalia paced back and forth, biting the side of her thumb. Two sets of bright blue eyes haunted her. What if she had pulled the trigger and orphaned those two precious boys? *You've orphaned other children.* Yes, but she hadn't met the other children of the scum she took out. Natalia jumped when the email notification sounded in the room. Rushing to her laptop, Natalia swallowed hard when she read Nix's response.

"This did not come from me. Cease looking into this man. Consider the contract null and void. You will be paid for your time. Feel free to accept a different job, but this time, make sure it comes from me."

"Damnit!" Natalia yelled to no one then sent a reply. "Is this man in danger?"

It took several minutes before she received a response. *"Do not concern yourself with it."*

How could she not? Maveryck was most likely an innocent man with a price on his head. But why would…? Gah! Natalia didn't know what to do. It wasn't like she could drive to the man's home and talk to him about it. Same issue as before; she would have to explain how she knew about the contract, and she couldn't do that. She had already warned him via the documents, so she would have to trust him to watch his own back. And that of his boys.

Before Nix's email, Natalia had been hungry. Now, she was afraid she'd throw up if she tried to eat anything. This wasn't like her. She'd been raised to be uncaring. To not worry about other people. To only concern herself with that of her father's well-being. Anatoly had done his best to train emotions right out of her. It hadn't worked. She'd held onto the love of her mother, hiding away the photo she had managed to save when her father tossed all her mother's things after her death. Anatoly had gotten rid of all evidence Bellona Volkova had existed. As hard as he tried, he couldn't erase Natalia's memories. Every day, she looked at the photo. Every day, she reminded herself of what she had shared with the woman who brought her into the world. Twenty years later, and Natalia could still remember what her mother's voice sounded like. How soft her hair was. The way she smelled.

Natalia always wanted to have a daughter so she could name the child after her mother. She wanted to honor the woman in more ways than hanging onto one photo. Natalia walked down the short hallway to her bedroom and picked up the photo she kept in a frame on her nightstand. "Mama, I wish you were here." Natalia often spoke to the photo, but some days, like today, she missed her more than ever. If her mother had lived, would Bellona have allowed Anatoly to turn Natalia into the killer she was? She liked to think not. She tried to imagine how differently her life would have turned out. How much better her life would have been. Natalia had plenty of money, but other than that? She had nothing. No one.

Hers was a lonely existence.

So, do something about it.

Yes, but what?

CHAPTER TWELVE

Maveryck

MAVERYCK COULDN'T SHAKE the feeling he had met Natalia before. She wasn't his usual type, but something about the female called to him. The same way the blonde on the sidewalk had. Those handful of minutes in the grocery store had been more than enough for Mav to know he needed Natalia in his life. As he watched her interact with the boys, he couldn't take his eyes off her. His Gryphon had pushed at him, saying she was theirs, but Maveryck couldn't make himself ask her out. The twins had just come into his life, and they needed to be his focus. She was pixie cute with her lavender hair. Her dark eyes were expressive, and she had made a hell of an impression on the boys.

When they finally got around to choosing a birthday cake, Marshall insisted on getting one with purple balloons, because they reminded him of Tolly. Major agreed, so that's what they got. The twins didn't stop talking about "Lollipop" all the way home.

When they got to the house, Mav tried to get their minds on something else, so he busied the boys with helping put the groceries away. At least the things they could reach in the pantry or fridge. While they did that, he told them a little about his brothers. He had asked them all to stagger the times they arrived so the boys wouldn't be overwhelmed.

War and Kerrigan were the first to show up. Mav had

asked them to come by earlier than the others so they would have some one-on-one time with the twins. All were equally smitten with each other. As soon as introductions were out of the way, the boys were pulling War and Kerrigan upstairs to see their bedroom. Maveryck stood in the doorway as Major animatedly talked about their new things, and Marshall silently nodded his agreement.

"War and Kerrigan are the ones who bought your toys and clothes. Can you tell them thank you?"

"Thank you!" they called out together. They insisted on showing Kerrigan each toy even though she'd helped pick them out.

War came over to stand next to Mav, a smile on his face. "They sure are something else."

"Right?" Maveryck turned away and wiped his eyes. War gripped Mav's shoulders and placed his forehead against the back of Mav's head. Blowing out a breath, he admitted, "I lost Marshall in the store today. I about had a heart attack."

"I see you found him, though. Where was he?"

Mav turned around, having his emotions under control. "The next aisle over. He ran into this really cute woman with lavender hair, and he called her a lollipop."

War barked out a laugh, and Mav shook his head. "War, I don't know what it is about her, but I think I made a mistake not getting her phone number."

"Why didn't you?"

"Because, I just got the boys. I have to focus on them right now, not a love life."

"Love life? Who are you and what have you done with my twin who only has one-and-dones?"

"Not the point. I don't have time for that either. Their lives have been uprooted, and until I feel they're settled, I'm going to be here with them every step of the way."

"I get that, but what about work? Are you going on hiatus?"

"Yes. No. Fuck. I don't know. This is all so new. Mom's already said she'll help out, but I'm not going to take on any new jobs for at least a couple weeks."

"Kerrigan and I will be glad to help. All you have to do is ask. We've already discussed setting up one of the spare rooms for them for when they need 'cool uncle' time away from their overbearing father."

Mav shoved War's shoulder, laughing. "I'll show you overbearing."

War got a funny look on his face when he turned his attention back to his mate and the boys. Mav asked, "You okay?"

"Yeah. Just reminds me of all the time I missed with Lucy. At least you only missed four years. I practically missed her whole life."

"So did Ryker with Mac. But hey. We've got our kids in our lives now, and all we can do is make sure they know they're loved going forward."

"You're right, but you and Ryker didn't have a choice. I did. And I made the wrong one."

Mav squeezed his twin's neck. "You've got to forgive yourself, Brother. Lucy has, so why can't you?"

Major walked up and asked, "Daddo! Is it time for cake yet?"

"Not yet, Buddy. We have to wait until everyone else gets here. Then we're going to eat burgers and hotdogs."

"That's gonna be foreeeeeeever."

"I tell you what. Let's go downstairs, and Uncle War and I will get the grill fired up. The others should be here—"

"The fun uncle has arrived!" Kyllian yelled from downstairs.

"And that would be me," Hayden said.

"Come on, boys. Looks like the party is getting started." Mav brushed his hand over Major's head as he took off toward the stairs.

"Wait for me!" Marshall yelled after his brother. Mav

114

and War stepped back so they didn't get run over.

"And here I thought they were going to be nervous about meeting everyone." Mav shook his head, grinning.

By the time he, War, and Kerrigan got to the living room, Hayden and Kyllian were sitting on the floor, each with a twin on his lap. "I grabbed your mail on my way in. I put it on the kitchen counter. There's an envelope you might want to check out," Hayden told Maveryck.

"Yeah, okay." Maveryck started toward the kitchen when a short knock sounded, and the front door opened. Ryker walked in, followed by their parents.

"Hey, boys," Sutton said.

Ryker stood just inside the room, staring down at the twins. "Well, there's no denying who these two belong to. I'm Ryker." His voice was gentle, and he was actually smiling. He took a step closer, squatting. "You must be Major," he said, touching the older twin on the knee. Major nodded, and Ryker said, "That means you're Marshall. I'm really glad to meet you."

The boys both gave Ryker little waves, but they didn't move to get up from where they sat on their other uncles' laps. Rory and Sutton sat on the sofa, asking the boys how they were. Marshall started telling them all about Natalia, and everyone laughed when the boys sing-songed the names they'd given the woman.

With the boys taken care of and talking animatedly, Mav moved to the kitchen to get lunch going. "If you want to start the grill, I'll get the meat ready," he told War.

"You got it." War kissed Kerrigan's temple before heading out to the deck.

"What can I do to help?" Kerrigan asked.

"If you want to get the tomatoes sliced and the lettuce washed, that would be great."

Maveryck went to work on the hamburger patties. He added a couple spices and some steak sauce to most of them. He left out the spicy sauce on two burgers for the boys.

When they were patted out, he washed his hands. As he was reaching for a paper towel, he noticed the mail. A manilla envelope with no postage or return address sat on top. Mav tore it open and peered inside before pulling the stack of sheets out. When he saw what it was, he fell back against the counter.

"Are you okay?" Kerrigan asked.

"Yeah, I... Ryker? Can you come outside for a second?" Mav didn't wait on his brother to follow. He needed air.

"What's up?" Ryker asked, closing the French door behind him.

Mav handed him the papers. "This was in the mailbox."

"What the fuck?" Ryker asked.

War closed the lid on the grill and joined them. "What is it?"

Ryker flipped through each page. "It's a contract. Well, it's what looks like a contract. These come in from Nexus via email. The identifying portion has been removed, but the format is exactly the same. Why would someone warn you about a hit taken out on you?"

"Better yet, who the fuck would take out a contract on you?" War asked.

"I don't know. But this looks like it came from Nexus. Why would they accept a hit on one of their operatives?" Mav paced the deck. Someone wanted him dead. "Fuck!" He grabbed his hair and pulled.

The back door opened, and Lucy and Tamian stepped outside. "Hey, Dad." Lucy stopped next to War and hugged him. When she opened her mouth to say hello to Ryker and Maveryck, she narrowed her eyes. "What's wrong?"

"Nothing we need to get into right now." Mav hugged his niece, and the growl from Tamian was low but still loud enough to be heard. "Ease up, St. Claire. She's my niece."

Tamian shrugged. "I know that, and you know that, but the beast still doesn't like it when someone else touches my mate."

War grinned. "He's not wrong. Doesn't matter who it is." Yeah, Maveryck had been on the receiving end of his twin's Gryphon warning him away from Kerrigan.

"So, that little matter of Tatiana Volkova?" Lucy stepped back over to Tamian, hugging him tight around the waist. "I have some information, but not enough. I was able to track her up until about a week after her father was killed. After that? The woman disappeared into thin air."

Mav scratched his beard. "That's impossible. Nobody can completely disappear."

"It's possible if they change their identity," Lucy said.

"Do you think that's what happened?" Ryker asked.

"It's the only thing that makes sense. If she were dead, I would have found that. I traced her to a hotel close to her family's home. She stayed there for six days. Then, *poof.* She was gone. Her bank account had been emptied, so it's possible she paid someone to make her disappear."

The back door opened. "We have some little boys in here who are threatening to eat their cake if they don't get some food in their bellies first," Rory said.

"Shit. Let's save this conversation for later." Maveryck followed his mom into the house and grabbed the burgers and wieners for the grill.

"Look, Daddo! Lollipop has a twin," Marshall said.

"What are you…?" Maveryck leaned over his son to see what he was talking about. The photos Lucy had printed out of Tatiana Volkova were spread out on the table, and Marshall was pointing at her. Upon closer inspection, Mav knew his son had hit on something.

"Holy sh… shingles," he said, catching his curse word. If there was ever a time to spout expletives, it was now.

"What is it?" Lucy asked. War, Kerrigan, and Ryker joined them.

"Did Tatiana Volkova have a sister?" Mav asked Lucy. The information sent on both her and her father had indicated she was an only child.

"No, why?"

"It appears we know where Tatiana Volkova is. Right here in New Troy."

"What?" Lucy asked. "How do you know?"

Maveryck explained their run-in with the woman at the grocery store who introduced herself as Natalia. "Because Natalia? That's her."

"'Cept she has purple hair now. Like a lollipop," Marshall said.

"Okay, let's get the food on the grill. I've got some boys who are hungry," Rory said, taking the photos and shoving them back in the envelope. She handed the envelope to Maveryck and told him to put it away. His mom was right. This wasn't a conversation they needed to have around the twins. Luckily, the boys had no trouble keeping the adults' minds off the contract. Both contracts. The one he had on Natalia, and now, the one that had been put out on him. He wasn't surprised he had a price on his head because of what he did for a living, but the fact that Nexus had taken it and released it? That shit was un-fucking-acceptable. Normally, Mav trusted Ryker with anything and everything, but in that moment, he needed his older brother to step up and figure this shit out.

When it was time to cut the cake, Marshall was the one to point out the purple balloons were because of Natalia. And wasn't that a kick to the balls? This assassin had been close to his sons. Too close. Had that been a coincidence? Or was she following Maveryck because she'd accepted the contract? He needed to focus on his boys, because this party was for them. About them. While everyone was singing "Happy Birthday," it dawned on Maveryck that in the two days since Jenna dropped the twins off, not once had they asked about their mother. Did they not miss her? He needed to have a chat with his ex and find out what she told them. He needed to find Natalia, and he needed to find out who was out to get him. He needed too damn much.

Ryker suggested taking the discussion to the clubhouse, but Maveryck didn't want to leave the boys. Not even with his mother. He was in danger, and the best way to get to him would be through them. Rory was helping clean up when she suggested the males and Lucy take their discussion out on the deck while she and Kerrigan kept the twins entertained.

As Maveryck spread the photos out on the patio table, he explained both about looking for Tatiana Volkova, a.k.a. Natalia, as well as the contract on him. They had all heard about him and the twins meeting Natalia in the grocery store, and he voiced his worry that she was the one who had accepted the contract on him.

"Hey, I know her." Hayden turned one of the photos around. "She pulled up alongside us at a stop light last week."

"And I don't believe in coincidence. If she's in the area, I'll find her. Tam, let's go home. I want to start looking for this woman. She's not going to get the chance to go after Mav and the boys." Lucy hugged Maveryck from behind. "I'll find her, Uncle Mav. I promise. And when I do, she better pray she is innocent." Lucy may have only come into their lives a few years ago, but she was one of them. Fiercely protective of all of them, the same way they were of her. When she and Tamian were gone, Mav stood from the table and looked through the back door. He could see through the house into the living room where the boys were on the floor, playing.

"I can't lose them," he whispered.

Sutton squeezed Mav's shoulders from behind. "You're not going to lose them, Son. Lucy will find this woman."

"What if it is a coincidence, and she isn't the one who accepted the contract?"

"Let me handle that." Ryker's demeanor was back to pissed-off. "I have a contact at Nexus I'm going to reach out to."

"How do you know you can trust them?" War asked.

Ryker hesitated, rubbing a hand down his face. "You'll just have to trust *me* on that."

And like the last twenty-something years, his older brother was still keeping secrets.

CHAPTER THIRTEEN

Maveryck

MAVERYCK WAS LEANING against the doorframe, watching the twins sleep. Marshall was curled in a little ball with one arm wrapped around the Aquaman figure. Major was lying crossways, having kicked off the covers, and was snoring softly. Neither one was aware of the threat their house was under. Ryker, before he left, called Tank, Shadow, and Spyder to come sit on the house. Mav and the twins were going to have round-the-clock protection until the threat was over. His phone vibrated in his back pocket. When he pulled it out, he read the text.

Lucy: *I have something.*

Mav walked across the hall to his room and called his niece. "Lucy? What did you find?"

"It took a bit, but I found her. Natalia's last name is Jones, and she lives about twenty minutes from you. She's been renting a house on the outskirts of New Troy for a few months. Since a couple days after Tatiana Volkova disappeared. Whoever set her up with her new identity is good. They didn't just wipe Tatiana off the grid, they gave her a back story, complete with travel documentation dating back to her teens, as well as school transcripts.

"I was able to get a good look at her car and license plate from the security cameras at the grocery store. I was worried she was the one after you, so I also checked the feed from the cameras at the compound. Natalia has been watching from across the street, every day for the past week. She's even followed the Hounds when they left. If it weren't for her using the same vehicle every time, I wouldn't be sure, because the woman was wearing a different disguise every time. Uncle Mav, I think she's the one who accepted the contract on you."

Mav sat down hard on the bed, blowing out a breath. "Then who put the copy of the contract in my mailbox? It had to be someone who wanted to warn me, right?"

"You would think so. I'm emailing some pictures I made from the videos, and I'm sending her address to your phone, but promise me you won't go after her alone."

"Lucy, I'm a Hound. I can take care of myself."

"Yes, and she's a trained assassin for the Russian mafia. You can't stop a bullet."

"Don't worry. She won't see me coming." He hoped.

"Promise you'll be careful."

"Always. And Lucy? Thank you. You are more important to our family than you will ever know."

"I do know that, but I appreciate you saying it. Now, I'm going to snuggle with my Gargoyle and get some sleep. I still have to find Josiah Talbert."

"Good night, Luce."

"Night." Lucy clicked off, and Mav dropped onto his back, staring at the ceiling. He had been a mercenary for over twenty years. He'd had several close calls, but back then, he didn't have as much to lose. Sure, his family would miss him if he were taken out, but now he had the boys. His sons needed their father, and he was going to make sure he was around long enough to watch them grow up. Find out if they were Gryphon. Help them acclimate to their shifter if they were.

To do that, he had to find Natalia Jones and deal with her. Find out if she was the one who took the contract. He had to get his head in the game. Be the professional he'd

122

been all these years and do what he did best – hunt. Something Lucy said niggled at his brain… *the woman was wearing a different disguise every time.* Maveryck lunged from the bed and stalked out the door. He stopped to look in on the twins. Marshall was in the same position, but Major had turned around so his head was on his pillow, still snoring.

Downstairs, Maveryck sat with the photos Lucy had printed off. He fired up his computer and opened the email. When he looked over the pictures, his breath caught. He should have known. Her smell on the sidewalk had infiltrated his senses, the same way it had in her bedroom. When he passed Natalia on the street in her white-blonde wig and big sunglasses, he felt it. This connection. Had she been stalking him back then? Or was she the one who took the shot? Why would she be after the same mark unless she worked for Nexus? Mav sent Ryker a text. It was the middle of the night, but his brother needed to know what Maveryck suspected.

Maveryck studied all the photos closely. Memorizing every look Natalia had. Long brown hair, shoulder-length blonde hair, red curls, all different looks. The photos weren't close enough to show her eye color, but Maveryck bet his Harley the woman wore colored contacts. But he had seen the real Natalia Jones with her candy-colored hair and chocolate brown eyes. That was the look he couldn't get out of his mind. The one he wanted to see more of. The one that made his boys giggle. No, he couldn't have that. There was no way he could allow an assassin anywhere near the twins. That kind of woman wasn't mother material.

Getting ahead of yourself, aren't you?

Don't tell me you didn't feel it. You were the one pushing me to ask her out.

I felt it. What I didn't feel was anything threatening. You saw her with our boys.

She's a godsdamned assassin. You want that kind of

123

woman around them?

You're also an assassin – a mercenary. And you're their father.

Fucking hell. His Gryphon was right. He felt the connection when their eyes met. But his beast was also correct in that he was getting ahead of himself. Just because he felt some strange pull to the woman didn't mean they were meant to be together. Yes, she had been gentle and charming with the twins, but that could have been an act. Mav used to think he was a good judge of character, but that went out the window when Jenna walked out of his life. Pregnant with his boys.

Forgetting about their connection, Mav got in the mindset he needed to go after Natalia as if she were the mark. *She is the mark.* How had he forgotten that? Ryker had accepted the contract on Tatiana Volkova. Was someone at Nexus pitting them against the other? According to Ryker, Nexus knew who the Hounds were. Not that they were Gryphons, but the MC members were the ones taking the jobs.

He had to get into Natalia's house without getting shot. That meant stealth. That meant using his eagle. Mav needed to do some recon, but with the boys upstairs asleep, he couldn't leave the house in the middle of the night like he normally would. He needed help, and there was only one person he trusted. Well, two, because with War came Kerrigan. Mav texted his twin and told him what he needed. If War felt comfortable leaving Kerrigan at home, he could come watch over the boys while Mav did what he needed to do. A minute later he had his answer. *They* were on their way.

When his brother and his female arrived, Mav ushered them into the living room. "Thanks for coming. I'm sorry to do this in the middle of the night, but I need to stake out her house while it's dark." He filled them in on what Lucy had found.

124

"No, don't apologize. This needs to be handled as quickly as possible. Go do what you need, and we'll watch over my nephews." War looked toward the stairs where his mate had gone. "She hasn't stopped talking about the twins. I think they're making her want a baby," War whispered.

"Yeah? How do you feel about that?"

Warryck's eyes softened. "I'd love to see her belly round with my child. But there'll be time to talk about that later. Go. Do what you need to do. We'll be here."

"Thanks, Brother."

Maveryck got in his SUV and drove toward the address Lucy gave him. When he passed by the little house, he continued on to find somewhere to park so he could shift. There was a wooded area not far from Natalia's home where he could hide his vehicle. After stripping, Mav shifted and took to the sky. The house was surrounded by trees, so it was easy for him to see all four sides from different vantage points. Knowing she was an assassin helped in what he looked for, and when he searched, he found several security cameras. He didn't know if Lucy had the ability to hack into the servers to cut the feed or put them on a loop. Julian Stone did, but Mav hesitated in asking Tamian's Clan for help even though they had willingly trained Lucy.

When he moved to a tree at the back of the house, Mav used his shifter vision to look into all the windows. One in particular. Natalia's bedroom window was open, the sheer curtains fluttering with the breeze. Mav zeroed in on the woman, asleep in her bed. She was lying on her stomach, one toned leg on top of the sheet, which was draped over her lower half. Her face was scrunched, like she was having a bad dream. In that moment, Maveryck felt the need to wake her. Take her in his arms and offer comfort. And wasn't that just fucked up? This woman who was most likely looking to take him out, he wanted her. He wanted to hold her in his arms and see her brown eyes alight with joy, the way they'd been when she was interacting with Marshall and Major.

Remembering why he was there, Maveryck flew to different branches, noting all points of entry. Two doors, front and rear, and several windows he could easily break into if needed. With security cameras watching the perimeter, he would not be able to walk right up to her home without alerting her he was coming. There was no second story where he could sneak inside. Maybe he would take a page out of her book and wear a disguise. That, or he could ask one of his brothers to cause a distraction while he entered her home. He didn't want Natalia harmed. At least not until he figured out if she was the one who'd taken the contract on him.

Mav considered getting several of the Hounds to roll up to her house on their bikes, but he didn't want to put their lives in jeopardy. She could pick them off with her rifle before they ever had their kickstands down. No, he needed to do this alone, that way he was the only one risking his life.

You could call her and ask her out.

And how would I have gotten her number?

That is a problem.

Indeed, it was.

She's asleep. Just shift and go through the window. It's already open.

Now that was an idea. Except he was naked.

Go back and get your clothes.

What if she wakes up before I get back?

Come back tomorrow night.

He *would* have the element of surprise on his side. She probably slept with a gun under her pillow, so he would be taking a big chance, but it didn't sound like a bad idea. So, taking his Gryphon's advice, Maveryck flew back to his vehicle, shifted, put his clothes into his carry pouch, shifted back, and returned to her home. Natalia was still asleep. The only thing that worried Mav about this plan was the cameras. If they were motion-sensor, they would detect his movement and wake her. Unless he aimed the cameras away from where he needed to walk.

Before moving to the cameras on the house, he double-checked the trees all around, making sure there were none hidden among the branches. When he found none, he once again studied the ones attached to the house. The cameras were pointed toward the ground, which meant he was able to fly above them, coming at them from a downward angle. Using his powerful beak, Mav pushed the cameras so they were pointing up. When that was done, he dropped to the ground and waited. Listening for any sign of Natalia waking. He walked until he was directly under her window, then lifted himself off the ground, gently flapping his wings. She was in the same position she'd been in, so Mav decided to take the chance on surprising her. After shifting back, he quickly dressed and folded his pouch, sticking it into the waistband at his back. He pulled his T-shirt over it so Natalia wouldn't see it. Not that she would know what it was, but still.

Maveryck stared at the screen, noticing the pins holding it in place were on the inside. With no other choice he extended a claw and sliced the mesh away from the frame, holding his breath. Natalia still didn't move, so he hoisted his body as silently as possible and slipped into her room. Landing without a sound, he eased his way to the opposite side of the bed, and using his lion's speed, he grabbed the woman from around the waist, pulling her from the bed. Her left hand came away with a pistol in her grip. Maveryck grabbed her wrist, keeping the gun pointed toward the ceiling. She pulled the trigger three times in rapid succession, and white dust rained down on their heads. Natalia kicked and wiggled, doing her best to get away. She set her feet to the mattress, pushing against his larger body, but it was useless. She was but a slip of a female, and he outweighed her by at least a hundred pounds. Plus, he was a Gryphon. She was no match for him.

"Shh. Calm down. I'm not going to hurt you." *Yet.*

"Natalia, settle," he coaxed against her ear. She relaxed in his embrace, her ass hitting right at his groin. Mav swallowed down a groan at having this feisty woman pressed against him. The scent of wildflowers assaulted his senses, and before he realized what he was doing, Mav turned his face so his nose was against her neck. He stupidly inhaled. Natalia shivered, and Mav held her tighter. He moved so he could stand, and when he did, she tried to wrestle the gun away again.

"Cho ty khochesh', suka!!" Mav didn't speak Russian, but he did understand pissed-off female.

"I said I don't want to hurt you, but if you continue pulling that trigger, I won't have a choice," he growled. He pushed her down onto the bed and used his weight to secure her while he took the weapon away, tossing it on the floor out of her reach. She wiggled beneath him, and his cock forgot who they were dealing with and why they were there.

"Ty cho ebanuti?"

"You can curse me later, Natalia. Or should I call you Tatiana?" That was the wrong thing to say, because she headbutted his nose. "Ow, shit. Calm down, woman. We need to talk."

"Get off me!" she yelled, doing her best to buck him off.

Mav rolled to his feet, taking her with him. He banded both his arms around her waist, locking her arms to her sides. He leaned his head against hers so she no longer had the advantage of the back of her head. "Like I said, we need to talk. I need answers, and I'd rather not hurt you to get them." Natalia sighed, and her body relaxed minutely.

"Who are you?" she asked.

"Maveryck Lazlo," he answered honestly. Natalia gasped and tried to turn her head to look at him. With his tight hold on her, all the move did was put her face against his neck. It was her turn to inhale, and Mav bit the inside of his cheek to keep from moaning.

Closing his eyes, he blew out a breath. "Here's what I know:

128

You've been staking out the clubhouse from across the street. You've also been following the Hounds. I know you're an assassin. Here's what I don't know: Why did you feel the need to get a new identity? Who do you work for? Did you follow me into the grocery store? Are you stalking all the Hounds or just me? And before you answer, let me just say, you have one shot to tell me the truth. You might be an expert with a rifle, but I don't need a gun to hurt you, or make you disappear. One chance, Natalia. One."

Chapter Fourteen

Natalia

Maveryck Lazlo was in her home. How? How had he found her? Or bypassed the alarm? The security cameras outside should have picked up his movement. Ever since getting home from the grocery store, she had spent all her time thinking about the man and his sons. She knew why he was there. He knew she'd been searching for him, or one of the Hounds. Her fear at being grabbed out of her sleep had turned into anger. When he laid out what he knew, the fear turned to resignation. He knew who she really was. Maveryck wanted answers, and she wanted to live. He told her she had one shot, so she opted to tell him the truth. If he knew she was the one who warned him, maybe he wouldn't kill her.

Natalia deflated in his arms. She turned her head away from his neck, because really, the man smelled too delicious. Not like cologne or aftershave. No, he smelled like clean skin and... She turned her head before she did something stupid like lick him. He was holding her hostage, for god's sake. Her body was doing its best to override logic.

"I..." She cleared her throat. "If you know who I am, then you should know why I needed a new identity. My

130

father was killed, and my cousin Mikael took over the family. He kicked me out of the house. Out of my home. The only home I'd ever known, and he said I needed to leave. He tasked me with finding my father's killer. I didn't know where to start looking. I was approached by… actually, I'm not sure who they are. I got a call one day from someone who knew all about me. About my work for the family. They said they would help me with a new life."

"What did they want in return?"

"For me to work for them. I knew Mikael would never let me have a moment's peace, and I needed a job. The little I had saved was in an account monitored first by my father and then by my cousin. I have no formal education, and I couldn't simply put out a resume with my experience." Natalia shouldn't admit to this stranger she was an assassin, but he already knew that about her.

"Why are you following me?"

"The people I work for, they put a contract out on you."

"And you accepted it? No questions asked?" Maveryck all but growled in her ear.

Natalia shivered. Again. "No. I mean, yes I accepted, but I had plenty of questions. Before I received the contract, I was sent photos. Pictures of you with your Club. I didn't know who you were, but I had seen you before. There was no note or any identifying information with the package, only the photos. I searched the internet, trying to find more about the Hounds, but your internet presence is lacking. I already had plans to go on vacation, so I put the photos aside and went. When I returned home, I was emailed a contract. Your contract. I began following the others when I couldn't find you."

"So, you followed me and my boys into the store?"

"No. That was purely coincidence. I have a question. Did you get a copy of the contract in your mailbox?" Natalia fisted her hands to keep from grabbing hold of Maveryck's thighs.

"Yes. Was that you?"

"Yes." Natalia leaned her head back against his chest. When his cheek pressed against her head, she jerked away.

"Why? Why did you warn me?" Maveryck's arms loosened a little.

"Because something felt off about it. I don't go around killing innocent men. I do have a code."

"And you? Who would want you dead, Natalia?"

"Wh-what?" It had to be her imagination. Because she could've sworn Maveryck brushed his lips across her hair.

"There's a contract out on you as well."

"Contract?" Jesus, could she not speak in sentences? "How do you know that?"

"Because I accepted it."

Fear chased down Natalia's spine.

"While I was off looking for you, you were hunting me," he admitted. "Who do you work for?"

A contract on her? Probably her *svoloch'* cousin. And she and Maveryck we're supposed to kill each other. Now that was fucked.

"Natalia?"

She saw no reason to lie at this point. Either she was going to die in the next few minutes, or she could convince Maveryck not to pull the trigger. "Nexus."

Maveryck sighed, and his breath tickled her ear. "We have a big problem then."

"You killed my father." She didn't know it was him, but she had that gut feeling.

"Yes. And since there's someone wanting you out of the picture, I'm guessing it's your cousin putting the hits out."

Natalia took a deep breath. "I'm glad your bike was faster than my bullets."

Maveryck chuckled. "Me too."

Natalia remembered the way her father and his guards had been killed. The same as the pedophile. Maveryck didn't use guns, so more than likely his weapon of choice was hidden somewhere on his body. That didn't bode well for her, especially with the position she was in. If he chose to take her out, she would never see it coming.

"Are you going to kill me?"

"Not today." Maveryck leaned his head against hers. Why did he keep doing that?

"Thank you, I think."

"I need to talk to my brother. He needs to know Nexus can't be trusted. If they're pitting their operatives against each other, we need to end our association with them."

"Maybe they're in it for the money. If the price is high enough, maybe they think anyone is expendable." Natalia hadn't worked for the organization long. "How long have you worked for Nexus?"

"Going on twenty years."

"Wow. You must have started young." She didn't know how old he was, but Maveryck looked like he was in his early thirties.

"I'm older than I look," he muttered.

"So, what now?" Natalia needed to disappear.

Again.

"Now, we come up with a plan, but I need to get home to my sons."

"Who's watching them?" He told her in the grocery store he didn't have a wife, and she hadn't seen a woman at his house.

"My brother and his ma... girlfriend." Maveryck turned Natalia, keeping her in his arms. "Are you still planning to kill me?"

"I never was. That's why I put the contract in your mailbox." Natalia's arms were caught between her chest and his, so she unfisted her hands, laying them flat against his chest. Maveryck sucked in the slightest of breaths, but she felt it. She felt a lot of things, and none of them good considering the situation. She wanted to lean in closer. Press her lips to his. Natalia wanted to get as close as possible. She

133

just plain wanted. She had ever since running into him in the store.

"Natalia," Maveryck groaned.

"Huh?" She took her gaze off his lips and searched those blue eyes that had been haunting her dreams. It was hard to see them in the dark room, but she didn't miss the way his breath tickled her face. Maveryck tightened his arms, and she slid her hands up his chest to his neck. She caressed his skin with her thumbs.

"This is a bad idea," he grumbled.

"A very bad idea," she whispered.

Maveryck gripped the back of her hair. "Fuck it," he said before touching his lips to hers, angling her head the way he wanted. Since she had never been kissed before, she hadn't known what to expect. She always thought kissing a man would be awkward, but this was anything but. Maveryck was soft yet crushing. Tentative yet demanding. Submissive yet controlling. In a word, it was perfection. When his tongue swept into her mouth, exploring, she met him stroke for stroke. Twisting, twirling, tasting. Fire stoked her belly, dipping lower. She had never felt such need clawing at her to be with a man. All the sex she'd experience before had lacked something. Now she understood what.

Passion.

This... this was everything, and it was only a kiss. With this stranger. A man she was supposed to kill. With their bodies so close, breathing each other's air, Natalia didn't want to kill him. She wanted to protect him. Protect his boys.

But who was going to protect her?

Maveryck pulled his lips from hers and pressed their foreheads together. He inched back, probably so she wouldn't feel his erection. Too late. He was breathing heavily, his eyes closed. One hand was rubbing a slow path up and down her spine while the other remained tight on her hip. Natalia rested her cheek on his chest. His heart was thundering, matching her own quick beats. There was so

134

much Natalia didn't know. Didn't understand. But in that moment, she knew she wanted him. Any way she could get him.

"Please tell me you don't have a girlfriend," she begged against his neck. She pressed a kiss to the pulsing vein. "Or boyfriend," she added, licking at his Adam's apple. Maveryck's hand on her back stilled, so she waited, resting her cheek against his. Squeezing her eyes closed, she held her breath.

"I have neither. The twins' mom walked out when she was six-months pregnant. She sent me a text with some bullshit excuse about needing to find herself. I know now that was a lie. What she needed was to hide my boys from me. For four years, she kept my sons a secret, until..."

Maveryck cleared his throat. "I still don't know why. Hell, I didn't even know she was pregnant. I wanted that. I wanted the wife and kids. The white picket fence. I wanted what my parents have. That forever spent with the one person who just gets you. Who has your back no matter what. I... Fuck, Natalia. So much in my life is upside down right now. Taking care of the twins. Making sure they know they're loved after their mom just handed them over like a cheap business transaction. Figuring out who wants me dead. Who wants *you* dead. I just—"

Natalia kissed him. She ran her fingers through his beard, scratching at his jaw beneath while she tried her best to comfort him with her lips. She carded her free hand through his dirty-blond hair. Hair that he'd cut since she chased him through the woods. Never had she been so happy to have missed a target. Twice. She wasn't shooting at him the last time, but she had a feeling her bullet had hit close when she shot at the pedophile.

Natalia ended the kiss and cupped his cheeks in both hands. "My life is upside down too. Has been my whole life. My mom died when I was six, taking with her any chance I had at a normal life. If normal was even possible to begin

135

with being Anatoly's daughter. I didn't understand until I was older why I couldn't go to school with my friends. Why I had a tutor instead. Why my father only spoke to me when he was training me to shoot a gun or take a punch. Why I wasn't allowed outside the grounds. When I was little and I fell and scraped my knee, I didn't have someone cleaning it off, putting on a bandage, and kissing it better. I was told to get up and not fall again if I didn't want scars. I learned to drive when I was thirteen. I could barely reach the pedals. But I didn't learn so I could take the car to the store or go visit friends. I had no friends. I was taught defensive maneuvering so I could get away from someone chasing me. Chasing him.

"On the outside I was Tatiana Volkova, my father's number-one guard. Later, his trained killer. On the inside, I was that little girl who missed her mother something fierce. Who loved playing dress-up. I guess I'm still that assassin, but I'm also that lonely little girl. So yes, your life might be upside down, but you have real brothers and your Hound brothers. I'm assuming you still have both your parents. And you have those precious little boys. Upside down or not, you have everything, Maveryck Lazlo. Me? I have nothing. I have no one."

Ryker

BETRAYED WAS TOO weak a word to describe how Ryker felt. He kept to the shadows, knowing she wouldn't be home for another week. At least that's when she was supposed to meet him there. He knew where the security cameras were. He had the alarm code, which was why he was able to get into the house in the first place. He called Lucy and had her disable the cameras. He didn't want to involve her, but he also didn't want to get caught. Ryker didn't want anyone in his family to know what he had been up to for the last several years. Or who with. But staying alive was more important than keeping his secret.

The first time he met his handler, they had done an assignment together. She had been an operative back then. Rarely did contracts call for more than one person, but his old handler, Mercury, had insisted. Ryker and Proxy, as she was now known, came close to losing their lives that night. They had met for three weeks prior, planning, scoping, planning some more. During those nights together, Proxy had tempted Ryker with her easy countenance, her long, slender legs, her strong voice. Nothing about the woman screamed "assassin," but that made her a good operative. No one saw her coming. Ryker sure hadn't. The sex had been nothing more than scratching an itch for both of them. Close proximity and all that. She easily seduced Ryker, and before he knew it, they were in bed more than they were out of it.

Four years later, and he still met her in this house once a month. Twelve weekends out of the year, his body was satisfied in ways it hadn't been since he lost Juliette. He wasn't in love with Proxy. That ship had sailed with his wife. But that didn't mean he didn't have needs like every other male. Proxy needed him just as much. In their line of work, it was hard to have a relationship. Not that he wanted one. Proxy did, even if she didn't say it aloud. He could see it in her eyes every time he walked out the door. And walk away he did. Every time.

Now, though, someone was gunning for him. Putting out a contract on his brother was the same as painting a target on Ryker. Maveryck was his brother. His blood. Part of his heart. All his brothers, along with his parents and older sisters, filled that void left by the death of his wife. Now, his niece and daughter filled more of the void. He was glad he hadn't let Proxy in. Now more than ever. She was playing with fire, and when he figured out why, she was the one who was going to get scorched. Ryker would turn the world to ash for his family. And when he got his hands on Proxy? She would rue the day they met.

He didn't want to believe she could be this cunning, but Ryker had seen the worst the world had to offer. He wouldn't take her out without proof, thus the reason he was there in that house they used for sex. But he was staring at it. The proof she had been using him all this time. He just didn't know why. He had a week to figure out what he was going to do about it. A week to figure out how to make a handler from a worldwide assassin organization disappear. When he did, her sai would be no good against the wrath he would bring to her.

CHAPTER FIFTEEN

Maveryck

MAVERYCK'S HEART ACHED for the woman in his arms. Hearing her tearful confession put his own life into perspective. She was right – he had everything while she had nothing. His Gryphon was trying to break free. To go after anyone who had ever wronged Natalia. It wanted to bring back Anatoly so they could make him suffer. The quick death had been too merciful. Now, she had someone wanting her dead in the same manner. Maveryck vowed then and there that would never happen. He wouldn't let it. His Gryphon wasn't the only one feeling protective. But more than that, Maveryck felt like this woman was his. His to protect. To cherish.

To love.

Until that moment, he hadn't understood why War felt the deep-seated need to find Kerrigan, a woman he'd only seen in photos. It didn't matter who she was, who she had lived with, who she had been before he found her. It only mattered she was his.

Now, Maveryck understood. Natalia was his. Russian mafia or not. Assassin or not. Tatiana or Natalia. None of that mattered.

"Come home with me," he blurted, surprising himself. He must have surprised her too, because Natalia gasped, jerking her tear-stained face from his chest. Maveryck used his thumbs to gently swipe at the moisture rolling down her cheeks. "Until we figure out who wants us both dead, please come home with me. I have two little boys who have talked nonstop about their Lollipop."

Natalia coughed out a laugh, but she sobered when she asked, "You trust me with them?"

"Yes, Princess. I do." He wasn't as sure he trusted her with himself. With his life, yes. She had warned him about the contract. It was his heart he needed to guard. As much as Jenna ripped a hole in it, Mav knew Natalia could shatter it into a million pieces and scatter them on the wind, never to be found. He also knew he would never be whole unless he at least gave her a chance. Gave them a chance. Now he understood the ache to go after her that day on the sidewalk.

"Let's figure this mess out together. You said you have no one in your life, but I do. I have my family and the Hounds. I—" Mav's phone vibrated. Probably War making sure he was okay. This was supposed to be a quick recon mission. "Sorry, I need to get this." He was right. He shot his twin a return text, telling him he was fine and would be home soon.

"So, what do you say? Pack a bag and come with me?"

"How did you get in my house?" Natalia asked instead. When Mav pointed to the open window, she frowned. Stepping away from him, she walked over to the window and looked outside. Leaning farther out, she looked around then up, no doubt at the security cameras. Mav was enchanted by her bare legs. He had admired those legs on the blonde from the sidewalk. They weren't long, but they were smooth and toned. Her ass was covered by silky red panties, and Mav pushed down on his waking cock. Maybe having her in his home wasn't such a good idea. How was he supposed to keep his hands and mouth to himself?

"You're good." Natalia was still frowning when she turned around. "Too good. How did you reach the cameras? I don't see a ladder, nor do I see many footprints. Tell me, Mayhem, how did you really get in my house?"

Well, shit. "Come home with me, and I promise I will tell you. I want to get home before the twins wake up."

Natalia bit her bottom lip. Mav wanted to be the one biting it. He wanted his mouth back on hers. Breathing her in as she'd done him. Sharing oxygen while saying with their lips and tongues what they couldn't put voice to. Not yet. They were strangers. Strangers who were supposed to kill each other. He only knew what was on paper and the little bits she'd shared about how she was raised. She knew less about him than he did her. You couldn't truly know someone unless you lived with them, and even then, unless you were a mind reader, you could never know what someone was thinking. What they were feeling deep down. Everyone had the ability to lie. To put up a front. To hide their emotions. But having someone in your space, your life, every day, gave a better understanding as to their likes and dislikes. Their quirks.

Maveryck wanted to know Natalia's quirks. What made her happy so he could ensure she had that daily. What made her sad so he could erase those things from her life. His Gryphon had felt their connection that day on the sidewalk, and now it was pushing Maveryck to keep Natalia close. Safe. To make her happy. Erase as much of the sadness from her past as he could. Yes, she was an assassin, but if his Gryphon trusted her around the twins, around him, he wasn't going to argue.

"Okay. But only until we figure out who's trying to kill us both." Natalia left the room, and when she came back, she was carrying a suitcase. He kept an eye on her. Not because he didn't trust her, but… Well, he was still a little wary. How could he not be? Then again, she was the one who warned him, not the other way around. He was the one who had

141

broken into her home and grabbed her in her sleep. And she was agreeing to come home with him, so it seemed her trust was easier to come by than his. Or maybe she was keeping her enemy closer. He wasn't her enemy, and he would prove it to her.

"I'm going to get my car. It'll only take a few minutes. I'll wait for you in the driveway."

"Sure." When Maveryck walked over to the window, she stopped him. "I do have a door, you know. Come with me." Natalia led him to the back door and punched in the code to the alarm. "There you go."

"Thanks." Mav grabbed the doorknob, but before he turned it, he pulled Natalia to him and kissed her softly. "I'll be right back." He felt her eyes on him as he took off jogging through the trees. He didn't take a chance on shifting, so he made his way on foot to his SUV. When he got back to her house, Natalia was waiting on the front porch. He got out and strolled up to where she was standing.

"I can follow you," she offered.

"I think it would be better if you left your car here. If someone is watching, they might wonder why your vehicle is in my driveway. If you need to go somewhere, you can take my car."

Natalia agreed, and Mav helped her into the passenger seat, then put her luggage in the back. He was nervous as he drove toward his own home. Having her next to him, with him, seemed like a turning point in his life. Another one. This was added to the list of those days he would remember as long as he lived. It was still dark out, but the sun would be coming up soon. Natalia had been calm and patient with the twins at the store, and he couldn't wait to see their faces when their lollipop was in their home.

He pulled the vehicle into the garage, shutting them away from prying eyes. He retrieved her bags from the back seat and led Natalia into the house via the kitchen door. "War, we're home," he announced.

"We? Who—?" War froze when he saw Natalia. Kerrigan stared between Mav and her mate, waiting for someone to say something.

"Natalia, I'd like you to meet my twin, Warryck, and his mate, Kerrigan. Natalia will be staying here until we figure out a few things."

War stared at his brother like he'd lost his mind. Mav stared back, silently promising to explain. "Come on, Princess. I'll show you to your room. Afterward, we'll have coffee while we wait on the boys to wake up. Then we can all have breakfast together." Mav wanted nothing more than to put Natalia in his room, but he didn't think either one of them was ready for that, so he showed her to the spare room next to the boys. "It's not much, but I think you'll be comfortable in here." He placed her bags on the bed. She looked around, leaning against the doorframe.

"It's nice, thank you."

"How about some coffee? My brother has questions, and I need to answer them before he runs and tells the family you're somehow forcing me into this."

"Sounds good." Natalia reached out for his hand, and Mav didn't hesitate to thread their fingers together. When they walked down the stairs, War was waiting. His eyes narrowed in on their hands, and he flashed a bewildered look at Mav's face.

"Coffee's ready," Kerrigan said from the kitchen. At least she was able to do something more than stare.

"I sure could use a cup," Natalia said, pulling away from Mav. He missed the contact immediately. Natalia followed Kerrigan, and War grabbed Maveryck's arm, pulling him into the living room.

"Please tell me you know what you're doing," War begged.

"I know what I'm doing. Do you remember how you felt when you saw Kerrigan's photos the first time sitting in Harper's Point? Remember how you knew you needed to

143

find her?"

"Yes, but—"

"There is no but, War. This is the same for me. As strange as the circumstances are, I know in my soul Natalia is my Kerrigan."

"But she's an assassin. A mafia princess... Ah, Princess."

Mav grinned. "Yes, I know very well what she does for a living, but how is that any different from what we do? Assassin and mercenary are basically the same thing. We just go after different types of evil."

"And you trust her with the twins?"

"I do. Wait until you see them together. You'll get it. I know it doesn't make sense, but I feel it. Here." Mav made a fist and rubbed his chest over his heart.

Four little feet pounded down the stairs, and before Mav could intercept, the twins ran into the kitchen.

"Daddo! There's a lollipop in the kitchen!" Marshall yelled. "Tolly! You're here."

"Lolly!" Major joined in. "You missed our party. But we have cake. You want some cake? It has purple balloons on it. Like your hair."

Maveryck and War walked to the kitchen were Natalia was on her knees with a boy in each arm. Kerrigan was smiling over the top of her coffee cup as she watched the three of them interact. War walked over to his female, sliding an arm around her shoulder, and pulled her close to his side.

"I would love some cake, but maybe I'll wait until after breakfast. Did you have fun at your party?"

"Yeah! Everyone was here. Pops and Rory. Hayden and Kyllian and Ryker and Lucy and T...T... What was his name, Daddo?" Major asked.

"Tamian."

"Yeah, him. Oh, and Uncle War and Aunt Kerrigan were there too. They bought us clothes and toys."

"They did? That sure was nice of them." Natalia's smile was genuine as she listened to them chatter.

Major nodded. He had stepped away from Natalia's embrace but remained close by. Marshall, though... Marshall was staring at Natalia like she hung the moon. It seemed Mav wasn't the only Lazlo smitten with the pretty Russian.

"How about I make us all some breakfast?" Kerrigan offered.

"You don't have to do that," Mav said.

"I know, but I want to. How about pancakes?"

"With booberries!" the twins yelled together.

The adults laughed, and Kerrigan said, "Booberry pancakes, coming right up."

Mav brushed his hand across Major's soft hair. "Why don't we let Natalia get some coffee? You can go turn on the TV while Aunt Kerrigan cooks for us."

"Cartoons!" Major rushed out of the kitchen, but Marshall seemed reluctant to let go of Natalia.

"It's okay, Marshall. I'll join you as soon as I get my coffee, okay?"

"Okay, Tolly," he whispered. Before he turned loose of her neck, he smacked a little kiss on her cheek. Natalia didn't move, even after Marshall was out of the room. She pressed her fingertips to the spot Marshall kissed and closed her eyes. Kerrigan elbowed War who was staring at Natalia. Mav squatted in front of her and placed a hand on her arm.

"You okay?"

Natalia opened her eyes. They were bright with unshed tears. "I don't understand. How could their mom... no, how could *that woman* just hand them over and walk away?"

"Come here, Princess." Mav held out his hand, and when she took it, he stood, pulling Natalia into a tight embrace. He set his chin on top of her hair. "I don't know. It's only been a few days. I got home from looking for you, and my mom called, telling me to get to her house. Jenna was there with the boys. She handed me an envelope containing legal papers and their birth certificates, then told me they were all mine. She signed them over to me, giving up all rights to them. She included a short note apologizing for walking away four years ago, but it didn't really explain anything."

"Are you going to confront her?"

"Eventually. Right now, it doesn't really matter why. They're here with me, and they're safe. We have bigger things to worry about than the excuses of my ex."

"Right, like what the hell is going on with you two," War said.

Kerrigan smacked him in the stomach with the hand not mixing pancake batter. "Warryck Lazlo. Mind your manners."

"What? I'm talking about the contracts. You did tell her, right?"

"Yes. I sent Ryker a text telling him he needs to figure this shit out."

"Lolly! Are you coming?" Major yelled. Maveryck was still learning their voices from another room, but that was the name his oldest twin had given Natalia for whatever reason.

"Be right there," she responded. "I know we have a lot to discuss, but right now, I have a date with two handsome blonds." Natalia winked at Mav. Kerrigan handed her a cup of coffee, and Mav pointed out the creamer and sugar on the counter. After pouring a little milk into her mug, Natalia left Mav alone with his brother.

"That was beautiful," Kerrigan said, sighing.

"You weren't kidding," War added, speaking to Mav. "Those boys are crazy about her. It just makes me wonder about their relationship with their mother."

"You mean, *that woman?*" Kerrigan snickered. "You're not wrong though. And it appears she's just as crazy about them. But I understand that. Those boys are perfect. I have a good feeling about all this." She turned back to the stove, and Maveryck closed his eyes.

He had a good feeling about it too. He just had to figure out who wanted them both dead. Before that happened, he wouldn't let himself get too caught up in what might be.

Not what might be. What's going to be.

Yeah, what his Gryphon said.

Chapter Sixteen

Natalia

MAVERYCK HADN'T BEEN kidding when he said he had a big family. Not only did all of his brothers and parents show up at some point during the day, several of the Hounds came by to meet the twins. Oh, god. The twins. Natalia was in love. Unequivocally, irrevocably in love with Marshall and Major. Major was the louder of the two. That was saying a lot, because Marshall made his voice heard above the noise in the busy house. But whenever it was just her and the younger boy, Marshall was more soft-spoken. Almost like he was afraid to raise his voice around Natalia. She had a feeling she knew the reason. If she ever got her hands on their mother...

Maveryck's two-story house was a well lived-in home. The furniture was nice yet gently used. He had photos on the walls of his family. It wasn't cluttered, but it also wasn't pristine. Love, camaraderie, and friendship all filled the home as it became overrun with his family and Hounds.

Natalia spent most of the day on the floor with the boys. She rose when newcomers arrived, greeting them all with a smile on her face. It was all overwhelming, especially meeting Sutton and Rory. They were a mystery to Natalia. This was the same couple she had spotted her first day sitting on the clubhouse. The same couple who couldn't be older than mid-fifties. Ryker was older than Mav and War, and they had six older sisters. There were four sets of twins in the eleven siblings, so Mav having twins wasn't a surprise. But how did his parents have that many kids who looked just like them when they didn't look old enough? Maveryck had promised to tell Natalia everything, but there hadn't been time. She knew he didn't have this much company all the time, because when she'd driven by looking for him, there were no cars or bikes except for the one brother she'd followed.

Hayden. Now there was a character. He was the one who winked at her the day she followed the bikers. He was still winking at her, and Maveryck was threatening his life every single time he caught his brother. It was all in jest, but every once in a while, she caught Mav staring at her with what she could swear was longing. Did he want her? If so, why? Because the boys loved her? Did he want a new mother for them? What did Natalia have to offer a man like him? She couldn't cook. She had no hobbies. Oh, but hey. She could hit a man between the eyes from a hundred yards out. Real mom material right there.

Speaking of moms... Aurora Rose Lazlo was scary. Major said everyone called her Rory because she could roar like a lion. Natalia didn't doubt it. The woman was intimidating. She hadn't been unkind, but she didn't go out of her way to welcome Natalia into the fold either. If Natalia was in Rory's place, she would probably feel the same way. Here was this strange woman who had accepted a contract to kill one of her sons – the father of Rory's grandchildren. While the men went outside to talk about the mess she and Maveryck were in, Kerrigan acted as a buffer between Natalia and Rory. The twins helped. Especially Marshall, who was never far away. When he kissed her earlier, her heart melted. She had fallen a little in love with them at the grocery store, but in that moment when they both hugged her, she was gone. All the way.

Sutton was a different story. Maveryck's father took one look at Natalia, clapped his son on the shoulder, and said,

"Yep." What did that mean? Yes what? He approved? She was a killer? His mom was going to hate her? Natalia had never been in any situation like this one. She'd never seen so many people in one house, not even when all her father's guards had been in attendance. Her father had definitely never said the word "yep," much less with a gleam in his eye.

The twins were watching an animated movie, sitting on the floor next to Natalia who was resting against the sofa, her legs stretched out in front of her. Marshall leaned against her, and her arm automatically went around the child. Next thing she knew, his head was on her lap. She ran her fingers through his hair, and soon, he was snoring softly. Major glanced over at his brother, then looked up at her. She winked at him, and Major smiled. He mimicked his brother and rested his head on her other thigh. She scratched her nails through his hair, brushing it off his forehead. It was the most peaceful she had felt since her mother passed away.

Kerrigan was curled on the other end of the sofa, chatting quietly with Rory. They were talking about Kerrigan's parents coming to visit. The couple lived in South Carolina, and it had been a few months since Kerrigan had seen them. Natalia loved Kerrigan's soft Irish lilt. Being born and raised in America and only allowed to learn English, Natalia didn't sound Russian unless she was cursing someone using Russian terms. That always amazed her – the fact that her father refused to let her speak in his native tongue. Everything else he taught her was true to his heritage. The only thing she could figure was he didn't want her privy to his conversations. She didn't need to know the business side of things, only how to take someone out. She didn't need to speak to do that.

"Natalia, are you—?" Maveryck smiled down at her with his boys asleep on her lap. She smiled back; this time it wasn't forced. He squatted next to her. "How are you doing, Princess?"

"Fine." She wasn't about to tell him she was ready to run. Ready to get away from the crowd and his mother's accusing eyes.

"Do you want me to take them upstairs for their nap?"

Natalia shook her head, her hands never leaving their hair. "No, please. I…" She looked down at their sleeping forms. "They're good where they are, if that is okay with you?"

Maveryck brushed his knuckles down her cheek. It surprised her he was touching her in front of the others. She didn't mind his touch. In fact, she welcomed it. Natalia had gone most of her life without hugs or affection. Without words of love or adoration. Not since her mother. It was one reason she wanted the boys to remain where they were. They had no idea how much their presence soothed her.

"It's more than okay. I have a feeling they need your touch," Mav whispered.

Natalia figured he was referring to Jenna. The twins had been with Mav for three days, and they had yet to ask about their mother. Hadn't mentioned her once. Some women didn't want kids. Some wanted kids, or thought they did, but then after they were born, the mothers weren't equipped to handle them. Natalia didn't know Jenna, but she selfishly was glad the woman had brought the boys back to Maveryck. Even if she was only in their lives for a week or two, she knew she would never be the same for knowing them.

"Mom, Dad wants to see you outside for a second." Maveryck stood and waited for his mother to follow him. Rory turned and looked down at the boys before she went out the back door.

"She can be a little intense," Kerrigan said, scooting closer to Natalia on the sofa so she could whisper. "She's a lioness, guarding her cubs. As long as you don't hurt Mav or the twins, she'll keep her claws put away."

Natalia looked over her shoulder at the pretty redhead. "I would never hurt them. I would protect them with my life.

151

Before I knew who Maveryck was, I gave him a copy of the contract. I just couldn't let him go about his day without warning him. But now? Now that I know about the twins? I'm ready to find out who put the hit on him and take them out myself."

Kerrigan smiled, brushing her hair behind her ear. "You feel it, don't you? That pull to him." Kerrigan didn't give Natalia a chance to answer. "I was kidnapped from my hometown. It was the middle of the night, and I had been beaten badly by my boyfriend. I escaped when he left me to 'think about what I'd done.' I was kidnapped and taken to a cult. Have you heard of the Ministry?" Natalia nodded. Everyone knew who those crazies were. "I ended up at one of their compounds. The leader, Gideon Talbert, decided he wanted me for himself. During that time, War retired from teaching, and he and Mav set out on their bikes. They started on the East Coast and were going to ride west. While they were eating one night at the bar I used to work at, my parents came in looking for me. War and Mav decided to get involved. War said he knew the moment he looked at my picture he needed to find me.

"Long story short, with Lucy's help, War tracked me down. I was running through the woods being chased by two of Gideon's men and a dog. War grabbed me right as the dog snapped his jaws down. I passed out, and when I woke, I was in War's tent. I was scared. I was in so much pain, but I knew. I had left an abusive relationship to fall right into an obsessive one with my kidnapper. I should have sworn off men for the rest of my life, but I felt this deep connection to War. He had been through some shit with his wife, Lucy's mother. That's a story for another day, but suffice it to say, he wasn't looking for a mate either. Didn't matter. The pull to one another was too great to ignore. And here we are."

"You said mate. Why?"

Kerrigan looked over the sofa toward the back door. "The Hounds think they're really animals." Kerrigan smirked like she knew a secret. "Animals have mates, not girlfriends or partners. One day, I'll be his wife, but until then?" She shrugged. "I don't mind being his mate."

"That sounds... really nice. And I'm happy for you. I don't know you, but I'm glad your story had a happy ending."

"I think your story will have one as well."

"I appreciate you telling me your history, but what does that have to do with Rory?"

"War's wife, Lucy's mother, didn't want their child raised in or around the MC, so he chose Harlow over his family. When she died, he allowed her family to adopt Lucy, and he continued on the path they chose. He became a professor. When War and I got together, he insisted we get to know each other without coming back to his family and the MC immediately. I thought for sure Rory would hate me because of her dislike of Harlow. She didn't. All she wants for all her children is for them to be happy. If you make Mav happy and you take care of him and the twins, she'll welcome you with open arms. As it stands now, she doesn't know you or your intentions."

"I can understand that. But Maveryck and I just met. And the circumstances surrounding us? They're crazy at best. We accepted contracts on each other."

"But neither of you plan on fulfilling those contracts. The Hounds are out there working on figuring this mess out. Once that's taken care of, the two of you can figure out the rest."

Natalia glanced down at the twins. She'd dreamed of having a man in her life. Children too. She never thought it was possible because of who she was and the life she lived. Maveryck knew all about her past and what she did now. She couldn't get her hopes up. Not yet. But he made her feel that – hopeful. And she was already attached to the sweet boys asleep on her lap. If some miracle happened and she was allowed to remain in their lives, Natalia would never walk away from them. Never hand them over for someone else to raise. They would never doubt her love for them. Because love them she did. Fiercely.

And if she got to love their father too?

Movement to her left got her attention. Maveryck stood at the entrance to the living room, silently watching her. She didn't know what he was thinking. Couldn't tell by his blank expression if it was good or bad. So, she waited, taking the opportunity to admire the man. He was definitely her type as far as looks and build went, but it was what he held inside that drew her to him most. The ink, the piercings, the strong muscles trapped beneath the black T-shirt, those were just icing on the cake. The powerful man exuded strength. He moved gracefully when he walked. No, not walked. He stalked. Like a lion. Kerrigan likened Rory to a lioness with cubs. Mav was one of those cubs, but behind his striking blue eyes she saw the gaze of a predator. She had no doubt he was all alpha. He killed his prey with a sharp blade. Or *sharp claws*.

Holy shit. Kerrigan was using metaphor, not speaking literally. Because those things didn't exist in real life. Shifters were myth. Legend. Major said they called Aurora "Rory" because she roared like a lion.

Maveryck licked his lips and... Natalia gasped and took a closer look at Maveryck's mouth. No. No freaking way had she seen sharp fangs. Her mind was playing tricks on her because—

"Princess? You okay?" Maveryck was kneeling beside her. When had he moved? How had he gotten across the room so quickly?

Natalia giggled. Laughter bubbled from her throat, waking the boys. She was going mad.

"Tolly?" Marshall sat up, rubbing his eyes with his little knuckles.

She ran her fingers through his sleep-flattened hair. Marshall gifted her with the sweetest smile she'd ever seen.

"Hey. I'm sorry I woke you."

Major pushed off Natalia's lap, yawning. "Hey, Daddo. Lolly makes a good pillow."

"And Lolly's butt is probably asleep. How about we let her stand and stretch her legs?" Maveryck held out a hand, and Natalia took it, letting Mav pull her to her feet.

"Where is everyone?" Natalia looked toward the back door. Where the house had been full of people and noise earlier, now it was disturbingly quiet. Even Kerrigan had slipped away at some point. Natalia was used to the silence in her own home. In her own life, but that didn't fit here in Mav's home.

"Most everyone has gone home or back to the clubhouse. Ace and King are guarding the front, and Kyllian and Hayden are out back." He was still holding her hand, and it felt like the most natural thing in the world. Being in his home with his sons. Sons who were now curled around each other on the floor, their eyes closed once again.

Natalia pulled away from Mav's hold and took pillows from the sofa, placing one under each of their heads. She didn't know much about kids. Actually, she didn't know anything about them, but she couldn't stand them sleeping on the floor like that.

When she faced Maveryck, he was staring at her again. Natalia blinked, and then she was in his arms with his mouth against hers. This kiss was different than the ones in her house. This was full of need. Want. Desperation. Maveryck owned her with his lips and tongue. His hands restrained her tightly, one on her ass and one threading her hair.

Need raced through her core. Maveryck's erection was hard against her stomach. Knowing she was the reason stole the air from her lungs. If it weren't for the twins at their feet, Natalia would beg Maveryck to take her to his room. Take her body and make it his. Take her heart and keep it safe. The last time Natalia begged for anything was when her mother was taken from her. She begged God to bring her mommy back. He hadn't listened then, so she didn't pray to that god now. Now, she prayed to any deity who would listen that Maveryck felt the same connection she did. If not, she was going to be on the losing end once again.

CHAPTER SEVENTEEN

Maveryck

MAVERYCK HAD TO stop before he couldn't. Breaking the kiss was close to impossible. He wanted more, so much more, but they needed to talk. "Oh, Princess. What are you doing to me?" he whispered against her mouth.

"I…" Natalia huffed out a little laugh. "You make me breathless."

"Same. But we need to talk."

"Those words never end well."

"I hope these will. There is something I need to tell you." Rory had warned Maveryck against telling Natalia the truth. His mother didn't trust his Princess, but that was on her. When she compared Natalia to Jenna, Maveryck had come close to telling his mother off. He had never raised his voice to the woman. Never felt less than unconditional love for her. She could spout all the hatred against Jenna she wanted, but he wouldn't stand for her saying one bad thing about Natalia. It was in that moment he knew why Jenna hadn't worked out. She wasn't the one he was supposed to spend forever with. Natalia was.

"Let's go outside." Maveryck took her hand and led her to the patio. Instead of putting her on his lap like he wanted, he sat next to her on the low sofa. Turning toward her, he did take her hands in his.

"Well, don't keep me in suspense."

"Ryker found out something. Mikael is the one who put the hit out on your father."

"That doesn't surprise me. The family business is ruthless. It's not like, say, a pack of wolves where the alpha is taken out by another, stronger wolf. Like Anatoly, Mikael will never get his hands dirty. That's what I was for. What a hired assassin is for. If he knew where to find me, I have no doubt he'd put a hit out on me."

Maveryck sighed, and Natalia gasped. "Mikael was behind my contract? But how? I have a new identity."

"And who got you that new identity? Nexus. Or, someone at Nexus. We don't know how many handlers they have or how their organization is run. You and I were both given contracts on the same pedophile. Who's to say that wasn't so we'd take each other out? It would seem your new identity has been compromised. What we don't know is if it's your handler or a different one."

"You knew that was me outside the mark's apartment?"

"Not until yesterday when I saw the photos of you in various disguises. Marshall was the one who figured that out, by the way. He saw the pictures and pointed out you have a twin. I should have known, though. When I passed you on the sidewalk that day, I should have known who you were."

"How?"

"By your smell."

"My what? No, I meant how did you get pictures of me in disguise?"

"Lucy. She's an expert with a computer. I went back to your family's estate to look for you. While I was there, she was searching for you via the web. When you put my contract in the mailbox, she started searching for anyone lurking around. She caught your pictures from when you were sitting across the street from the clubhouse. Then Marshall noticed 'your twin,' and Lucy found footage of you getting in your car at the grocery store. You never swapped vehicles, so she was able to trace your new information to your house."

"Some assassin I am," Natalia muttered.

"Don't say that, Princess. I have no doubt you are excellent at your job. It's just that Lucy is that good with the computer. I'm glad she found you, or else we never would have met like this, and we wouldn't know the truth." Mav rubbed his thumbs across her knuckles. "If something were to happen to Mikael, who would be in charge?"

Natalia looked out into the backyard. "Hmm, I guess Ivan would take over, because Viktor isn't a leader even though he's older. But neither one has what it takes to keep the business running smoothly." She turned her gaze to Mav. "Is something going to happen to Mikael? Because if it is, I want in. He doesn't get to take a contract out on me with no retaliation."

Mav's first instinct was to say "hell, no," but this was Tatiana Volkova sitting next to him. The successful Russian mafia hit woman who knew where the bodies were buried. The anger-infused determination in her eyes was as sexy as it was scary. His dick twitched. Who knew talking about murdering someone could be foreplay?

"Relax, Princess. I would never take this away from you. My question is, do we need to include the brothers in the hit, or will they implode themselves without Mikael leading them? Is there someone else to come behind them and take over?"

"Anatoly kept all his proverbial eggs in one basket. He had me take out anyone strong enough to step into his place. Other than me, Mikael is the only one who knows everything about the family business. If we take him out, Ivan and Viktor will make a mess of things. They don't know who Anatoly's contacts were, and I doubt Mikael is stupid enough to share with them, brothers or not."

"So, we let them live and implode? What if they come after you too? We don't know what Mikael has or hasn't shared with them. I'm not good with that. I want you safe,

Princess." Mav didn't realize he had grabbed Natalia's arm until she looked down at his hand. "Sorry," he said, releasing his grip.

"It's been a long time since someone was concerned about my well-being." The sheen of wetness covering her lower eyelids had Mav's heart stuttering.

"Think you could get used to it? Because your well-being is important to me. *You* are important to me." Mav placed his hand on Natalia's cheek, brushing his thumb back and forth.

"Why?" she asked, blinking the tears away.

Maveryck wanted to tell Natalia what he was feeling even if he didn't understand why, but the twins came barreling out the back door. "Daddo?" Major called.

"We're over here," Mav responded.

Major marched up to them with Marshall following, leaning against Natalia's legs. She ran her hand through his sleep-rumpled hair.

"Can we have cake now?" Major asked.

Mav and Natalia needed to finish their conversation, but the boys needed their attention more. "We need to eat lunch first. What do you say, Princess? Would you like some cake?"

"I would. I've never had birthday cake before."

Maveryck mentally shook his head. Natalia's life had been so different from his. He wanted to know what else she'd never been allowed to have and give it to her. "Then you should have the biggest piece." Major did a little dance, and Marshall took Natalia's hand, leading her back into the house.

Lunch consisted of sandwiches and chips. While Mav was fixing them, Natalia admitted she couldn't cook. "It wasn't in the requirements for my job," she said. "Whenever I asked Marta to teach me, she would shoo me out of the kitchen. I've only recently been learning via online videos. You really can find anything on the internet."

160

"I'll be more than happy to teach you," Mav told her. "Mom is an excellent cook, and she made sure all us boys knew how so whenever we moved out, we wouldn't live on pizza and takeout. As a matter of fact, we can cook supper together. What kind of food do you like?"

"Anything without beets in it. Marta only ever cooked Russian dishes, but while I was out on jobs, I made sure to try something new each time. I like steak and fried chicken. Spicy pasta dishes. Hmm, let's see. I ate a fried bologna sandwich once, and I liked it so much, I ordered a second one. I like tacos and lasagna. Any kind of pasta, really."

Mav got the boys settled at the table with their food. His mom had bought new booster seats to replace the worn-out ones Jenna had left for them. He still had a lot to learn about what his twins needed. He had a lot to learn about what his Princess needed too. "What have you learned to cook from your videos?"

"So far, just spaghetti, stir fry, tacos, and chicken alfredo. I can't get the hang of fried chicken."

"It's one of my specialties. How about we cook that for supper?" Maveryck wanted Natalia in his kitchen. Jenna hadn't been a great cook, so she'd usually left that duty to Maveryck. He didn't miss Jenna, and he hadn't for a long time, but he did miss the domesticity of having a woman to do things with.

"I'd like that." Natalia smiled up at him from where she was sitting beside Marshall. Maveryck took the seat next to Major, and the four of them ate lunch as if they were a family. Maveryck wanted that. He wanted to see Natalia sitting with him and his boys at every meal.

The doorbell rang, and Major jumped up, running to the front of the house. Mav followed, because all his family had keys and let themselves in without knocking. He looked through the peephole, and his Gryphon growled. Major jumped back. Mav looked down at his son. "Go back into the dining room with Lolly." Major took off running. He hated

161

he had scared his son, but it couldn't be helped. The bell rang again, and Maveryck opened the door, pulling up to his full height. It was a struggle to keep his lion from breaking free.

"Jenna, what are you doing here?"

Not caring about the danger she was in, his ex pushed past him into the living room. "I wanted to check on my boys. See how they're settling in."

Maveryck got between his ex and the rest of the house. "They're not your boys. You made that clear. And legal. You don't get to worry about them. You don't get to stop by and check on them."

"I'm still their mother, and I'll wor— Major?" Jenna tried to step around Mav, but a hand on her bicep stopped her. Mav looked over his shoulder, worried how his son would take seeing his mom. Since neither twin had mentioned their mother, he didn't know if they missed her or not. Mav had no clue what Jenna told the boys, and that was a conversation they were having before he let her leave.

Major all but ignored Jenna. He only gave her about three seconds before he said, "Can Lolly play with us in our room?"

"Yeah, Buddy. That's fine." It wasn't fine, because then Marshall would have to pass the doorway to get to the steps, but maybe that's what needed to happen. Major turned and yelled, "Come on, Lolly! Daddo said we get to play!"

Mav kept his tight grip on Jenna's arm as he waited.

"Maveryck..." Jenna's eyes narrowed when Natalia, holding hands with both boys, walked by. "You got a nanny? That's good. You'll need the help. They're too much—"

"Stop," Natalia gritted out. The boys immediately froze. Her face softened as she knelt beside them. "I'm sorry. I wasn't talking to you." Wrapping her arms around their waists, Natalia softened her voice. "Go on up to your room and pick out what you want to play with. I'll be there in a few minutes."

"Okay, Lolly." Major took off up the steps, but Marshall eyed Jenna over Natalia's shoulder. He blinked a few times before looking back at his Lollipop.

"Marsh? You okay?" Natalia asked.

He nodded and smiled. "Love you, Tolly."

Jenna gasped, and when Natalia told Marshall she loved him too, Jenna tried to wrench her arm free. Mav didn't let go. Not until Marshall was up the stairs and his pretty Princess was inches from Jenna's face. He should probably have put himself between them, but he was interested in what Natalia had to say.

"Those precious boys are not 'too much' anything. Not for their father and not for me. You don't get to toss them away then come in here spouting bullshit like anything you have to say matters. You were given a gift in those two. There is no excuse good enough for not being the best mother you could be. Nothing and no one should come before them. Yet something did, and I'm telling you one time and one time only – I *will* be the best because they deserve nothing less." Natalia was shaking, and Mav was... in love. Not the best time to realize he was in love with his Princess, but there it was.

"Are you...? Is she a...?" Jenna narrowed her eyes. "Does she know what you are?"

Maveryck did step between them at that point, because Natalia knew Mav was a mercenary, but Jenna could be hinting about him being a shifter. This was not how he wanted Natalia to find out. He had to tell her the truth and soon, because he didn't want there to be secrets between them. Natalia pushed Mav out of the way. Not a small feat considering how much larger he was than her. Hell, Jenna probably outweighed Natalia by thirty pounds, but in that moment, the feisty Russian was larger than life.

"I know all about him. And there's nothing that could make me walk away from him or the twins. Nothing. Now, I'm going upstairs to play with *my* sons." She stepped back and turned to Mav. "Deal with her. Or I will."

Feisty! And now his cock was twitching again. He and Jenna both watched Natalia stalk off.

"Outside. Now." Mav opened the front door and not so gently ushered his ex out. "I want answers. I want the truth. All of it, because this is the last time you will come here. You gave up your parental rights to them, which means you gave up the right to see them. Truth, Jenna. Start with why you didn't tell me you were pregnant. Why you kept them from me for four fucking years. What bullshit excuse you gave them before you dropped them off without so much as a goodbye kiss or mommy loves you. And finish with why they didn't run to you when they saw you. Speak!" Mav used his shifter voice on her, the one which gave the recipient no choice but to comply. But he couldn't feel guilty about it, because he didn't trust her to tell the truth.

Standing completely still, Jenna complied. "You were never home. I thought you were sleeping around on me. Then I found out I was pregnant, and I waited. Waited for you to notice. But you never touched me. Even when I started showing, you didn't notice. I didn't want a child to be ignored either. So, I left. I thought you would come after me if you missed me, but you never did. If you didn't want me, you couldn't want my child. Children. I didn't know I was having twins until they were born. Marshall hid behind Major in all the ultrasounds."

Jenna took a deep breath and continued, still not meeting Mav's eyes. "I kept waiting on you, but after a while, I knew you weren't coming for me. So, I got on with my life. Except raising twins is hard when you have no money. Childcare is expensive. What little I made barely put a roof over our heads and food on the table. I met someone. He... he didn't want kids, but I told him we were a package deal. I tried. I tried so hard to make it work, because having someone help pay the bills had to be better. But he never accepted the boys. Couldn't because they weren't his. He convinced me to give

164

them to you."

"Why didn't you at least ask for child support? You know me, Jenna. I never would have skirted my responsibilities."

"Did I? Did I know you? You weren't there for me in the end. For six months, I waited for you to look at me. Make love to me. See me. You didn't."

"Did he hurt them? This man, did he hurt my sons?"

"No. He never laid a hand on them. He ignored them."

Maveryck was shaking on the inside. He dug his fingernails into his palms, his claws itching to burst forth. "What did you tell them? Before you brought them to me?"

"I..." Jenna cut her eyes to his. She must have seen the fire burning behind his normally blue eyes. He had never seen his own face when he shifted, but he had seen his brothers. The color matched the animal. Golden eyes for the lion, black for the eagle. A strange mixture of the two for the Gryphon.

"I told them I couldn't handle them anymore. Said they were going to live with their father."

"Have you told anyone about the Gryphons?"

Jenna looked into his eyes. "No. I swear it."

"I want pictures. Every single photo you have of them from the time they were born up until you dropped them off. Send them to me. My email address hasn't changed. After you do that, you will forget they are your sons. Jenna Monroe, you will leave here and never come back. You will forget all about the Gryphons. Your sons are no longer yours. After you send me the photos, you will forget them. Now go."

Jenna blinked the fog away and walked down the steps to her car. She drove away without looking back.

CHAPTER EIGHTEEN

Natalia

HOLY SHIT. HOLY fucking shit. Natalia had claimed the boys in front of their mother. She basically insinuated that she and Maveryck were together. He hadn't stopped her from getting in his ex's face, but he was probably pissed at her words. She had spoken the truth. Major and Marshall were hers, no matter whether she and Maveryck had a future or not.

When she heard Maveryck ask Jenna what she was doing there, it was all Natalia could do to remain where she was seated. But it wasn't her place to confront the woman. At least not until she heard the bullshit words coming from Jenna's mouth, saying they were too much. There was no way she could stand by and let that woman spew garbage, especially when they were within earshot. *Nanny, my ass.*

Natalia worried about the boys not reacting to their mother. Worried what had been said for them to ignore the woman. To willingly want to spend time with Natalia instead. Was it something as simple as she showed them they were loved? They were precious to her?

When Major returned to the dining room, she watched his little face closely. He didn't seem traumatized. He wasn't sad. He was excited they got to go upstairs and play. Maybe she didn't know enough about how brains of children worked, but she couldn't imagine being separated from her own mother at that age and not reacting to seeing her again.

166

Major just wanted to play. But Marshall? Maybe his little four-year-old heart understood more than Natalia realized. He ignored his mother and told Natalia he loved her. Had he been giving the woman a big "fuck you?"

All Natalia knew was she hadn't been lying. She might not be their mother, but she would be the best at whatever Maveryck allowed her to be in their lives. If they never called her "mom," she was okay with that. She was their Lollipop. Tolly and Lolly. Different titles for different boys. She loved them differently, because they weren't the same child, but she didn't love either one of them more than the other. Major, the louder, older boy, was funny. Marshall was quieter and just a little bit sweeter. Natalia had only been around Maveryck and his twin a few hours, but they, too, were different. Like their father and his brother, Major and Marshall were their own person with their own personalities.

"Hey, Daddo! Come play with us," Major said. Natalia looked over her shoulder, waiting for the disdain. Instead, Maveryck winked at her. He came into the room and lowered himself to sit next to her on the floor where the three of them had been playing with trucks. Maveryck bumped her shoulder with his arm as he reached for one of the toys. Natalia sighed to herself. Maybe she hadn't screwed up.

Natalia waited for Maveryck to say something to the boys about Jenna, but he never did. He pretended like the shitshow downstairs hadn't happened. Was that the best way to approach the situation? She didn't know, but he was their father, and she would follow his lead. They played on the bedroom floor until Natalia's phone vibrated. When noticed it was her alarm at home, she opened the app that let her look at her cameras.

"Fu… fudge nuggets!" She jumped to her feet.

"What's wrong, Tolly?" Marshall asked.

"Uh, nothing. I just have to pee." As she raced out of the room, she heard Major ask, "What's a fudge nugget?"

Maveryck said something about little pieces of

167

chocolate. She was digging through one of her bags as Major said he wanted some fudge nuggets. If her world wasn't bursting into flames, she might have laughed. Her phone rang, the security company calling to tell her what she already knew.

"Princess?" Maveryck asked from behind. "Everything okay?"

She held up her hand. "Hello? Yes, this is she. Yes, I know. I'm on my way." She disconnected. "I need my keys."

"You rode with me. Princess, stop a second. What's going on?"

"My house is on fire. I need to go."

"No, you need to stay here. It's not safe. Not with the contract out on you."

"I'm going, Maveryck. Everything I own... all my weapons... I'm going."

"I'll drive you. Let me get my shoes on."

"Maveryck. You can't. The boys."

"Shit." He brushed a hand down his face. "I'll call War and Kerrigan. As soon as they get here, I'll meet you there." That didn't explain how she was getting home. Maveryck pulled his phone out of pocket and punched in a number. As he walked away, he was saying, "Hayden, meet me inside. I need you and Kyllian to drive Natalia to her house. It's on fire."

Natalia shoved her feet into her shoes and stopped at the boys' room. "I'm sorry, but I have to go take care of something at home."

"Are you coming back?" Marshall whispered, his eyes flooding with tears.

Natalia went to him and hugged him close. "As soon as possible." She didn't give him a time or make it a promise, because she would never break a promise to these kids if at all possible. "I love you both." After wiping Marshall's tears and kissing the top of their heads, Natalia raced down the steps where Maveryck was waiting with his two younger

168

brothers.

"I'm sending Hayden and Kyllian with you. Hayden will drive. This is non-negotiable. I'll be there as soon as I can."

"You ready?" Hayden asked. The younger Lazlo was dressed as he normally was in faded jeans, white T-shirt, his Hounds kutte, and biker boots.

"Yes, let's go." She turned to follow, but Maveryck stopped her.

"Princess…" Maveryck kissed her softly. When he stepped back, his eyes were on his brother.

"I've got her," Hayden said. Maveryck nodded and blew out a breath. "Go, I'll be there soon."

Natalia followed Hayden out to the garage where Kyllian, dressed identically to Hayden, was holding the passenger side door open. She muttered, "Thank you," and climbed into the front. Hayden had already started the SUV. As soon as Kyllian's door was shut, the garage door rolled up, and Hayden maneuvered the large vehicle out of the driveway.

Once they were on the road, Hayden said, "I'm going on record to say you shouldn't be anywhere close to your house. Having said that, I know better than to argue when a woman gets something in her head. When we get there, I don't want you running off. You need to stay in the SUV until we know there is no threat."

"You seriously think whoever did this will hang around?"

"Someone wants you dead, Lollipop. Maveryck didn't do the job he was hired for, so it's obvious whoever took the contract out on you is getting impatient. If this is another assassin, they're going to need you dead to get payment. Since you didn't come running out of your burning house, they're probably going to realize you aren't home. This is probably their way of smoking you out. Literally."

"Fucking Mikael," Natalia muttered.

"That bastard needs to die," Kyllian said from the back

169

seat.

"I know you're a badass assassin, Lollipop, but say the word, and I'll take your cousin out," Hayden said, sounding both proud and pissed off at the same time.

"It doesn't bother you what I do for a living?"

Hayden grinned at her, looking more like Maveryck in that moment than she'd ever noticed. "Nah. Like I said – badass. I hope when I find my mate, she's half the woman you are."

Mate? That wasn't the first time that term had been used by someone in Maveryck's family. Kerrigan likened it to animals having mates, possibly since the bikers were Hounds. Natalia looked over at Hayden. He thought she was badass. What did his brother think about her?

Hayden was focused on the road, and when they were taking the exit toward her house, Natalia realized she hadn't given him directions. They were a family of mercenaries with a niece who was a computer hacker. Maveryck hadn't said that's what Lucy was, but it was apparent she wasn't merely a programmer working in an IT department somewhere. Not if she'd tracked Natalia down using cameras around town. Natalia had yet to meet Lucy, but if she was anything like the rest of the Lazlos, Natalia would like her. They were what Natalia always imagined families to be. Loving. Loud. All up in each other's business, but not in the way her father and Mikael had been in hers. Not controlling or stifling.

The Lazlos were mercenaries, but they took down those people in society who hurt others. People like her father. Natalia had never taken a life she felt was redeemable. Those members of the Russian mafia she'd killed when she was younger had been no different than Anatoly. They had an agenda that included making money any way they could. Drugs. Guns. Humans. Natalia grew up hating her family while protecting them. She'd wanted to learn the business so when her father was gone, she could dismantle it from the inside. Maybe he realized that early on, and that was why he didn't groom her to take his seat. He hadn't given Natalia a choice in what she did. It was either kill or be killed. He never said those words, but he didn't have to. It was clear being a Volkov meant she was either loyal to the family, or there was no room for her in it. And one didn't leave the family alive. That fact was something Mikael was making sure of with the contract on her.

The red and blue flashing lights of all the first responders filled the windshield before they reached her house. It wasn't hers, since she was renting, but it had been the first place she lived alone. Natalia needed to call the property management company and let them know. She had renter's insurance, so her things could be replaced. Some of her things. Luckily, she had stuck her mother's photo in her bag she packed to take to Maveryck's. It would have broken her heart to lose it. Her guns and ammo should be safe in the fireproof cabinet. Her pistol, however…

Hayden couldn't get close to the driveway with so many vehicles in the way. Natalia released her seatbelt as a policeman walked in front of them with his hand up. Hayden rolled down his window, and the cop stepped up. "I'm afraid you're going to have to turn around."

Natalia leaned over the console. "That's my house."

"And you are?"

"Natalia Jones."

"Do you have any identification on you?"

"Yeah, it's… Shit, I left it at Maveryck's." In her rush to get home, Natalia left her purse in the guestroom.

"Sorry. Without ID, you can't come any closer."

"I'm on it," Kyllian said. The cop walked off, pulling out his phone. As he made a call, Natalia watched the firefighters. The house was no longer burning. Her car didn't look as if it had been damaged, but the house was mostly gone. Black, charred wood stood like ominous sentinels around the edge of the structure. The room on the side closest to her was tilted inward, covering the kitchen. The most damage was at the back where her bedroom was. All her clothes and shoes destroyed. They were material things which could be replaced. Her weapons would be fine. She just had to get to them.

"Maveryck has your ID. He's—" *CRACK!*

Natalia screamed as she ducked. Hayden already had the car in drive, turning away from the house. Another bullet shattered a different window, and Kyllian cursed from the back seat.

Natalia leaned over the console to check on him. "Kyllian?" Mav's brother was slumped over on his side. The white sleeve of his T-shirt was now dark red. "Kyllian! Shit. How bad is it?" Natalia started to climb over into the back seat, but Hayden jerked her backwards.

"Get your pretty ass down, Lollipop. You're not dying on my watch."

"But Kyllian…" Hayden's hand on her shirt had Natalia sliding back down until her head was no longer visible.

"Kayos? How you doing back there? Talk to me, Brother."

"Rory's going to kill me," he slurred.

"Yeah, I wouldn't be thrilled if one of my sons was shot either," Natalia said, glad to hear Kyllian talking, even if it was strained.

"Nah. She's gonna be pissed at the blood on my shirt. Says it's a bitch to get out. Might as well toss it."

"You need the hospital?" Hayden asked, driving like the hounds of hell were on his tail.

"Nah. It's just a scratch." Kyllian groaned, and Natalia was pissed. Her fucking family did this. Forget what she said about taking Mikael down and leaving Ivan and Viktor alive. One of them was probably the shooter. Mikael wouldn't take the risk of coming after her himself.

"Talk to me, Havyck." Mav's voice was inside the vehicle.

172

"Two shots fired. Kayos is hit, but he's talking. Lollipop is secure. I'm headed to Lucy's."

"Princess?" Maveryck's voice was shaky.

"I'm fine, but I'm going to fucking kill Mikael. This shit ends tonight."

"Easy, Princess. Let Hayden get you somewhere safe. I need eyes on you, then we'll talk about your cousin. I'll meet you at Lucy's."

"Call Ace. Tell him to lock down your house. I'll call Ryker and Lucy," Hayden commanded.

"Hayden..."

"With my life, Mayhem."

"Thanks, Brother. Princess? I'll see you soon."

"I'll be waiting," she said. But in all honesty? Natalia would be finding a way to get back to Mikael. Fucker didn't get to shoot at her family and get away with it. And yes, she knew she was referring to the Lazlos as her family. She had only just met them, but in her heart, she knew she would do anything to protect Mav and the twins, even if they couldn't be together. There was no one more perfect for her than this strong, gentle man and his two precious boys. If she couldn't have them, she could at least keep them safe.

Natalia zoned out, planning her revenge against her cousins, while Kyllian sat quietly in the back seat, and Hayden called several people while he drove. He pulled up to an iron gate, punching in a code. When he drove through and up a long driveway, Natalia looked around.

"This is where Lucy lives?"

"Yeah. Her dad was filthy rich," Hayden said, his voice perturbed.

"Warryck?"

"No, her adoptive dad. He was a scientist."

Natalia figured there was a story there, but they pulled up to the garage, and Hayden cut the engine.

"Come on, Brother. Let's get you inside." Hayden went to the back and put an arm under Kyllian's, helping him

173

walk.

The front door flew open, and a pretty brunette ran down the steps. "What the hell, Uncle Kyllian?" Behind the woman, who Natalia assumed was Lucy, was a tall man who made Natalia stop in her tracks. Partly because his eyes took in all of them while scanning their surroundings. The other part was because he moved Hayden out of the way and picked Kyllian up like he weighed nothing. "Hi, Natalia. I'm Lucy. The handsome one is my mate, Tamian. Please, come inside."

There was that word again – *mate*.

Natalia followed Lucy into her house. It was just as large as the one she grew up in. The difference? This one was a home. Soft colors. Photos of the Lazlos. Love. She felt it every time she was around this family. No matter if it was a couple or all of them. These people loved each other. Natalia hoped she could get rid of her blood relatives so she could keep experiencing everything this family had to offer.

CHAPTER NINETEEN

Maveryck

MAVERYCK WAS SHAKING. His Princess and two of his brothers had been shot at. Natalia was right about ending her cousin. Mikael wasn't going to stop. Maveryck made the necessary calls, one of them being his twin. He gave War a rundown of what was happening, and War assured him he would guard the boys with his life. Ace was calling in reinforcements to guard the outside of Maveryck's home.

When he arrived at Lucy's, Maveryck barely had his bike on the kickstand before he was running toward the door. It was quiet when he entered, so he called out to his... to Natalia. He didn't know what they were to each other. He just knew she had to be okay. "Princess?"

"I'm here," Natalia said from the top of the stairs. He ran up them two at a time and dragged her into his arms, burying his face in her neck.

"Fuck, Princess." He pulled back and held her face gently between his hands. "You sure you're okay?"

"I'm fine. Someone called Rev is in with Kyllian. It was just a graze on his bicep. He's getting stitched up. I'm so sorry." Natalia leaned her forehead against his chest.

"Shh, none of that. Let's place blame where it lies – with your cousin." Mav kissed her temple then took her hand. "Come on. I want to see Kyllian for myself."

The large bedroom was filled with shifters. Lucy stood

175

off to the side, wrapped in her Gargoyle's arms. Hayden was sitting on the side of the bed next to Kyllian. Rev was putting a bandage on Kyllian's arm. Maveryck figured that was for Natalia's benefit. If it was just a graze, Kyllian would already be healing. If he shifted, he would heal that much quicker.

Hayden jumped up when he noticed Maveryck. "We need to end this fucker. Tonight. I won't have him gunning for my family!" Hayden's eyes were flashing from blue to golden. The lion was too close to the surface.

Maveryck stopped his brother's pacing with hands on his shoulders. "Why don't you take Kyllian outside while I talk to Natalia?"

"Yeah. That's… Come on Kayos. We could both use some fresh air." Hayden waited for Kyllian to climb to his feet. When he did, the two of them hurried from the room. Lucy's estate was twenty private acres. Plenty of room for two lions or eagles to get lost in the woods for a bit.

"Rev, thank you for coming so quickly."

"No thanks needed, Brother. You know that. You need anything else? Need me to look Natalia over?" Maveryck growled, and Rev held up his hands, grinning. "Enough said. If you don't mind, I'm going to hang around. I'd like to be in on taking down a Volkov." Rev flashed his eyes to Natalia, his brows dipping between his eyes. "Shit, no offense."

"None taken, but I'll be going after my cousin alone. I won't have any more of you hurt on my account."

"Fuck that noise." Maveryck got in Natalia's face. "You will not be going in alone. I know you are more than capable, but I won't have you hurt to protect our family. Now, let's go downstairs and put a plan in motion."

Natalia crossed her arms over her chest, scowling. He loved how fierce his Princess was when she was pissed.

"Why don't you guys head downstairs and wait for Ryker. I'd like to talk to Natalia," Lucy said. Maveryck didn't want to let Natalia out of his sight for even a second, but Lucy was giving him the death glare.

"Fine. But I'm getting into the good liquor."

Tamian laughed and clapped him on the shoulder. "I think I have just the thing." Maveryck and Rev followed the Gargoyle, but he turned to look at two of the most important women in his life. Lucy shooed him out the door with her hands, and he shook his head. Girl was definitely a Lazlo.

"Jasper, one of our Clan, sent us home with a case of special stock Jameson. It's pretty damn good," Tamian said when they were downstairs. He led Maveryck and the other Hound into the game room and gestured toward the sitting area. "Have a seat." Rev fell back into an overstuffed armchair. Maveryck had planned on pacing, but he felt compelled to do as the other shifter said. He knew of Tamian's special abilities. The Gryphons could coerce humans into doing as commanded, and they could make them forget. Tamian could control humans, shifters, and animals alike.

Tamian poured three tumblers full of the amber liquid and handed one to Maveryck then to Rev. "She's the one, isn't she?"

"Yeah." Maveryck took a sip of the whiskey and moaned. "Shit, that's good."

"Have you told her about Gryphons?"

"No. I need to, because with everything that's happening, the truth is bound to come out sooner rather than later, and I don't want her to be surprised."

"I wasn't sure if you had said anything. That's why I put the bandage on Kyllian's arm," Rev said, sipping his own Irish whiskey.

"Jenna stopped by earlier, and I thought she was going to spill the news then."

"What the hell did she want?" Rev asked. All the Hounds were aware of the way Jenna left. And now, they all knew about the twins and how Jenna just dumped them on him.

177

"Bitch wanted to check on *her* sons. Man, I wish I could have recorded what happened when she saw Natalia. Jenna said it was good I'd hired a nanny because the boys were too much. She didn't get to finish whatever she was going to say, because Natalia was in her face. My little Russian basically told Jenna she'd fucked the pooch with no lube. Told her she was no kind of mother, and that Natalia was going to be the best for the boys because they deserved nothing less."

"Ooh, feisty," Rev said.

"She is that. Plus, she already loves the twins, and they are completely smitten with her. Marshall gave his mother about two seconds of his attention before telling Natalia he loved her. After what Jenna did, I'm kind of glad my kid cut Jenna down with three words directed at someone else. But yeah, Jenna asked Natalia if she knew what I was. Natalia said she did, but I think Jenna was hinting at me being a shifter and not a mercenary."

"We're back, bitches," Hayden announced as he and Kyllian strode through the patio doors. "Where's the lollipop?" he asked, looking around.

"Upstairs with Lucy," Tamian said.

"Oh, shit. That's not good." Kyllian laughed until Tamian growled at him. "Easy, big guy. But you know your mate as well as I do. She's either tearing Natalia apart with her claws for bringing danger to our family, or she's making plans to have a girls' weekend. There's no in-between with her." Tamian grinned, raising a glass to toast his mate, because Kyllian was right.

"Maybe I should go check on them," Maveryck said.

"Maybe you should calm your tits, Uncle Mav." Lucy strolled into the room with Natalia behind her. "Ryker's coming up the driveway. I know you all have a lot to talk about, but I'm hungry. So, I'm going to start supper while you guys have your little powwow. If you need my computer skills, those will have to wait until I've eaten." Lucy walked over to Tamian and took his glass from him, downing the

178

contents. "Shit, that's good. Hayden, pour Natalia a glass of this or whatever else she wants. She's going to need it," Lucy said, glaring at Mav.

Maveryck wished he was a mind reader in that moment. What the fuck had she and Natalia talked about? "You okay, Princess?"

"Hmm? Yes, but I don't need any alcohol. I want to have a clear head for this."

"This?" Mav asked.

"My mission."

"Our mission," Maveryck and Hayden said in unison.

"We have a mission?" Ryker asked, striding into the room. Their older brother looked calmer than Mav had ever seen him, and that wasn't necessarily a good thing. Ever since he lost Juliette, Ryker was the most stoic, pissed-off male Maveryck had ever known. Even more so than War when Harlow had been killed. For the last twenty years, Ryker hadn't smiled. He was barely tolerable on most days. He had eased up some since finding out his daughter was alive. Being around Mac was softening his edges, but this was different. Ryker almost looked… resigned. He walked directly over to Lucy and kissed her temple. "Thank you, Little Dove."

"You're welcome, Uncle." She grabbed Tamian's hand and pulled him out of the game room.

Maveryck wondered what he was thanking their niece for, but they had other things to worry about. Like going after Mikael Volkov. "Okay. So, we're all in agreement to go after Mikael. Natalia and I talked about whether or not to leave the other two cousins alone or take them out at the same time."

When everyone looked at Natalia, she walked over to stand beside Maveryck. She seemed distracted. He wanted to get her alone and find out what she and Lucy talked about. Had Lucy threatened her? He didn't think his niece would, knowing how Mav felt about Natalia. When she pressed against his side, he didn't hesitate to wrap his arm around her waist. She smiled up at him, staring intently at his eyes before turning serious again.

"Neither Ivan nor Viktor are smart enough to lead the family. If we leave them alive, they'll most likely self-destruct before one of the other leaders takes them out when they learn Mikael is no longer alive. But that news won't travel fast since most of the other families are still scrambling from their own losses. I have no doubt Mikael has shared the fact that I have a new identity, and neither of my cousins has any love for me. They will make it their mission to finish the job, so I say we take all three out at the same time."

"What happens to your family's empire once those three are gone?" Hayden asked.

"*They* are not my family," Natalia hissed. "But for the sake of conversation, the family's estate and all the money will just sit there. Maybe we can get Lucy to do her special brand of manipulation and move the money into an account we can use for the twins' future. I don't want or need the money. Well, I could use some new shoes. Fucker burned down my house."

The males in the room laughed, and Maveryck pressed a kiss to her purple hair. He might have inhaled while he did so.

"As for the house and contents, it will sit there until one of the other families decides to take it over for themselves, unless I sell it first, because I sure as hell don't want it."

"What about Marta?" Mav didn't want to kill the woman, and he didn't think Natalia was cold enough to do so either.

"We can make sure she has enough money in her account to live on comfortably. She has family she can return to, but whether or not she does will be up to her."

"And your father's contacts? His business deals? Do you know what will happen when Mikael is no longer around?"

180

Ryker asked, pouring his own glass of Jameson.

Natalia shrugged. "They'll look elsewhere to do business. I can give you those names. My father thought by keeping me from learning to speak Russian I would blindly obey. I learned the language on my own, and I listened in on every conversation he had when at all possible. While he was teaching Mikael about the business, he was unknowingly sharing his secrets with me. Anatoly was old school. He kept everything in ledgers. Unless Mikael has transferred the information to a computer, it will be easy enough to obtain."

"So don't burn the place down. Got it," Hayden said, winking. Maveryck growled at his brother, who laughed. One of these days, Maveryck was going to get Hayden back. When Hayden found his own mate, Mav was going to make his baby brother's life hell.

Natalia looked up at Mav. "Is it possible to use that information to take down those drug dealers, gun traders, and human traffickers my father worked with?"

"Yes. We will hand the information over to Sutton. He will put together teams, make the long-term plans that are required for things of this nature."

"Good. That was my plan growing up. To take over the family and dismantle it once he was gone. Of course, that was before I learned I wouldn't step into his seat. As soon as Anatoly began grooming Mikael, I knew my plan was moot. I had to continue being the good little soldier until such a point came where I could escape."

"How did you escape?" Ryker asked. He didn't sound accusing exactly, but he wasn't the most trusting male. He'd already given Maveryck his opinion of allowing Natalia into his home. If he could have seen her giving Jenna the verbal ass-whooping, Ryker would probably be as proud of her as Maveryck was.

"Mikael said my services as guard were no longer needed, but honestly, I believe he saw me as a threat. He said since I didn't get along with Viktor, I should find somewhere else to live. He promised to give me enough money to find a place. When he pushed me out the door, he said my only job was to find my father's killer. When I accomplished that, he would keep me on the payroll as family assassin. This will be the only time I ever say I appreciate something Mikael did. If he hadn't kicked me out, I would have never found all of you."

"Aw, you like us, Lollipop?" Hayden asked, grinning.

"Hayden, I swear to Zeus…" Maveryck pulled away from Natalia to lunge for his youngest brother, but her hand on his wrist stopped him

"I like most of your family. You? Maybe you'll grow on me," Natalia threw back at Hayden. Maveryck returned his hand to Natalia's hip, and she relaxed against him. "You have to understand. I was an only child. My mother died when I was six. My father pulled me out of school, so the only people I was around were my cousins, my tutor, and Marta, the housekeeper. She wasn't any better, though. The only one who showed me any amount of decency was my tutor, but she was afraid of my father, so it wasn't like she was stepping in as a mother figure. I know the way I was raised isn't normal, but it's all I knew. Being around your family is like something out of a movie to me. Anyway, back to my cousins. I say we take them all out at the same time, if possible."

"Then that's what we'll do," Maveryck assured her. The sooner they took care of the threat to her, the sooner Maveryck could make sure she was always part of their family.

CHAPTER TWENTY

Natalia

MAVERYCK WAS A Gryphon shifter. All the Hounds were Gryphons. Lucy was a Gryphon. Natalia would have thought she was losing her mind had Lucy not shown her the truth. When Lucy stripped out of her clothes and transformed into a lion, Natalia fell backwards onto her ass. Lucy was a beautiful tawny beige, and her paws were huge. When she shifted back, she stood unabashedly naked. Then she showed Natalia her eagle. She was larger than a normal eagle with gorgeous red and gold wings. When she was once again in human form, Lucy explained about the Gryphon as she put her clothes back on, but said there wasn't room upstairs for her to fully shift without causing chaos in the room.

"I know Uncle Mav will eventually tell you, but I thought you should know what you're getting into with the family. I want to know if you can handle what we all are, because if you can't, you need to step away before the boys and my uncle fall any harder for you," Lucy said.

Natalia appreciated how protective Lucy was of her family. Some things now made more sense. Like Kerrigan calling Rory a lioness. Major saying his grandmother roared like a lion. The term mate being tossed around. The way Maveryck rumbled deep in his chest when Hayden winked at her. Why Jenna wanted to know if Natalia was aware of what Maveryck was.

"And you trust me with this knowledge?"

"I do. Gryphons have the ability to alter someone's mind so they forget what they know about our kind, but I don't think that will be necessary. Uncle Mav was hurt badly when Jenna left. I don't think he ever planned on falling in love again, but here you are."

"We've known each other a handful of days."

"Are you saying you don't feel anything for him?"

"No, I'm saying it's crazy how much I feel for him. And the twins. It's too soon to say he's in love with me."

Lucy sat down on the edge of the bed. "Is it? Who has the right to tell someone how they feel? Or how much time it takes to know for certain the feelings are real? I felt the pull to Tamian immediately. Sutton and Rory knew immediately. War fell in love with Kerrigan from a photo. Is our love and commitment to one another dismissible because we didn't wait months before we let our feelings be known?"

"No. It's just so new. I thought I would never have a chance at a relationship because of my job. I refused to date because I would have to lie to my partner about my occupation. I might be a killer, but I'm not a liar. Now, here is this amazing man who knows what I am. He knows who I am. It's too good to be true."

"Let me ask you something else. Are you only interested in Mav because of the boys?"

"Of course not. Those boys are precious, but so is Maveryck. All three of them deserve the best in a partner – mate – and a stepmother. I don't know if that's me. I love those boys, and I want to be in their lives. But I know nothing about being a mother figure. I don't know how to be a mate. I can't cook. I've never been very social because I wasn't allowed. The only thing I know how to do well is take someone out with a rifle or knives. Besides all that, I have a price on my head. I've already brought danger to their door. So maybe I should walk away and let them find someone more appropriate."

"Let me tell you what makes an appropriate mate and a good mother. Love. Unconditional love. If you can give that to the three of them, you'll be perfect for them. Relationships aren't easy; just ask Tamian. He was somewhat of a loner when we met. He has a sister who he's close with, but she has her own mate. He has other family, but they're nothing like the Lazlos. You've already seen them when they all get together. Not only are Mav and the twins a package deal, but so is the rest of the family. And the Hounds. If you can handle that, you're golden. Besides, the Hounds bring their own danger to the door by doing what they do. If you allow yourself to love Maveryck, you'll have a group of badass bikers watching your back. There's a lot more to being Gryphons, but I'll let Maveryck fill you in if you decide to give him a chance. Right now, we need to get downstairs, because I guarantee both Mav and Tamian are going nuts wondering what we're doing."

It was hard for Natalia to pay attention once she was downstairs with Maveryck and the others. She kept wondering what they all looked like in their various shifter forms.

Maveryck and his family listened as Natalia talked about her own family. About how she was ready to take her cousins down. These were men – shifters – who basically did the same thing, only they went after bigger targets. "If your family mostly hunts down the Ministry, why do you take contracts too?"

Ryker, who was more relaxed than before, answered, "For the money. Going after the cult, finding safe places for those we rescue, takes money. The mercenary work we do funds that. We take down the evil while helping the victims ease back into life outside the sheltered existence they'd been forced to live. Since Kerrigan has been on the inside of a cult, she is now working with Sutton and Rory by helping with the victims."

Everything Ryker said made sense, and Natalia was impressed with the Hounds. She wanted that – a purpose. Sure, she eliminated bad men with her rifle, but the paycheck sat in her bank doing nothing more than buying more weapons and clothes. "I want to help," she blurted.

"We wouldn't think to leave you out of taking down your cousins," Mav said, misunderstanding.

"No. I know that. I meant with the Ministry. I want to help your family there. Not like Kerrigan does, because I'm not good with people. I want Lucy to wipe out my family's accounts and transfer it to wherever your parents need it. If that's possible without the government finding out."

"Why?" Ryker asked. "You could take the money and go anywhere. Do anything."

"Because it's the right thing to do. I can't atone for my past sins by going on a permanent vacation. I wouldn't want to anyway, because I'd be bored after a week. But apart from putting some money aside for the twins, I don't need it. You know the kind of bank I bring in working for Nexus. That's more than enough for a single person." Except Natalia didn't want to be single. She wanted a life with Maveryck.

"I can absolutely make that happen," Lucy said. "Let's discuss this over dinner."

When all the men headed toward the dining room, Natalia grabbed Mav's hand. "Can we call and check on the boys?"

Maveryck cupped her face and pressed a soft kiss to her lips. He might have meant it to be sweet, but his touch had her body tingling in all the right places. Or wrong places, considering where they were and who was in the next room. Mav pulled out his phone, smiling like she had offered him the world. "I'll send War a text and have him call on video chat."

"Everything okay?" Lucy asked.

"Yeah, Luce. We re gonna talk to the boys right quick. Y'all go ahead and start without us."

Natalia cocked her head to the side. "What?" Mav asked.

"The way you speak is…"

"Twangy?"

"I was going to say southern."

"With the exception of Kyllian and Hayden, the rest of us were born in Texas. Does my twang bother you?" Maveryck hadn't lost his southern accent in all the years he'd lived in New York.

"No. I think it's sexy." Natalia ran her fingers through his beard.

"I think you're sexy," he whispered.

Mav's phone made a funny chirping noise, and he tapped a button. When he held the phone out in front of them, two happy faces shone from the screen.

"Daddo!" Major yelled.

"Tolly," Marshall added, somewhat quieter.

"Hey, buddies. We're at your cousin Lucy's. We're gonna be here for a while, but we wanted to call and say hi."

"Kerry let us make pasghetti," Major said.

Natalia smiled, but she was a little jealous that the pretty redhead was able to help the boys with something Natalia couldn't do. She wasn't mother material. But hadn't Lucy said being a good mom only took love? That she had in spades, so why did she feel so inadequate? What if Lucy was wrong? Natalia wanted the best for the twins, and she really doubted that was her.

"Tolly, I saved you some," Marshall said.

"Thank you." Natalia blinked so she wouldn't cry. This little man owned her completely. They both did, which made needing to walk away so hard.

"We need to go now, but we'll be home later. Be good for Uncle War."

"'Kay, Daddo. Bye, Lolly." Major ran off, but Marshall pressed his little lips to the screen, making a smacking sound. Natalia caught a sob behind her hand. She turned her back as Mav talked to his twin. Strong arms surrounded her from behind. "What's wrong, Princess?"

How did she tell him she loved his boys and wanted to be everything Jenna hadn't been?

When she didn't respond, Mav tightened his hold. "I get it." Mav set his chin against the top of her head. "I've only had them a few days, but they're already so deep inside my heart I'm afraid I'm gonna wake up and find out it's all just a dream. And I know you just met us, but I want you in our lives, Princess. Is that something you might want too?"

"I want what's best for the three of you."

"And you don't think that's you? Because it's so new?"

Natalia merely nodded as best she could under his chin. She couldn't bring herself to tell him the real reason. Yes, this was all new. Brand new. But she was lacking, and it would only be a matter of time before he figured that out.

"In our family, we just kind of know when it's right."

Natalia turned so she could look up at him. "But what about Jenna? Didn't you think it was right with her?"

Mav blew out a breath, looking at the ceiling. "I don't want you to take this the wrong way, but Jenna was supposed to be a one-night stand. She ended up staying the weekend. Same thing happened the next few weekends, and before I knew it, all her things had migrated to my house. I loved her in time. I thought we would get married. I actually had a ring, but before I could ask, she left. I think I was more pissed off than brokenhearted. I gave her three years, and I didn't understand how she could just walk away. I didn't go after her, though. I think if she had really been the one I was destined to be with, I would have tried harder to get her back. Hell, Princess, I didn't try at all." Maveryck caressed her face again. "I think…" He swallowed hard. "I *know* if you left me, I'd follow you to Hell to get you back."

She didn't understand what he saw in her. She knew what it was about Maveryck that drew her to him, but something so one-sided would never work. He might think he had feelings for her now, but he thought he loved Jenna too. He was going to marry her. If he spent three years with the woman who wasn't right for him, how long would it take for him to figure that out about Natalia? *But Jenna was the one to walk away. Not Maveryck.*

Maveryck bent over and grabbed her ass, lifting her into his arms. Natalia wrapped her legs around his waist, holding onto his shoulders. When she went to protest, Maveryck cut her off with his lips. His tongue sought out hers. Maveryck kissed her deeply, moaning into her mouth, setting a smoldering fire ablaze in her core.

"Take that shit upstairs," Hayden called from the dining

room.

Maveryck panted against her lips. "Damn, woman. You make me forget myself." He set her feet on the floor and adjusted himself behind his jeans. "Let's go eat and figure out a plan for taking out your cousins." Lacing their fingers together, Mav led her into the dining room. Hayden and Kyllian were smirking, but the others did their best to ignore what they'd heard.

Lucy offered Natalia some wine while asking Mav if he wanted his usual. She should have been embarrassed, but she wasn't. When Hayden winked at her, Natalia smirked back at the man. He threw his head back and laughed. "She's a keeper, Mayhem."

Maveryck took a long pull of the beer Lucy handed him. "Damn straight she is."

While they ate, Maveryck, who was familiar with her family's home, suggested going in a day before they hit her cousins to do recon. He asked her questions about entry points he might not be aware of. Then she asked the question she'd wondered ever since he'd taken out her father. "How did you get in last time?" Mav opened his mouth then closed it, looking around the table.

Natalia poked him in the side. "Well? This is no time for secrets."

Lucy sighed. "This is where I tell you she knows the truth."

"What truth? Lucy, did you—?"

"Yes, I did. You can be pissed later. I needed to know if she was all-in. If she couldn't handle knowing, I would have zapped her memory."

Maveryck turned toward Natalia. "And you're okay with it?"

Natalia smiled up at him. "Why wouldn't I be? Sure, it was unbelievable until she shifted. The proof was right there in front of me. I can't wait to see your lion. But if I'm right, I've already seen your eagle."

"When? The only time I've shifted around you was… Wait. You saw me leaving your father's house?"

"I thought it was odd for an eagle to be carrying a bag. So, I followed you into the woods."

Hayden laughed. "You're slipping, Mayhem." Maveryck threw a roll at his brother who caught it before it could hit him in the face. Hayden stuffed it in his mouth, tearing off a chunk and chewing around his smile.

Tamian, who had sat quietly through the meal, told Lucy, "I'll clean up. Why don't you call Julian and see if he can't get satellite images of the estate? Make sure Mikael hasn't made any changes."

"Who's Julian?" Natalia asked.

"One of my Clan," Tamian responded.

"You're a Gryphon too?"

"No. I'm a Gargoyle. We only became aware of the Gryphons when Lucy and I mated. The Gryphons, however, have known about our kind for a while, but they kept our secret."

"What other kinds of shifters are there?"

"That, we don't know. We could be the only two species, and then again, there could be any number we haven't found out about. Gryphons have been around as long as the Goyles, and if Lucy hadn't been my fated mate, they would probably still be a secret."

"Is it rude to ask what you turn into? I know about the Gryphons, although I've yet to see one. Lucy only showed me her lion and eagle."

"Considering you are family, it's not rude. Gargoyles don't have an animal, per se. When we shift, we remain in our human body, but we have wings, claws, and fangs." Tamian held out his hand, and sharp claws extended from his fingertips. Lucy held out her hand and did the same, showing the difference.

"Rory really could claw my eyes out," Natalia whispered.

"If you don't harm any of her family, you don't need to worry about our mother," Ryker said. "Now, enough show and tell. Go call Julian, Little Dove. The sooner we get the intel, the sooner Maveryck and Natalia will be safe."

Lucy left the room, and Natalia and the others helped Tamian clear the table. She was still trying to wrap her head around the knowledge there were shifters in the world. She could have walked past any one of them and never known it.

Kyllian offered to help with the dishes, so the others retreated into the game room. Maveryck pulled Natalia off to the side. "Are you mad I didn't tell you?"

"No. We met two days ago, and that was a fluke. We are supposed to be taking each other out, not… whatever it is we're doing." Natalia shrugged.

"I should have known," he started. "When I passed you on the sidewalk that day, I should have known who you were."

"How?"

"By your smell. It was the same one I caught in your bedroom when I went after Anatoly. You smell like wildflowers. I caught a whiff of that delicious aroma, and it was all I could do not to turn around and follow you. But I couldn't. I had to get out of town."

"You were in my bedroom? Wait. How did you get up there without killing all the guards? I never saw you on the ground."

"You already said you saw my eagle. That's how. I shifted in the woods, stored my clothes in the bag I was carrying, then shifted back on the roof. I lowered myself down to your window. Afterwards, I left the same way."

"I can't wait to see your lion," Natalia whispered.

Maveryck smiled. "Hang on." He left the room, and less than a minute later, a large lion was stalking toward her. Natalia dropped to her knees and held out her hand. She had never seen a more stunning creature in her life. When Maveryck stopped right in front of her, he lowered his massive head, and Natalia dug her fingers into his thick mane. Two days ago, she was lonely. Alone. Drifting with the exception of her job. Now? She was falling in love with a man who was also an animal. A man with two darling little boys and a loud, loving family.

This couldn't be real. This could not be her life. But Tamian had said she was family. Could he be right?

CHAPTER TWENTY-ONE

Maveryck

MAVERYCK'S LION WANTED to roll around on the floor with Natalia. Her hands in his mane was heaven. At first, he had been upset with Lucy telling Natalia about the Gryphons, but he understood why she did it. The girl was just as protective of their family as they were of her. Having Natalia know the truth was freeing. Lucy had done him a favor, really. His niece smiled when she came into the game room and found his lion on the floor.

"You want to shift back so we can talk?" Lucy asked.

Maveryck nudged Natalia with his nose making her giggle before leaving the room to shift. When he returned, Natalia was sitting on one of the sofas, so he took the empty spot next to her. Rev was sitting in an oversized armchair, and Ryker was leaning against the pool table with his arms crossed, Hayden mimicking their older brother. Ryker's eyes were unfocused, and Maveryck wanted to know what was on the male's mind, but his oldest brother was a private person. He only shared what pertained to the club.

When Tamian and Kyllian joined them, Lucy opened her laptop. "Julian was able to get shots of the Volkov estate. Natalia, you'll need to take a look since you're most familiar." Lucy handed the laptop over, and Natalia turned it so Maveryck could look at the screen too.

"The gate is new, as is the guard shack."

Mav rubbed his beard. "Since I'll be going in through the woods, that won't be a problem."

"And I can take the tunnel," Natalia added.

Maveryck nor his Gryphon wanted Natalia anywhere near her cousins, but he knew she could handle herself. Having her rifle would be a plus in the numbers column. "Tunnel?"

"Yes. There's a secret passage no one knows about. Well, my father did, but I don't think he ever shared its existence with my cousins."

"Then how do you know about it?" Ryker asked.

Natalia smiled, her eyes soft. "My mother. She would take me on walks around the property when she wanted to get out of the house. I was young, so it might be me remembering things a certain way because of what I now know about Anatoly, but I don't think she was happy with my father. I often heard them arguing, and it was always about me. She never smiled unless it was only the two of us. She and I spent a lot of time outdoors. My father never seemed to mind it either. He would often suggest us going for walks, and I think it was so he could talk freely about his business without the chance of her overhearing. Anyway, one day, we were walking in the woods, and she asked me if I wanted to play a game. Of course, I did, so she told me we were going to pretend to run away. Looking back, I think she knew. Somehow, she knew I would one day need a way to escape.

"She made me promise to never speak of our games to anyone, and showed me a secret door. It was covered by brush. I wasn't quite tall enough to reach the lever, but she explained how it worked. When she pulled it a certain way, the brush opened up, a heavy steel door sliding with it. We walked into this tunnel. We always took a picnic with us, but on that day, she pulled a flashlight out of the basket, like she'd planned on showing me the tunnel all along. We walked the entire length. It's about a quarter-mile long, but

194

back then it seemed like a massive journey to someone my age. The tunnel is just wide enough for a vehicle to pass through. The other end opens up on a path just outside our property. It has the same type of covered door. That was the only time we ever visited it, because she said it was too special to risk anyone else finding our secret."

Lucy leaned back against Tamian's chest, biting her lower lip. "Luce, what is it?" Maveryck asked.

"Natalia, please forgive me if this is painful, but what happened to your mother?"

"She was in a car wreck. I went to school as usual, a somewhat normal child, and instead of finding my mother waiting to pick me up afterward, my father was there. When I asked where Mama was, my father told me she was gone. That she'd been in a wreck driving home after dropping me off that morning. I was devastated. I didn't speak for a couple months. Not only had I lost the only person in my life who loved me, but my father pulled me out of school, and I guess I was depressed. The fact that I wouldn't talk to him pissed him off, and that's when my life changed even more. He demanded I have an English tutor and forbade me from speaking Russian. You know the rest of it."

Lucy's eyes narrowed, and Maveryck knew the wheels were turning. She, like him and probably everyone else in the room, assumed Anatoly was responsible for Bellona Volkova's demise.

Natalia cleared her throat, and like she hadn't relived the most painful time of her life, she stood and said, "Mikael is mine. I don't actually care what happens to Ivan and Viktor, because they'll eventually get what's coming to them when they screw someone over with their stupidity. If they happen to get caught in the crossfire – or crossclaws – it's not going to be a huge loss."

Maveryck normally looked to Ryker when it came to who partnered on jobs, but this shit was personal, and they needed the best. "We'll be taking Rev, King, and Ace."

Hayden pushed away from the pool table. "And me. I'm going, so don't even think about pulling the 'you're too young' shit with me."

Ryker grabbed their younger brother by his nape. "Settle down, Havyk. You're in. You will be with Natalia coming in through the tunnel. The other five of us will be going in from the treetops." Maveryck arched a brow, but Ryker waved him off. "This is too important, so of course I'm going. Lucy, please send the satellite images to the computer at the clubhouse. I'm going to send Digger to the estate tonight to sit on the house and make sure the cousins don't leave. The rest of us will all get some sleep tonight, and we'll meet first thing after breakfast to get Ace and King up to speed. If we're all in agreement, we'll hit the estate tomorrow night."

"Are you good with that, Princess?" Maveryck asked.

"Yes. I'm used to doing more recon, but I already know the layout as well as the mark. Tomorrow night is fine. I just... I need to go back to my house for my weapons."

"But your house is mostly gone," Ryker said. "I had Sultan and Hawk swing by there to monitor not only the fire, but to also see if they couldn't find the shooter if the cops didn't get him. I've got a score to settle with that one."

"You and me both," Kyllian muttered.

"With the exception of a pistol I sleep with, my weapons are in a fireproof cabinet, so they should be okay."

Ryker pulled out his phone and made a call. "Sultan, Natalia has a gun cabinet that contains her weapons. I need you and Hawk to retrieve it, drop it off at Mav's, and put it in the garage. Thanks." When he disconnected, he told Natalia, "They're on it."

"Oh, uh. Thanks."

Lucy walked over to where the laptop was and picked it up, taking it to the bar. "Natalia, if you don't mind sharing your old bank account information with me, I'll get started tracking down Mikael's other accounts so I can work on wiping them out. Depending on how encrypted they are, I may not be able to move the money before you hit them tomorrow night, but I'll do my best."

"I don't mind." Natalia went to join Lucy. While the females were busy with that, Ryker inclined his head to Maveryck. Maveryck stood and followed his brother to the far side of the room.

"Are you okay with me taking lead on this?" Ryker asked.

Maveryck shoved his hands in the back pockets of his jeans. "Yes. I feel like this is the most important job I've ever taken, and I want it to go smoothly. That means I want the best at my side."

Ryker's eyebrows shot up, and Maveryck bristled. Did his brother not know how much Mav admired him? "You might be a grumpy bastard, but you are the best of us besides Pop. I'm honored to have you take lead."

Ryker looked at the ceiling, blinking. Maveryck had only seen Ryker get emotional one time in the past two decades, and that was when he found out his daughter was alive. Not wanting him to feel embarrassed, Mav clapped his hands. "Now, I'm ready to go snuggle two little hellions." Natalia and Lucy had finished going over the account information, so he held out his hand. "Ready to go home?" He knew all eyes were on them at the way he worded his question, but he didn't care. Natalia's rental had been torched, and if he had his way, her staying with him and the twins would become permanent.

When she took his hand, he held out his free one to Hayden. "Keys," he said, making a give-me motion.

"I'm not riding bitch," Kyllian grumbled.

Rev chuckled. "You can ride with me." The Hound's bike had a sidecar even though Mav had never seen anyone ride in it. Bethany, his wife, rode behind him, and his kids were almost grown.

"Or you can take one of my cars," Lucy offered. She still had her parents' vehicles in the garage.

Kyllian grinned. "Nah. After getting shot, I need the wind in my face." He clapped the big Hound's shoulder. "Besides, the sidecar needs to actually get used."

Rev grunted. "It gets used."

"By an ass in the seat. Your dirty laundry doesn't count," Hayden joked. Rev reached out to smack Hayden, but the shifter quickly jumped out of the way.

"How's your arm?" Natalia asked Kyllian as they watched him try to fold his long legs into the sidecar.

Kyllian pulled his still-red sleeve up. "Good as new. I just needed to shift for it to heal since the bullet only grazed me,"

"Then why the charade of Rev patching you up?"

"You didn't know about shifters yet."

Natalia grinned. "Makes sense."

They all said goodbye to Lucy and Tamian, thanking them for everything. When Mav and Natalia were on the road, Natalia asked, "Why didn't we take your bike?"

"You wanna ride with me, Princess?"

"Yes. I've never been on a motorcycle, but it looks fun."

"After we get these hits off us, we'll go for a ride. Guess I'm gonna need to get a sidecar too so the boys can go with us. But as for why I didn't take the bike home, you were shot at a few hours ago. At least with the SUV, even with a couple bullet holes, we have some protection. Out in the open on the Harley? Not so much." Maveryck reached over and took Natalia's hand. "How are you doing? You've had a pretty shitty day."

"Let me think." Natalia tapped a finger against her chin. "I was pulled out of bed by a hot mercenary. I met your family. All your family. Your ex came by, and I wanted to beat her within an inch of her life. My house was burned down, which means I'm now homeless without clothes, shoes, my computer, or disguises. I found out about shifters. We've plotted murdering not one but three of my family. *But* I got to spend most of the day with two extremely cute boys,

198

and I got to meet your lion. I wouldn't say it was all bad."

"You think I'm hot?"

Natalia laughed, smacking Maveryck on the bicep. "You know you are."

"Do we need to go shopping before we get home?" Mav asked, once again referring to his house as hers.

"Not tonight. I'm ready to see the boys. But I will need to get something to wear for tomorrow night. I can't very well do a job wearing shorts."

"You could, but I'd hate to see those pretty legs get scratched up."

"My legs are too short and skinny. I'm skinny."

"Princess, you're perfect. No, you aren't tall, but your legs are toned." Maveryck didn't care that Natalia was short, or that her tits were on the small side. She was perfectly proportioned. "And I love your hair. Do you keep it short because of the wigs?"

Natalia leaned back against the headrest, but turned and focused on him. "My hair was really long when I was younger. I thought the brown was boring, so I colored it red. Anatoly had a fit and chopped it all off. And when I say chopped, I mean he did it himself and none too carefully. I let it grow back out, but never as long as it had been. When Mikael kicked me out, I had it all cut off and colored lavender just because I could."

"Well, I like it. And I know two boys who bought a birthday cake with purple balloons because they were intrigued by it."

"Was their birthday recent?"

"No, it was a couple months ago. Since they didn't get to celebrate with Jenna, I wanted to make up for it."

Natalia narrowed her eyes. "Speaking of that woman, I may kick her ass if she ever stops by to see the boys again."

Maveryck grinned at his feisty Princess. "You don't have to worry about that. I told her to forget about them and never come back."

"You think she will?"

"I know so." Maveryck wasn't sure if Lucy shared about the shifter voice, so he asked, "What all did Lucy tell you about Gryphons?"

"Not much. I know you can alter human thinking. Is that something I need to worry about?"

Maveryck squeezed her hand. "No. I would never use my persuasion on you, unless you threatened to tell others about the Gryphons. I shouldn't have used it on Jenna, but she seriously pissed me off keeping the boys from me."

"What are you going to do when the boys ask about her? Ask why their mother never comes around."

"I'll make up some bullshit excuse if they're not old enough to understand the real reason. If they are old enough, I'll tell them the truth. You saw them when she came by. Neither one ran to her like they missed her. Hell, Marshall all but gave her the finger when he told you he loved you in front of her. As long as you're around, I don't think they're going to miss her."

Maveryck didn't want Natalia to think he wanted her around only for the boys. "My home is yours as long as you want it, Princess. I know it's not the kind of house you're used to, but it's plenty spacious enough for all four of us."

"When you were breaking in to kidnap me, did you happen to notice the type of house I was living in? I'm not a material person. Don't get me wrong; I do love my clothes and shoes. But I only lived in Anatoly's three-story manor because it's where I was raised."

"I wasn't going to kidnap you. Just get some answers."

Natalia groaned. "And if you didn't like those answers, you were going to kill me."

"No, I wasn't. I don't go around killing women or children. Never have, never will."

"But you took the contract."

"So no one else would. And I'm so very glad I did." Maveryck didn't believe in coincidence, and Gryphons didn't have fated mates. But he believed all the way to his soul he met Natalia because she was supposed to be his.

Chapter Twenty-Two

Natalia

IT WAS LATE when they got home. Not home – Maveryck's house. He said she could stay for as long as she wanted, but she couldn't believe he wanted someone like her. Still, she was glad to be there. Her day might have had shitty parts, like Maveryck said, but it hadn't been her worst. Not even close. The boys were waiting up, and they both ran to her and Maveryck when they walked into the kitchen from the garage. War and Kerrigan followed, and when War asked how things went, Maveryck grabbed them a couple beers and went out back where they could talk freely. That was after spending a few minutes listening to his sons go on and on about what they'd been doing.

Natalia sat down on the sofa with a twin on either side. Marshall had asked her to read them a story, and Natalia couldn't say no. Every so often, she'd glance at Kerrigan and find her staring almost wistfully. By the time she got to the end of the book, the boys had scooted down so their heads were on her lap, and they were both snoring softly. Natalia set the book aside so she could run her hands through both boys' hair. When she felt Kerrigan staring again, Natalia asked, "Is everything okay?"

"I admire you." Kerrigan's eyes were kind, and her smile friendly. "You're this kickass woman. If you want it" — Kerrigan motioned around the room — "this is all yours for the taking. Don't get me wrong. I love War with everything I am. But I was a bartender before I was kidnapped. I've never led an exciting life. You, on the other hand, could probably write a book."

"Do you honestly think if given the choice as a young girl, I'd have opted to"— Natalia knew the boys were asleep, but she looked down to make sure — "I'd have chosen my particular occupation? I can tell you I absolutely would not have. I wasn't taught anything other girls my age were. Until a few months ago, I'd never cooked or cleaned a day in my life. We always had Marta for that. I don't see it as being spoiled. I see it as being hindered. I had to watch a video online to figure out how to wash my clothes. I'm a twenty-six-year-old woman with no life skills.

"I'm good at what I do because it's what I was groomed for from the time I was seven. My father gave me a year to grieve my mother's death before he started instructing me in how to fight. I can throw a punch without breaking my hand, and I can take a punch without it knocking me out cold. I held my first rifle when I was nine. I took my first life at sixteen. That isn't something to admire. It's something that should disgust you."

Natalia hadn't cried since she was six, but being around Major and Marshall, and now Kerrigan, was making her tear up. She closed her eyes tight, willing the wetness to go away. "I admire *you*, Kerrigan. You're working with Sutton and Rory, using your experience with the cult for good. You helped the boys cook spaghetti tonight. You're not a criminal. You are the kind of woman these boys need as a stepmother. Not someone like me," she whispered, losing her battle with her tears.

Kerrigan moved from the chair to drop to her knees in front of Natalia, pulling her hands from the boys' hair. Her own tears fell when she choked out, "I'm so sorry. I didn't… I didn't mean to offend you. But I don't think you're a criminal. If I did, I would have to think the same thing about the Hounds, War included. You're wrong about the kind of woman the twins need. Yes, they helped me with supper, but the whole time we were in the kitchen together, they were talking about you. Lolly this. Tolly that. Do they make purple noodles? War mentioned them going to bed, and Marshall almost threw a tantrum. Said he had to wait until you got home so you could read to them. I offered to read them a story, and Major told me no. Flat out." Kerrigan squeezed Natalia's hands. "They are so in love with you. You could feed them peanut butter and jelly every meal as long as it was grape jelly, because it's purple." Natalia laughed and squeezed back. "You've been in their little lives less than a week, and you've captured their hearts. They love their Lollipop. All you have to do is love them back."

Kerrigan released Natalia's hands and wiped her face. "I still admire you. Even more so now that I've heard your story."

The back door opened, and Natalia quickly wiped her own face with her fingertips. She smiled at the other woman so Kerrigan would know Natalia wasn't mad.

AFTER WAR AND Kerrigan left, Maveryck and Natalia got the twins into bed. She didn't want things to become awkward. Natalia had never spent the night with a man, not that she knew Maveryck's intentions. The few times she had taken a lover to bed, she was the one to walk away in the middle of the night after making sure the man was asleep. But this wasn't a one-night stand, and Natalia had her own room. The chemistry had been there when they kissed, and they were both young. Maveryck was all male. She had no doubt he had a healthy sexual appetite. But she still wasn't going to assume anything.

Just as she opened her mouth to say she was going to turn in, Maveryck's phone rang. When he hung up, he smiled. "Your gun cabinet is here." He held his hand out, and she automatically took it. She shouldn't have. Natalia shouldn't get comfortable being here in his home. *You're already comfortable.* Mav hit the garage door button on the wall, and the two Hounds who Ryker had watching her house were standing there holding the heavy cabinet. "Set it over here," Mav instructed.

When the safe was in place and the males stepped back, Natalia noticed it was fairly clean. One of the Hounds said, "We would have been here sooner, but we stopped by the clubhouse to clean the soot off the cabinet."

"You didn't have to do that, but I appreciate it." Natalia placed her hand on the scanner, and the lock clicked. When she opened the door, Maveryck whistled. She glanced over her shoulder. Mav was closer than she expected, and she took a step back. He narrowed his eyes, and she felt bad at her reaction. She wanted to step closer, not farther away, but she couldn't allow herself to fall for the male any more than she already had. Turning to the Hounds, Natalia held out her hand and introduced herself. "Natalia Jones."

Maveryck shook his head. "Sorry. Natalia, this is Sultan and Hawk." Each male shook her hand, looking from her to Maveryck and back. She wanted to know what the looks were for, but she wasn't about to ask.

Natalia turned her attention back to her weapons. She checked each one over while the three males watched. That didn't make her nervous at all. Natalia saved her rifle for last. Since it was still broken down in its case, it had extra protection from the fire. She dragged out the case, holding her breath. She pressed her thumb to the sensor and raised the lid. Natalia carefully inspected each piece. When she didn't find any markings or a speck of damage from the fire, she let out a breath of relief. She had a lot of money tied up in her babies, and it would have been a shame if they had been damaged. "Glad I spent extra on a top-of-the-line cabinet," she said. "At least that's something I don't have to replace."

"I take it you didn't catch the shooter," Maveryck said.

"Actually, we did. Ryker said he would take care of him," Hawk replied.

"Do you know who he is? Was it one of my cousins?" she asked.

"The man was Russian, but he isn't one of the three cousins we know about. His name is Yuri."

Natalia sighed. "He is one of the guards at the estate. Where is he? Ryker shouldn't have to deal with him. This is my problem."

Hawk looked at Maveryck then back at Natalia. Mav crossed his arms over his chest. Ignoring the way her stomach fluttered with Maveryck's eyes studying her so intently, she waited on Hawk to answer her. When Maveryck nodded at the male, Hawk smiled at Natalia. "Ryker said you had more important things to do tonight, and he would handle it."

"Oh, here you go." Sultan handed her the pistol she kept under her pillow while she slept. "I cleaned it up, but you can see the bluing is pitted. I'd probably take it to an expert to have it tested and restored if it means a lot to you. If not, I'd get a new one just to be safe."

Natalia knew all this, but it made her feel good the Hound felt the need to warn her.

"I'm not attached to it. If it had been my rifle, however, I'd probably be in the fetal position crying like a baby." Anatoly had insisted Natalia use a Russian Dragunov rifle, but when she got her first paycheck from Nexus, she purchased a Savage 10 BA Stealth and had it modified for use with her personal suppressor. It had taken a while to find someone she trusted to do the work, since the man she used before knew her as Tatiana. Now that she wasn't sure what was going on at Nexus, being sold out was a possibility. Just another reason to stay away from the twins. She would never knowingly bring danger to their door. *But you already have.*

"We'll get out of your hair. Mayhem, let us know if you need us tomorrow." The men inclined their heads to Natalia, and she thanked them again.

"Thanks, Hawk. You too, Sultan." While Maveryck walked the Hounds to their truck, Natalia closed the safe and made sure the lock engaged. She didn't wait on Maveryck. Instead, Natalia went upstairs. She looked in on the twins and couldn't stop the tears when she took in the way Marshall snuggled a stuffed toy to his chest, or the way Major was angled crossways. After a few minutes, she made her way to the spare room where her bags were, closed the door, and sat down on the edge of the bed. She was tired, physically and mentally. It really had been a shitty day. And now more than before, she knew what she had to do. It was going to kill her, but Natalia had no other choice.

The house was quiet, so she heard when Maveryck closed the door from the garage. She waited for him to come upstairs and knock on her door. After sitting there for twenty minutes, Natalia figured he had decided to remain downstairs. She didn't know what the male's routine was at night. Maybe he sat outside on the patio drinking. He might turn on the television and watch a movie. If she had been home, she would have poured a glass of wine and read a book to lose herself in an imaginary story to try and forget the events of the day. She didn't have that luxury tonight. She had a job to plan. Ryker might be in charge where he and the Hounds were concerned, but it was Natalia's fault they were involved in the first place.

Since she didn't have wine, and her e-reader was probably melted and under a pile of rubble, Natalia opted for a shower. She grabbed her sleeping clothes out of her bag along with her toiletries. Just as she stepped out of the bedroom, Maveryck was entering his. Either he didn't see her, or he was avoiding her, since he shut the door behind him. Natalia had retreated without a word, so if he was giving her space, it was probably because he figured she wanted it. She did, and she didn't. Natalia wanted Maveryck. Wanted to spend time with him. Kiss him. Get closer to him. But that wasn't what he needed.

When Natalia walked out of the bathroom, finger-combing her damp hair, Maveryck was leaning against the opposite wall. Since she didn't know him all that well, she couldn't tell what kind of mood he was in since he wasn't smiling.

"Is everything okay?" she whispered.

"You tell me. You're the one who disappeared while I was telling Sultan and Hawk goodbye."

"I was giving you some space. I appreciate you letting me stay here, but I don't want to intrude on your routine." That sounded legitimate, didn't it?

Maveryck's eyes hooded as they traveled from her face down her body to her toes. "I haven't gotten into a new routine since the twins showed up." His eyes did a slow perusal back up to her face, and Natalia didn't miss the heat in his gaze. "And I don't need space. Not from you."

"I…" Natalia had no idea what to say. Maveryck didn't give her a chance to figure it out. He stepped close enough to cup her cheek. Tipping her chin up, Maveryck leaned over and pressed their lips together, nibbling on her mouth. Since she'd left her toiletries on the bathroom counter, her hands were free. Free to grab onto his hips. Free to fist his T-shirt. Free to untuck the soft cotton from his jeans and slide her hands along the skin underneath. Mav sucked in a breath at the first contact of her fingers on his sides.

"Princess," he murmured against her mouth before plunging in, teasing her tongue, tracing her teeth, exploring every inch he could reach. When he licked the roof of her mouth, Natalia sucked on his tongue, pulling on it like she would if she were giving a blowjob. Or at least how she thought she would give one, since it was something she'd never done. All previous thoughts of staying away from Maveryck fled her brain as her body took over. Would it be so bad if she gave in to her lust?

Maveryck grabbed Natalia's ass, lifting her off the floor. She wrapped her legs around his waist, and with their mouths still fused together, he walked her into his bedroom. Mav closed the door with his boot and pressed her back against the wall. His erection was nestled in the juncture of her legs, and she couldn't help but writhe against him. Her body ached with need. Using his strong thighs, Maveryck held her aloft while tearing her T-shirt over her head. Since she'd planned on sleeping, she had forgone a bra, so now her small breasts were bare. Natalia held onto his shoulders as Mav bent his head and latched onto one of her nipples. His soft beard tickled her skin, but the sensation was quickly replaced with just the right amount of pain as he sucked hard. Natalia's head banged against the wall with each lick and nip. The more he worked it, the wetter she became.

Mav moved to the other bud, giving it the same rough treatment. Her fingernails dug into the skin of his back as she wiggled her ass, looking for friction. One of his hands moved between them, and Mav released the button on his jean before lowering the zipper. "Are you on birth control, Princess?"

He wasn't asking permission to keep going, but that was the point where she could have told him to stop. Should have told him no. "Y-yes," she managed to stammer. Natalia wasn't having sex very often, but she didn't trust a stranger to keep her safe. She always insisted on condoms as an added layer of protection. But she trusted Maveryck. She knew he wouldn't do anything to put her at risk.

With his erection freed from his jeans, Maveryck slid it against her sleep shorts. Natalia gasped as she felt something different. When she looked down, there was a large piercing threaded through the end of Maveryck's cockhead. *Wow.* The thin barrier of her shorts was the only thing keeping him from entering her. He rubbed back and forth against her clit, and her shorts were getting wetter with each slide of metal. She tried to push her shorts down her legs, eager to have him inside her, eager to see how the piercing felt, but her position made it impossible. Maveryck growled low in his throat, and he leaned back, releasing the claws of one hand to shred her shorts. He ripped the material away from her body, and in one fluid motion, his hard cock entered her wet heat.

"Oh, god," she moaned. Maveryck wasn't huge, but he was larger than any of the men she'd been with or the toys she played with. The real thing was so much better. Mav rocked his hips, filling her, then slid almost all the way out before slamming back in. All Natalia could do was hold on.

"Fuck, Princess. I've never..." Retreat, slam. "Felt anything..." Retreat, slam "So fucking good." Retreat, slam. "It's like you were made just for me." Retreat, slam.

Natalia's slickness made it easy for Maveryck to slide in and out, and the harder he gave it to her, the more she wanted.

"Please," she begged.

"What do you need, baby?"

"More. Harder," she begged.

Maveryck wrapped his arms around her back, his cock buried deep, and walked them over to the bed. He placed her gently on the edge and pushed her calves over his shoulders. "Hang on, Princess." Maveryck gave her what she asked for. He kept his eyes on hers. The tingles started soon after he laid her down, and she fisted the bedding beside her hips as she used her ankles to dig into his shoulders, meeting him thrust for thrust.

"Mav... oh... god... Mav!" She gasped when her orgasm tore through her core, her channel gripping him tight as she pulsed through her release, her eyes squeezed tight.

"Look at me," he demanded. When she did as commanded, Mav's lion was in his eyes, and his sharp teeth dug into his bottom lip as he pumped into her, grinding his groin against her mound. The friction against her clit had her coming again.

Maveryck gritted his teeth. Veins pulsed, pushing at the taut skin of his straining neck, and a guttural cry left his throat as he found his release, spilling his seed inside her. He shortened his strokes with each pulse of cum he pumped into her body. Natalia had never seen anything more exotic. Had never felt anything as powerful as Maveryck Lazlo making love to her.

His harsh breath mingled with hers as he brushed his beard against her cheek and nuzzled her neck. Her previous question came back to her as he released her legs and lowered his body so they were chest-to-chest. *Would it be so bad if she gave in to her lust?* Yes. Now that she knew what being with Maveryck was like, she would never be able to give her body to anyone else without remembering what just happened. Natalia would never be able to give her body to another man, because Maveryck now owned it.

Chapter Twenty-Three

Maveryck

Maveryck hadn't planned to have sex. When he went upstairs, he only wanted to make sure Natalia was okay after the day she'd had. But his Gryphon had other ideas when she came out of the bathroom in her barely-there sleep shorts. He had to taste her, so he kissed her, but when she sucked on his tongue, his plan to talk went out the fucking window. When she writhed against his dick and he scented her arousal, all rational thought was gone. If he never got to touch her again, he had to have her in that moment.

When their breathing returned to normal, Mav slid down her body, pushing her thighs apart, and licked at her folds. Natalia gasped, grabbing for his hair. As he lapped up every bit of wetness, she writhed against his face. It wasn't his intention to bring her to orgasm again, but it didn't take long once he focused on her clit. Natalia rode his face, and Maveryck licked and sucked, giving her no quarter. He had no idea if they had more than one night together, and he was going to make the most of it. When her body convulsed, Mav shoved two fingers in her slick pussy, massaging the top of the entrance where one of her pleasure buttons was. Her head was rocking back and forth as she muttered incoherently.

He removed his fingers, sucking them dry. His spend was mixed with her juices, and it was the best thing he'd ever tasted in his life. His beard was soaked. Mav placed soft kisses to the insides of her thighs. One side then the other, until she relaxed her hands at her sides. He kissed his way up her flat stomach, stopping to lick inside her cute belly button, and when she giggled, he smiled against her skin. He didn't put his mouth to her breasts because he wanted them to come down from their high. When he reached her face, he looked into her eyes. Eyes that were bright. Not with tears, but something else. Something he refused to hope for.

Mav picked his Princess up and took her into his bathroom. He held her close as he started the shower, and as soon as the water was warm, he stepped under the spray sideways so it rained down on them both. He turned his face toward the water to rinse his beard, but Natalia grabbed his jaw, turning it back toward her. When she leaned in and sucked at the strands, he just about came again, right then and there. His Princess liked his beard. He already knew that, but having her suck their juices from it? That was something he'd be jerking off to for years to come.

She released his whiskers and found his lips. As much as Mav wanted to make love all night, he needed to hold her more. He slowed their kisses before setting her on her feet. They washed the evidence of their lovemaking from each other, and then took turns drying the other off. When they returned to the bedroom, he set her on the edge of the bed and picked up her T-shirt, sliding it over her head. He grabbed a pair of briefs and put them on. "I'll be right back." Mav went into the guest room and dug through her bag until he found another pair of shorts. Before returning to his room, he checked on the twins. Thankfully, they were still asleep, because in his haste to have Natalia, he'd forgotten to lock the door.

He helped her into her shorts and pulled back the covers. Mav turned out the light and slid into the bed, pulling Natalia down next to him, wrapping an arm around her shoulder. She rested her cheek against his heart and drew circles on the smattering of hair between his pecs.

Neither one said anything for a few minutes. He was afraid of what she would say if she found her voice. He didn't want what just happened to be a one-off, but with her silent retreat earlier, he didn't know if Natalia felt the same way he did. When thirty more minutes passed and she was still quiet, he thought maybe nothing needed to be said. Maveryck pressed a kiss to her damp hair before closing his eyes. Once again, he sent up a prayer to Zeus. First thanking him for his boys, then thanking him for bringing Natalia to the three of them. Just before sleep claimed him, Natalia pressed her lips to his skin and snuggled closer.

THE MORNING HAD not gone like Maveryck expected. First, he'd woken up alone. It not only bothered him that Natalia had slipped out of bed at some point during the night, but he hadn't woken when she did. When he went downstairs to start coffee, she was already dressed and sitting on the patio with a cup cradled between her hands. The twins were dressed and running around the backyard. He poured his own cup before joining them.

When he stepped outside, she glanced up at him, smiling, but it didn't reach her eyes. Was she regretting the night before?

"Daddo!" Major yelled. Maveryck couldn't help but smile at his son. Both boys were so full of life, but Major ran at full throttle twenty-four seven.

"Morning, Buddy." Maveryck took the seat next to Natalia. "Y'all been up long?"

"About an hour. The boys were hungry, but since I didn't want to traumatize them with my cooking, I gave them cereal."

Maveryck hated the defeat in her voice. "I love cereal. Always have. Especially the kinds with marshmallows. Did you eat?"

Without looking at him, she nodded. "They insisted."

"Natalia—"

"What time are we expected at the clubhouse?"

"Natalia," he tried again.

"Don't, okay?" She finally looked at him. "Last night was wonderful, but let's concentrate on getting my cousins taken care of, yeah?"

Maveryck didn't understand. Here he was, hoping to have her in his life, but she obviously had other ideas. Things had been tense after that. Other than talking to the twins, Natalia hadn't spoken one word. He thought maybe he'd hurt her during sex, but she said it had been wonderful, so he was at a loss as to why she'd basically ghosted him in his own home. Now, they were sitting at the oak table in the clubhouse after dropping the twins off at his parents', and she still wouldn't meet his eyes.

After introducing her to the Hounds she hadn't met, the seven of them sat down to hash out their plan for that night. It was odd having a female sitting in the room where the Hounds held church. Rory often came by, but she was never allowed to sit in on their meetings since she wasn't technically a member of the MC. Not even Lucy sat in the meetings with them. She called in from her home office and would remotely take over the computer while she was on speakerphone, which she was currently doing.

It took a couple of hours before they all decided on a course of action. Digger had called and let Ryker know the cousins were at the estate, and he was going to stay there to keep watch. Ryker was in charge, but Natalia challenged him on several issues. Maveryck knew they both made good points, and as much as he wanted to side with Natalia, he didn't know if they had a future. Ryker was not only his brother but also his Pres, and Mav couldn't challenge his

215

authority for a woman he might not see after tonight. So, he sat quietly while the two of them hashed things out. Several times, Natalia looked to Maveryck for help, but he kept his face turned toward the opposite wall. He could feel her frustration, but there was nothing he could do to help without completely pissing off his older brother.

When they had a solid plan in place and the meeting was adjourned, Lucy told Mav to call her before she disconnected from the conference call. Natalia had excused herself to the restroom, so he stepped outside and called his niece.

"Hey Luce. What's up?"

"That's what I want to know. Why didn't you speak up when Ryker was talking over Natalia? I know you had to have your own opinions about tonight."

"You know how these things work. Ryker is President."

"But this isn't club business. This is personal. How mad is she?"

Mav sighed and ran a hand down his face. "I don't know. She's in the bathroom."

"Oh, she's pissed then. You need to talk to her and explain why you didn't argue on her behalf."

"She's not going to be around long enough for it to matter." Gravel crunching behind Maveryck had him turning around. When he did, there was no one there.

"What makes you think that?" Lucy asked.

"Just something Natalia said this morning." Mav wasn't going to discuss his sex life with his niece, no matter how old she was. "I don't think she wants to be with me."

"Listen, I don't want to betray Natalia's trust, but she doesn't think she's good enough for you and the boys. You know how she was raised. She doesn't think she has anything to offer you. So, I don't know, maybe try to reassure her how you feel. You *do* want her to stay, right?"

"Yeah, I do. And like I told her, I'll follow her wherever she goes and bring her home. Listen, I need to go find her and apologize. Thanks, Luce."

216

"Good luck."

Maveryck looked inside first, and when he didn't see Natalia, he headed out back. When he caught up to her, she was standing with Hayden.

"Natalia," he said, but she ignored him.

"I need to go shopping, and since I don't have a car, I'd like for you to take me," she said to Hayden.

Hayden looked at Maveryck over her shoulder, his eyebrows raised. Mav shook his head, and Hayden gave Natalia one of his flirty smiles. "No can do, Lollipop. I have a couple bikes I need to work on this morning. But my big brother isn't doing anything right now. I'm sure he would love to take you shopping." Hayden walked off, but not before scowling at Maveryck. Why was everyone pissed at him?

"Come on, Princess. There's something I need to talk to you about. We can chat while we're driving." Natalia glared at him, but she followed him to the SUV. When he went to help her get in, she ignored his hand. Maveryck sent a prayer to Zeus for patience as well as the right thing to say. "Where are we going?" he asked once he was seated.

"The army surplus store over on Madison." Natalia was leaning against the door, looking out the window.

"I'm sorry I didn't back you up in there."

"Why didn't you?" she asked, still not looking at him.

"Ryker is my President. When we're sitting at that table, he's ultimately in charge. I realize now what we were discussing wasn't Club business, and I should have offered my opinion. I should have had your back."

Natalia waved her hand in the air. "It really doesn't matter. I'm not your mate. I'm just someone who was supposed to kill you, not..." The sadness in her voice said it did matter.

"Not what?"

"Forget it. Like I said, it doesn't matter." Her voice was soft. Too soft. He had been around enough women in his life

217

to know she was probably fighting back tears. He couldn't handle tears, especially if he was the cause of them.

"Did I hurt you last night? Is that why I woke up alone?" Mav hadn't planned on bringing up sex, but he had to know why she wasn't cuddled up to him when he woke. Was that something she didn't like doing?

"What? No, you didn't hurt me. I already told you it was wonderful. But we didn't discuss sleeping arrangements, and I didn't want the boys to walk in on us if that was something you weren't ready for. After I got dressed, I heard them talking and giggling, so I took them downstairs with me."

The store where Natalia wanted to shop was close to the clubhouse, so it only took a few minutes to get there. When he put the SUV in park, she said, "I won't be long."

Maveryck didn't let her dismissal sway him from following her inside. She'd been shot at the day before. There was no way he was letting her out of his sight. He fully expected his Princess to take her time. He had been shopping with Jenna, and by the time she'd looked at everything and tried on so many clothes she never bought, he was ready to gouge his eyes out. But Natalia was like a machine. She had obviously been in this store before, because she walked directly to the clothes she wanted and rifled through them to find her size.

Tactical pants, T-shirts, socks, boots, holsters, sheaths, knit caps, and gloves, all in black, found their way into Mav's arms as she grabbed several of each item except for the boots. When Natalia was finished, she walked to the counter and opened her purse. When she pulled out a roll of cash, Maveryck wanted to grab her hand and shove it back in. "I'll pay," he said.

"But it's my gear," Natalia countered.

"Yes, but—"

"I've got this," she insisted. Maveryck dropped the items on the counter, deciding it was better to let her pay than make her any madder than she already was. The

218

cashier's eyes were laughing. If he thought it odd that Natalia, who looked like she should be perusing the racks at a high-end fashion boutique instead of getting geared up for a covert mission, was shopping in this particular store, he didn't say anything. He didn't bat an eye when he rang up the two different types of gun holsters or the sheath for Natalia to hide her knife. Or knives. He didn't know how many she had.

After paying, Natalia picked up two of the bags, leaving the rest for Mav. Before he could walk away, the cashier asked, "Man, does she have a sister?"

Mav grinned. "No, I'm afraid not."

"You've got yourself a good one."

Mav didn't correct the man. He just inclined his head and hurried outside, not wanting Natalia to wait outside the car. He hoped the cashier was right. He wanted Natalia to be his. Now, to convince her.

He pressed the unlock button on his key fob and opened the back door. After the packages were secure in the cargo section and they were seated, he asked, "Are you hungry? I'm hungry."

"I could eat." Once again, she was staring out the side window.

"Is there anything you're allergic to or don't particularly care for?"

"Not really. I mean, I'm not allergic, but I'll eat just about anything."

"Excellent. One of the Hound's wives owns a little Mexican restaurant. Most of us eat there at least once a week, sometimes twice. Not only are we supporting a fellow Hound, but the food is delicious." What Maveryck didn't tell Natalia was the building was secure with bulletproof glass. Maveryck also hadn't told her they had two Hounds following in an SUV. She would know soon enough, because when he parked right in the front door, Tank pulled in beside them. He and Ripper got out of their vehicle and followed

219

Mav and Natalia. Once they were inside, Mav introduced them.

Tank's wife, Martina, walked out of the kitchen, and Tank's face lit up. "Come here, *Mamacita*." Martina was eight-months pregnant with their second child, and when she reached the big Hound, he dropped to his knees, cradling her round belly, and spoke softly to the baby inside. It was something he did every single time they came to eat there, and it always made Maveryck smile. Martina was shorter than Natalia, and Tank was a couple inches taller than Mav. She was Latina, and he was a pale-skinned redhead, but somehow, they matched each other perfectly.

"Who do we have here?" Martina asked Mav, looking at Natalia.

"This is Natalia. Natalia, this is Martina, Tank's better half."

Martina smacked Tank on the shoulder. "Let me say hello, you big goof." Martina's family was originally from South America, but she and her siblings had all been born in Texas, where she met Patrick "Tank" Murphy. People didn't expect a southern drawl to come out of her mouth when she spoke. When Tank stood, Martina stepped forward and grabbed both of Natalia's hands. "Well, aren't you just the prettiest thing? Come, sit down. Tank, go tell Donny to get his butt out here and wait on us. Me and Miss Natalia need to get acquainted."

Natalia looked over her shoulder at Maveryck, her eyes wide. Mav just shrugged and grinned, because if there was one person in the world who got whatever she wanted, it was Martina Murphy.

CHAPTER TWENTY-FOUR

Natalia

NATALIA HAD NEVER laughed so much. As she pulled on her new boots getting ready to head toward her old home, she smiled, thinking about Martina and the way she made Natalia feel like they'd been friends forever. Martina's life hadn't been an easy one. The young woman had lost her parents when she was seventeen, having to do whatever it took to keep her and her siblings together. She didn't hesitate to tell Natalia everything, and that included selling her body to buy food. She struggled until she met her Gryphon. Martina had propositioned a handsome cop, not knowing what he was, and instead of tossing her in jail, he took her home with him, fell in love, and married her.

Martina made Natalia forget about what was going on in her own life, and it had felt good. It also gave her a lot to think about. Being around Maveryck and everyone he'd introduced her to had shown her what was missing in her life. Friends. Family. Laughter. Love. It made Natalia's chest pinch when she thought about leaving all those things behind.

When she woke in the middle of the night being spooned from behind, Natalia had wanted to stay there forever. She'd wanted to roll over and kiss Maveryck awake, begging him to make love to her again. When Natalia remembered the twins were across the hall, she made herself get up and go back to the guest room.

Not being able to cook a good breakfast for the boys hadn't set well with her, but she assumed if Mav had cereal in the house, it was okay to feed it to them. When he told her he loved cereal, she thought it was his way of telling her it was okay she didn't cook. He had offered to teach her, and she was more than willing to learn. She wasn't one to feel sorry for herself. Natalia figured out a long time ago if she wanted to learn something, she could. Like speaking Russian. So why not cooking?

But she'd overheard Mav on the phone saying she wasn't going to be around long enough for anything to matter, so learning to cook was no longer important. He couldn't have hurt her worse if he'd used his claws to reach into her chest and pull her heart out.

Natalia did her best to forget about her future, or lack of one, with Maveryck as she adjusted the straps on one of her new holsters before sliding it over her shoulders. Since she didn't know what they were going to encounter later, she opted for the one which held two guns. She had already wrapped the knife sheaths around her thighs. They were going in after dark, so Natalia didn't feel the need to hide her blades in her boots or under long sleeves. Plus, having them on her legs gave her quicker access.

Last, she grabbed one of the knit caps and pulled it down over her hair. She didn't bother looking in the mirror. Natalia already knew what she looked like decked out to blend in with the darkness. She wasn't looking forward to the four-hour drive, but she was ready to get the night over with. Mikael had underestimated her, and tonight, she was going to show him he screwed with the wrong Volkov.

Natalia bypassed the twins' room without looking in as she made her way downstairs. When she walked into the living room, several sets of eyes stared at her. Most of the Hounds gawked at her appearance, seemingly surprised, because Ace muttered, "Holy shit," and Hayden said, "Bad.

Ass." But one set – Mav's – gave her goosebumps while setting her on fire. If they had been alone, she had a feeling he would have removed every stitch of black from her body and taken her back upstairs. She shivered at his intense gaze, and when Ryker cleared his throat, Natalia found her feet. Instead of saying anything, she strode out to the garage to her weapons cabinet.

She grabbed the rifle case and set it aside, then she chose two 9mm Sig Sauers and slid them into the holster. She had several knives to choose from, but she picked up her favorites, spinning them in her hands before sliding them home in the sheaths on her thighs. The double-edged Shaitans were larger than most of the other knives in her arsenal, but these were the best-balanced for throwing. She opened the drawer at the bottom of the cabinet and loaded her black duffel with more ammo than she would need, but Natalia liked to be prepared.

She closed the cabinet, making sure it locked, then picked up her case and duffel. When she turned around, those same six sets of eyes were staring at her again. "Where are your weapons?" she asked.

"Lolly, we are the weapons," Hayden crowed, grinning.

Maveryck shoved his brother. "They're already loaded. Here, let me take those." He added her things to whatever they had in the vehicle. Since there were seven of them, Maveryck and Natalia slid into the back seat of his SUV with Hayden driving and Rev riding shotgun. Ace, King, and Ryker got into the other vehicle. Natalia didn't see who was driving. She figured it would be Ryker, since he liked to be in charge of everything.

"You nervous, Lollipop?" Hayden asked after they got on the road.

"Yes," she admitted. Sitting beside Maveryck in the dark back seat was both exhilarating and heartbreaking. She was confused as to why he could say she wouldn't be sticking around then look at her like she was his favorite

223

dessert he wanted to devour. So, yes, she was nervous, and it had everything to do with the male sitting next to her with his powerful thigh pressed to her smaller one. His arm was spread across the back of the seat, and she had to remind herself not to lean her head back and use it as a cushion.

"Really? I thought a badass like you would be all calm and collected."

"Usually I am, but I'm used to working alone. I don't have to worry about anyone other than myself. I know my job. I get in, get out. Tonight, I'm going to be worried about all of you getting hurt."

Mav reached over and took her hand in his. "You do realize this is what we do for a living, right? You're not the only one who knows how to get in and out without getting hurt."

"I didn't say my nervousness was logical; I merely spoke the truth."

"What's your ritual, you know, to get in the zone? Do you have a playlist to get you pumped?" Hayden asked. The younger Lazlo, Natalia found, rarely stopped talking. It was a blessing in that she didn't have to come up with something to talk about, but he asked questions she didn't always want to answer. This one, she didn't mind.

"No playlist. I'm more of a Zen person before a job. I sit somewhere quiet and find my center, going over what I'm about to do in my mind. I try to see every possible outcome and prepare for it."

"Huh. I might need to try that. Ryker says I talk too much."

"No, not you," Rev joked.

"What about you?" Natalia turned and looked up at Mav. "Do you have a pre-slash ritual?"

"Pre-slash?" Mav smirked, letting his hand drop down to her shoulder. He rubbed circles against the cotton of her T-shirt. "I take my bike to a lot of jobs, so I guess the ride is my ritual. The rumble of the motor beneath me teamed with the wind in my face; that's my Zen."

Rev nodded in the front seat. "Same here, Brother. Nothing better than the open road other than shifting and soaring above the trees."

"That makes sense considering you're an air Gryphon. Me being an earth Gryphon, I prefer padding through the woods in my Lion," Mav said.

"What does that mean exactly? Being an earth or an air Gryphon?" Natalia asked.

"Gryphons take on one of the four elements. The element dictates the color of our eagle's wings and the power we have. I can manipulate anything on the ground, like dirt or rocks. Rev being an air Gryphon can manipulate the wind. Hayden's a water Gryphon, and you get the picture."

"Can I ask you something?"

"Of course." Maveryck turned a little, giving Natalia his full attention.

"Your parents look young, but they have to be a lot older than you since you have so many siblings. How old are they?"

Maveryck grinned. "Pop is one hundred and five. Rory is two years younger. My sisters are in their eighties. Pop wanted boys, but they kept popping out sets of girl twins. After Dahlia and Iris were born, he gave up. Then Rory unexpectedly got pregnant with Ryker, and they kept going until Hayden was born."

"That was when Rory said 'enough,'" Hayden joked.

"He's not wrong." Mav laughed. "Gryphons can live two to three hundred years unless something happens, like getting shot. We don't succumb to human disease, but we aren't immortal."

Natalia chewed her bottom lip, curious about something, but not sure how to ask. Mav tugged her hand. "Ask whatever it is on your mind."

"What happens when you marry a human? You live so much longer than they do."

Maveryck's smile was sad. "We love them until they die, and we take all the memories into the rest of our days."

"That's..." Natalia turned away, not wanting him to see how the answer upset her.

"That's beautiful, is what it is," Rev said. "Even knowing I'll most likely outlive my Bethany, I wouldn't trade loving her for anything. Plus, I have my kids, and then I'll have grandkids, and so on. They'll help keep her memory alive."

When he put it like that, it *was* beautiful.

Natalia didn't ask any more questions. They were getting closer to the estate, and she needed to think about the job. While it wasn't technically a job, she had to treat it like one. Working with the Hounds was going to be a distraction, because she didn't want anything to happen to them. She and Ryker argued about who was going into the house, but she finally relented when he explained how they could get inside from upstairs, and she couldn't unless one of them carried her, and that would be risking too much.

They had agreed to only take out the guards if they had to. Same with Ivan and Viktor. Ryker offered to use his Gryphon voice on them, but after discussing it, Natalia said that would be crueler than killing them. These men didn't know any other life. If Ryker were to make them forget about who they were, they would have no way of making a living. Ryker argued it was no less than what they deserved for being on a mafia payroll. She asked if it was what she deserved, because she was no better than them.

It was Hayden who had spoken up on her behalf. He said she was forced into the life. Her father hadn't given her a choice, and now she was doing her part to make the world a better place. Hayden's words, Lucy's, Kerrigan's, and even Martina's, had given her a lot to think about. They had given her hope that maybe, just maybe, she was good enough to be in the twins' life. Then Maveryck went and shot it all down. So why, if he didn't want her to stick around, was he

226

touching her? Smiling at her like she mattered? Introducing her to his family and friends? Maveryck leaned over and pressed his lips to her temple, like he cared for her.

"We're here, Princess," he whispered against her ear.

Natalia didn't look at him. She got out of the SUV and strode around to the back. When Hayden released the hatch, Natalia grabbed the rifle case and her duffel, taking them around to the front where she sat both on the hood. The first thing she retrieved was a multi-threat vest. She rarely wore it considering she was usually in disguise, but tonight she wanted the extra protection. The vest was specially made to prevent both bullets as well as blades from piercing her skin. Her pants were designed to store extra ammo. Natalia chose four magazines for her pistols and slid two into the pockets on each side of her thighs.

Next, she opened her rifle case and assembled the weapon, adding the suppressor to the end. She popped the ten-round magazine into place then slipped the strap over her shoulder. Finally, Natalia removed two spare magazines, adding one to each utility pocket of her pants. She closed the case, zipped the duffel, and returned both to the back of the vehicle. Once again, the males stared at her, but she ignored them, except for the new male in the group. His perusal of her body wasn't one of intrigue. This male looked pissed.

"Digger, this is Natalia," Mav said, introducing them. Since he didn't give her the impression he was friendly, Natalia didn't offer her hand or say hello. They had a mile hike ahead of them, and she planned on using that time to get her head in the game, not worry about a stranger's perception of her.

"The cousins are in the house. There are three guards. No one has entered or exited the premises since last night," Digger said.

"Thank you. I would like for you to remain with the vehicles and keep your phone on in case we need you," Ryker instructed. The man inclined his head then held out his hand, palm up. Ryker passed him a set of keys before giving the male his back, looking toward the trees.

Maveryck stepped up beside Natalia and stared out into the darkness. "Princess, I know you can handle yourself, but promise me you'll be safe." He turned to face her and lifted her chin so she had to look at him. "I'm not ready to lose you," he whispered. She couldn't let her emotions get in the way of what she had to do, so she nodded once.

"Everyone ready?" Natalia left Maveryck standing there and walked past the rest of them. Since she knew where the tunnel was, she was leading the way with Hayden at her side. He had come to mean a lot to her in the last couple days, and she would do everything in her power to make sure the youngest Lazlo returned to his family unharmed.

It had been so many years since Natalia had been in the tunnel that she almost couldn't find the entrance. Once she did, Maveryck had to push the lever because it was stuck. Before she stepped inside, she addressed the Gryphons. "Please be careful, and do whatever you need, but don't forget – Mikael's mine." She looked at Maveryck one last time. She should have turned around, but nothing in life was guaranteed. Getting out of this night alive wasn't a sure thing. Natalia grabbed Maveryck's T-shirt and stretched up on her toes. "I'm not ready to lose you either," she whispered before pressing a soft kiss to the side of his mouth. Not waiting on his reaction, she turned and stepped inside. The flashlight illuminated a scant four-foot path. Considering she had a quarter of a mile to go, it did little to ease her nerves. It had been twenty years since she walked through the darkness. Twenty years since she'd felt loved. There was no love in this tunnel. Only the harsh sounds of breaths in an otherwise silent tomb. It was as sinister as she remembered.

Hayden joined her, and just as Ryker pushed the door back into place, the Hound's lion was front and center in his eyes. She assumed the animal's night vision allowed him to see without the need of a flashlight, but she didn't have that luxury. They trekked the quarter mile in silence, having already planned what they were doing on the other end. When they reached the door that opened onto Volkov property, Hayden placed his hand on the lever and whispered, "Ready?"

Natalia turned off her flashlight and set it on the ground. She took a deep breath, pulled both her Sigs from the holster, and flipped off the safeties. "Ready." Hayden pressed down on the lever and slid the door open. Natalia took a deep breath and stepped outside. The night was inky, with the moon giving a soft glow to the area around her, but it wasn't nearly as dark as the tunnel had been.

Before she could fully get her bearings, bullets sprayed the stone wall beside Natalia's head. She squatted, raising both guns, firing in an arc. One body fell, but more bullets sprayed the ground around her. Natalia ran as fast as her short legs would take her, shooting in the direction the bullets had come from. She dove behind a tree, rolling to her knees with her guns up. That was easier said than done with a rifle hanging around her chest. More bullets were fired, and bark from the tree exploded, some hitting her in the face. Natalia fired several shots in the general direction she guessed the shooter to be. She paused, and as soon as the man came out of hiding, she put a bullet between his eyes. Natalia turned to check on Hayden, praying he was within the safety of the tunnel. She caught sight of Ivan and Viktor, and she aimed her pistols at their heads.

"Ah, Ah, Ah," Viktor taunted, pointing to her right. She was too late.

"Hello, Tatiana." Mikael had a gun pressed against Hayden's temple.

"I'm sorry, Lolly." Hayden's eyes were filled with both sadness and anger.

"Shut up," Mikael growled, hitting Hayden's temple with the butt of his gun. Hayden growled back, his lion threatening to break through. Natalia knew if the Hound shifted, he wouldn't be fast enough. Hayden wouldn't be able to attack Mikael before her cousin could shoot him.

Debris danced at her feet when a shot rang out. Natalia jumped back, spreading her Sigs out, searching to see which one of her cousins had a death wish. She should have known. Viktor was laughing. "Payback's a bitch."

"You're laughing now, Viktor. But when I put a bullet in your head..." Natalia shrugged, turning her attention back to Mikael.

"Big words for such a little girl. It seems your tutor forgot to teach you how to count. In case you haven't noticed, you're outnumbered."

Maveryck would come for her as soon as he realized her cousins weren't in the house. Natalia needed to buy him some time. He would come for her. He would make sure they got out of this shit alive. And when he did, Natalia was going to do whatever it took to have a future with him and the twins.

CHAPTER TWENTY-FIVE

Maveryck

NATALIA'S WORDS GAVE Maveryck hope for a future together. Why she thought she wasn't good enough for him and the twins didn't make sense. Natalia was fierce, she was kind, and she loved with her whole heart. He knew that by watching her with the boys. He knew she felt lacking because she couldn't cook, but she wasn't the only woman who wasn't an expert in the kitchen. There was so much more to being a good partner and mother figure than making a five-course meal. He had judged her when he first met her, thinking she didn't need to be around the boys because she was an assassin, but he had been mistaken. He didn't want her to be a step-anything. He wanted Natalia to be a full-time mother to the boys. A full-time partner with him.

"Where's your head, Mayhem?" Ryker asked.

"Wondering what the fuck is up with Digger," he said. It wasn't exactly a lie. He had been thinking about what came next with Natalia after they took out her cousins, but he hadn't missed the way the Hound scowled at Natalia.

"I noticed that too. Maybe he has a thing against Russians."

"Natalia was born here in the States. She's as American as you and me."

"Yeah, but she was raised by a notorious Russian

mobster. Some prejudices run deep."

"Well, he can get over it." Mav was leading the way to where he shifted when he took out Anatoly. The plan they discussed with Natalia was to leave the guards alive if possible, but Ryker had a different idea in mind. It was one reason Mav was glad Natalia was going to be watching from the woods instead of being in the middle of a firefight in the house. The Gryphons didn't carry weapons, since they were the weapon.

Maveryck stopped. "We'll shift here." He and the four other Hounds removed their clothes and stored them in the bags. Once they were all in eagle form, he launched into the trees with the others following. They stopped several times, scoping out their surroundings. When Maveryck felt it was safe, he continued toward the house. As per the plan, he and Rev landed on the rooftop first, while the others watched from a nearby perch. Mav intended to enter the house through Natalia's old bedroom like he'd done before. He shifted, keeping close to the floor of the roof. After putting his clothes back on, he lowered himself to the window, placing his feet against the rough stones for purchase. When he got the window raised, he pulled himself inside once he made sure the room was empty.

He whispered to Rev to do the same. When the other Hound was safely inside, Mav motioned for the other three to follow. While he and Rev waited, Mav noticed the room had been completely emptied of anything of Natalia's. Her wildflower scent no longer filled the air. When all five men were dressed and ready to move, Mav eased the door open and listened. They spread out, checking each of the rooms on the third floor. Finding them all empty, they kept to the edge of the carpet against the wall until they reached the top of the stairs.

The air was still. Too still. Mav's Gryphon was vibrating to be released.

Something's wrong.

232

Yeah, I feel it too.

Mav looked at his brother and raised his eyebrows. Ryker nodded. He also sensed it. Silently, they eased down the steps, and when they reached the second floor, Ryker gave the hand signal to spread out. They checked every room, not finding anyone.

"Where is everyone?" Ace whispered.

"Let's keep going," Ryker responded.

Mav had a sinking feeling they weren't going to find the cousins downstairs. He was right. After searching the lowest level, no one was inside. Not even the housekeeper. Mav's Gryphon was getting harder to control.

We need to get to Natalia.

Hayden's with her.

Hayden's not her fucking mate.

Mav agreed, but he couldn't take off running out the door. He would be a sitting duck, and then it wouldn't matter whether or not they were meant to be together. The boys would lose their father, and he could not let that happen. He had pulled War aside and asked that he and Kerrigan look after the boys should something happen to him, but it wasn't in writing. Until that happened, Rory would try to take over. Mav loved his mother, but he would rather his twins be raised by his own twin.

When they reconvened in the den, Ace, Rev, and King reported there were guards standing just outside the exterior doors. Where were the fucking cousins? Digger said they were in the house when he left. But it took approximately fifteen minutes to get from the house to where the SUVs were parked. Plenty of time for them to head outside and go where? Shit, the tunnel. Just because Natalia didn't think her father shared its existence didn't mean he hadn't or that Mikael had somehow discovered it at some point.

"Don't kill them all. We might need answers," Mav instructed.

Maveryck and Ryker stood watch while Rev, Ace, and

233

King used their lions' stealth to sneak up on each of the guards. Mav had his eye on Ace as he eased open the door. Wrapping a large arm around the man's neck, the Hound subdued the guard, keeping a hand over his mouth as he instructed the guard to stand down. Stronger minds often fought the voice, but this one complied instantly. Mav headed to the side door where Rev's guard was struggling. The man fired his handgun wildly until Rev snapped his neck. King dragged his guard inside and dumped his body beside the dead one.

"He's alive, just unconscious."

They had two alive, and that was enough. Ryker retrieved the gun from the dead guard, picking it up with a gloved hand. The weapon had a silencer screwed to the end, so the soft *pftt* when it fired hadn't been loud enough to alert someone outside.

Ryker extended his talons and grabbed one of the guards around his throat. "Tell me where Mikael is."

With blank eyes, the man responded to the shifter command. "At the tunnel."

"Fuck!" Maveryck took off running upstairs with Rev on his heels. They were stripping as they went. As soon as he reached the open window, Mav shifted and launched himself into the sky. Shots rang out and Mav didn't try to keep his Gryphon contained. For the first time in four years, Mav unleashed the beast. It was harder to shift midair, but he was determined to get to Natalia and Hayden before anything happened to either one of them.

The Gryphon took over, headed for the ground. Mav tried to keep them in flight, but the beast was too strong.

We will be no good to them if we get shot out of the sky.

Mav wanted to argue, but he wasn't thinking straight. His heart was in his throat. He had just found Natalia. No way was he going to lose her now.

The Gryphon shifted into the lion, and Mav yelled at it.

No! She needs the Gryphon!

And we need the element of surprise. Trust me.

Mav did trust his beast. Usually. But this was his love. His mate. More shots rang out. They were coming from a handgun, not Natalia's rifle. That wasn't good. When the lion stopped running, Mav's blood ran cold at the scene before him. Mikael was holding Hayden's arm with one hand, the other held a pistol pointed at his head. There was blood running down Hayden's face, but he wasn't harmed beyond that. No, he was pissed.

Natalia had both her guns pointed at her other cousins, arms stretched out to her sides. Ivan and Viktor had their guns pointed at her in a standoff. The lion scented blood, and Maveryck looked around to see where it was coming from. Two guards were down, multiple shots to each of them.

"You are a disgrace, Tatiana. You had one job – to kill your father's assassin. But instead, you get into bed with him."

Natalia met his lion's eyes. They were filled with fire. "You do not understand how being an assassin works, Cousin. Sometimes you have to play with your food before you eat it."

"Just kill the *blyad'* and be done with her!" Viktor yelled, spit assaulting the air in front of him. Oh, Maveryck was going to play with his food all right.

"You'll be dealt with soon enough." Natalia didn't look at Maveryck when she spoke, but he knew her words were for him. "Have you ever seen a lion in the wild? Sometimes it just pounces, but other times it calls on the elements."

Maveryck shifted back to human so he could do as she suggested. His lion could use the earth, but not as well as when he was in human form. Maveryck held out his hands and called on the earth to rumble. When small tornados began swirling around Ivan and Viktor, Mav knew Rev was calling on the air to help. Mav added dirt and debris to Rev's wind, keeping the brothers' attention occupied.

As Viktor and Ivan were frantically looking around trying to figure out what was going on, Mikael yelled, "Where is Maveryck Lazlo?"

"Right behind you." When Mikael turned to look back, Natalia yelled, "Hayden, shift!"

Hayden didn't hesitate to do as she said. His lion came forth and crouched low to the ground. Natalia shot Mikael and Ivan at the same time. Mav ran at Viktor, shifting mid-leap, and his lion pounced on Viktor, latching onto his gun hand. The Russian screamed, but Mav didn't let it distract him. Rev ran to check on Ivan, while Natalia and Hayden, who had transformed back to his human, kept an eye on Mikael.

"He's dead," Rev announced. Mav's Gryphon bristled at the male being naked around their mate, but Mav wasn't worried. She was his mate, and she was going to see the others shift from time to time. He had to get used to it.

"Tatiana... what...? What the hell is happening?" Mikael's eyes were wide. His shoulder was bleeding where she shot him, and the front of his pants were wet where he pissed himself.

"I will tell you what the hell is happening, Cousin. You put a hit out on me after you put a hit out on Maveryck. When we didn't take each other out, you burned my house down. Shot at me. You missed."

"Fire... what... I didn't burn down your house." Mikael licked his lips, glancing around, his eyes wide. "What... that's a lion. Why is there a lion here? And why are these men naked?"

"Don't worry about them. Hayden, please tell Mikael to speak the truth," Natalia requested, never taking her eyes nor her guns off her cousin. She was asking Hayden to use his shifter voice on Mikael.

"Mikael, tell us everything you have done since you kicked Natalia out of her home."

"Who's Natalia? Tatiana, what's he talking about?"

236

"I'm Natalia. It's not like you didn't know that." Natalia raised both pistols, aiming them at Mikael's head. "I believe he gave you an order."

Mikael held his hand against his shoulder, trying to stop the bleeding. "I waited for you to find Anatoly's killer and take him out. I couldn't contact you, because you disappeared. Someone sent me a file about a month after that. It named Maveryck Lazlo as the killer and gave me the name of someone to contact to take a hit out on him. I sent Ivan and Viktor to find him. Why spend a quarter million when we could kill him ourselves? But they couldn't find him, so I contacted someone called Oz. I don't know if they're a man or woman. Their voice was distorted."

"Did you take a contract out on me?" Natalia asked.

Mikael shook his head. "Tatiana, please…"

"Answer the question," Hayden demanded. "Truthfully."

"They sent me pictures of the two of you together. You, Lazlo, and two kids."

Maveryck's lion roared, releasing Viktor. When Viktor tried to grab his gun with the hand that wasn't mangled, Natalia shot him in the chest. If he didn't die instantly, it would only be a matter of time until he bled out. Trusting Maveryck to watch Viktor, Natalia turned and shot Mikael in the knee, sending him to the ground. "Owww, fuck!" Mikael panted through the pain, and tears rolled down his face.

"Did you take out a contract on me? I'm not going to ask you again!"

"Yes! Fuck, yes. But—" A bullet hit Mikael in the center of his forehead, and he slumped to the ground.

"You crazy fucking bit—!" Natalia silenced Viktor with one final shot.

She slid both pistols into the holster. "Who is this Oz?" Natalia asked Maveryck as soon as he shifted back to his human form.

"My guess is someone from Nexus. We need to get

237

Ryker and the others. I need to get back to the cars and call my parents. The boys..." Maveryck couldn't get the words out.

"Ryker's here, Brother." Hayden pointed to the sky. Three large eagles flew over the trees and landed several feet away, shifting into their humans.

"It's Digger. Motherfucker sold you out!" Ryker yelled. "I'm going to kill him."

"The boys!" Natalia yelled. "You have to warn your parents. Go. Use the phone in the house."

"I'll go call Sutton and warn him. The rest of you get to the SUVs. I doubt Digger stuck around. If he didn't, he has at least an hour head start. Maveryck, call Lucy and get her to charter a flight. We need to get back home before Digger does. I'll gather our bags and bring them after I call Pop." Ryker shifted back to his eagle and took off.

"I'll hang back with Lolly. You all go ahead," Hayden offered.

"No. I'm not letting her out of my sight." Maveryck looked at Natalia and asked, "Do you trust me?"

"With my life."

"Good. Hop on." Maveryck shifted, turning the Gryphon loose.

CHAPTER TWENTY-SIX

Natalia

NATALIA HAD KNOWN Mav's Gryphon was going to be spectacular. This so-called mythical beast was real. Standing around ten feet tall, the majestic eagle head, wings, and front legs were blended seamlessly with the body, tail, and back legs of the lion. The black eyes blinked at her before it opened its mouth and squawked.

"Up you go, Lolly." Hayden helped her climb onto Mav's back, telling her to hold onto his feathers. She straddled his back as she would a horse, tucking her knees behind the massive wings. She didn't want to hurt him, but there wasn't anything else to grab onto, plus she didn't want to fall off. It was surreal. Not just riding a Gryphon, but all of it. Seeing the Hounds in their various animals. Killing her cousins. Finding out someone else at Nexus was at play in the whole thing. Knowing the boys were in trouble. The Gryphon's wings flapped, their feathers brushing against her knees, and within seconds, they were accelerating into the sky. She looked down just as Hayden and the other Hounds shifted into their eagles and took flight.

Hayden's wings were blue, where Rev's were solid white. The two others' wings were both a golden yellow. When she'd been talking to Mav's lion, she'd never been happier that he had explained about their elements on the ride there. If she hadn't known he could manipulate the

239

earth, they might not have been able to distract her cousins long enough to gain the upper hand.

At least this part was over. Now they had to figure out who the fuck Oz was, why Digger betrayed his own kind, and make sure the twins were safe. Natalia dug into Mav's feathers and leaned forward so she was lying against his back. As exhilarating as flying with his Gryphon was, she needed to be close to him more. "I'm through being an idiot," she muttered. The Gryphon squawked. She didn't know if Mav was fussing at her, telling her she wasn't an idiot, or if he was agreeing with her.

The SUVs came into view, and Natalia saw the flat tires. "Damnit!" As soon as Mav touched down, Natalia slid off his back and pulled her guns. She knew Mav and the Hounds didn't use guns, but if Digger wanted to take them out, shooting them would be the perfect way. He was outnumbered, but picking them off in their eagles would have been the perfect opportunity.

Mav and the others shifted into their humans, and all five males cursed the condition of their vehicles. Hayden dropped the bag he'd been carrying and dug the keys out, hitting the unlock button. He opened the door and retrieved his phone, tossing it to Maveryck. Hayden and the other Hounds walked around to the other side of the car, probably to hide their nudity. Not that she'd looked. None of them held a candle to her Mayhem.

Maveryck leaned his elbows on the hood of the SUV. "Tell me," he demanded.

"One of the guards admitted it was Digger who warned the cousins we were on our way. He didn't know why, just said the man was pissed at you, Natalia, the Hounds, and basically the world," Ace explained.

"Fuck!" Maveryck yelled into the air. He punched in a number on the phone and put it to his ear. "War, hey. Digger has lost his fucking mind! He warned Natalia's cousins we were coming... I don't know why... No, listen. He's

240

sabotaged our cars. He has a good hour head start. Ryker's already called Pop, and I was going to call Lucy to charter a jet, but we don't have a car."

"Yes, we do." Natalia placed her hand on Mav's arm. "There are at least three cars back at the estate."

Mav nodded. "Yeah, okay. That's good. We have transportation to the airport. I'm going to call Lucy, but War, I need you to get the boys. No, War. I know you want to be here, but I need you to take care of my sons. Take them somewhere... What? Fuck, that's perfect. Take Sutton and Rory with you. Kyllian too. Okay, thanks, Brother. I will. You too." Just as Mav disconnected, he grabbed Natalia's hand and pulled her behind the SUV. "What is it?" she asked.

"There's a car coming."

Instead of hiding, Natalia handed Mav her pistols. When he took them, she pulled the rifle over her shoulder and aimed it at the approaching car.

"Princess Badass, the Gryphon Rider," Hayden whispered. Natalia winked at him, and Maveryck growled. She knew Mav would have smacked his brother if his hands were empty.

A familiar face rolled down the window. "Don't shoot. It's me," Ryker yelled. When Mav and Natalia lowered their weapons, Ryker got out of the car, holding several bags of clothes from where they had stripped. He strode to the SUV and handed them out. The Hounds looked through the pouches, handing over the correct one to whoever it belonged to. While they got dressed, Ryker ran a hand through his brown hair. Where the twins and Hayden were blond like Rory, Ryker and Kyllian had darker hair like Sutton.

Natalia went to the back of the SUV, removed her vest, and broke down her rifle, storing it in the case. She took her pistols from Mav and put them in her holster. When she walked back to where the males were talking, she stood with her arms crossed over her chest, but Mav maneuvered her so she was standing in front of him. He settled his hands on her shoulders, massaging her neck with his thumbs. She bit the inside of her jaw to keep from moaning.

"What the ever-loving fuck is going on?" Mav asked Ryker.

"Have you called Lucy?"

"No. I just got off the phone with War. The boys' safety was my first priority."

"You know that's going to piss Rory off."

"I don't give a shit. Besides, I told War to take Sutton and Rory with him. Kyllian too."

Ryker stroked his beard. "Call Lucy, then we'll talk while we're on the way to the airport. Hayden, you're with us. The rest of you head back to the house. There're more vehicles to choose from. Take care of the men in the guard shack, if they haven't fled. Don't kill them; just instruct them to find another line of work in a different state. Afterwards, go home and protect your families. If any of you hear of something that'll help us figure out this shit with Digger, give me a call."

"If you head through the woods there between those two trees, there's a path that leads directly to the property," Natalia instructed. Rev and the other Hounds took off jogging through the trees. While Mav called Lucy and told her what they needed, Natalia walked to the back of the SUV. When she returned, she was carrying her case and duffel. Ryker took them from her and put them in the trunk of the car he'd commandeered.

Natalia leaned against the car, staring off into the woods. She had thought when her cousins were taken care of, things would be over. They would go home to the twins, and she would start on her plan to prove to Maveryck she was worthy of him and his sons. First, they had a rogue Hound to hunt down. When Mav hung up, he opened the back door for her. She removed her holster and sheaths before climbing in. She

242

placed them on the floorboard so she would have her weapons close, just in case. Mav levered himself into the back seat and buckled up.

Hayden turned around and looked at Natalia. "I'm really sorry, Natalia. I let you down."

"You did no such thing. I'm the one who didn't scope out the area before I charged out of the tunnel. We're both alive. That's all that matters."

"Can I just say I'm glad you're on our side?" Ryker asked, looking at Natalia through the rearview mirror. "I admit, I doubted your sincerity in the beginning. But you saved my baby brother's life. I'm in your debt."

Natalia pressed against Mav, placing her hand on his. "You help us keep the twins safe, and consider the debt paid." That was all she wanted from any of the Lazlos. Safety for the twins. Anything else wasn't necessary. She'd taken care of herself for so long, and the only one she wanted something from was Maveryck, and that was love.

Mav put his arm around her shoulder and kissed her temple. "Lucy's going to call back when she gets us a jet. She's also going to see if she can't get a location on Digger."

"That bastard's as good as dead," Hayden seethed.

"I agree. He's been distancing himself from the club for months now. I didn't question him whenever he said he needed time on his bike. We all have those moments when nothing but the open road will soothe the soul."

"It obviously didn't work. I haven't done anything to him for him to turn against me." Maveryck got quiet, and Natalia figured he was thinking about his relationship with Digger.

"While we're looking for your Hound, we need to also look into Nexus. Whatever is going on has something to do with them. I can feel it." Natalia's gut hadn't led her astray yet. Ryker didn't respond. Neither he nor Mav spoke the rest of the way to the airport. Hayden found a rock station on the radio and they all let the music fill the empty space.

Natalia had a feeling she was getting a glimpse into the lives of the Hounds. Granted, she was the one who shot at Maveryck, but he and the others took jobs all the time. This couldn't be the first close call they'd had, even if it was one of their own putting them at risk. Before she met the Gryphon and his boys, all she had to worry about was her cousins and herself. Now, she had a whole family she cared about. If she pursued a relationship with Mav, she would be bringing more danger to their door. But she could also be another line of defense standing guard. Gryphons weren't immune to guns, and if this Digger was coming after them, she would stand on the front line for all the Lazlos. She would protect Martina's Tank. She hadn't met the other mates, but Rev, Ace, and King had gone with her to fight her cousins, even though they didn't know Natalia. She would gladly repay these males, and in turn their women waiting at home by being the best guard to them she could be. Even if Mav decided he didn't want her as a mate, she silently vowed to protect them.

When they arrived at the airport, they boarded a small jet. Maveryck led Natalia to the plush leather seats in the back of the cabin. She had flown first class on a commercial plane, but she'd never flown on a private jet. Ryker and Hayden sat in the front, giving them what privacy they could. When they were in the air, Natalia asked, "Where are we going?"

"The cult we are hunting has a compound in New Basom. When we went in to take them down, they had fled. Lucy's still trying to figure out where they moved to, but their old compound is in the middle of nowhere. We are going to meet up with the rest of my family until we figure out our next move. It's not a five-star hotel, but if hundreds of people can live there comfortably, we should be okay for a few days. War and Kerrigan are stopping by our house to grab some things for us and the boys. I know this isn't your fight, but—"

"Stop." Natalia placed her hand on Mav's arm. "Going up against my cousins wasn't your fight, either, but you and your Hounds joined me anyway. It almost got Hayden killed."

"That's different."

"How? How is you being there for me any different than me wanting to protect you and fight alongside you? If you haven't noticed, I'm pretty good at what I do. And one more person standing between danger and my boys is a good thing, in my opinion."

Maveryck grinned. "Your boys, huh?"

"Oh, well, I mean——-"

Mav leaned over and kissed her. "I'm glad you're claiming them, because they've already claimed you." Maveryck unbuckled Natalia's seatbelt and pulled her onto his lap. She clasped her hands behind his neck while he held onto her hips. "And what about their Daddo? Do you think you might want to claim him someday?"

Natalia studied his eyes looking for any sign he was joking. All she found was sincerity. "I——"

"Sorry to interrupt, but Lucy wants to talk to us." Ryker motioned toward the front of the jet where a low table sat in front of one of the sofas. Natalia wished she and Mav could continue their conversation, but it could wait. Knowing he wanted her was enough.

When they were seated, Ryker tapped a few buttons on a laptop, and Lucy's face appeared on the screen. "Go ahead, Little Dove." Natalia smiled at the endearment.

"We have a problem. I asked Hawk to drive by Digger's place since he lives in the same neighborhood to see if he had taken his bike or his truck. Both are in the garage. I tapped into all the local rental companies, and I can't find where he rented a car. I don't know what he's driving, so I can't find him. Do you know someone who would have loaned him a car?"

"He was closest to Monk before Monk took off. He

245

really hasn't been very social with anyone since."

Lucy frowned. "Have you heard from Monk?"

Ryker rubbed his hands down his face and sighed. "Yeah. He sent me a message about a month ago. He's not coming back."

Natalia didn't know who they were talking about, but it was clear by the way Lucy turned away from the screen she was fighting her emotions.

"This isn't your fault, Little Dove. But look at it from his perspective. You're around all the time, and that means Tamian is too. He needed to put space between you so he could move on. I know you cared for him, just not the way he wanted."

"Do you…" Lucy cleared here throat. "Is it possible he's helping Digger? Would my rebuke make him turn against all of you?"

"If you had asked me that yesterday, I would've said no. But I didn't think Digger could do something like this either. Monk was supposed to have packed up his house and taken everything with him to New Mexico. I never thought to make sure that happened. Why don't you ask Hawk to drive by and take a look?"

Lucy nodded and picked up her phone. They waited while she made the call. When she hung up, she asked, "Did you tell them about your contact at Nexus?"

"Not yet. She, uh," Ryker glanced over at Maveryck and Natalia.

"What?" Maveryck said. "Wait. You said 'she.' I thought y'all didn't know if your contacts were male or female." Ryker leaned forward in his seat and clasped his hands together. "Something you need to share, Brother?"

Ryker stared at the top of the plane when he responded. "I know my contact. Before she took that position within the company, she was an operative. We worked a couple jobs together."

"And?"

Ryker blew out a breath. "And she's the one who recruited Natalia."

"She told you that?"

"It doesn't matter how I found out. What matters is I'm pretty sure she's the one who sent Mikael the information of who to contact to put the contracts out on the two of you."

Mav clenched his fists against his thighs. Natalia reached over and covered one of his hands with hers. He released his fist and turned his hand so their palms met. "I think it matters. Mikael admitted to taking out the contract on Natalia, but he said he contacted someone called Oz. If that's the case, Oz and your contact are working together. Natalia was recruited days after I took out Anatoly. Someone had to know Natalia's background. She wasn't already an assassin for hire. She only took out other mafia heads."

Natalia had never put much thought into how Nexus found her. She had been focused on how she was going to get away from Mikael. How she was going to survive.

"If she recruited me, she knew me somehow. Knew what I did for the family."

Maveryck squeezed Natalia's hand. To Ryker, he said, "And if she knows you, worked jobs with you, she knows me. She... what's her name? I can't keep saying she."

"Fuck!" Ryker stood and carded his fingers through his hair. "Her code name is Proxy. Her real name is Cassandra. Cassandra Valentino."

Natalia gasped. "Oh my god." Natalia lurched from the seat and ran to the lavatory. As soon as her knees hit the floor, she threw up.

Chapter Twenty-Seven

Maveryck

"WHAT THE FUCK?" Maveryck followed Natalia. When he reached the small bathroom, he dropped to his knees behind his Princess. She hadn't eaten anything since yesterday afternoon, so she was vomiting bile. Maveryck wet a paper towel and pressed it to Natalia's nape. When she stopped heaving, he helped her stand and waited while she rinsed her mouth with water.

"Are you okay?" She obviously wasn't, but he asked anyway.

"No. Let's go sit back down. I don't want to explain this twice."

Mav followed her back to the front of the jet. Ryker looked pissed while Hayden looked worried. Mav sat next to her and took Natalia's hand in case she needed his strength.

"Cassandra Valentino is Marta's daughter. When we were younger, she lived with us. This was after my mother died. She's a couple years older than me. When my father took me out of school, I wanted to hang out with her, but my father wouldn't allow it. As we got older, my father did let her train with me, but it was so I had someone my size to spar with. She was bigger than me, so I had to learn to be tougher. Quicker. Anatoly wouldn't allow her near the guns or knives, and that pissed her off. He didn't hesitate to remind her she wasn't a Volkov but the daughter of the hired help." Natalia looked around. "I need something to drink."

Hayden jumped up. "Do you want water or something stronger?"

"Water's fine. Thank you."

Hayden went to the galley and returned with a bottle of water. "Here you go, Lolly." Maveryck smiled to himself. His baby brother had also fallen under Natalia's spell.

After taking a few sips, Natalia continued. "I was good at being invisible. I knew where to hide so I could eavesdrop on Anatoly's conversations. I listened in on his phone calls, his meetings, and most importantly, his arguments with Marta. When I was younger, some of those arguments didn't make sense, but as I got older, I understood what was going on. Not only was Marta the housekeeper and cook, but she was also his mistress. Cassandra was his child. He didn't deny it, but he didn't – wouldn't – claim her. Marta wanted her daughter to have equal treatment. He claimed she did, and other than the training, I agreed. The two of them lived in our big house, he paid Marta handsomely, so she had plenty of money for her daughter. Most of the time, I was jealous of the girl. She still had her mother, and she wasn't being trained to become a killer. Those were the two things I wanted more than anything."

Natalia drank more water, and Mav rubbed small circles on her back. She gave him a tired smile. "Cassandra tried at every turn to get me into trouble, but my father never believed her lies. I overheard him tell Marta if Cassandra didn't change, they both could find somewhere else to live. That worked for a while, until my cousins came to live with us. Anatoly made it clear to them that Cassandra was off limits without telling them why. Viktor was always a stubborn shit, and being a Volkov, he felt he should be able to do as he pleased. He hated me immediately because my father was grooming me to be his number-one guard. Viktor, being younger than Mikael, knew he'd never take over, but he needed to feel important. When he found out Cassandra

249

hated me, the two became thick as thieves. They would sneak off in the middle of the night. Sometimes they would have sex, and when my father would leave the house, Viktor would take her out into the woods to teach her how to shoot."

Hayden interrupted. "Wait, did they know they were cousins?"

"Cassandra knew, but she didn't care. I don't think she ever told Viktor. Since I was already good at spying on my father, following them and listening in on their conversations was easy. When I overheard them plotting for me to have an accident, I knew it was either them or me. I began taping their conversations as well as their trysts. One night, when I knew they had snuck off to have sex, I put the recordings on my father's desk. I wasn't about to go to him and tell him all I knew, as badly as I wanted to let them know it was me who outed them. I shouldn't have been able to get into his office. He was the only one with a key, and if he found out I could pick the lock..." Natalia closed her eyes and took a deep breath.

"I hated my life. I hated my father and everyone else in the house, but as the saying goes, better the devil you know. I had no idea what would happen to me if he kicked me out. *If* he kicked me out. He didn't abide disloyalty, and he would have seen me breaking into his office as that. By then, I already knew what happened to those who opposed him. Anyway, he found the recordings. I had no idea what he would do, but I think since he didn't know who managed to get into his office, he wanted to save face that his sanctuary had been breached. He told Marta she had a choice to make. Either Cassandra left alone, or Marta could go with her. Either way, Cassandra was out. He didn't tell her about the recording being in his office, but he told her he had proof of her daughter's transgressions, although he didn't elaborate. Being the head of a Russian family was all about control. Marta had been with him long enough to know how that

250

worked. Long story short, Cassandra left, Marta stayed, and Viktor hated me more."

Mav pulled Natalia closer. "That explains why she went after Natalia, but why me? Why does she want me dead?"

Ryker squeezed his eyes shut and shook his head. Mav grew impatient waiting for his brother to respond. "Ryker, for fuck's sake. Spit it out."

"To get back at me!" He stood and beat his chest with a fist. "She did it to hurt me. Fuck! At least that's what I thought. Now that I know about her connection to Natalia, she was probably just using me."

"Using you how?" Hayden asked.

"She… I've been meeting her once a month to… We'd spend the weekend together," he whispered.

"You've been fucking your handler?" Mav asked. He didn't begrudge his older brother a little sex. If anyone needed to get laid on the regular, it was Ryker.

"Where does Digger come into all this?" Hayden asked.

"She's probably been sleeping with him too." Natalia didn't shrink back when Ryker growled. "Cassandra is a beautiful woman. At least she was when we were teens. I can't imagine that's changed. If she went from being an operative to a handler, she's still cunning. Ryker, I'm assuming since you only saw her once a month, it was nothing more than scratching an itch for you. You don't strike me as the type of male to hide someone you care about. If I'm wrong, I apologize."

"You're not wrong. It's just, I should have seen it."

"Why? Why should you think she wasn't scratching an itch too? That isn't reserved for men. People in our business don't make good partners."

Maveryck wanted to disagree, but he also wanted to hear Natalia's opinion. Lucy had said Natalia didn't think she was good enough for Mav and the twins. This was probably why. He kept quiet as she explained.

"People like us – assassins – we either lie to those we

251

love about what we do, or we live a solitary existence. If we get into a relationship, we make excuses for where we've been. We have to lead a double life. You can't have a wife or husband and bring home your stash of weapons, and in my case, disguises. You have to hide them. You keep your home life and your business separate. That has to eat at you. At least I would think so. Since I've never been in a relationship, I'm just speculating. Maybe that's just me. Maybe there are those assassins out there who have no trouble leading that double life."

Maveryck turned Natalia's chin so she could see the sincerity in his words. "And maybe they find someone who is in the same line of work as them. They can compare notes on jobs. They can take turns going on jobs while the other stays home with the kids."

"Mav—"

"So you're saying I was just a fuck buddy and she *wasn't* using me?" Ryker was lost in his anger and didn't realize Maveryck was trying to get Natalia to see they could have a future together.

"Not at all." Natalia ran her fingers through Mav's beard, letting him know she heard what he was trying to say. But she understood this was about Ryker and his feelings too. "I'm saying if this were anyone other than Cassandra, that's exactly what you two were. A weekend here and there to get what you both needed. Having that would be so much better than trying to find some stranger to hook up with. But this *is* Cassandra."

Mav's Gryphon was pissed thinking of Natalia having one-night stands, but anything or anyone she did before they met didn't matter. Hell, he had been planning to marry someone else.

"I'm saying, this isn't your fault. It's hers. She used you, and for that, I'm sorry. I'm sorry my father didn't claim her. I'm sorry she felt like I was the enemy. I'm sorry she felt the need to get revenge on me and used you to do so."

252

"But why wait?" Ryker fisted his hands against his thighs. "If she wanted her revenge against you, why not go after you before now?"

"Maybe because I was still living at home? She knew the layout. She knew how to get into the house, but there were always guards around."

"Maybe she knew how much of a badass you are and figured she couldn't take you out herself," Hayden said.

"Possibly, but she could have enlisted Viktor's help. He was pissed when Anatoly made Cassandra leave. Pissed at me, because he said it was my fault somehow."

"Whatever the reason, we need to figure out a way to take her down." Maveryck massaged Natalia's neck while he spoke. "Ryker, does she know you're aware of her deceit? If not, we can use that. If so, we're going to have to figure out if there's anyone at Nexus who can help. And we can't forget about Digger. We've got to watch our front and our back."

"Unless she has cameras I'm not aware of, she doesn't know I'm on to her. I snuck into her home a few nights ago with Lucy's help. As for taking her down, I can do that when I meet her next week."

"You have to be absolutely certain. If there were cameras, and she knows you were in her house, she's going to be waiting on you. She won't fight fair. If she's your handler, she has seen the way you take out your targets. You don't use guns, but she will. When you go to her, I'm going with you," Natalia said. "She might have used you, but the bitch tried to kill me. She tried to kill Mav. I owe her one."

Hayden was grinning, and Maveryck shook his head. "Don't say it," Mav warned.

"Say what?" Ryker asked.

"Nothing," Mav said at the same time Hayden said, "Princess Badass, the Gryphon Rider."

"That's Princess Lollipop to you." Natalia stuck her tongue out at Hayden. Maveryck wished she wouldn't encourage his baby brother, but he knew they were forging a bond like no other. When someone you cared about came close to dying, and when you took out the person threatening your loved one, that brought two people closer than almost anything could. He wouldn't begrudge either of them their growing bond. If anything, Hayden's loyalty to Natalia was a good thing. His brother would protect Natalia with his life. And with the upbringing she'd had with family who didn't love her, she could use a new family. Hell, she had one. She just had to accept it.

"I'll take you with me on one condition," Ryker said. "Mav comes with us. I know you can handle yourself, but I want someone else there just in case." Ryker didn't say just in case what. They knew. Cassandra was a wild card, and if she was hellbent on seeing Natalia dead, she would play dirty. And if she knew Ryker was aware of her using him to get back at Natalia, she wouldn't hesitate to take him out the first chance she got. "And just so you know, when we worked a job together, she didn't carry guns; she used a sai and a short sword."

"I'm fine with Mav going, and I have also trained with sai. I prefer knives because they're easier to hide. But I have a question. If Cassandra is using Digger to get to you, does that mean she's aware of the Gryphons?"

"We don't know she is using him. But at this point, I think we have to assume she is. There are too many variables to understand why Digger would choose to go along with her scheme. Maybe she seduced him, and he's in love with her. I doubt it's about money, since we all have more than enough to live on comfortably." Ryker ran a hand through his hair. "If he told her the truth, we'll deal with that next week and pray she hasn't revealed the truth to anyone else."

"Guys," Lucy called out. Mav had forgotten she was still on the video call. "I have something. While you were talking, I hacked into Cassandra's security system. Uncle Ryker's not the only one who has been meeting her at her home. Digger has too. There's no audio, but from the video, it's evident they're more than business partners. The system she uses doesn't keep information for more than a month, so I have no idea when their association began. I looked into Digger's bank account. There haven't been any deposits made other than those he's earned from his regular job, so either she's paying him in cash, or he's doing it for a different reason."

Ryker sat down, then stood up again. "I hate to ask this, but did it look like they were merely having sex? Or did they seem, I don't know, close?"

Mav knew his brother had to be hurting. Even if he and Cassandra had been nothing more than fuck buddies, to know she had used him had to cut him to the quick. Mav couldn't wait to take the bitch down. There would be no mercy. Not for her or Digger.

"This is not the kind of porn I would choose to watch, but I knew you would want to know that answer. It's clear she's using Digger, but it's also evident by the way he looks at her, he's in love. If not in love, he's falling. There's no telling what she promised him. If he wasn't a traitor, I'd feel sorry for him."

"So, what's the plan?" Mav asked. "If we take Digger out, Cassandra will know because she won't hear from him."

"We have to find him first," Hayden said.

"Or, we could lure him to us." Maveryck had an idea, but first he had to protect the rest of his family. "Lucy, we're going to need Tamian's help."

Chapter Twenty-Eight

Natalia

As far as plans went, it was solid. Natalia had never been impressed with Anatoly's money. She'd often thought the old adage about money being the root of evil was correct. Now? She welcomed the fact that both Lucy and Tamian were loaded, and Tamian had his own jet and pilot. Whatever it took to keep the twins safe, Natalia was all for it.

While Maveryck and the others chatted with Lucy on how to lure Digger and Cassandra to them, Natalia used the restroom and then stopped by the galley to see if there was something to snack on. Her stomach was empty since she'd thrown up, and she needed fuel if she was going to fight Cassandra. Natalia wouldn't underestimate the woman. Revenge was a strong motive. For all the reasons Cassandra felt Natalia deserved to die, they weren't nearly as strong as Natalia's reasons for wanting the other woman to pay. Natalia could understand feeling slighted by Anatoly. Having a parent who didn't recognize you as his own had to be a hard pill to swallow, but it wasn't Natalia's fault. Nothing her father had done was for any reason other than he was a selfish bastard.

If Cassandra were out to get revenge for a family member Natalia had taken out, she could understand. Natalia had looked over her shoulder for many years waiting on someone to retaliate for her role in her Russian family. Then again, maybe those other families felt the way she did – the world was better off without the criminals in their lives. There was no love lost for Anatoly when Mav eliminated him. Just like she didn't feel one ounce of guilt in taking out her cousins.

After finding a bag of peanuts, Natalia returned to the seating area. Mav held out his hand, and she took it. If anyone had told her a month ago she would be falling in love with her father's murderer, she would have laughed. Hell, falling in love at all hadn't been on her radar. She'd never known romantic love, but she wouldn't discount what she felt for the Gryphon. Just meeting him for the first time in the grocery store had drawn her to him. It wasn't only his looks. She'd had sex with handsome men, but not once had her stomach fluttered when she thought about them afterwards. When Natalia witnessed the way he panicked when he lost sight of Marshall, her heart went out to him. Being around them in their home, watching them interact, seeing the love he had for his sons in such a short amount of time, those were the things she admired the most.

Having met his parents, Natalia understood why Mav was who he was. Sutton and Rory didn't hide their love from any of their kids, even though they were grown. She didn't know how they had raised their children, but from the way his siblings came together to welcome the twins, it was evident the elder Lazlos had instilled in them all the essence of a true family. They might have taught them how to fight, but it was so they could do good in the world. Protect the weak, not prey on them. Like she told Maveryck and the others, she wanted to be part of that. Being an assassin went a long way in ridding the world of evil, but she wanted to do more.

When there was a lull in the conversation, she pulled away from Maveryck and sat down in front of the computer. "Lucy, were you able to get into Mikael's accounts?"

Lucy's face lit up. "Yes! I've transferred seventy-five

257

percent of the money into the account Sutton uses to help with those they save from the Ministry. The other twenty-five I put into a separate account for the twins, like you asked. I'll give you the account number next time I see you. I called Julian to help with a few other things, since he's better at hiding his digital footprint. As of about half an hour ago, your cousins' cars and the house were transferred into your name. This way, when you decide what to do with everything, you won't have any issues."

"That could have waited. I hate that you're all working when you should be sleeping, but thank you." She had worried the Lazlos wouldn't accept the money considering how it was obtained, but Maveryck assured her it was welcomed.

Lucy waved her hand in the air. "We can sleep later. I've also been in touch with your leasing agent as well as your insurance company. The agent assured me they had insurance on your rental, and they were just glad you weren't injured. Your own insurance company needs a list of everything you lost in the fire before they can do an assessment and cut you a check. And don't worry. I did that during business hours yesterday."

"Wow, I..." Natalia's chest tightened. Mav sat down next to her and hugged her to him, kissing her temple.

"Thank you, Lucy. For everything," Maveryck responded on Natalia's behalf. "When this is all over, we'll have you and Tamian over for dinner."

Natalia really hoped she was included in the "we" part of that statement.

"You know thanks isn't necessary, but I'm not going to turn down any opportunity to spend time with the twins. It'll give me practice," Lucy said with a wink.

"Is there something you need to tell us, Little Dove?" Ryker asked.

"Nope. Not yet anyway. I've got to learn how to be Queen before I can worry about little princes or princesses

258

running around."

"Fair enough. We should be getting ready to land soon, so we'll call you back when we're on the road."

"Sounds good. I wish I was there with you. I'd really like to see Natalia kick this Cassandra's ass."

"I'll video it for you," Hayden offered.

Lucy laughed at her uncle. "You do and *I'll* kick *your* ass. You have your Gryphon ready to create some havoc."

"Will do. Talk soon." Hayden turned off the video.

"What's this about her being queen?" Natalia asked.

"Tamian's father is the current Italian Gargoyle King. He's ready to pass the crown to Tamian," Mav explained.

"Do Gryphons have kings?"

"No. We've never needed something so formal to police our own. When someone like Digger betrays our kind, whoever is in charge of that area deals with them. Most Gryphons in the States formed Motorcycle Clubs back in the mid-nineteen hundreds as a cover for gathering our kind, and even though Sutton stepped down as President, he's still the one other Gryphons in our area turn to when they need advice or for someone to dole out punishment. Just like with humans, there are good and bad in every species, but there's less evil in the Gryphons. We were created to be good, and most of us are honorable. This is the first time I can remember one of our own turning on us."

"What about Monk? Was that his name?"

"Yes. He didn't turn his back on our kind. He had his heart set on Lucy, and when she didn't return his love, he left to find his place somewhere else. To me, that was honorable."

The pilot announced they were preparing to land, so the four of them fastened their seatbelts. Mav took Natalia's hand. "When this is all over, we need to take the twins on a vacation. Just the four of us."

"Really?" Mav nodded, and Natalia smiled. "I'd like that." She raised her face, and Mav didn't hesitate to kiss her. He pressed his palm to her nape and pulled her closer, deepening the kiss. Natalia forgot about Cassandra and Digger. She forgot about Mav's two brothers sitting a few feet away. She got lost in the feel of his hand on her neck and his tongue making love to her mouth. When someone cleared their throat, Mav sighed into her mouth then kissed the tip of her nose.

"And very soon, we're going to go away where it's just the two of us. I want at least forty-eight hours without interruptions."

"Just forty-eight hours?" she whispered.

Mav grinned. "You don't think you'll get tired of me by then?"

"I don't think I could ever get tired of you."

"Okay. Save the mushy shit for later. We've got asses to kick and an hour drive before we get there," Hayden said.

Back before the near-apocalypse caused by the Ministry, there were plenty of airports servicing all areas of the country. As the world began rebuilding, not all business reopened, airports included. They could have landed at one of the defunct locations, but they had chartered a private plane, and as such had to abide by the rules. The New Rochester airport was an hour's drive to the compound Josiah Talbert and his people had abandoned. It was the perfect place for them to lure Digger and Cassandra. The plan was to scout the area so they had the upper hand in knowing the layout. Natalia was intrigued by this cult. Not that she agreed with how they operated, but the fact that people lived off the grid in self-sustaining mini towns. Growing up with money, she'd never thought about where her food came from. She had everything she needed without question. And although she'd never really had a social life, she couldn't imagine living somewhere there were no theaters or bars. Or where the men dictated how their world was run and the women meekly obeyed.

Wait. Yes, she could.

The original plan had been for War and the others to bring the twins to the Ministry compound. After Natalia told them who Cassandra was, they asked Tamian to take Maveryck's family somewhere else. Somewhere neither Cassandra nor Digger would know about. That left the four of them to take on Cassandra and Digger, if they took the bait. Since Ryker wasn't sure who he could trust within Nexus, if anyone, they let Lucy handle getting word out as to where they would be hiding. Natalia had no doubt Lucy would be successful. She was smart and good at what she did. Natalia could see them becoming friends, and that was something else she was looking forward to. It had been twenty years since she'd had friends, and she wanted that with Lucy, and with Kerrigan.

After transferring from the jet to the rental car, Hayden drove them to the first restaurant they came to open for breakfast. Natalia's stomach had been rumbling for an hour, and it was getting ridiculous. Even Ryker chuckled the last time it happened. Natalia felt bad for the male. She didn't know him well, but he seemed like a good person. She hated the fact that Cassandra had gotten her hooks in him. If he was meeting her monthly for sex, did that mean he didn't want a relationship? Maybe he felt he'd had his one shot at love with Juliette. Natalia couldn't imagine what losing a spouse would be like. She remembered when her mother died, and her father hadn't been broken up about it, but Anatoly was not one to measure others by. Jenna had walked away from Maveryck, but that hadn't been a death. From what little he told her, he had been hurt, but not enough to go after his ex.

After eating, they stopped at a Walmart to grab some toiletries, food, and bottled water. The males didn't know if there was still running water at the compound, so they stocked up. When Natalia caught Maveryck in the condom section, she sidled up to him and whispered her contraceptive shot was good for another few months. She didn't imagine them having time or privacy for sex with his brothers around, but she was glad to know he was thinking about it. She was too. Every time he touched her or kissed her, heat pooled in her stomach. Natalia had never thought of herself as a wanton woman, but Maveryck could turn her on with just a look.

When they reached the compound an hour later, Hayden parked on a service road half a mile away. While she and Maveryck waited in the car, Hayden and Ryker went in to scope the area, making sure the cult members hadn't returned. When they deemed it secure, Hayden drove the car onto the property and parked in one of the barns. The little town was nothing like she had expected. Natalia felt like they'd gone back in time and were in the midst of an Old West setting. If she closed her eyes, she could imagine cowboys hitching their horses to posts outside a saloon and women dressed in bustles carrying parasols walking down the sidewalks.

Except there were no hitches or sidewalks. There was nothing except for empty buildings. She had never been anywhere so quiet. There were no noises, save a handful of birds calling to each other in their morning songs. It was almost eerie. When Hayden began whistling a song Natalia didn't recognize, she was glad for the noise. As isolated as her home had been growing up, there was always someone talking or her father's classical music coming from his office. Natalia loved music, but she had never been allowed to listen to the latest pop songs. One of the first things she did when she moved into her rental house had been to listen to all kinds of music. She had even purchased a subscription to an online music service that played all genres. The station Hayden had turned on in the car had been some heavier rock, and she found herself tapping her fingers on her thigh to the beat while Hayden sang along. She even caught Mav singing to himself a few times.

There were small buildings scattered throughout the

compound. The four of them investigated each one. Cabins which contained bunkbeds lined several unpaved streets, and there was a larger house that sat back away from everything else.

"This reminds me of The Sanctuary," Ryker said.

"What's that?" Natalia asked.

"It was the compound where Mav and War found Kerrigan. Considering its leader, Gideon, is brothers with Josiah, the leader of this place, it doesn't surprise me. They probably have a blueprint on how to build the perfect cult town."

"That makes sense. If they've been doing this for over thirty years, they had to have learned how to create an efficient town." Maveryck opened the door to the house, and Natalia stepped inside. Walking through the house, Natalia was surprised at how modern everything was. She had expected the inside to be as utilitarian as the small bunkhouses. There was a coffee maker in the kitchen which had leftover liquid inside. Green globs of mold on the surface had her cringing.

"Hayden and I can share the master if you two need your own rooms," Ryker offered. Maveryck silently asked Natalia what she wanted.

"That's not necessary. I wouldn't want to be the cause of you two large men fighting over the covers," she said.

Hayden chuckled, his eyes alight with mirth. "*Right.* Thanks for taking one for the team, Lolly."

Chapter Twenty-Nine

Natalia

NATALIA WINKED AT Hayden. "I'm going to clean the kitchen. It looks like they left in a hurry, and that coffee pot is disgusting." She knew they didn't expect her to be the maid, but Natalia needed something to keep her mind off sharing a room with Mav.

Maveryck offered to unload the supplies they had purchased while Ryker and Hayden went to have a more thorough look at all the buildings. During their initial walkthrough of the compound, they discovered a well system for the water and generators for power. There were hordes of oil lanterns and candles as well. She was drying the last of the dishes when the three brothers returned from outside. Hayden placed a piece of paper on the island. She glanced down at a rough sketch of the compound.

"Did you do this?" she asked.

"Yeah. I always liked to draw, and it kept me from getting beat up when I was younger." Natalia arched a brow, and he elaborated. "Being the youngest meant I wanted to do everything my brothers did. Seeing there's such a big gap in our ages, the others didn't always appreciate it when I followed them everywhere. Rory found ways to keep me occupied, and drawing was one of them."

"What about Kyllian? He's not that much older than you."

"He's a lot more outgoing than he used to be. Back then, he mostly stuck with Pop. Yeah, he played with me sometimes, but he has always been more focused than the rest of us. Even at ten, he hung onto every word our father said. Gaining every bit of knowledge about every subject. Straight-A student, top in his class. He's smart. Observant. While he read everything he could get his hands on, I preferred to draw." Natalia heard the pride in Hayden's voice when he spoke of Kyllian.

Natalia hung the damp towel over the oven door handle and turned her attention to the map. She was impressed with the detail. "This is amazing."

"Thanks. This is just the town proper. I want to shift and get an overhead view of the surrounding area. When we were here before, we were only looking for people. I want to find every access point. Every potential hiding place or trap."

Ryker pushed away from the wall he'd been leaning on. "I'll come with you. That'll give me a chance to watch for Tank."

The other Gryphon was coming to bring the bags War had packed for them. Since they didn't know if or when Cassandra and Digger would take the bait, they could be waiting for days. While the two brothers headed outside to shift and take to the air, Natalia studied the map.

Maveryck stepped up behind her, wrapping his arms around her waist. He looked over her shoulder. "I can't imagine living like this. I can understand wanting to be able to survive simplistically if you have to, but to choose living this way without the amenities available on the outside isn't something I would do willingly. Going camping with War was always a treat. Just the two of us would pack our bikes and hit the road. We would catch our food and cook it over a campfire. Sit around the fire at night enjoying each other's company. Don't get me wrong. I love all my family, but the bond between twins is special. I've already noticed it with Major and Marshall."

"So have I. Do you think Major takes the lead because he's older?"

"Not necessarily. I think that's just his personality. Marshall is the quieter of the two, but with me and War, he's older and has the same demeanor I see in Marshall." Maveryck nuzzled her cheek with his nose, the small diamond stud scratching lightly against her skin. "I know we just met and haven't been able to spend much time getting to know one another, but what I feel for you is real, Princess. I want the chance to see where this goes. No pressure here, but the boys love you, and I'm not far behind them."

Natalia turned in his arms and threaded her fingers through his hair. "You think the kind of woman I am is who they need in their lives?"

"You mean someone whose heart is as intense as her skills in the field? A woman who puts the boys first? Someone who makes them laugh and do little wiggly happy dances? Absolutely." Maveryck ran his hands down her back, cupping her ass. He lifted Natalia and placed her on the island, moving to stand between her legs. "You're a good woman, in spite of how you were raised. Maybe because of it. When you were talking about assassins having to hide from their partner, you don't have to do that with me. And I don't have to hide any part of myself from you. That's the beauty of this. We are alike, you and me. I was drawn to you the day we passed on the sidewalk. My Gryphon recognized you as someone special. We didn't know how true that was. Then in the grocery store..." Mav grinned. "My Gryphon was pissed when I didn't get your phone number. But the boys had been in my life less than twenty-four hours, and I was still trying to come to terms with having kids I hadn't known about. It wasn't like being there when Jenna was pregnant, having the nine months to prepare for being a father. I was scared shitless. Still am. I needed to focus on them and not my love life."

"What changed?" Natalia needed to know why he was

willing to allow her in only a few days later. "It's not like you've had months to get used to having them with you."

"You changed. Well, not you as in your personality, but being around you, seeing how drawn the boys are to you, how drawn *I* am to you… It just feels right. I'm not glad your house was destroyed, but I am glad that gives me a reason to keep you with us in our home. And when I say our, I'm including you in that. We already know the sex is incredible, and that was our first time. It can only get better while we learn each other's bodies. You're beautiful on the inside as well as out. I want the chance to show you who I can be on the inside."

Mav pressed a soft kiss to her lips. "What do you say, Princess? Will you give me a chance?"

Natalia didn't have to think about it. Her response was immediate. "Yes." She untucked his T-shirt from his jeans so she could touch his skin. Skimming her fingertips up his abs and over his pecs, she toyed with the barbells in his nipples. "I like these," she said, tugging. Mav groaned, his blue eyes darkening. She pushed his shirt up and leaned over, biting the metal between her teeth and flicking her tongue on the hard nub. After blowing on it to take the sting away, Natalia looked up, licking her lips. She had no idea where the sudden courage was coming from, but the way Maveryck responded made any doubt fall away. "How much time do we have before your brothers return?"

"Not enough." Mav grabbed her wrists, removing them from his chest. "Not nearly enough for all the things I want to do to you." He stepped back and adjusted his hard-on. Natalia's eyes tracked the movement, remembering the feel of the metal piercing threaded through the end of his dick sliding over her clit. In the few times she'd had sex, Natalia had never given a blowjob. She tilted her head to the side, imagining having the piercing hitting the back of her throat.

"What are you thinking?" Mav asked, his eyes dancing as if he knew where her mind had gone.

"Why the piercings?" she asked instead of telling the truth.

"Because the fucker never learns not to bet with Kyllian," Hayden said as he and Ryker strolled into the room.

Maveryck rolled his eyes, but he was smiling. She loved the way these two teased each other. She had noticed Mav interacting with each of his brothers. With Hayden, he was sarcastic. With War, the bond shined through in every word or touch. With Kyllian, he was playful, and with Ryker, there was respect, even if they didn't agree.

"What do you bet on?" Natalia jumped off the island as Hayden pulled the drawing to him and started adding to it.

"Usually video games or shooting pool. The kid's good, I'll give him that. Just never, ever bet against Lucy at billiards. She kicks all our asses," Mav said with pride.

"Considering I've never played the game, I don't think that will be a problem,"

"Don't worry, Lolly. I'll teach you," Hayden offered, his attention on the paper.

"You have a table?"

"There's one at the clubhouse. Now that you're family, I'm sure you'll be coming by a lot."

Natalia looked at Mav, and he nodded his agreement.

"I'm going to take a shower," Ryker said gruffly.

"I don't think he likes me," she whispered to herself.

"It's not you. Ryker doesn't like anyone," Hayden said, not looking up.

"That's not true." Maveryck took her hands between his, pressing his lips to her knuckles. "Being here has to remind him of Juliette."

"Why would this place make him think of his wife?"

Maveryck's face grew solemn. "When we went in to take down Gideon Talbert, Ryker learned the truth about what happened to her. Josiah has kidnapped Juliette outside a bar while Ryker was out of town. He was told she, along

268

with their unborn daughter, died in a fire, but without proof, he never knew for sure. He had no body to bury. No closure. Gideon took Juliette to his compound and considered her to be his woman. She had the baby, but Gideon gave the child to a relative outside the cult to raise. Juliette escaped one night, but her car went off the road while she was being chased. She ended up dying by fire. Kerrigan found pictures of Juliette when she was snooping. The truth came out that his daughter, a young woman named McKenzie, was living at the compound with her adopted family. Mac chose to leave with Ryker and get to know him."

"And now this mess with Cassandra." Natalia felt for the oldest brother.

Hayden tossed down his pencil and went to the fridge. "Beer?" he asked. Natalia declined, but Mav said yes. It was barely lunchtime, but she didn't judge them for drinking on behalf of Ryker's pain.

After drinking his down in one go, Hayden tossed the empty bottle in the trash can and pointed to the drawing. "Here's what the place looks like from all angles."

Once again, Natalia was impressed with Hayden's eye for detail. "You should be an artist."

"He is," Mav said. "Hayden drew all his own tattoos and most of mine."

A pretty blush colored Hayden's cheeks, and he turned to get another beer. As cheeky as the man could be, she loved his modesty at being praised. When he turned around, he popped the top off the bottle and winked at her. "My next tattoo is going to be a lollipop."

Maveryck groaned and reached out to smack his brother. Hayden danced out of the way, grinning. He wasn't done though. He bounced on his toes and added, "A lollipop wearing a crown riding atop a Gryphon."

Natalia laughed, and both brothers joined in.

269

Ryker

RYKER EXITED THE house through the back door. He walked far enough away he wouldn't be overheard as he made the call. He trusted Lucy to come through for them, but he was ready for this shit to be over. Having a contingency plan made him a good leader. As soon as the electronic *Hello* came through, he said, "I have a problem."

"And that is?"

Ryker started to say, "Maveryck's gone and fallen in love with Natalia," but instead he said, "Digger's turned against us."

"Turned against you how?"

"He's helping someone from Natalia's past try to kill both her and Maveryck. I know I agreed to let you walk away, but I don't know who else to trust."

Ryker was afraid they had hung up when there was nothing but silence. Finally, they said, *"What do you need?"* After telling them his plan, they said, *"One last job, Ryker. Then you have to let me go. For good this time."* The call disconnected, and Ryker hung his head. Blowing out a breath, he made his feet take him back inside. He didn't have clean clothes, but he stepped into the shower anyway. Being here at this compound brought back memories he swore he would bury. Losing Juliette the first time had been devastating, and then he'd found out the truth. It was like losing her all over again. He didn't feel like he was cheating by fucking Proxy. His wife had been gone too long for guilt, but knowing who Cassandra really was and that she was using him tore a hole in his soul he didn't think he'd ever come back from.

It wasn't that he was in love with her. His one love had

died with Juliette. Being with the woman had given him a false sense of being wanted. Needed. It made him believe he wasn't so far gone that he was no longer capable of feeling something stronger than lust. Ryker thought he and War had something in common, sharing the loss of their wives, and then War fell in love with Kerrigan. Did that mean War's feelings for Harlow hadn't been as deep as Ryker's love for Juliette? And now, Maveryck had gotten caught up in Natalia after he swore "never again."

Feeling sorry for himself did no good, but neither did trusting his Gryphon when it tried to convince him there was someone out there for them. Ryker turned his face toward the water so he couldn't feel the tears. He hated himself in that moment of weakness. Hated he let Proxy's betrayal eat at him. But it was better to get it out of his system in private than to show his brothers how affected he was. He was a fucking Gryphon. President of the Hounds. He wasn't allowed to be weak.

Ryker grabbed the new bar of soap and bathed. He didn't have to ignore his dick because it hung limp against his thigh. He doubted it would ever get hard again.

After drying off and putting his dirty clothes back on, Ryker returned to the kitchen amid laughter and the scent of something on the stove.

His brothers and Natalia were laughing at two excited voices coming from the computer. Ryker couldn't help but smile as the twins told their lollipop all about flying in Uncle Tam's plane. Tamian's pilot, Santiago, had flown the rest of their family to New Atlanta, where they were hiding out in Tamian's home there. Major turned the phone around, focusing on a familiar redhead. If Maveryck wasn't in love with Natalia, Ryker would bet money his brother would be flirting with Tamian's sister, Tessa, even though she was happily mated to Gregor Stone, brother to the American King. Tessa was another feisty female, and Ryker had to admit she was indeed *the shit*.

271

Ryker checked to see what Hayden had left unattended on the stove. He stirred the hamburger meat simmering with onions and peppers. He dumped the noodles into the forgotten boiling water, and added a little salt. Hayden was as good in the kitchen as he was with his art. Maveryck had been pissed when Ryker began training their baby brother to go on missions. Mav wanted Hayden to pursue an art career. But Hayden wasn't having it. He said art was his escape just like building motorcycles. Ryker understood where Mav was coming from, but after talking it over with Sutton, he gave in to Hayden's wishes. Even Rory thought it was a good idea for Hayden to know about being a mercenary. She said they never knew when one of them would need backup.

"Uncle Ry!" one of the twins yelled through the computer screen. He hadn't learned to discern which boy was speaking, but by the volume of his voice, Ryker would bet money it was Major. He turned, and sure enough, the older twin was smiling.

"Hey, Major. Having fun?"

"Yes! Aunt Tessa said there's fish here. We get to go see them tomorrow with some new friends."

"Wow. I'm jealous. You'll have to take lots of pictures and show me when you get back from your vacation." It didn't surprise Ryker that Tessa had insinuated his family into hers. War and Kerrigan had stopped in New Atlanta to visit Lucy when she was training with Julian Stone. The Gargoyles had welcomed them all into their Clan.

"Okay!" Major turned and yelled, "Uncle War! I need a camera!" Major took off running with the phone. The picture was bouncing all over the place.

"Tell your Daddo and the others bye," War said.

The twins went through telling them goodbye individually, and before they handed the phone off to War, Marshall got close to the screen and kissed it. When he whispered," Love you, Tolly," Ryker was afraid the tears were going to fall again.

Ryker had thought Maveryck falling in love with Natalia was a problem, but in that moment, he recognized it for what it truly was – a blessing.

CHAPTER THIRTY

Maveryck

MAVERYCK KNEW HE was making the right choice with Natalia. After the way Jenna left, he'd sworn off getting into another relationship, but there was no way he was letting his Princess go. She was the perfect mixture of tough and sweet. She reminded him of his mother, and that was a good thing in his opinion. Rory was the standard all women should be held to. He only hoped that one day soon his mom would embrace Natalia the way she had Kerrigan. He also prayed to Zeus his older brother would eventually find the one woman who would heal Ryker's heart. Mav hated knowing Cassandra had used Ryker. That had to be devastating. When Ryker returned from taking his shower, he was more withdrawn than usual. He laughed at the twins on the video call, but weariness was etched around his eyes.

Tank arrived just as they sat down to eat lunch. He called from the access road so they would know it was him driving onto the property. After unloading all their bags, he parked his SUV in the barn beside the rental. Once they finished eating, the five of them walked through the town, marking the places they planned to hide. Lucy had sent word to the Hounds about Digger's betrayal. With Julian's help, she set up an alert that notified her of any call immediately made once the Hounds read their notification. Mav didn't agree with betraying their trust in such a way, but Ryker explained if there was one traitor in their midst, it was possible there were more. And since Digger wasn't using his personal phone, they couldn't track him.

They entered the building which had been used as a school. There were four chalkboards, one on each wall. By the different levels of lessons written on each, the one room was used to house all ages of children. "How many kids do you suppose were here?" Natalia asked.

"If this group is anything like his brother's, I'd say around twenty or thirty. From what Mac told us, couples who come into the group usually already have kids. There aren't as many couples who get together on the inside, because men like Josiah and Gideon have a say in who can or cannot be a couple. Mac had been promised to one of Gideon's guards, so when she and Elijah fell in love and Mac got pregnant, Elijah was sent away, and Mac's baby was given up for adoption against her wishes." Ryker leaned against the desk, looking around. "I can't believe my baby girl was raised in this shit and that my grandchild is out there somewhere and I may never see her."

"Does McKenzie want her daughter back?" Natalia asked.

"She's torn, because she doesn't know if the couple who adopted the baby is aware of the circumstances. If they are, Mac doesn't give a shit about their feelings. If not, she hates to think of taking their dream from them. She's more worried about us finding Elijah right now." Ryker pushed off the desk. "The closet in here is large enough for one of us to hide in, but there's only one exit. Let's keep looking."

The next building they chose appeared to be a dining hall. It was set up like a school cafeteria. There were three sections, and from what Kerrigan told them, couples sat in one section, men in another, and women in the final section. Unmarried men and women weren't allowed to mingle. They were even segregated in their jobs. The kitchen contained stainless workstations. The refrigerator was empty with the

275

exception of a few vegetables that were no longer edible. There were three ovens, but all smaller appliances had been removed. There were no utensils. No pots or pans.

"They must have been planning to move well before they actually did. Hawk and Spyder said it felt like they were gearing up for something, and that something was them moving. You can't pack up a whole town, even one this small, in the few days it took between when Hawk and Spyder scouted and we all came back," Ryker said.

"Josiah knew he'd be on our radar after we took down Gideon." Maveryck opened a door and stuck his head in.

"This just proves they have something to hide," Hayden said.

"I think we need to put this building on the list. The kitchen has plenty of hiding spots where they won't see us until it's too late," Maveryck said. "There're two entry points as well."

Tank ran a hand over his head. "What about the cabins? We could each take one and put Natalia on a roof with her rifle."

Mav shook his head. "Digger is probably going to come in his eagle. He will see her and alert Cassandra."

"Not if I pick him off first," she said. Natalia's phone rang. "This will be Nix. No one else has this number."

"And if they use the same voice distorter, we don't know if it's really your handler or if we can trust them," Ryker said.

"One way to find out." Natalia answered the phone, putting it on speaker. "Hello?"

"Natalia. Where are you?"

Natalia looked at Mav and narrowed her eyes. "Did you find out who put the contract out on Maveryck Lazlo?"

"I told you not to concern yourself with that. I also told you I need you to do your job."

"That's kind of hard to do when there's a contract out on me."

276

"What are you talking about?"

"I'm talking about the fact that one of your fellow handlers is pitting Maveryck and me against each other."

"And how do you know this?"

"Let's just say we compared notes."

"You... I need to call you back."

"Don't bother. I'm done."

"What do you mean?"

"I mean I'm no longer working for you."

"You owe us, Natalia. We put a lot of resources into creating your new identity."

"An identity that was supposed to keep me safe. Not only did one of your fellow handlers allow a contract to be put out on me, but they involved my cousin. He is no longer a concern, and as far as your resources go, I don't need them; I now have my own. With my cousins out of the picture, I'm ready to step into the role that should have been mine in the first place. Besides, I will not work for an organization that allows someone like Proxy to dole out assignments." Ryker was shaking his head, so Natalia muted the phone.

"What the fuck are you doing?" he asked.

"Calling Cassandra out. This is not my handler," Natalia said, waving the phone.

"Proxy? Are you certain?"

Unmuting the phone, she said, "I'm positive." She muted it again, waiting for them to come to a decision. Natalia looked at Ryker. "Do you want to end this or not?"

"Let her do this," Mav said. He trusted Natalia.

"Fine." Ryker shook his head. "I hope you know what you're doing."

"Natalia?"

"I'm here, and yes, I'm sure. She's not going to stop until I'm dead."

"Then let me help you. Tell me where you are."

"I'll text you my coordinates. But Nix? If you don't come alone, I'll put a bullet in your skull."

"I'll be there in three hours." The call disconnected.

"How the hell would she know how soon she could be here without the coordinates?" Tank asked.

"Because someone has already tipped her off," Ryker said. "And how did you know it wasn't Nix?" he asked Natalia.

"Nix has never once called me Natalia. It's always *Myshka*. And how do *you* know someone has tipped her off?"

If Maveryck hadn't been looking at his brother, he would have missed the tiny flinch. "Yes, Brother. How do you know? We haven't spoken to Lucy." Ryker narrowed his eyes at Maveryck, but Mav wasn't backing down. "This is our lives on the line," Mav said, gesturing between him and his Princess. "If you know something, now's the time to share. You might be my Pres, but this isn't MC business. This is fucking personal, Ry."

"You think I don't know that? You think I don't feel guilty that Cassandra used me to get to you?" Ryker took a deep breath and when he continued, his voice was softer, but his face was still haunted. Ryker's phone rang. When he looked at the caller ID, he sighed. "Talk to me... Fuck... No, that's it."

"Who was that? Was it Lucy?" Maveryck's Gryphon pushed to be turned loose. He would never fight his brother, no matter how pissed he got.

"No. It was Monk. I called him for a favor, but he said he was too late. Digger told Monk to forget he ever knew him."

Maveryck couldn't be around his brother right then. "I need some air." Maveryck left the others in the kitchen, but as soon as he stepped outside, he knew he'd made a mistake.

"Don't make a sound," a woman's voice said behind him at the same time a blade was pressed against his throat.

Fuck that noise. "Cassandra," he said while looking around for Digger. He didn't see the traitor anywhere. Now he had to stay alive long enough for the others to come looking for him. He didn't want Natalia to fight this woman, but he wouldn't take that away from her. He would deal with the former Hound if he lived long enough. And by former, he wasn't talking about the MC. Digger's deceit was a death sentence.

"So, you know who I am."

"I do. And I have to say, I'm impressed you found us so quickly."

"You don't work for the world's top assassin organization without having a few tricks up your sleeve. I should have known Tatiana wouldn't do the job she was hired for. She's not as good as she thinks she is."

"She's pretty damn good." The blade cut into his neck when he swallowed. Taunting this killer wasn't smart, but he couldn't let her speak badly of his Princess.

"Let him go, Cassandra." Ryker stepped into view. Tank was behind him, scanning the area. Where was Hayden? Better yet, where was Natalia?

"Hello, lover." Cassandra's voice dripped with disdain.

"I wouldn't go that far. Lover is a term reserved for people who give a shit about each other. You and I were nothing more than fuck buddies," Ryker sneered.

"Always so serious. But I'll give you that. I always knew you were incapable of feeling."

"So why continue fucking me?" Ryker was calm. He kept his eyes on Cassandra until Tank took a few steps backwards. Mav cut his eyes to the side, expecting to see Natalia. He was almost disappointed when Digger walked from between two buildings.

"You know you're dead, right?" Ryker told the male.

Digger shrugged as if the finality of Ryker's words meant nothing. Before he opened his mouth to argue, the most beautiful sight in the world appeared before Mav.

"Ah, Tatiana. So nice of you to join us. Take one step closer and I slit his throat," Cassandra purred in Mav's ear.

279

Hmm. Sadism as foreplay? Not Mav's style.

Natalia stopped walking, but she was smiling. It was eerie the way her eyes darkened with something sinister. Mav had seen Natalia happy. He'd seen her sad. He had even witnessed her anger when taking on her cousins. This was a whole new level of malevolence he prayed he never encountered again. Gone was the woman he'd come to love, and in her place stood someone he didn't recognize. She was dressed differently than she had been just a few minutes ago. While he'd been wondering where she was, he now knew. Natalia had slipped back to the house and changed clothes. She still wore the black tactical pants, but now she had on a long-sleeved black T-shirt.

"Thank you, Cassandra." Natalia wasn't purring, but her tone was low. Seductive. Hmm. Maybe the foreplay depended on the woman. Mav's dick should not be getting hard with a blade at his throat, but his female was sex on legs when she was ready for battle.

"What the fuck are you thanking me for?" The blade loosened just a fraction. It was no longer cutting into his skin but was still close enough that one flick of the wrist would end his life.

"For helping me get what was rightfully mine. With Mikael out of the way, I can now take over the family business."

Cassandra scoffed. "Like you would know anything about that. Our father trained you to be a killer, not head of the family."

Natalia grinned, cocking her head to the side. "So you think. So *he* thought. By keeping me in the dark, he taught me so much more than shooting a gun. Or taking a punch. Or how to make it so the bodies were never found. You see, *Sister,* our father taught me how to be invisible. I learned how to hide. How to listen. How to find all the best places in the manor where voices carry. Where to stash money so no one else could find it. Where to place listening devices that

280

recorded everything. I have to say, fucking our cousin? There's not enough bleach in the world to wash that image from my brain." Natalia did a full-bodied shiver. Mav wasn't sure taunting Cassandra was the best idea, but he couldn't tell her so without risking his life.

"I knew you had something to do with Anatoly finding out about us! I should have killed you then."

"Tell me, *mor cectpa,* why *did* you wait so long to come after me? Why recruit me into Nexus? Why try to get me to kill Maveryck?"

When had Natalia moved closer? And had Cassandra noticed? Damn, his Princess was good.

"When Father sent me away, I trained harder than ever. I spent years becoming the best. But when I approached him, he threatened to have you kill me. I knew then he would never accept me as a Volkov, so I convinced Viktor to put the contract out on him, under the guise of Mikael ordering the hit." Cassandra was lost in her conversation with Natalia, and the blade dipped lower, settling against his chest. She still gripped his nape, but her hold had loosened. Digger stood with his arms crossed, his rapt attention on the woman he was going to die for. Or because of.

"Getting Father out of the picture was just the first part of my plan. I made sure Ryker took the contract. It just happened to be Maveryck who did the job. Once that happened, it was a matter of biding my time for Viktor to convince Mikael to let me back into the family. Only that didn't happen. He was too focused on finding Father's killer. By making you disappear, giving you a new identity, it convinced Mikael you were a traitor to the family. He was so lost in his hatred he never questioned how Nexus knew all about you."

"How did you come to work for them?" Natalia asked from a step closer. Zeus, she moved like the wind.

"The man I found to train me was a former operative. He was impressed with my skills and contacted his former

281

handler. Nix really shouldn't be allowed to remain in the organization. He was too easy to sway after a night of debauchery." Cassandra laughed as if she had cornered the market on seduction. Digger uncrossed his arms, his lion showing on his face.

"Digger," Mav warned.

Digger's eyes snapped away from Cassandra to meet his gaze. The lion retreated, but Mav knew the Gryphon was close to the surface.

Natalia got Cassandra's attention when she asked, "Why Ryker? Why did you single him out for the contract?"

The blade fell away when Cassandra gestured wildly with it. "Because I wasn't enough for him! I was good enough for a monthly fuck, but it was never more than that. I gave him years! Years to realize what we had could be so much more. We did jobs together. Working seamlessly taking down our marks. We were the perfect team, but after the high of the kill wore off, he walked away, going back to his family. His precious club. I was good enough to fuck but not good enough to take home to meet the parents. So, I set you up to take out his family." Cassandra flung her hand out toward Digger. "Found another man who gave up secrets after a night in bed."

Maveryck took advantage of Cassandra's focus on Digger to step back several feet. Natalia's face briefly flashed with relief before returning to her focused demeanor. Squaring her shoulders, she smiled at the other woman. "Too bad your plan didn't work. Your days of treachery are over."

"You think so?" When Cassandra turned, she was holding a sai in one hand and a short sword in the other. Maveryck wanted to shout at Natalia to run. Why would she go into a fight unarmed?

"Yes. I do."

Cassandra sneered at Natalia. "As you wish."

CHAPTER THIRTY-ONE

Natalia

WHILE MAVERYCK WAS cooling off, Hayden decided to look out the back door. When the youngest brother returned, he was pale. "She's here," he whispered. "At least, I think it's her. Tall, scary-looking, with a blade to Mav's throat."

"I need my knives. Can you buy me some time?" Natalia asked.

Ryker nodded. "I'll go with Natalia. Hay, you and Tank go outside with Mav."

"I think you should go outside. Maybe since the two of you have been doing the horizontal mambo, you'll be a bigger distraction," Hayden countered.

Ryker thought about it for a moment. "Yeah. You're right. Tank, keep your eyes peeled for Digger."

The big Hound inclined his head. "Be careful," he said to Natalia.

Natalia promised she would, then she and Hayden slipped out the back entrance. Hayden scanned the area, both down low and up high. Natalia was glad she had studied the map. She ran the quickest route to the house where she wasted no time grabbing her knives and the special sheaths for her forearms. She checked her Sig before shoving it in the back of her pants. When she tore her shirt over her head, Hayden choked, turning his back.

"A little warning there, Lolly. I know we're family and

283

all—"

"Sorry. No time for modesty. Besides, I'm sure you prefer a woman who doesn't look like a boy," she said as she secured the blades to her arms before pulling on first her vest, then a long-sleeved tee. Knife fights weren't like what was depicted in the movies. With blades, someone was going to get cut. Wearing the vest lessened Cassandra's chance at slicing Natalia's torso.

"Uh, not that I noticed or anything, but believe me, you're all woman."

Not that she wanted Mav's brother's attention, but his words made her feel good. "Let's go." Natalia ran back toward the dining hall, only this time, she took the route that placed her in Cassandra's line of sight. She thanked Zeus for keeping Maveryck alive. Zeus might not be her god, but he was the Hounds'.

Natalia knew the best distraction was conversation. Not only did talking give her time to get Cassandra's attention away from Maveryck, but they all got answers to questions they had. When Maveryck was safely away from the other woman, Natalia took a deep breath and focused on the fight before her. It had been many years since she had sparred with anyone, but her blades were like an extension of herself.

Natalia had trained with Cassandra's weapons of choice on the off chance she would one day come up against them. Never was she gladder than that moment she had. Every time Anatoly sent Natalia out on a job, she spent extra time away from her father training in weaponry he didn't feel she needed to learn. His thought was why let someone closer than what a bullet could stop?

The only way to take out your opponent using either weapon was up close. The proper mentality of using blades was knowing you were going to get cut. You just had to be able to strike more blows than your opponent. Natalia closed her mind from everything around her other than Cassandra. She trusted the males to stay out of her way.

While Cassandra twirled her sai in her hand, grinning, Natalia flicked her wrists and released her knives. Cassandra was momentarily distracted at the sight of Natalia's blades. Natalia flipped one knife so it was aiming toward her forearm in an icepick grip while keeping the other in a hammer grip. The alternate holds gave her the ability to parry against the sword with one and slice with the other. Natalia's fists were tight around the hilts of her double-edged Shaitans as she stepped in close. Cassandra's arrogance was a mistake.

Natalia moved both hands with a speed born of practice and necessity. She hit Cassandra with several quick slashes across her torso, but Cassandra came at Natalia with a sword to her chest. The weapon hit Natalia's vest where it was thickest, thus doing its job. Cassandra scowled and tried to find purchase again, but Natalia drove her knife across the top of Cassandra's forearm. Going on a quick offensive once again, Natalia arced her left hand downward, but Cassandra caught the blade in one of the tines protruding from the hilt of her sai. Cassandra tried to remove the knife from Natalia's grip by slicing Natalia's arm with her left hand. In doing so, she managed to cut Natalia's forearm, but Cassandra had angled her body away from Natalia, giving Natalia the opening to stab the other woman in the side. Cassandra, who was not wearing body armor, yelled out, but she didn't stop.

Cassandra, in her thirst for revenge, wanted to make Natalia pay for everything that happened when they were younger. She wanted Ryker to pay because he hadn't fallen in love with her. Natalia wanted retribution for all the damage her half-sister had caused. Attempted murder was a death sentence in Natalia's world. If it was just the fact that Cassandra had used Ryker's family because she was scorned, Natalia would let the male deal with his lover himself. But it was so much more than that. She had tried to make it so the twins didn't have their father or Natalia in their lives.

Blood dripped down Natalia's wrist, loosening her grip

on her left hand. She flipped the knife in her right hand around so it, too, was pointed up. This was necessary to be able to block as well as strike. Cassandra was quick, but she was losing a lot of blood from the gash in her side. Natalia knew if she didn't finish this, she would lose the grip of her left hand completely, so she took a deep breath, found her resolve, and went in for the kill. Natalia felt they were pretty evenly matched, but her nemesis was weakening with the blood loss, and she didn't have as much to lose as did Natalia.

When Cassandra raised her sword, Natalia dropped low, slicing through the back of Cassandra's knee before diving to the side, barely missing the tip of the sword as it swung down in an arc where Natalia had been seconds before. With the artery cut, Cassandra stumbled, trying to remain on her feet. Natalia strode forward and executed a roundhouse kick, sending her opponent to the ground.

"You fucked up." Natalia pointed her knife at the downed woman who was struggling to get to her feet. "I just severed your popliteal artery. You have about three minutes before you bleed out, if that long."

"No!" Digger yelled, shifting into his Gryphon.

"Tank, Hayden, stay with Natalia," Maveryck yelled before he and Ryker both turned their Gryphons loose.

"Fuck you!" Cassandra yelled, tears streaming down her face. Her chest was heaving with each breath. "Fuck... You," she repeated.

Natalia squatted, but far enough away Cassandra couldn't reach her with her sword if she somehow managed to find the strength. "I can almost understand you coming for me, but you went after my family. That I could not abide."

"You killed your family," Cassandra managed to choke out.

"No. Maveryck is my family. His sons, his siblings, his parents – they're my family. Going after the man I love? That, *mor cectpa,* was your final mistake."

"Rot in hell," Cassandra whimpered, slumping over. Her breathing became shallow until she finally stopped moving, and her hazel eyes stared unseeing at the chaos around her.

Natalia stood, and with shaking hands, returned her knives to their sheaths. "Save me a seat," she muttered, turning her gaze to the magnificent display in the sky.

Hayden ran over to where she was standing. "Lolly, are you okay? You're bleeding. You're, holy fucking hell, I…" Hayden looked her over. "Of course you're not okay. You're bleeding. I already said that, but *you're fucking bleeding.* Let's get you back to the house—"

"No. I'm not going anywhere. The wounds are mostly superficial. I've had worse."

"You have? Of course you have. You're the badass princess who rides Gryphons. Holy hell. I—"

"Hayden, breathe. I promise you I'm okay. I'm still running on adrenaline. Now hush and let me watch my Maveryck."

"Right. Your Maveryck. He's the one—"

"On the right. Digger's on the left, and Ryker's the one hanging back."

"How do you know that?"

"I'm a badass princess, remember? I know my Gryphon. Plus, I saw Digger shift. His wings are gold where Ryker's are blue."

"Damn, you're good."

The two Gryphons circled each other, talons swiping out, trying to gain purchase. Each flap of their wings rustled Natalia's sweaty hair. Maveryck clamped onto Digger's leg, snapping at the other creature's face with his beak. Digger kicked out with his hind legs, claws extended. They found their mark in Mav's stomach, and his grip faltered. It was fascinating how the eagle's wings were strong enough to keep the weight of the lion's body aloft.

As the two continued to dive in and retreat, Tank appeared next to Natalia. "Here you go," he said, holding out a wet towel. "Since you won't go back to the house, I thought you might want something to wipe the blood."

"Thank you. I don't want to miss this," she said, looking up at the two Gryphons.

"I know you don't, but Maveryck can smell your blood, and I know for a fact it's making him crazy."

"Crazier than Digger? Because I just killed the woman he loved."

Hayden sliced a hand through the air. "Bitch got what was coming to her, and if Digger was paying attention, he heard her say she was using him."

Tank shrugged. "Sometimes the heart overrules the head."

Natalia pressed the towel to the deepest wounds. "I don't want to distract Mav, but I can't not watch. And why isn't he calling on his element?"

"They're both earth shifters." Hayden grabbed Natalia's belt loop, pulling her back a few feet. "Let's give them a little more room. I don't like the way Digger keeps looking down here."

Natalia took her gaze off Mav to look at Digger's Gryphon. Hayden was right; Digger was more focused on her. Tank took a few steps back, putting himself closer to Natalia. The next thing she knew, both he and Hayden were shifting, clothes landing at their feet. Tank was knocked backwards as Digger slammed into him. She jumped sideways as large talons grabbed for her. Natalia squeezed her eyes shut, bracing for the pain, but two distinctly different squawks had her opening them. Maveryck's talons were embedded in Digger's feathers, pulling him backwards. The two beasts tumbled ass over head with Maveryck landing on top of Digger. Natalia blinked, and Maveryck had shifted into his lion. His gorgeous mane shook as he fastened his powerful teeth around Digger's neck. His sharp claws were slashing every part of the downed Gryphon he could reach.

Maveryck released Digger's neck and roared, the sound echoing all around. His mighty jaws clamped down on his opponent's back, and with a jerk of his massive head, he snapped the vertebrae of Digger's spine. Blood coated his golden fur as he ravaged the dead shifter's body.

"Maveryck, it's over," Ryker yelled. When Mav's lion continued mauling the Gryphon, Ryker yelled again, "Mayhem! Stand down."

"Shit. He's lost in his blood lust," Hayden said, now back in his human form. "Lolly, talk to him. You're the only one who can reach him."

Natalia knew Maveryck would never hurt her, but she wasn't sure he was in there. Still, she had to try. "Maveryck?" When he released his grip, she called out to him a little louder. "Mav, baby, look at me." The lion turned its head toward her. "I need you, Mav. I need my male."

Maveryck stood, stepping on the dead Gryphon, and stalked toward her. Hayden eased closer to Natalia, and the lion growled.

"It's okay, Hayden. He won't hurt me." Natalia stepped around a now-naked Hayden and strode toward her lion. "Come back to me, Mav. Come back to me so we can go get our boys."

Mentioning the twins did the trick. Fur turned to skin, and four legs became two. The other males started closing the distance, but Natalia held up her hand. Keeping her eyes on her male, she didn't stop walking until she was in his arms. Maveryck held her tight, burying his face in her neck.

"I'm sorry, Princess. I never wanted you to see that side of me,"

Natalia kissed his jaw that was surprisingly free of blood then looked up so she could see his eyes. "Do you think less of me because I killed Cassandra?"

Mav straightened and cupped her face. "What? No. You were fierce. Did I want to step in? Yes, but I knew it was your fight. I've never been prouder than I was watching you

289

kick her ass."

Natalia placed her hands against Mav's bare chest, caressing the muscles under his skin. "Likewise. Well, not the stepping in part, because those talons are fucking scary." Natalia kissed his chest before looking up, grinning. "Is it weird I'm a little turned on right now?" The scorching look he gave her said no, it wasn't weird.

"Aaand, that's our cue to leave." Hayden bent over to pick up his shredded clothes. Natalia closed her eyes and buried her face against Mav's chest, laughing. She really didn't need to see all Hayden's bits and pieces. "We'll just grab our clothes and head back to the house. Give you two a few minutes."

"It'll take more than a few," Mav replied huskily.

Hayden huffed. "While I'm not doubting your prowess, don't forget Lolly has wounds that need tending."

Natalia groaned, because she knew sexy time would have to wait. Mav stepped back, checking her over. "Fuck, Princess, I'm sorry. How bad is it? Let me see—" Natalia cut him off with a kiss.

"Natalia," he mouthed against her lips as he gripped her wrists to try and move her back. She couldn't help but hiss at the pain where his palm covered one of the deepest wounds. "Shit!" Mav dropped her arm like it was on fire and stepped back, running his hands through his messy hair.

Natalia sighed. "Grab your clothes. The sooner we get me cleaned up, the sooner we can get on with that vacation you promised me." She crossed her arms over her chest, giving him her sternest look, but the misery on his face had her backing down quickly. "Oh, Love. Come here," she whispered.

Maveryck shook his head. "I'm sorry. I never want you to feel pain, especially at my hands."

"And I never want to be the cause of *your* pain." She placed her palm over his heart. "Especially here." She moved her hand up, running her fingers through his beard. "I only want to bring a smile to those blue eyes of yours."

"You do. You have brought so much joy back to my life. You've taught me how to love again, and if you'll let me, I promise to make you smile every day for the rest of your life. I love you, my Princess."

"And I love you, my Gryphon."

CHAPTER THIRTY-TWO

Maveryck

WHILE MAVERYCK CLEANED Natalia's wounds as best he could without a proper first-aid kit, the others went to dispose of Cassandra and Digger. Since both Natalia's and Maveryck's DNA were on the bodies, they decided to torch them. They were in the middle of nowhere, and a fire wouldn't be suspicious, especially since there was already a burn pit at the back of the property.

As much as Mav wanted to pull Natalia down onto the bed there at the compound, he wanted her home in their bed more. Plus, he had two little boys he was missing greatly. Mav undressed his Princess as gently as possible, cringing at the sight of each new wound. The blood was stark against her pale skin. She was a trooper though, only flinching when he dabbed at the deepest cut, the one he had unintentionally grabbed. "This needs stitches," he muttered.

"I wish I was a Gryphon. Your wounds have already healed."

Mav pressed a kiss to her wrist. He wished that too, with all his heart. He would love Natalia until her dying breath, but then he'd have to find some way to go on without her. He just prayed to Zeus that didn't happen for at least seventy more years. To keep the melancholy out of his voice, he joked, "I don't think the world could handle it if you were any more badass."

Natalia pulled on shorts and a T-shirt with short sleeves so the fabric wouldn't abrade her cuts. "When are the boys coming home?" she asked. Maveryck had called War while Natalia asked for a minute alone in the bathroom to pee.

"Not for a couple more days. War didn't know how long it would be before we finished up here, and he promised the twins they could play with their new friends a while longer. Plus, Rory's in heaven spending time with Kaya. She's Rafael's – the King's – mate, and they have a new baby. She and Pop met Rafael and Kaya when Lucy was missing. Mom's never met a baby she didn't fall in love with."

"I miss them," Natalia said wistfully.

"Me, too. But that gives us time to take you shopping and replace some of your clothes and shoes."

"It also gives us time for other things too," she said, wiggling her eyebrows.

Maveryck laughed and kissed her on the nose. "It sure does. I also want you to feel free to redecorate our bedroom. I know the bedding is kind of boring, and since it's now your bedroom, I want it to reflect your style. Same goes with the rest of the house. It's your home, and it needs your touch."

"You don't think it's too soon?"

"Nope. I refuse to spend even one night apart."

"Okay, but when all my shoes and boots overtake your closet, I don't want to hear you complain."

"Well, let's see. There are two guest bedrooms you can use for all your many shoes and clothes. If those get full, I'll build you a new closet."

Natalia wrapped her arms around his neck and kissed him softly. "Deal."

"Are you two decent?" Hayden yelled as he entered the house.

"No, but we have our clothes on," Natalia yelled back.

Maveryck chuckled. "Don't encourage him."

"What?" she asked, innocently.

"You know what, you cheeky minx. Come on. I'm ready

293

to go home." Maveryck took their bags to the living room where the other Hounds were waiting. "Any problems?" he asked.

"Besides the smell? No." Ryker ran a hand through his hair. "We found the rental car Digger was driving. Cassandra must have ridden with him, because we couldn't find another vehicle."

"How did they find us so quick? It's a good three-hour drive from home, and Lucy's message wouldn't have been circulated that fast," Hayden asked.

"Cassandra said working for Nexus allowed her a few tricks. She probably traced our phones." Maveryck sat on the arm of the sofa and situated Natalia between his legs with her back to his chest. "What are we going to do about Nexus? Mikael mentioned Oz, Nix isn't to be trusted, and your handler's dead."

Ryker looked at Natalia. "Did you mean what you said? Are you really done working for them?"

"Yes. I have plenty of money saved up for now, and I'd really like to spend my time with the twins until they start school." She looked over her shoulder. "If that's okay with you?"

Maveryck's heart swelled. His Princess was going to be the perfect mother. He was ready to officially make her a Lazlo, and he hoped she would be willing to adopt the boys. "I think that's perfect."

"With the money we got from Natalia's family, Sutton and Rory are set for a while. Sutton has an old buddy who started his own organization, but I didn't see a need to go elsewhere. Until now. I'll get in touch with him and see what he has to say. But for now, we'll all take some well-earned time off. You have two boys you need to spend time with. I need to locate Josiah and find my daughter's boyfriend. And we all need to hit the road on our bikes. It's been too long since we took off together for the hell of it."

"Hear, hear," Tank said. "Martina's got plenty of help at

the restaurant, and she's been itching to ride."

"Then let's get home and make that happen," Ryker said.

On the way back to New Troy, Tank dropped off Digger's rental car at the local branch so the authorities wouldn't be notified of a stolen car when it wasn't returned. That left Cassandra's disappearance as their only concern, but when they spoke to Lucy during the drive, she assured them she and Julian would be able to make it look like the woman had fled the country.

They stopped off and got some bandages and antibiotic ointment for the worst of Natalia's injuries before they sat down at a steakhouse for dinner. Maveryck tried to get Natalia to go to a local hospital, but she asked if they could call the Rev instead. So, on the way home, Mav made the call and asked him to meet them at their house. Once her arm was stitched up and the Hound said his goodbyes, Natalia closed and locked the door, leaning against it. She bit her lip and looked up at Mav with heated eyes.

"I want to call the boys, and then I want their Daddo to take me to bed," she said.

Maveryck pulled his phone out of his pocket so fast he had to juggle it to keep from dropping it. "Then get your fine ass over here, Princess."

Natalia joined Maveryck on the sofa where they spent twenty minutes listening to their boys recount their day with their new friends, Connor, Rain, and Amelia. Major was smitten with Amelia, and he asked Mav if boys wore tutus. Marshall, with his tender heart, asked if Rain could come home with them because he needed a Lollipop since his own mom was with the gods. War assured Mav he and Kerrigan would explain to Marshall that Rain had plenty of females around who loved him and that he'd be okay. By the time they got off the phone, Natalia was a mess.

"That boy," she whispered, sobbing against Mav's chest.

"That boy loves you. They both do. Thank you,

Princess. Thank you for loving them the way they should be loved."

"I do. I love them both so much. And I love you."

"Let's go to bed so I can show you how much I love you in return."

Instead of the heated passion of their first time, Maveryck stripped Natalia down and kissed every inch of her skin, taking extra care with her wounds. His Gryphon was pushing Mav to take her hard and to mark her. Mav wouldn't do that until they talked about it. The mating bite was reserved for the one being a Gryphon wanted to spend the rest of their days with. He had never marked Jenna. Never planned on it even though he was going to marry her. That should have told him something. But now... Mav wanted to bite Natalia. To claim her for as long as she was alive.

"Mav, is something wrong?" Natalia was on her elbows, frowning.

"What? No. Nothing's wrong."

"Are you sure? Are you having second thoughts?"

Mav lowered his head and nipped at the skin above her hip bone. "Definitely not. It's just..." Mav studied her beautiful face. Her dark eyes were wide as she waited. "We haven't talked much about the Gryphon side of me. I know Lucy explained some of it, but did she tell you about mates?"

"Just that it's the term shifters use for their significant others."

"There's more to it than that. With the Gargoyles like Tamian, they have what's called fated mates. One being chosen by the fates for them. When they find their one, they'll never be able to love someone else. With Gryphons, we don't have that. We are given the choice as to who we take as our mate. With both species, we mark our mate with a bite. That seals the bond. Unlike marriage, it's permanent."

"Was Jenna not your mate?"

"No. I was willing to marry her, but for whatever reason,

I never intended to mark her. Now I know why. You are the one I want for the rest of my life. I want to marry you. Raise my boys with you. Spend my life growing older with you. Marking you isn't necessary for all that to happen; it would just make my Gryphon incredibly happy if you one day accepted the bite."

"Your Gryphon? What about you? Do *you* want to bite me?"

"More than anything."

"I'm past worrying about how fast we came together. I love you, and I can't imagine there being someone else more perfect for me. So, if you want to claim me, do it. Make me yours."

"Are you certain? Because once I do, you're stuck with me."

Natalia carded her fingers through his hair. "I'm sure."

His Gryphon roared in elation, and Maveryck pushed against the beast to calm the fuck down. Natalia was still injured, and his plans to make love gently hadn't changed. Maveryck resumed pressing kisses to her torso, working his way up. He stopped at her breasts to lick each one, remembering how Natalia reacted last time. When he bit the tip, she grabbed onto his hair, holding his head in place. When he tried to kiss higher, Natalia pulled harder. Mav chuckled around the nub.

"Mav…"

He looked up, and her eyes were even darker, if that was possible. "Yes, Princess?"

"I need you," she husked.

"You've got me." Licking a line from the center of her chest to her neck, Maveryck released his fangs and scraped her skin. When Natalia gasped, he kissed the spot where his sharp teeth had touched. "Easy, Love. I promise when I bite you, it won't hurt." He climbed her body, her legs already open to accommodate him. Settling on one forearm, he touched the point on her shoulder where he would claim her.

"I'll bite you here, but not until we're both ready to come."

Natalia nodded and licked her lips. "Kiss me."

"Gladly." Maveryck pushed down on his erection so it pointed toward her mound, and as he tasted her sweetness with his tongue, he rolled his hips so his piercing rubbed against her clit. He kissed her slowly, keeping rhythm with his lower body. Maveryck called on his shifter's control to keep his orgasm at bay. He drove Natalia to the edge then eased off, kissing her neck so she could take a breath.

"Mav, baby…" Natalia raised her hips, searching for the friction that would take her over the edge. Maveryck didn't give it to her. He wanted her to experience the explosive orgasm she'd have with the mate bond. Angling his hard-on so it pressed against her entrance, he slid into her wetness, relishing the way she molded to him perfectly as if she were made solely for him.

He propped up on his forearms so he could watch her face. Natalia kept her eyes on him as he glided in and out slowly, wanting to prolong the feel of being inside her. "You're perfect for me. The way your body surrounds my dick, it's like nothing I've ever felt before."

"Yes, I… Mav… I need…" Natalia closed her eyes and begged with her body for him to give her more. His Gryphon was demanding he take more. It amazed him how his beast had never tried to get him to claim Jenna. Mentally shaking his ex from his brain, Mav increased the intensity, thrusting a little harder. A little quicker.

"Are you ready to be mine, Princess?"

Natalia opened her eyes and looked at his mouth. He released his lion's eye teeth once again, and Natalia nodded. Maveryck thrust harder, pumping his hips with purpose. When he couldn't hold off any longer, Mav lowered his mouth to her shoulder and sank his fangs into the muscle. Natalia's startled shout turned to moans as her pussy clamped down around him. His own release exploded as her blood coated his tongue. He retracted his canines and licked her skin, the two holes closing with his healing saliva. His dick pulsed, still releasing his seed deep inside her. He'd never felt more alive than he did becoming one with his mate.

Her warm, dark eyes met his blue ones, shining with love and wonderment. Yeah, she felt it too. "Hello, mate."

Natalia smiled, cupping his face, running her fingers through his beard. It was something she did often, and the caress was as good as her saying "I love you."

"Hello, my Gryphon. That was…" Natalia bit her bottom lip. "I don't even know how to describe it."

"You don't have to."

"You felt it too?"

"Oh, yeah."

"Did you know I could see the lion?" Natalia touched the edge of his eye and caressed the skin there.

"Does that bother you?"

"No. It's amazing how there are these different sides of you. Three animals buried within this human shell. All three spectacular, but I have to say, the lion is my favorite."

Maveryck pushed up so he was on his hands and brought forth the animal. His face transitioned and the long mane touched her chest. He shook his head and called it back. Natalia laughed, her eyes glinting with joy. "Like I said – amazing. Will the twins be Gryphons?"

"We won't know for quite a while." Maveryck's soft dick slid from her body as he rolled over to his back, taking her with him so she was lying against his side. "The Gryphon doesn't come out until puberty, if it manifests at all. We'll hide what I am until they're old enough to understand how important it is to keep that part of us a secret. But we will tell them so they're prepared if their bodies start changing in ways they aren't expecting."

"Will you love them as much if they remain human?"

"They're my sons, Princess. My love for them is unconditional. If Major gets home and decides he wants to wear nothing but tutus, I'll buy him a different color for every day of the week. If Marshall were to tell me he was in love with Rain, I'd give him my blessing. I know bikers have a stigma of being homophobic assholes, but that's not me. It's not the Hounds' way. Yes, we're mercenaries, but we only rid the world of those who don't deserve to walk among the innocent. We were created to protect. To love. And I love those two boys with my whole heart, the same way I love you."

"I love you as much. I know I'm not their mother, but I want to be. I want them to know they are cherished every single day. And I promise you, I'm going to be there for them, for you, until my dying breath."

"In that case, I think your last name should be Lazlo, too."

"Are… Are you asking me—"

"Will you marry me and adopt our boys?"

"Yes. Yes!" Natalia giggled and slid her body over Mav's, straddling his lap. "You know, we're going to need to practice being quiet while we have sex. We don't want to wake them up every night with our lovemaking."

Maveryck's dick liked the sound of that. It also liked the feel of her ass pressing down on it. "Is that right?" Natalia smiled, sliding her slick folds back and forth. "Then I guess we commence to practicing." Maveryck lifted her hips and slid inside. They found out it was going to take a lot of practice to learn to be quiet.

CHAPTER THIRTY-THREE

Maveryck

LAUGHTER COMING FROM the living room had Maveryck bounding down the stairs. The joy their sons found in Natalia's love was something he never wanted to get used to. She kept her promise, and every day, Natalia showered both boys with all the love she had to give. Thankfully, she had plenty to share with Mav, too.

The last month hadn't been without its trials, but those had nothing to do with the four of them. Everyone in the family was vying for time with the twins. Maveryck understood his parents and brothers wanting to spend time with them, but damnit, he did too. If he had been part of their lives for the first four years, he might not be as hesitant in letting them go for sleepovers. When anyone asked for a night with the boys, Mav would open his mouth to say no, but his Princess was there to remind him they could use the time to not worry about being quiet.

The sex had only gotten better as they discovered all the different ways to please one another. Natalia had been hesitant at giving blowjobs, but her enthusiasm made up for her lack of experience. Now, if her mouth got anywhere near his dick, he struggled not to blow his load in the first fifteen seconds. She was that good. Or maybe it was because it was her. Maveryck never expected to love Natalia as much as he did. It was as wonderful as it was humbling.

Natalia not only put everything she had into their sex life, but she was doing everything she could to become the perfect mate and mother. She watched video after video to learn how to cook delicious meals, and she was getting good at it. When they ate with his parents, Natalia spent her time in the kitchen with Rory to watch how his mom made each dish. Rory had warmed up to his little Russian assassin as soon as she learned how Natalia had given most of her family's money over to their cause. Respect was hard won from Aurora Lazlo, but not when it came to his Princess.

Jenna had emailed photos of the boys, and together, he and Natalia chose quite a few to print off and frame. Those pictures, along with new ones of all four of them were added to the myriad of family photos around the house. Maveryck's favorite picture was a drawing Hayden had done of their little family. It was framed and had the place of honor over the fireplace.

Instead of Maveryck taking Natalia shopping like he promised, Lucy and Kerrigan intruded for a girls' day out as soon as War had returned with the twins. They even included McKenzie in their shopping spree. Usually, Mac chose to hide out at Ryker's because of the scar on her face, but she was getting more comfortable with the others' encouragement. While the females were raiding the mall, Mav and his brothers took the boys swimming at Lucy's, with Tamian joining them. Natalia had met some of the other mates, the ones with smaller kids. She took the twins for playdates, and their boys were thriving. Having friends there in New Troy meant they didn't miss the Stone Society kids as much.

Natalia had talked to Sutton about her family's estate. She offered it to him and Rory to use for those people they rescued from the cults as a temporary place until they found something permanent. Since it was three hours away from New Troy, Sutton asked if she'd be willing to sell it so they could build something closer to home. So, that's what she did. Rafael Stone was the premier architect in all the States, and he had agreed to design the new home when he and Kaya brought their baby, Sebastian, for a visit. When the house was being cleaned out so the furnishings could be offered in an estate sale, Natalia had gone through the office first to gather anything Sutton could use to take down all Anatoly's contacts, including her ledgers. The estate sold for upwards of nine million, and that went a long way in building the new halfway house.

When Natalia was going through the house, she noticed Marta's things were gone. Mav had Lucy look through security footage to see if she had been at the house the day they took out Natalia's cousins. She hadn't been, but when Marta did return, there had been nobody there. Lucy tracked the woman down and found her, along with a toddler, living in Connecticut with her sister. Ryker paid Marta a visit to "convince" her to forget everything she knew about the Volkovs, but not before he inquired as to the toddler's identity. Marta admitted the little girl was one Anatoly had his men kidnap as part of his trafficking business. Marta hid the child because the girl was so young, and had taken her to her sister's after Anatoly was killed. When Ryker asked why she hadn't returned the child, she said she didn't want to go to jail. In the end, Ryker told Marta to call the police and admit to everything.

Mav told Natalia about seeing the amber alert and then stepping on a little shoe when he went looking for Natalia in the beginning. Ryker hung around Connecticut until the authorities showed up and the child was returned to her family.

Maveryck had so many days he would never forget that he stopped adding them to his list. Every day with his mate and their boys was one to remember. His home was filled with the sounds of laughter, the scent of wildflowers, and the taste of cake at least once a week.

Now, the Hounds were going on their group ride. It had

303

taken a month to make it happen, mostly because Maveryck had a surprise for his family. He and Natalia had taken to backroads on those days and nights the boys were visiting his family. She was a natural riding behind him, and when he asked if she wanted to learn to ride her own bike, she declined, stating how much she loved riding with him. She enjoyed looking at the scenery and pressing against him, holding on tight.

Hayden had been working his ass off to get their surprise ready, and now it was. He was on his way with it. The twins knew about the group ride and were excited about sleeping in the woods. Mav explained they would be in a tent, and he even set up a small one in the backyard so they knew what to expect. They loved it so much they begged to go camping every night, even if it was just out the back door.

"Lolly!"

"Major!"

Major giggled every time she responded that way.

"How many more sleeps?"

"Just one more. Tomorrow when we wake up, we'll eat breakfast then meet everyone else."

Both twins jumped up and yelled, "Yay," doing the little butt-wiggle dance. Natalia jumped up and mimicked them. When she grinned at Maveryck, he strode through the room and wiggled his ass right alongside them.

"Daddo!"

"Marshall!" Mav called back, picking up his quieter son and twirling him around. They might look nearly identical, but their personalities were completely different. Major was wide open from the time his feet hit the floor until he went to bed. Marshall had his moments where he was as boisterous, but most of the time, he sat and observed those around him.

When he placed Marshall on his feet, Mav told them, "I have a surprise for you."

"What is it?" Major asked, jumping up and down.

"Go look out the front window. Uncle Hayden's on his

way with it." The twins ran to the window, pulling the curtain aside so they had an unobstructed view.

"What did you do?" Natalia wrapped her arms around his waist and set her chin to his chest, giving him her chocolate gaze.

"You'll have to wait and see." He kissed her forehead and hugged her tight. Holding his mate was one of his favorite things in the world. Right up there with playing with the twins and making love.

"He's here! He's here!" The boys ran to the door, but Mav had to go unlock it. After finding the boys playing in the front yard when they were supposed to be sleeping in, Mav had installed a dead bolt toward the top of the door. One day, they would figure out they could reach it by climbing on a chair, but for now, it kept them safely locked inside. Mav took Natalia's hand and led them outside where Hayden was climbing off a new Harley Ultra. Mav kept his Dyna for when it was just him and his mate, but a family of four needed more room, thus the shiny, black sidecar attached to the touring bike.

"Daddo! Look! Uncle Hayden has a side cart!" Major exclaimed. Mav had given up explaining it was a sidecar.

Marshall looked up, his eyes wide. "Is that our side cart?"

"It sure is. Now we can all ride together." Major bounded down the steps, lunging at his uncle, knowing Hayden would catch him.

Marshall tugged on Mav's jeans. "You're the best Daddo in the whole world."

Mav's eyes burned, but he blinked a few times to keep the tears at bay. That was the best praise Mav had ever received, and he didn't take it lightly. He picked Marshall up, snuggling him close. "And you and Major are the best sons in the whole world. I love you, Buddy."

"Marsh! Come look!" Major yelled.

"I love you too." Marshall didn't wiggle to get down. As

305

excited as he was to see the bike, he never rushed to get out of hugs. Maveryck placed a kiss on his son's blond head and set him on his feet. Marshall grabbed Natalia's hand. "Let's go look."

Mav had picked out the factory-painted bike, so he was surprised when Natalia pointed at the gas tank. "Hayden, did you do this?"

Maveryck looked at his brother who wouldn't meet his eyes. When Mav saw the specialized paint job, he found it hard to swallow. Instead of being solid black with red pin stripes, there was a Gryphon with gold wings covering the portion of the tank below the gas cap. When he looked closer, he noticed a crown sitting atop the eagle's head.

"What's it say?" Major asked, pointing to the cursive writing.

Natalia squatted down. "That's your name and Marshall's name," she said, pointing to each one as she identified them.

"There's more over here," Maveryck said. Natalia and the twins walked around the bike. They couldn't get as close because of the sidecar, but she leaned over and pointed to the two names. "This says Mayhem, and that one's Lollipop."

Hayden rubbed his hand through his hair and sheepishly indicated there was something on the outside of the sidecar. Mav raised his eyebrows, and when he walked to where his baby brother was standing, he wrapped his arm around Hayden's neck. The words "Double the Mayhem" adorned the boys' ride in a funky, cool font.

"That's perfect," he said. "Thank you, Brother."

Before Mav had time to get too emotional, several bikes and an SUV pulled up to the curb. Rory climbed out of the vehicle as Sutton, Kyllian, Ryker, and War, who was doubling Kerrigan, shut off their bikes. Sutton climbed off Hayden's Harley, smiling.

"What do you think?" his dad asked.

"I think we need to take it out for a spin. What do you

say boys? Wanna test out your sidecar?"

"Yeah!" they shouted, wiggling their butts. The adults laughed at the two youngest Lazlos.

"Let's go grab our helmets," Natalia told the boys.

While they waited on his little family, Mav asked his dad, "Where's your ride?"

"Right there," Sutton responded, thumbing in Rory's direction. "We've got some shopping to do, but we'll meet y'all bright and early in the morning." Sutton clapped Mav on the shoulder.

When Natalia and the boys returned, he helped Major with his helmet, while Natalia fastened Marshall's on. Maveryck lifted the boys into their tricked-out sidecar and buckled them in.

"Ready to test out your new ride, Princess?"

"I'm ready." Natalia climbed on behind Maveryck and relaxed against the wrap-around seat. Maveryck knew getting the bigger bike meant Natalia wouldn't be wrapped around him like she usually was, but as he pulled down the driveway next to Ryker, she placed her hands on his waist. With his boys and his mate riding with him, Maveryck Lazlo rode the wind, and he didn't need his eagle to do it.

The End

A Note From The Author

This was such a fun book to write. I've known about the twins for a long time. When they first came to me, they both were these rambunctious balls of energy, but Marshall quickly let me know he had a softer heart. I also intended for Natalia to keep working, but she let me know right away that wasn't happening. Yes, the characters have their own minds, and I always listen.

Next up in this series is Ryker's story, and I can't wait to meet his mate. She is going to be something special. Someone who can pull Ryker out of his past. Release date is August 8th. Click below to preorder.

Coming Soon

ABOUT THE AUTHOR

Multi-genre author Faith Gibson began writing in high school, and through the years, penned many stories and poems. As her dreams continued getting crazier than the one before, she decided to keep a dream journal. Many of these nighttime escapades have led to a line, a chapter, or even a complete story.

"Love is love, and there's not enough love in the world." This belief she holds strongly, and it's the prevailing theme in her works, all of which come with a happy ending.

Faith believes her purpose in life is to entertain the masses, even if it's one person at a time. Living just outside of Nashville, Tennessee, with the love of her life and her pit bull pup, when she's not hard at work writing her next adventure, she can often be found playing trivia while enjoying craft beer, listening to live music, or off on an adventure of her own.

www.ingramcontent.com/pod-product-compliance
Lightning Source LLC
Chambersburg PA
CBHW072344020726
47506CB00004B/1003